The
Captain's Wife

The Captain's Wife

A NOVEL

Douglas Kelley

DUTTON

DUTTON
Published by the Penguin Group
Penguin Putnam Inc., 375 Hudson Street, New York, New York 10014, U.S.A.
Penguin Books Ltd, 27 Wrights Lane, London W8 5TZ, England
Penguin Books Australia Ltd, Ringwood, Victoria, Australia
Penguin Books Canada Ltd, 10 Alcorn Avenue, Toronto, Ontario, Canada M4V 3B2
Penguin Books (N.Z.) Ltd, 182–190 Wairau Road, Auckland 10, New Zealand

Penguin Books Ltd, Registered Offices: Harmondsworth, Middlesex, England

Published by Dutton, a member of Penguin Putnam Inc.

First Printing, September, 2001
1 3 5 7 9 10 8 6 4 2

 REGISTERED TRADEMARK — MARCA REGISTRADA

LIBRARY OF CONGRESS CATALOGING-IN-PUBLICATION DATA
Kelley, Douglas.
The captain's wife : a novel / Douglas Kelley
p. cm.
ISBN 0-525-94619-5
1. Patten, Mary Ann Brown, 1837–1861 — Fiction. 2. Patten, Joshua A.,
1826 or 7 –1857 — Fiction. 3. Neptune's Car (Clipper ship) — Fiction.
4. Ship captains' spouses — Fiction. 5. Women and the sea — Fiction. 6. Ship captains —
Fiction. I Title.
PS3611.E44 C36 2001
813'.6 — dc21
2001017346

Printed in the United States of America
Set in Cochin
Designed by Eve L. Kirch

PUBLISHER'S NOTE

For
Jan, Anna, and Sam

The
Captain's Wife

Cape Horn

Looking aft from the quarterdeck rail, Mary Ann Patten saw the helmsman at his post, feet apart to steady himself on the wet and rolling deck. His tanned hands, red with cold, gripped the ship's wheel. He stood alert, watching the sea and the sails for the effects of the wind. A new gust came across the waves, manifesting itself by blowing the frothy foam from the tops of the white capping waves. The helmsman watched the sea to judge the wind's arrival at the ship, where it would whip the straining canvas and deliver yet another surge of seawater across the deck. Just before the gust arrived, he spun the wheel, making a preemptive correction.

Overhead, the masts were mostly bare, with minimum sail out to maintain directional control and provide a hint of forward progress. Still, as the gust hit, the ship gave in and leaned away from the wind, tilting the masts and deck at aberrant angles to the sea. With the wind came the water, in yet another twenty-foot surge. It broke over the bow and port rail in what had long ago ceased being spray and foam and was now the ocean itself, tons of soaking Antarctic water coming on board like an unruly and uninvited guest. It washed over the deck, ready to carry away anything or anyone not secured to the ship.

Mary Patten gripped the rail above the steps leading down to the main deck. The long bowsprit of the clipper ship *Neptune's Car* reemerged from the smothering wave and rose again toward the cold gray sky, riding up the crest of the swell. The deck cleared as the seawater ran amidships and out the starboard scuppers. Mary saw a man dressed in an oilskin coat leave the foremast rigging and move forward to the bow, where he bent to some task as the ship fell into the next trough. The bow crashed into the oncoming swell. Mary watched the sailor drop to one knee and wrap his arms through the jib rigging, hanging on for his life. A second later he disappeared under the overrunning wave. She anxiously waited — then the ocean subsided to reveal the kneeling form, his pose unchanged.

The water ran away from him across the slanted deck, and he went back to work.

The dim figure in the bow was wet, but so was Mary. So was almost everyone on board. Her dress, once new and pretty, was now fit only for rags, but she saw no benefit in putting on anything else. Like the crewmen working before her, she would only be wet again. And cold. Water swept endlessly over the ship, and the spray of every breaking wave added another layer to the ice coating the lines and rigging, like a candle dipped repeatedly into wax.

The ship rose and fell, straining to beat its way through the frigid sea and endless gales. So far the vessel was holding together, and the crew steadfastly resolved to carry on despite the hardships of the weather.

Mary was trying to do her part. The crew of *Neptune's Car* was a good one, but they were still only common sailors, many of them foreign at that, and required someone to be their captain. Mary deplored the role. She deplored her situation. She deplored Cape Horn and its weather. She hoped the Pacific would live up to its peaceful name.

She wondered again about their position. There had been no sun or stars for days, and without the light of other worlds she could not know where they were on this one. She felt someone beside her and turned to see the young second mate, his hat pulled low over his eyes, hiding most of his expression. His face was wet, with water trickling down his cheeks and dripping off his chin. His lips were blue with cold, and when he spoke, his words came out stiffly.

"What do you think, ma'am, of coming a couple of points to for a while?"

Mary looked at him. The mate was only twenty-one, just two years older than she, but his time spent at sea had left him with the tanned and weathered skin of a seasoned sailor. His eyes, though, still shined with youthful exuberance. He had proved eager to aid her as she struggled against the misfortunes that had put her on this windswept deck, and she admired his character. He was her link to the crew and to the ship. Without him, the situation would be untenable. She relied upon him and upon his practical knowledge. If he wanted to come into the wind, that was good enough for her.

"Yes, Mr. Hare, let's do that."

The second mate turned to the helmsman and delivered the order. The big wheel spun counterclockwise, and the bow, nearly two hundred feet ahead, turned slightly to face the swells more head-on. On this new heading, the ship was more stable, with less rolling and wallowing. It would also move through the water more slowly, but when the seas were as high as had been experienced for the past few hours, the amount of forward progress on any heading was, at best, debatable.

After a few minutes *Neptune's Car* settled into her new course and took the swells a little better. There was less rolling now, but the ride was still rough as the bow rode up the face of the swells only to drop more sharply into the following trough. Mary felt better about the ship's ability to withstand the beating it had been taking. Perhaps this latest storm would soon abate and they could resume speed.

Mary sighed. She had been hoping that for days now. She looked at the clouds hanging low and ragged over the ship. There was no sign of a break. The first mate spoke again.

"I can watch things here. Why don't you go below for a while. Tend to the captain."

She wanted to go below. She wanted to go below and not come back up. She wanted to sleep, and she wanted to be dry. She wanted her husband to stand here on the quarterdeck and guide this ship and crew. She wanted many things.

"Yes. Maybe I will." Her words came out in a monotone. "You have the ship, Mr. Hare."

Below deck the still air was damp and chilled. The wind was banished from here—banished, but its effects were still felt and heard. The waves beat against the hull, and the wash ran over the deck boards. The thick timbers and planking creaked and groaned in long wooden moans. Nothing loose stayed in place, and lanterns swayed from their bails.

Mary stepped into the cabin she shared with her husband, steadying herself in the doorway for a moment as the ship rocked through a swell. Then she moved to the side of the bed and knelt upon the floor. She took her husband's hand and held it tightly. He stirred under the blanket and a sound escaped his lips, but for the third day in a row he did not open his eyes. Mary watched him for a while, then slipped off her coat and slid into bed beside him.

How, she wondered, had they gotten into this situation? How had a voyage with her husband the captain, meant to be so sweet and wonderful, turned so fearsome and deadly? She wished she were at home in Boston. She wished she could turn back time to before they had left New York. That July day had been so warm and pleasant, not at all like the wintry gales through which the ship was now struggling.

She rubbed a curious hand over her belly, feeling the faint beginning of a new roundness. Worry filled her mind. Exhaustion pushed away the worry, and she slept.

CHAPTER 1

The Captain

The last day of June in New York can be hot and humid. The pleasant airs of spring may still drift in and out, like an old friend who does not feel the need to knock, but more frequently the days speak the language of summer. It was on one of those warm summer days that Joshua Patten, captain of the extreme clipper *Neptune's Car*, left his room at the Battery Hotel and walked down Fulton Street to the docks of the East River. Here, at the lower tip of Manhattan, New York met the world.

As he neared the river, the business and commerce around Captain Patten shifted quickly from shops and stores of the city to the sights and sounds of the sea trade. Sail makers and ship's chandlers replaced the haberdasheries and shoe stores. The soft aromas of the fruit stands were overcome by the much stronger odors of the fish market. The jingle of trolley bells was left behind. Now were heard the sounds of ships. Loose rigging slapped against the masts, and ship's bells rang messages across the water.

At South Street, which paralleled the docks from the Battery up the river, Patten turned right and left behind all vestiges of city life. Before, behind, and all around him lay the South Street Seaport. He was in his element here. As the seaport surrounded him, he became more alert, more alive. His walk became lighter, more confident, his eyes sharper, more observant. In the city he was just a man walking down Fulton Street, but here he was captain.

Joshua Patten was a handsome man. Twenty-nine years old, of medium height, he had the sun-bronzed face and hands of a man who lived on the sea, his hair bleached to a lighter shade of brown by the sun. He was young for a captain, but had made the most of his career. He liked to think he was respected among his peers, and he was right.

On his left were the docks. Along the docks were the ships. The masts and yardarms lined the East River, standing at attention, bare of sail, inert. The ships, tied to their moorings, waited for the next cargo, the next sail. Every day vessels came and went, loaded and unloaded by strong men. Goods and merchandise were hauled on and off the docks in wagons pulled by draft animals steered by rough-voiced teamsters.

On Patten's right, opposite the busy docks, were the red brick offices and warehouses of the shipping business. The work was done on the docks, but the business was conducted across the street. It was to one of these offices that Patten was headed.

A short walk, hampered occasionally by long wagons crossing in front of him, brought him to a building on the corner where Wall Street ended at South Street. Its brick was identical to that of its adjoining neighbors, as was typical of the shipping district. A small brass plaque by the door announced the presence of the firm of FOSTER AND NICKERSON, which owned *Neptune's Car.*

He stepped inside and closed the door behind him. The brass doorknob was tarnished to a flat brown. The air within was cooler than the hot day outside, but to the captain it seemed stale and musty. A life spent outdoors made indoors seem a vastly inferior place. He looked with pity at the fresh-faced clerk behind the desk. The poor fellow would be miserable, Patten thought, if he knew how unfortunate he was.

"Good morning, Captain" said the clerk. "Mr. Wiley mentioned that you would be in."

"Good morning, Jules." Patten smiled. "And a good morning it is. It's a shame to be inside."

The clerk smiled wanly. "It's the curse of a secretary."

Patten thought for a moment. "I believe that Meriwether Lewis was a secretary. He wound up spending very little time behind his desk."

"Yes. Well." The clerk was a slight man, his hairline already receding to produce a high pale forehead above the wire rims of his eyeglasses. "He was a secretary to the president. Hardly the same as this." Smiling, he swept his arm across the little office.

Patten decided not to pursue the conversation. The clerk was satisfied with his position or resigned to it, and it really did not matter which. He changed to the business at hand.

"Is Mr. Wiley in?"

"I'm sorry to say he is not. He has stepped out for a moment." The clerk seemed genuinely unhappy that the captain was being inconvenienced. "He will be back shortly. You are welcome to wait in his office, if you like."

Patten said that he would, but instead stayed in the front room, watching passersby out the window and making small talk with Jules, who seemed not to mind a break from the papers on his desk. There was, however, only so much a captain and a clerk had in common, and eventually the conversation died out. Patten was about to leave and check on his ship when the door opened and Stephen Wiley came in.

Wiley, twenty years his senior, was the local shipping agent for Foster and Nickerson. His large graying head was tilted forward on rounded shoulders, perpetually bent as if ready to look over papers. He was a short man, which combined with his bent posture required him to look up and over the glasses on the end of his nose.

"Hello, Joshua. Sorry to keep you waiting."

"I just walked in."

"Good. Has Mary arrived from Boston?"

"Yes. She came in on the train yesterday afternoon. It's good to have her here."

"She is well, I hope."

"Very well, thanks. And looking forward to the trip. She's at the hotel, resting. Probably wants to go shopping later."

Wiley smiled. "She's a fine girl, Joshua. Lucky man to have her for a wife."

"I think so."

"Indeed, indeed. So, are we about ready to sail?"

"I hope so. The ship is ready, or will be by later today. There's still provisions to load, water and such, but that should be no problem. The articles have been signed by most of the crew. The rest will be signed on by this afternoon. I've kept over half from the last trip, and the new ones seem willing to work."

Patten paused, giving Wiley a chance to speak. He did not. A bad sign. Patten ventured: "How did you do with the mate from the *Rainbow*?"

"I'm afraid I was unable to get him. The master of the *Rainbow* made it worth his while to stay."

Patten frowned. His first mate had contracted malaria during the previous voyage. He was making a recovery but felt he was not ready for a return to work. Unfortunately, until only a few days ago, the mate had told Patten he would be ready. A setback in his recovery had changed that, and now Patten was faced with finding a new first mate at the last minute.

Finding a good mate was not nearly so simple as finding a ready seaman. The first mate was the second in command of a ship, and the person in charge whenever the captain was not on deck. A good first mate should be able to hold to the captain's style of running a vessel, so that the crew could expect the same orders regardless of who was giving them. This continuity of command was very important. The first mate needed to be competent to handle the ship, and the captain needed a mate he could trust. Wiley had hoped to obtain the services of a first-rate man from the clipper *Rainbow*, just in port for repairs and not expected to sail again for a while. Now that avenue had become a dead end.

"All right, then," Patten said. "The *Car* may not be ready to sail tomorrow after all."

"It has to," said Wiley. Patten heard a note of anxiety in his voice.

"She doesn't *have* to do anything," he replied. "We can't go without a mate. You don't think I can just walk into the nearest saloon and pick one up off the floor, do you? A deckhand, yes. A mate, no." He faced Wiley squarely, feet apart. He was in command on his ship, and he was in command here.

Wiley seemed to sag a little, and he slid around Patten toward a closed door at the back of the room. "Let's go into my office."

Patten followed warily, suspecting that Wiley was trying to use his office as home turf, where he could have some command of his own. They left the clerk in the outer room.

Wiley slipped off his coat and hung it on a hook. Patten noticed a ring of perspiration under the agent's arm, and wondered if it was entirely the result of the warm day or if partly from the worry of placating an unhappy sea captain. He had virtually promised to deliver the mate from the *Rainbow*.

"Coleman expects the ship to sail tomorrow," he said. "I think we should do our best to see that it does."

The cargo of the W. T. Coleman and Company—everything from butter and shovels to liquor and furniture—was loaded into the hold of *Neptune's Car*. It had been a hard sell, and Patten supposed that Wiley had made certain concessions and promises to close the deal. The gold rush was over, and with it the days when goods for the new Californians were wanted quickly, at any price. The shipping business was glutted right now, with more capacity than cargo. *Neptune's Car* had been in port since April, nearly three months, and was in need of revenue. Shippers like Coleman knew that and took advantage when bargaining for rates and shipping times.

"We can't go without a mate," Patten said.

"I know, I know," Wiley said, sitting down at his desk. "I'm just saying that it would be very detrimental to business not to go on schedule."

Patten took a seat in one of the chairs facing the desk. "What's Coleman to do, off-load fifteen hundred tons into another ship? That certainly wouldn't get them out tomorrow."

Wiley looked exasperated. "I'm not just talking about this trip, Joshua. Yours is not the only ship Foster and Nickerson owns. We have an overall reputation to defend here."

Patten looked across the desk. Wiley was twirling a pencil in his fingers. These office types certainly seemed nervous, worrying over a load of mundane supplies as if a cask of nails or a bolt of cloth were the most important thing in the world. He felt a little sorry for Wiley. If not tomorrow, Patten thought, then within in a few days

I'll be at sea, where I'm less encumbered by what others think. Poor Wiley will still be here, behind this desk, trying to keep everybody happy. He sighed.

"Listen, Stephen, I want to sail as much as you do. We just have to find someone."

Wiley stopped playing with the pencil. "I do know of someone. I'm just not sure if he would do."

"Oh? Who would that be?"

"His name is Keeler."

Patten wondered why the name had not been brought up before. "What's wrong with him?"

"Maybe nothing. He's been on several ships, though, and I know he usually isn't signed back up. He may be troublesome."

"Where is he now?"

"He just came off the *Comet*. Arrived three days ago from London. I talked to the *Comet*'s owners this morning. They know of no problems with him."

"*Comet*? That's Bob Beech's isn't it? Have you talked to him?"

"No. I haven't had the chance. Besides, I thought you might get a more straight answer."

"I might. I don't know Beech well, but I know him. I'll go to the *Comet* when I leave here. See what I can learn. I'd rather not have a troublemaker on board."

"No, of course not. Still, let's remember. We need to sail."

Wiley looked like he was about to begin groveling, but he stopped short, and only frowned. Neither man spoke for several seconds. Joshua fingered a nick on the arm of the chair, but looked steadily at the man behind the desk. He was determined not to give in. The agent had a job to do, but so did he.

The room was quiet enough to hear the door off the street close, and then an unintelligible voice in the outer room. Wiley cocked his head, trying to hear who had entered. They heard Jules's voice outside the door, followed by a knock.

"Yes!" Wiley spoke loudly enough to be heard through the door. It opened halfway, and Jules stuck his head in.

"Gentleman to see you, sir."

"Who is it?"

"A Mr. Keeler."

Wiley looked from the clerk to Patten. "Wasn't too hard to find, was he?" To Jules he said, "Show Mr. Keeler in."

Jules withdrew, and a moment later his place was taken by the newly arrived visitor. Patten made a quick visual appraisal. The man in the doorway looked to be in his thirties, of average height, perhaps an inch or two taller than himself, but heavier by twenty or thirty pounds. His hair had a very dark, almost black sheen; his tanned skin an olive color. His upper body was out of proportion to the lower, with a barrel chest and thick arms straining the checked shirt common to sailors, while dark dungarees hung loosely from narrow hips. Patten glanced back up to his face, studying the countenance for clues to the man inside. Keeler offered a smile, but the expression seemed forced and not compatible with the dark, unsmiling eyes. He struck Patten as someone who was difficult to get to know. That would, however, be of no matter on board ship. It only mattered that he be trusted to do his job well. Still, Patten wished he'd had time to ask around about this fellow before meeting him.

Wiley seemed to harbor no such reservations. "Come in, come in," he said, rising out of his chair and moving around his desk. He extended his hand. "I'm Stephen Wiley, and you are Mr. Keeler, is that right?"

"Yes. . . ." Keeler seemed surprised by the cordial reception. He recovered, offered his hand, and said, "William Keeler."

Wiley shook his hand and said, "Allow me to introduce Joshua Patten, master of *Neptune's Car*."

Patten also rose and offered his hand, though not as gleefully as Wiley. "Pleased to make your acquaintance."

"The pleasure is all mine, sir," said Keeler. Once welcomed into the office, his demeanor softened, his face relaxing a little. Patten was pleased to see this. Keeler smiled again. "I came here to ask how to find you, Captain, and here you are." He had a deep voice befitting his barrel chest.

Patten offered a flicker of a smile, but said nothing.

Wiley jumped back in. "I suppose, then, that you have heard we are in need of a good man to serve as mate.

"Yes, I have. Is the position still open?"

Before Wiley had a chance, Patten answered. "We are not sure. We have just concluded an interview with someone else who is to discuss our offer with his current employer. If he becomes available, I'm afraid the post will be his."

Wiley, to his credit, did not contradict Patten and quickly fell in line. "Of course, should that not happen, it would be to our advantage to have other possibilities lined up. So please, have a seat and tell us about yourself."

Patten wished Wiley would stop being so eager, but said, "Yes, please do," and motioned toward the other chair. He returned to his seat and said, "How did you come to hear of our opening?"

"It was being talked about around the waterfront last night. Word is it would be a good job, that the *Car* is a good ship with a good master. And a man can always use a good job."

Patten nodded acknowledgment of the compliment but wondered if by waterfront, Keeler had meant the docks or the Waterfront Tavern.

"You came in with Beech on the *Comet*, is that right?"

Keeler seemed surprised by Patten's knowledge of him. His face clouded for a fleeting moment, but he shook it off and put on a brighter look. "Yes, I did. Can I take that to mean you have some interest in me?"

"You were mentioned as being possibly available." This was Wiley speaking. He appeared ready to gush again, so Patten stopped him before he could.

"Will you not be sailing again with the *Comet*?"

Keeler glanced Patten's way. "I don't think so. I think Captain Beech has someone else in mind."

Patten pressed. "Was he dissatisfied with your work?"

"Maybe. We didn't always see eye to eye," Keeler replied, quickly adding, "Beech is a fine captain, don't get me wrong. Can't say anything against him."

Patten observed this attempt to hide any sign of conflict with the captain. Keeler knew he had said the wrong thing. Patten threw him a little line.

"Probably just a little personality conflict," he offered.

Keeler took the bait. "Yes, I suppose so. Just a little personality conflict."

"Not much room on board for that kind of thing," Patten said, jerking the line away.

Keeler scowled but checked himself. "I feel exactly the same way. That's why I don't think I'll stay with the *Comet*."

"So it was your decision to leave?"

"Yes." Keeler hesitated. His face clouded again. "Beech might say it was his. One might say it was mutual."

"I see."

"I have served under other captains who thought I was a fine hand. I can offer references."

"I would like to have those references," Patten said.

"Of course. Sir, may I say this?" Keeler leaned forward and clasped his hands tightly together. "I know you haven't much time to find a mate. If you already knew I came in with Beech on the *Comet*, you probably have heard we had some trouble getting along. You may have already talked to him."

"I have not," Patten said. "Yet."

"Well, let me say that any master who has any trouble with me has had other troubles besides. What I mean to say is that those captains have been generally unsure of themselves and indecisive in the handling of their ships. When I would try to improve on things, which I'll admit is not my place, that is when they had grievances with me. With good captains I have had no trouble. And you, sir, are reputed to be a good captain."

Keeler sat back in his chair, looking satisfied that he had made a good case for himself.

Patten knew of inept captains. They fall into their positions and blunder along, their success more by accident than design. Eventually they are caught up with, but sometimes not until the loss of their ship. It was a touchy subject. Still, it was not the place of an applicant to criticize former employers.

"How many different captains have you sailed under?" he asked.

"Altogether, or as mate?"

"As mate."

"Six."

"And how many would you consider poor captains?"

Keeler pondered and said, "Probably three."

Patten raised his eyebrows. "Do you suppose that ratio extends to all captains? Are you saying that half the captains of the seas are inferior?"

Keeler was back on the defensive. "No, of course not. I guess I've just had . . . bad luck, I guess."

Patten looked at him without speaking. Keeler glanced away, then back, then away again. At Wiley. At the office walls. The captain let him suffer for a moment and then changed the direction of the conversation.

"Have you made the San Francisco run before?"

Keeler seemed relieved to change the subject. "Yes, sir. Several times. Most recently with Howard on the *Western Star*. One hundred and five days to the Golden Gate. Then to Singapore and London. It was in London that I joined the *Comet* to get back here. Howard was an excellent captain. I enjoyed working with him."

"Why did you not stay then?"

"Half the crew had malaria. I didn't like the air. The *Star* was going to be in port for a while, and *Comet* was ready to go. So I went with it."

"You've been at sea a long time. Will you be ready to go again as soon as tomorrow?"

Keeler shrugged. "I've got no one to keep me here. If I stay, I'll just spend the rest of my pay. I've spent enough already." He gave Patten a knowing wink. "If I can find me a woman for tonight, I'll be ready for sea tomorrow."

Patten allowed himself a smile. *The man is a sailor, all right.* He thought about tomorrow's sailing date. He was not enthusiastic about Keeler, but he might do. If Keeler's trouble was with inept captains, Patten was confident he would have no trouble on *Neptune's Car*. It would just have to be made clear from the start who was in charge. He needed to talk to Beech. He didn't have much time, though. He would have to make a decision today. He decided he had learned all he could with this conversation.

"Well, Mr. Keeler," he said, standing up. "Mr. Wiley and I do thank you for coming in. We may possibly have use of your services—depending, of course, upon what becomes of our other applicant. You mentioned references. If you would be so kind as to list one or two it might be helpful."

He drew a blank sheet of paper off Wiley's desk and handed it to Keeler. The swarthy mate took the paper and leaned over the desk to write. Patten watched. He could have simply asked the names, but he wanted to see how skilled Keeler was with a pen. He assumed the man could write, having served as mate, but he wanted to see for himself. The names went onto the paper slowly but neatly, the mark of a sailor trying to improve himself. Patten had to approve.

As Keeler finished writing, Patten quickly considered what he had learned during the interview. Except for not particularly liking him, Patten saw no problem. Keeler could probably do the job and be all right. Being an unknown quantity, he would just bear watching. It was unfortunate, though, to have to decide so quickly. Once at sea it would be too late for a change of mind.

Keeler put the pen back by the inkwell and straightened up, handing Patten the paper. The captain glanced at the names. Except for Beech, of the *Comet*, the names were unknown to him. He wondered if he would have time to check these references. At the end of the short list was the name of a rooming house.

"I assume I can find you here?"

"Aye, sir, unless that woman drags me off somewhere else."

"Woman?"

Keeler winked, as he had a few moments earlier. "You know, the one I hope to find tonight."

Patten laughed politely, catching up with the joke. "I'll try to let you know if I'll be needing you before that happens."

Keeler thanked the two men for seeing him. He hesitated, as if he was trying to think of some other thing to say in his behalf, and then left the office. Patten watched him through the doorway as he passed through the outer office and out the front door.

Patten turned back to Wiley, who was looking at him expectantly.

"Well?" Wiley asked. "What do you think?"

"I think I need to go check on my ship and then go see Captain Beech." He picked up his hat. "Then I think I'll have lunch with Mary."

Patten knew Wiley wanted more, but he started to leave the

agent hanging. Just as he reached the door, he felt sorry for him and turned around. "If I find nothing too negative about him, I'll take Keeler."

He stepped out the door and inhaled deeply. The air smelled like ship's tar and the harbor, with just a hint of the sea. It sure beats being inside, he thought. He walked the few steps to the corner and crossed South Street to his ship.

CHAPTER 2

The Captain's Wife

After her husband left to see to his ship, Mary Ann Patten remained in bed, lazing dreamily in its softness. She enjoyed the quiet of the hotel room, resting from the train trip of the day before. She had left Boston, seen off at the station by her parents, and made the daylong journey to New York to rejoin her husband. The modern efficiency of rail travel was much more pleasant than the stage, but still wearisome. There were the crowds at the stations and porters to deal with, and the talkative seatmates. A young lady traveling alone always attracts the attentions of the traveling men.

Through the room's open window, muted by thick draperies, sounds of the city streets drifted in to remind her of where she was. Boston had its own city sounds, as did other large cities she had visited, but no place she had ever been to sounded like New York. There was an urgency to the voices, a need of instant results to whatever was going on. And there was always something going on. With the sounds through the window came the warm air of mid-morning, wafting around the drawn curtains to remind her that summer was upon the city.

New York was warmer than Boston, and a good bit more humid. She wondered what the attraction was that brought so many people

to live here. There were, of course, advantages. She smiled to herself, thinking of the shopping she had planned for the afternoon. For
now, she had nothing more pressing than to relax while waiting for
Joshua to return. Deferring to the warm air, she lay with only a
sheet over her, luxuriating in the crispness of the linens. She had always felt that the mark of first-class accommodations was the quality of the sheets and knew that she had better enjoy them.
Tomorrow she would be at sea, and she had learned on her previous
voyage that linens on board a cargo ship do not stay fresh for long.

Thinking back upon some aspects of the trip made Mary wonder
why she would want to go again. At sea for months at a time, living
with too much heat or too much cold, terrible storms or madden-
ingly flat calms, eating the same bland food and drinking stale warm
water; why would she subject herself to the hardships if she did not
have to? One reason, she decided, was simply because she had the
opportunity. Many people wished to see the world, and she had the
chance to do so. The water may be warm, she thought, but at least
she would not find herself to be an old woman having never taken a
drink.

Another reason, and the main one, was her husband. By sailing
on his ship she was able to be with him, and she could think of no
place she would rather be.

She had married Joshua Patten when she was sixteen. He was
twenty-six, and just named captain of the large clipper ship *Neptune's
Car*. He was young and good-looking, cutting a dashing figure
whether on the deck of his ship or waltzing across a ballroom floor.
They met at a party in Boston celebrating the launching of a new
ship by her father's shipbuilding firm. The room had been full of nautical wheelers and dealers, with captains of industry and captains of
ships gathered together for social merriment. Mary's mother had insisted that she go, saying, "One never knows whom one might meet."

Faced with these social obligations, Mary usually said, "Oh,
Mother!" But she always went. The truth was that she agreed. One
never did know, and Mary had developed into a beautiful young
lady who reveled in the attention she inevitably received. She
turned a lot of heads, but no one, until she saw Joshua Patten, had
ever turned hers.

She first saw him across the room, and hoped to catch his eye, but every time she looked he always seemed to be turning away. She finally caught him looking at her, as she knew he had been, and she took her turn at feigned indifference. They kept an eye on each other, but by protocol did not speak until properly introduced. She was pleased when she saw him approach a mutual acquaintance and tilt his head her way.

Trying not to appear obvious in their intentions, Joshua and his newly recruited liaison made a circuitous path around the ballroom and after several minutes made their way to Mary's side. The friend performed the introductions, as he had been commissioned to do.

"Mary," he said, "I want you to meet Joshua Patten. Joshua, this is Mary Ann Brown."

Mary smiled and made a slight curtsy. The young sea captain was even more handsome up close. His dark brown eyes showed a deep and thoughtful nature yet held a smile as he took her hand, kissing it lightly.

The friend was forgotten. He discretely took his leave, and Mary and Joshua spent the rest of the evening together. She was taken with his mix of youthful good looks and mature mannerisms, and as he told her about himself, he seemed the quintessential success story. Born in Rockland, Maine, on that state's rocky coast, he grew up by the sea. Inhaling the salt air, he said, made the sea a part of him, and he became part of it. He left the land for the sea when barely in his teens, and by the time he was twenty he was considered captain material. After proving his worth on small coastal schooners, he advanced to larger vessels and learned to handle men as well as he handled ships. His skills in commanding both became well known and admired.

A few days after the dance, Joshua visited the home on Terrace Place of George and Elizabeth Brown to see their daughter. When he left, Mary noted the approving tone of her father's voice.

Watching her suitor departing down the porch steps and into the street, George Brown said, "That young man is going to be very successful at what he does."

Standing beside her father in the doorway, Mary felt a tingle of excitement.

It was, she thought as she lay in her bed at the Battery Hotel, very much like the feeling she had experienced this morning. Joshua had roused her from sleep with gentle kisses and soft touches and spent an hour loving her before he slipped out of bed and got dressed.

She had lain under the sheet, still basking in the satiety of their lovemaking, and watched him shave. He stood over the basin in his dark blue trousers, bare from the waist up. She admired his flat stomach and the light curls of hair on his chest. Joshua was not a big man, but rather slender, with none of the filling out that would come with age. As he washed and dried his face and buttoned his shirt, Mary was intensely proud to have him for her own.

Once dressed, he became Captain Patten, ready to go out and be in command. She lay with her dark hair spread across her pillow and smiled as he leaned over to kiss her good-bye. She brushed his hair back with her hand.

"Hurry back, Captain."

"I will. Be ready for lunch. I know a nice place."

He touched a finger to her lips and slipped out the door, leaving her to linger between the sheets.

Mary and Joshua had been married on April 1, 1853, in Christ's Church, Boston, by the same minister who had baptized Mary as a child. The honeymoon had been brief, with Joshua leaving soon after for Portsmouth. He was only away for the summer, on that trip across the Atlantic and back, and he was home for all of autumn and early winter.

They spent those months together in Boston, taking up residence in an apartment not far from the harbor. They made several excursions to the outlying areas, to Cambridge and Somerville, looking for a place to build a home. They came close to settling on an area in Everett, on the bay's north shore, but stopped short of making the final agreement. Plans for a house were put on hold when Joshua was retained by the firm of Foster and Nickerson to take command of the clipper ship *Neptune's Car*, scheduled to depart New York in late January of 1855, bound for San Francisco.

The ship, of the sleek and fast class known as the extreme clipper, was far larger than anything he had commanded before, but

Joshua was not intimidated. Quite the contrary, he looked forward to the challenge.

Mary lay in bed a while longer, then rose and slipped into her dressing gown. As she opened the curtains to look out across the city, there was a soft knock upon the door. She turned as a chambermaid eased the door open.

The maid, a woman of about fifty in a pale blue dress, did not come into the room but stopped at the threshold, one hand on the doorknob. Cradled in her other arm was a stack of thick white towels.

"Pardon me, ma'am," she said. "Extras for the bath."

"Of course. Thank you," Mary said. "Just put them by the tub."

The maid did so and backed out of the room. The idea of a long bath suited Mary. Just as she had relished the comfort of the bed, she would not pass up the chance of a leisurely warm bath.

The Battery was one of the newer hotels, and had that newest fixture of luxury—running water delivered to the individual baths. A small table beside the tub held a variety of soaps and oils to clean and treat the skin. Within a few minutes, Mary had the tub filled with warm water.

She slid deep into the tub, immersing herself in the soothing water, and rested the back of her neck against its round lip, savoring the moment. Once the ship left port, she wondered how long it would be before she could again enjoy such comfort.

She remembered the first voyage she had taken with Joshua. When he had taken command of *Neptune's Car*, the ship was due to sail from New York to San Francisco and across the Pacific to China, continuing westerly around the world to England. Such a sail might take a year or longer, and Joshua did not look forward to leaving Mary for so long.

It was not uncommon for a captain's wife to accompany her husband, and he invited Mary along. She agreed to go without hesitation. Despite growing up in a family of shipbuilders, she had actually spent little time on ships, her travels limited to a coastal passage as a young girl to New York and one slightly longer voyage to visit extended family in Nova Scotia. The trip to Halifax seemed to the adolescent girl like a true ocean voyage, despite losing sight of land for only a day. Still, the experience sparked a desire to see more. She became aware that there was a big world out there, beyond the low hills and harbor of Boston, and she wanted to see it.

That desire had lain dormant, waiting to be aroused. Now, to circle the globe aboard a swift clipper ship such as *Neptune's Car* provided the opportunity for her wanderlust to be reawakened and nourished with adventure. She would be able to see the world, and she would be with her husband. She could imagine nothing more perfect. Once her ambition to see the world was realized, she could settle down to a more conventional life in Massachusetts.

After some delay in arranging enough cargo to fill the ship, they set sail. Mary's excitement at going to sea with her young and handsome husband soon turned to agony. For the first ten days of the trip she had no idea that a person could become so seasick. The ship had hardly left the sight of New York Harbor when she felt the first uneasiness in her stomach. She tried to ignore the queasy feeling, but within the hour she was on her knees. By the time she got her sea legs and appetite back, the ship was halfway down the Atlantic.

Once accustomed to the motions of the ship, though, she began to enjoy herself. The stormy weather of the North Atlantic was left behind. Once able to hold her head up and look at this new world around her, Mary began to appreciate what it was that Joshua loved about his seafaring life.

She learned to walk on the sloping deck and began to enjoy the feeling of the ship moving under her. As a passenger, and especially as the captain's wife, she had no duties and little was required of her. She was free to spend as much or as little time on deck as she chose, and come and go as she pleased. She could while away the days in a chair brought out into the sun, reading and writing letters or writing in the journal she kept of the voyage. In pleasant weather she often stood by the weather rail, admiring the seascape and feeling the sun and wind on her face. Other wives had warned her of days of boredom, and she brought materials with which to sew, and often did so, but more often simply spent the day watching the sea go by.

Much of her time was employed watching the crew climb the rigging and cross the yardarms, adjusting the sails for every change in the wind to send the vessel ever faster forward. It seemed that the men were always working, moving up and down the masts or back and forth along the slanting, pitching deck that, as the ship ran before the wind, tilted at steep angles. Mary marveled at their ability to move about with such alacrity.

A backdrop to all this activity was the ocean, with its never-changing horizon. The sea was always there, with the sharp bow of the ship cutting cleanly through the waves. Flying fish often led the way, jumping up from under the bowsprit and streaking across the waves. Above the horizon was the sky, its dome as blue and constant as the sea. Mary was thrilled by the sight from the quarterdeck of the canvas straining before the wind. With all sails out, she could hardly see the tops of the masts — masts so tall they seemed to scrape the sky.

In the center of it all was the captain. Nothing on the ship happened without his command or approval. He had only to express a wish, and it was carried out. A captain attains this position of authority by virtue of his skill and knowledge in handling ships and men, and Mary was extremely proud to be this captain's wife. To be on board was to see Joshua Patten in what was clearly his element. This both pleased and saddened Mary. During their life together, he would be leaving for months at a time. As much as she would hate it when he was away, she knew she could never deny him this, his vocation and avocation.

San Francisco was made in an even one hundred days. It was a reasonably good time, and good enough to earn its captain the bonus awarded for a fast passage, but the success, for Joshua, was tainted by the arrival only five hours earlier of the clipper *Westward Ho!*, which had departed Boston on the same day *Neptune's Car* had left New York.

Joshua had lost the San Francisco race, but he exacted his revenge on the next leg, arriving in the Chinese tea port of Foochow a full eleven days ahead of his rival. He was thus in a position to obtain a better commission for carrying tea back to England.

The harbor of Foochow was crowded with junks and sampans, all filled with round yellow faces beneath wide coolie hats. As busy as the harbor was, the city was even more so. Going ashore to tour the crowded streets, amid the encompassing babble of unintelligible language, made Mary all too aware of how far she was from the familiar world of New England. Having never been away from English-speaking society, everything seemed alien to her. Unable to understand the shopkeepers or even conversation on the street, she felt out of place. Nevertheless, and to her great delight, Mary found that she reveled in the adventure.

A brief stop in Singapore, where many cultures came together to make the beginning of a large port city, showed the people and dress of this British holding to be more varied than those of the Chinese masses. There, in microcosm, could be seen the diverse peoples of Malaysia, each different from the other and all very different from the world familiar to Mary. A few short hours away from the ship served to introduce her to social classes that she hardly dreamed existed. As Joshua escorted her for a short visit to the marketplace, beggars snatched at her dress hem and street vendors pressed in close, offering anything they might want and many things they did not. Joshua was alert and on guard, and more than once foiled pickpockets at work in the crowd. Even back on board *Neptune's Car*, they were not immune from the attention of the populace. Peddlers converged upon the ships in canoes, catamarans, and, just as in China, sampans, to sell whatever they thought the crew might buy.

The long passage across vast empty ocean made the velvet green of the Dutch East Indies and the Sunda Islands seem especially beautiful. *Neptune's Car* departed Singapore, slid past islands that seemed as tranquil as paradise, and slipped through the dangerous straits of Borneo and Sumatra. These were the havens of Malay pirates, hiding in the lee of any one of a hundred islands, and Mary thought she would never again see such a lovely and fearsome place.

After crossing the wide Indian Ocean and rounding Africa's Cape of Good Hope, they ran up the Atlantic to London with their cargo of tea. After months in the Orient—though still across the ocean from New York and Boston—it seemed to Mary that she was almost home. She had seen strange and exotic sights; now she was ready to see the familiar. They had been away for over a year when they slipped away from the docks of London and set sail for New York.

Midway across the Atlantic, a violent storm sent a bolt of lightning to the foremast, severely injuring a half dozen seamen and sending crewmen and splinters of wood raining down onto the deck. With all other hands busy battling the storm, Mary went forward to tend the wounds of the injured. Finding them lying dazed, some suffering burns, others with broken bones resulting from the fall from the rigging, she ignored the storm and went from one to another, gathering her courage and her wits as she went. She administered such aid as she knew how to give, or at least offered comfort as she knelt by each man in turn on the wet, pitching deck. When the ship had weathered the storm and the damaged mast was sufficiently tended, she ordered the injured taken below deck, where she kept a makeshift sick bay until arriving in New York. In caring for the men, she felt the crew come to regard her as more than a mere passenger.

News of the storm was reported in the New York papers, and Joshua was quoted as saying, "Mrs. Patten is uncommon handy about the ship, even in weather, and would doubtless be of service, if a man." That was all very nice, but the more Mary thought about it, the more she wondered what being a man had to do with it.

Returning to the present, she stayed in the bath until the water cooled, and then reluctantly got out and dried off. Making a selection from the bathside table, she applied a lotion to her skin. The cream had a nice fragrance and a soothing feeling, better than lotions available in Boston, and she wondered where she could buy some to carry onto the ship. She decided to look later, while shopping. Perhaps the chambermaid could tell her where to find it.

She slipped back into her dressing gown and sat before the mirror of the vanity. She relished the moment, slowly brushing her long brown hair, just as she had enjoyed the soft bed and soothing bath. She was eager to be on board Joshua's ship, but that was a much different life, and she clung to the familiar while she could.

The regulator clock on the wall chimed the noon hour, reminding Mary that her husband, if his morning was going well, would soon be returning.

She pinned up her hair to look its best under the hat she had picked to wear and cocked her head toward the mirror as she inserted modest silver studs into each earlobe. Leaning forward, she touched her round cheeks with a little powder. Satisfied with her appearance, she took from her trunk the dress she had chosen for the day, its deep green fabric meant to contrast with the white of her hat. The bodice was of a lighter green silk, edged with a narrow lace collar.

Slipping off her dressing gown, she stood naked before the mirror for a few seconds. She traced a finger under the curve of one of her breasts, and her eyes wandered down to the flare of her hips. She glanced at the narrow growth of hair between her legs and thought briefly about slipping back into bed to wait for Joshua. Instead, she took up her undergarments and carefully dressed. She wanted to look her best as she and Joshua were walking the streets of New York together.

She had enjoyed her morning of leisure, but enough time had been spent within the confines of the hotel room. She was impatient to see the city. She was also impatient to see the ship, which struck her as ironic, as she would soon be seeing more of *Neptune's Car* than she could stand.

She returned to the window and looked out over the buildings and streets of the city. It was a very different scene, she reflected, than the one she would see tomorrow. Tomorrow and for many days to come.

She thought of those long and leisurely days at sea. And they were leisurely, for her. The captain and mates spent long hours on duty, and the crew worked hard in all kinds of weather, but Mary had only to relax and enjoy the sail. On the last trip she read, slowly, to savor the words and make the books last as long as she could. She wrote letters to give to any ship they met going back to New York, and she wrote in her diary. She sewed and quilted. The time she spent on deck in fair weather, enjoying the sun and balmy breezes, seemed like time spent in paradise. Even the foul weather days seemed to be only exciting variations of pleasure.

At the same time, though, she knew that endless days on a ship could get to be tedious, especially for a passenger such as herself, with no duties to occupy her time. The journey across the Pacific and Indian Oceans to round Africa had seemed to take forever. The world, she found, was a very large place, and even a fast clipper ship was not fast enough for her.

To help pass the time, she learned how to use a sextant, the instrument that was the key to navigation. Daily, Mary watched Joshua carry the brass sextant from the cabin to the deck to take his sights. She became curious about the operation of the instrument. She watched as he held it up to his eye and peered toward the horizon, and then read from the curved scale some result that sent him to his tables and charts. To her, it seemed a mysterious process, but one that she was sure she could learn, if only she knew the secret.

The first time she asked about it, he dismissed her curiosity, saying she would not understand. Mary listened and then said, "Show me."

Joshua tried to discourage her. "There is no need for you to know this."

"I realize that," she answered. "Show me."

Joshua sighed. Surely, Mary thought, he did not expect her to ignore the world around her simply because she was told she should. Inquisitive by nature, she had long harbored an adventurous streak, which was one reason she was on the vessel in the first place.

"Show me," she said.

Joshua saw that she was not to be denied. "Very well," he said.

He picked up the instrument, an eight-inch-high triangle of brass, its bottom side curved and marked in degrees of arc on a graduated scale.

"We use the sextant to find the angle of the sun above the horizon. It works like this."

He showed her how an arm, hinged at the apex of the triangle, moved an index mark along the curved scale. There were two small mirrors, one attached at the top of the movable arm, and another on the forward leg of the instrument. This second mirror, called the horizon glass, was only half silvered, the other half being clear glass. Attached to the rear leg was a small cylindrical sight tube, lined up with the forward leg's horizon glass.

"As the adjustable arm moves," Joshua said, "its pointer moving along the scale, the top mirror also moves."

He handed Mary the instrument. "Try it," he said. "Hold the sextant so that you can see the horizon through the tube, lined up with the clear half of the horizon glass."

Carefully holding the sextant, Mary put the sight tube up to her eye. Through the tube, and through the small rectangle of clear glass, she saw the distant horizon of the sea.

"I see it," Mary said. "Now what do I do?"

"Now, being careful to keep the instrument vertical, move the arm until the mirror on top reflects the image of the sun into the mirror half of the horizon glass."

Mary did, and as the arm moved forward, the sun came into view, its brightness masked by dark shades flipped into position between the two mirrors. When the sun was in approximate line with the horizon, she followed Joshua's instruction and carefully fine-tuned the vernier knob until the bottom edge of the sun's disk was lined up exactly with the line of the horizon.

"And now," said Joshua, "you have the angle of the sun above the horizon marked on the scale. There you are. That's all there is to finding the angle of the sun."

"I assume there is more to it," Mary said.

"More to what?"

"More to the art of navigation."

Joshua laughed. "Oh, much more."

"Such as?"

Joshua's eyes twinkled. "Well, if you insist. What you have is actually just the observed angle. To find the true angle, useful for navigation, we must first make several corrections.

"First, the index error must be corrected to compensate for any error with the sextant itself. Then we allow for what is called dip error, taking into consideration the height of the observer above the sea. It is a small correction, but important. Then, whenever the sun is not directly overhead, the refraction of the sun in the atmosphere must be compensated for. The lower the sun, the more refraction there is. Then of course, all calculations are based upon the center of the sun, not the lower limb as we have measured, so we have to determine what one half the diameter of the sun is. Shall I go on?"

Mary knew he was trying to discourage her. "Yes," she said. "By all means."

"Not only are the calculations based upon the center of the sun, but we must also reduce our position, not merely from the deck down to the sea, but to the center of the earth. That is particularly important when sighting the moon. It is all very complicated."

"Then show me," said Mary.

Giving up on discouraging her, Joshua had her take another sight, this time noting the time of the observation. Then he took her below, where he showed her how to use the nautical almanac to allow for all the errors he had described to determine the angle of the sun. As they stood close by each other, examining the tables of the almanac, Mary leaned to brush her shoulder against Joshua's arm, feeling his warmth.

"I thought you wanted to learn this," Joshua said teasingly.

"I do. Please go on," she said softly, still touching.

Joshua smiled. "I'll try."

Once all the corrections were done, the angle as measured by the sextant became true altitude of the sun. If the observation was made precisely at local noon, when the sun was at its highest, simple consultations with the almanac revealed the difference, for that time on that day, between the sun's angle relative to the equator, and its angle to the ship.

"This difference between the angle, or declination, at the equator and the angle we have here on the ship gives us our latitude," said Joshua. He then added smugly, "Of course, if the observation is taken at any other time besides noon, it becomes more involved."

Mary refused to be deterred. She found it to be great fun to use the sextant, and soon felt quite at home in finding not only latitude and longitude but using that information to plot their position on the ship's charts. She practiced often, comparing her results with Joshua's. They were usually very close, and on occasion it was her plots that Joshua entered into the log.

At the window of her hotel room, Mary's thoughts left the ship and turned again to the brick and stone of the city. Leaning close to the glass she could see the street, three floors down, and the pedestrians rushing along the sidewalk. Everyone seemed to be in a hurry.

She was looking down, her forehead pressed against the glass, when the door opened and Joshua walked in. She turned to greet him and left the window, meeting him halfway across the room.

"I'm sorry I was so long," he said, reaching out to her. She slid into his arms. The strong hug and long kiss belied the fact they had only a few hours ago separated.

As he released her, and she him, their fingertips lingered on each other for a second. Their night together in the hotel notwithstanding, they had been apart for most of the last month, and the pleasure of being together again was still new and fresh.

She turned toward the dressing table. He dropped into a nearby chair.

"Busy morning," he said. "So much to do. But it's coming together." He looked at his wife. "How about you?"

Mary sighed heavily and waved a weary arm in a sweep about the room. "I am all done in. It has been one thing after another. Exhausted. That's the word. I'm exhausted."

Joshua smiled. "I don't feel so bad, then. I've only had to deal with recalcitrant shippers and overbearing agents and a crew still drunk with last night's rum. Add to that the problem of finding a new mate when no good ones are about and chandlers telling me at the last minute that they don't have what I ordered weeks ago. It goes on and on. Still, that is nothing compared to what you have had to do. Why, you have had to . . ." He looked around the room. "Tell me again what you have done."

"I have had a bath."

"Oh, poor thing. However did you manage?"

"Intestinal fortitude, I believe is the phrase."

They both laughed. Joshua looked across at Mary, who had sat back down to arrange her hat.

She carefully inserted a long pin to hold the hat in place, turning her head from side to side before the mirror. "Has it been that bad?"

"No. I mean, all those things did happen, but they always happen. Except for the problem of a first mate."

"You don't have a first mate?"

"Well, you know Charlie Rhodes is not able to go. It's unfortunate, since we worked so well together. I've got a man available, and he might work out."

Mary studied his reflection in the mirror. "You don't seem too sure."

Joshua shrugged. "Who can say? Are you ready to eat? I'm starving."

Mary made a last adjustment to the hat, a white straw with a wide brim that dipped over her eyes. Its pale blue band held a small spray of silk pansies.

"Yes, I'm ready. You can tell me more about your morning as we walk. You said you know a good place?"

"I think you'll like it. There is no salted meat on the menu."

Mary thought about the meals she would be facing on the ship and said, "Sounds perfect."

CHAPTER 3

Neptune's Car

The day spent in New York was a pleasant one. Mary wanted it to be perfect, and it very nearly was. A lingering lunch at the Astor House, at a table by the hotel's large windows overlooking the sidewalk, was spent in soft conversation, young lovers leaning over the soup to speak words meant only for each other. Joshua spoke of the ship and the coming voyage, and Mary of news from home, but anyone watching from the street would have thought they were speaking of the most intimate love, so closely did they hover over the small table. As far as Mary was concerned, that lunch could last forever.

Joshua had been in New York since early June, and Mary had stayed in Boston. There was much to catch up on. The roast beef had been cleared from the table and they were into the bread pudding before she finished most of her news and he had told of his weeks at the port. He finished by telling her the events of the morning, of the search for a suitable first mate and the queries made along the docks about William Keeler. Opinions of those who knew Keeler led Joshua to decide that while he may not be the ideal mate, he would probably not be too difficult to deal with. It seemed that the worst of Keeler's traits was a propensity toward strong opinions and a reluctance to have his mind changed. Hardly insurmountable problems, Joshua thought.

"And the ship is ready to sail," he said to Mary. "As hard as it is to fill the hold these days, it's best to go on time."

Mary took a bite of pudding and looked across the table at her husband. The light coming through the large front window was good, and she could see tiny worry lines on his face.

"You think Mr. Keeler suitable?"

"He will probably do just fine. I just don't like going off around the world with a mate I just met today. The fact that he doesn't always get along with his captains doesn't help."

"Perhaps you should tell Mr. Wiley that you cannot go until you are more sure about this Mr. Keeler. We are already a week later than originally planned. One or two more days will not hurt."

"I wish I could agree. The fact that we are already late is part of the problem. We booked this cargo with Coleman and Company by assuring them that we could leave New York before *Romance of the Seas*, which sails tomorrow. Not only that, but my old friend Horatio Gardner is ready to go with his new ship, *Intrepid*. It will be that ship's maiden voyage, and you can be assured that his departure will be noted in the papers. If we are still sitting at the dock when those two depart, it will not look good."

"You would rather take a chance on trouble after you are at sea than here in port?"

Joshua looked a little stung. He prided himself on a well-run ship, and Mary was suggesting that he was willing to compromise to appease businessmen behind big desks.

"I think I can take care of my ship."

Mary had not intended to be harsh. She completely trusted her husband's ability to deal with adverse situations, both at sea and in port.

"I'm sorry, dear. I did not mean to say that you could not." She paused, choosing her words carefully. "I just want this trip to go well. I want it to be perfect. It may be my last time to accompany you. Soon there will be children, hopefully, and a home to maintain. A woman's place, and all that."

Joshua smiled. "There are those captains who take their entire families to sea. It often works out quite well."

"I do not think I would like that. To be with you would be grand, but children need something more than a deck to play on, and more than vulgar sailors to play with."

"Not all sailors are that bad," said Joshua. "Some are quite civilized."

Mary was not swayed. "The best have been corrupted by the worst. They all lack social graces."

"I think I should be offended," Joshua said in mock indignation. "I was once a common foremast hand myself, you know."

Mary smiled sweetly. "Yes, dear, but you dragged yourself up from that gutter. If you had not, we would not be sitting her in this nice hotel having this splendid lunch. You would be carrying your duffel from your squalid room down to the docks to sign on with some ship or another, while the captain of that ship was here with me." She lifted her cup and daintily took a sip of tea.

Joshua feigned hurt. "You mean to say that you wouldn't have married me if I were an ordinary seaman?"

"Oh, I would love you no matter what you were. But if you were an ordinary seaman, we likely would never have met. The fates that raised you from the forecastle also steered you toward me. You lucky man."

Joshua laughed. He was a competent sea captain but was no match for the quick wit of the young woman sitting across from him.

"Very well. No children raised at sea. Besides, I rather like the idea of having a home to come back to. After this voyage, I will not sail again until we are settled into a house. Meanwhile, don't worry about me and my mates. Everything will be fine."

"You plan to take on Mr. Keeler, then?"

"If it is just his opinions that cause our Mr. Keeler trouble, I think I can keep him in line. Besides, I doubt anyone else will come along, and it is important to get under way. You know how the shipping business is these days."

Despite it not being a woman's business, Mary did know. The demand for fast transportation of goods to the California goldfields had peaked in 1850, but the building of the fast clipper ships had not peaked until 1853. One hundred and twenty clippers were built that year, one being *Neptune's Car*, from the Virginia shipyard of Page and Allen.

Unfortunately, demand for fast shipping was past. Many clippers lay idle at their anchors for months at a time, awaiting a commission. For those ships that did sail, profits were not as great. In 1850, when supplies were needed in California at any price, the cost of shipping goods around the Horn was about sixty dollars a ton. Now, in 1856, the rate had dropped to less than fifteen. The gold rush was over.

With falling freight rates and a scarcity of cargoes, ship owners were obliged to accept business they would never have considered in better times. Some were reduced to hauling bird guano from islands off Chile. Ship captains, too, were sometimes forced to do things they might not like, such as taking on inferior and untrained crews: many seamen had made the trip to California a one-way affair. Once in San Francisco, they jumped ship to pan for gold. The reduced pool of experienced hands also meant fewer men qualified for first mate.

Mary knew Joshua was not happy about being rushed into taking on a mate of questionable ability, and as she took her last bite of dessert she decided not to bring up the subject again.

"Ready?"

Mary looked up from her musings. Joshua had finished with his pudding and was patiently waiting for her. "Yes," she said, putting down her spoon. "Let's go."

The couple stepped back out onto the street. The next few hours belonged to Mary, to do what she would have no chance to do after this day. If shopping was in order, there was no better place to do it than New York City. They strolled up and down the avenues, looking at window displays and wandering into the stores. Purchases were considered and made—a new dress, a hat, shoes to match the dress—and couriers were dispatched to deliver bundles back to the Battery Hotel. At a shop on Fifth Avenue, she found bath oils like those she had used at the hotel. Joshua, while eager to get back to his ship, dutifully tagged along.

It was late afternoon when Mary felt she had shopped enough. She was also aware that Joshua wanted and needed to return to his ship to check last-minute preparations. It was very sweet of him, she thought, to take the time to accompany her along the busy avenues of this most metropolitan of cities. At a little past four she announced that her purchases were complete.

Joshua promptly hailed a passing cab, and they climbed in. "South Street Seaport, driver," he called out.

From the high bench came a "Yes, sir," and then a sharp "Hi!" to the horse, which started the cab with a soft lurch. As they traveled down Broadway and Fulton Street to the port, Mary thought the horse's hooves seemed to be tapping out *clipper, clipper, clipper,* along the pavement. She started to point this out to Joshua, but refrained, afraid he would think it childish. At twenty-nine years old, he was ten years her senior, and she wanted not to remind him that she was still in her teens.

The red brick buildings of the city hid the port until the last moment, so that when the cab turned onto South Street, Mary was treated to the sudden view of tall-masted ships. As far as she could see in either direction up and down the wide East River, ships lay waiting for cargoes and crews. To Mary, the masts and yards were as thick as trees in a winter forest, trees devoid of leaves. Bare rigging hung like vines. But unlike the trees of nature, with limbs and branches bent and twisting, these trees were uniformly straight and tall, their limbs exactly horizontal.

Below the rows of masts and yardarms were the ships themselves, long dark hulls docked side by side. A ship at sea, seen at a distance, might seem sleek and trim, but up close became almost incredibly huge. Ships docked two or three blocks away down South Street did not seem especially imposing, but those nearby, approached in turn by the horse-drawn cab, rose up in height and breadth to take command. All along the busy wharf the huge hulking forms were nosed in, their long bowsprits jutting out far over the heads of all who passed beneath. Sailors and stevedores, teams and teamsters, high-sided wagons and pushcarts—all were dwarfed by the overshadowing bows of ships.

Those who worked in these shadows of the ships were accustomed to their presence, but Mary could not help but feel a certain thrill at seeing the large numbers of big ships lining the port of New York. On her first voyage with Joshua, she had seen other crowded ports of the world, but she felt that this city had the most ships, as well as the largest, of any port she had visited.

Joshua was also watching out the open window, but with a more critical and less excited eye. Presently, he spoke loudly enough to be heard up on top.

"Here is fine, driver."

The carriage pulled to a stop, and the driver hopped down to open the door and help Mary down to the street. While Joshua paid the fare, she looked along the row of ships. For a moment she was unable to pick Joshua's ship out of the crowd, one clipper being pretty much like another. Then some familiarity showed itself, and she recognized the bow of the ship nearest them. Her heart swelled with pride.

Joshua beamed. "Well, here she is. Home away from home."

"You were reading my mind."

He glanced over at her and raised an eyebrow. "Second thoughts?"

Mary smiled. "None at all."

That was not quite true. She had considered staying home, but the thoughts had been fleeting ones. The first voyage with her husband had been difficult at times, especially starting out, but in the end she had adjusted well to the life. The intervening months at home were a welcome respite, but now she was ready to go again. It was said that the salt gets in your blood, and she could see how it could happen.

"Let's go aboard."

Joshua took her arm, guiding her down the dock beside the long black hull of the extreme clipper *Neptune's Car*. Mary looked at the railing along the side of the ship. She would be spending a lot of time standing there, watching the sea rush past. The rail glistened a bright white in the afternoon sun.

"New paint?"

"Stem to stern. The ship is in fine shape." There was pride in Joshua's voice.

The ship did look good. From the long bowsprit all the way back to the stern post, the entire hull, as common among clippers, was painted black, topped with a six-inch gold stripe just below the railing. The masts were likewise black as high as the topgallant yard, two-thirds of the way up. Above that they were whitewashed. The yardarms themselves were painted in the same scheme, lower ones black and the high white. Arrayed all about the vessel, hanging from masts and yards and stretching from bow to taffrail, the rigging and lines of the ship were coated with a mixture of linseed oil and black tar, so fresh that Mary could still smell the strangely sweet odor. The tar was intended to protect the hemp from the elements, but a secondary benefit was that the dark color further enhanced the appearance of the ship. Clipper ships were sharp and fast, and they looked it.

Neptune's Car, heavily loaded, sat low in the water, but even so, the side of the ship rose higher than the dock. A ramped gangplank led up to the side of the ship. In the *Car*'s heavy state, the slope was gentle, rising only a few feet, and Joshua and Mary stepped up to the ship hardly needing to use the iron handrails. Upon reaching the railing, Joshua led the way down a set of temporary steps to the deck and turned to aid Mary as she stepped down.

Mary was always reminded of a ship's size when she first stepped onto the deck and realized how high the sides were. Those unfamiliar with big ships usually think of the deck as being at the top of the hull, with the railing necessary to keep one from falling overboard. In reality, on the main deck, the bulwarks of the ship rose to near shoulder level, and was more of a wall than a railing. Only near the bow and along the raised quarterdeck at the stern were the sides of the ship low enough that a railing was really needed for safety.

The oak wood of the deck, freshly scrubbed with holystones, seemed instantly familiar under her feet. She noticed that in many places the oakum caulk that filled the gaps between the planks had been replaced with new. She looked forward, along the cluttered deck toward the faraway bow, impressed as always with the distance. Not only was *Neptune's Car* a tall ship, she was long.

Turning aft, Mary looked up over the poop of the quarterdeck. It was there that she would spend almost all of the next few months. Four steps led up through a waist-high railing that separated the raised deck from the main, or weather, deck. Behind the rail, the quarterdeck extended aft fifty feet to the stern's taffrail. This elevated quarterdeck was the domain of the captain and his officers. Unless duties required their presence, no seamen, except the helmsmen standing at the huge wheel by the stern, were allowed on the quarterdeck.

Likewise, the captain himself rarely went forward among the crew. Mary remembered, at the beginning of her first voyage, thinking that to be an odd arrangement, but after a while saw the advantages. A clipper captain worked his ship and men hard, at the limits of the capabilities of both, and it was best to keep some distance. If a captain got too familiar with his crew, he might soften toward them, not driving them hard enough to gain that extra knot of speed, and might not maintain the required hard edge of discipline.

By the same token, it was best that the captain not become too familiar to the crew. Not all ship's masters were totally worthy of the position, and close contact might more readily reveal their faults. It was better to keep the captain above and away, to make him more godlike. The captain ruled his ship like a Zeus, casting commands from the quarterdeck like oracles from Delphi.

This was the world in which Mary would live while at sea.

She was still taking this first look about the ship when a voice from midship called out for Captain Patten, and she turned to see a man with a sheaf of papers coming toward them.

"Pardon me, Captain," he said, "but if I could have a word with you." Then, remembering his manners, he turned to Mary and tipped his hat. "Good afternoon, miss."

Mary smiled and nodded politely. The man appeared to be concerned with things on his papers, so to save Joshua the trouble of introductions, she motioned that she was going aft and left the two men together. A few strides took her to the steps leading up to the quarterdeck. She climbed them carefully, holding the skirt of her dress to avoid tripping over the hem. At the high varnished rail, she turned and looked forward. Joshua was close by the man's elbow, and both were studying what she surmised were lists of something. Joshua stood with his hands on his hips, coat pushed back, revealing his slim torso. Once, he frowned and scratched his head above his ear, under the edge of his hat. The man was obviously trying to explain something to Joshua's satisfaction, but Joshua seemed unconvinced.

All about, at scattered locations around the deck, other men were working. Some were sailors, putting finishing touches to preparations for sea. Others were dockworkers and stevedores, dirty and sweaty from last-minute labors. The decks were clear of cargo, it having all been put below in the holds, and all but the most perishable of provisions were also on board and stored. It took a great deal of food and water to support a crew of thirty-seven and one passenger for the three or four months it might take to get to San Francisco. With no plans to stop at any port en route, it all had to be carried out of New York. The only additional food would be fish that the men caught from the sea, and the only other source of fresh water would be rain.

Directly in front of her, some forty feet away and near the midpoint of the ship, stood the mainmast. So large in circumference that two men could barely reach around it, the mast rose through the deck from its base down by the keel to reach 150 feet into the sky. Made of thick pine from the tallest of trees, it was actually several pieces of timber banded together with iron hoops but rounded and smoothed to appear as one giant trunk. At intervals were the yardarms, or yards, five long horizontal cross-members that, with accompanying lines of rope running down to the deck, held the sails.

Beyond the mainmast, toward the bow, stood the foremast. Behind Mary, rising from the floor of the quarterdeck, was the mizzenmast. Like the mainmast, each had a series of yards and lines. The mizzen also had two long booms for the spanker sail that extended aft toward the stern.

Each mast had its own set of rigging. For climbing there was the standing rigging, ladders of stiffened rope six feet wide at their base but narrowing as they went up. The running rigging, long lines from deck to yard, held the sails to the wind. Including studding sails, spanker, and jibs, there might be thirty or more sails out at once, each with its own set of lines. The lines were everywhere, covering the ship in a web of rope, and the array was bewildering. After sailing all the way around the world on *Neptune's Car*, Mary still did not know where every line went without carefully tracing its path.

Beyond the foremast, the deck stepped up to the low forecastle and tapered to the point of the bow, where the long bowsprit and jib boom jutted out over the water. From Mary's vantage point, this farthest forward extension of the ship, nearly two hundred feet away, was almost hidden from view by all the intervening masts and rigging.

As she looked over the ship, waiting for Joshua to take care of his business, the sights and sounds of the port filled the scene around her. The working men shouted to and fro. Wagons moved slowly along the wharves, and somewhere, a ship's bell rang. In the air overhead, seagulls patrolled the docks, coasting on bent wings, squawking their shrill call.

A breeze came off the East River, holding the gulls aloft, and Mary imagined being at sea, the now bare poles filled with billowing sail. The urge to be sailing again returned, stronger this time.

She rubbed her hand along the railing at her waist, feeling its smooth rounded surface. This rail, and every other piece of woodwork on the quarterdeck, was varnished to a flawless finish. *Neptune's Car* was a beautiful ship, freshly painted and scrubbed, every line tarred and in the best of repair. Even the name, Mary thought, was beautifully appropriate. What better way to ride across the waves than on the carriage of the ruler of the sea?

Once on the open ocean, free of the bindings of land, her beauty of form would blend with the beauty of function. All sails would be set, filling the warm sky above the canted deck with clouds of canvas. The sleek clipper would heel before stiff breezes, plowing its foamy furrow through the seas, white spray off the bow holding rainbows almost within reach.

Not all days would be ideal—there would be storms, perhaps even deadly ones—but that was part of the allure. After the storms, after the cold and the danger, there would be the reward of sunshine and life, and it thrilled Mary to contemplate sharing those rewards with her captain.

Tomorrow they would begin.

CHAPTER 4

Setting Sail

The first day of July began in the same way that the last day of June had ended. Joshua and Mary Patten had fallen asleep in the languid afterglow of making love and woke the next morning to soft touches that began the intimacy again. Still half in their own dreams, eyes still closed, each of their hands slipped over the close form of the other.

Using fingers, lips, and tongue, Joshua explored the contours of Mary's slender body, feeling the softness of her cheeks, the round point of her chin, tasting the sweep down toward the gentle rise of her breasts. She sighed softly in her half-awake state and arched her back toward Joshua's caressing lips.

His hand traveled down her side, into the swale of her narrow waist and up over the rise of her hip. He slid his reach around behind her and pulled her tight against him. His hand wandered down the back of her thigh, and he used his thumb to gently rub the depression behind her knee. She liked that, and the soft moan told Joshua that what he was doing was good.

He moved his face back up to hers, kissing her soft open mouth, and she tasted his lips and searched for his tongue with her own. Their lovemaking settled into a steady rhythm, both of them caught up in its intensity. Both knew that once at sea even the closed door of their cabin would not provide the private solitude of this hotel room with its luxurious bed. Here, Joshua need not be ready to leave the bed at a call from deck. Here there would be no interruptions, no distractions. Here they could simply be husband and wife, not captain and wife.

Afterwards they rested together, softly talking and tenderly touching. For Mary, it was her favorite part of making love.

It could not last forever. That afternoon *Neptune's Car* would be casting off and setting sail, and there were matters her captain must attend to. It was out of great necessity, but with great reluctance, that Joshua pulled himself out of the arms of his wife to prepare for the day ahead.

Mary sighed. For the last day and a half, he had been hers alone. Beginning today, though, she would once again have to share him with a ship and the sea.

After a few more minutes of basking in sheets that still smelled of their love, Mary rose and had a bath. It would be her last luxury until reaching San Francisco. This bath was much more brief than the lingering soak she had treated herself to the previous morning; then she, too, began readying for the day's events.

She spent the morning packing her trunk and valise, making room for the purchases of the day before. She could easily have made use of more luggage, but was trying to practice economy of space. *Neptune's Car* was a large ship, but even so, room in the cabin was at a premium. She also remembered the roll of Joshua's eyes when she appeared for her first voyage with baggage enough for six.

Without waiting for her husband to return, she sent down for a bellman and arranged for delivery of their belongings to the ship. She knew Joshua's day would be a busy one, and taking care of the luggage was one duty of which she could relieve him. She considered going on down to the ship but was afraid she might miss Joshua on his way back, so she waited. Her wait was an impatient one. She was ready to be on her way. It was with some difficulty that she occupied her mind, listening at every sound in the hallway to determine if her husband was coming for her. She tried to take advantage of these last hours in port to write some letters, but her heart was not in it. She penned short notes to her mother and brother, and one to a childhood friend, but they were uninspired and lacked the warmth she had intended. When Joshua finally reappeared, she had long since put away the ink and was ready to go. All that remained was for her to put on her hat.

Sitting before the dressing mirror, she slipped a jade hat pin into place. The pin had been given to her by a friend she had made on the last voyage, during the stop in Singapore, and it went well with the wide green hat she had chosen for today. Before she rose, she made a last check of her appearance. She wanted to look good for her husband when she went aboard his ship.

Mary and Joshua left the hotel and walked the few blocks to the port, stopping halfway at a small restaurant for lunch. Joshua pretended that he was in no hurry, but Mary knew otherwise and did not tarry over her food. The lingering lunch at the Astor House and the romantic dinner at Delmonico's was yesterday. Today was sailing day, with little time for genteel dining. For his part, Joshua ate as quickly as politely possible and then filled her in about his morning.

The new first mate, William Keeler, had been hired and was at the moment on the ship, overseeing preparations in Joshua's absence. The rest of the crew, totaling thirty-one men and four boys, had been signed and were on board. Provisioning was complete, including livestock in pens on deck and casks of water stored below. The holds were full of cargo. All that remained to be done was the filing of shipping articles and obtaining clearance to depart from the customs officer. Once those paperwork details were completed and the harbor pilot was brought on board, *Neptune's Car* would be ready for the tug. High tide was a little after one o'clock, and Joshua planned to ride it out. The weather was perfect, with a light but steady breeze from the south. Once away from land, a better wind could be expected, and he was impatient to set sails before it.

As they left the restaurant, Mary learned of another reason he was impatient to depart. Another clipper, *Romance of the Seas*, which Joshua had been determined to beat out of port, had left the dock well before noon, also bound for San Francisco, and was probably even now dropping its pilot and raising sails. *Romance of the Seas* had been built by Donald McKay, whose shipyards were earning a reputation of building ships of unbeatable speed. Joshua wanted to prove that *Neptune's Car* was just as fast, and it annoyed him that *Romance* should be getting a head start. Not only that, but a new William Webb clipper, the *Intrepid*, with Captain Gardner in command, was also departing this same day for its maiden voyage. Gardner was still in port, but no doubt wished to get under way for California before Patten. The coming voyage might take months, but for today the race was to get out of New York Harbor.

Joshua and Mary walked the few blocks to the port, finding *Neptune's Car* a hive of activity. Men moved quickly about a deck cluttered with coils of line and other gear, calling back and forth to each other, doing whatever the duty of the moment required. As the captain and his wife stepped aboard, seamen were working to bring a long roll of sail up from below. A rope looped through tackle hung high above deck hoisted the sail up through an open hatch while men guided it up and out of the opening. With a cry of warning to clear the area, the sail swung clear of the hatch and rose to its place high on the fore topgallant yard.

Mary looked up and saw two men waiting on a yardarm to take the sail and begin fastening it in place. Most of the sails were already up, with tiny figures of men crawling all over the high masts and yards working to finish the job. She noticed that one of the figures was more tiny than the rest. That would be one of the young boys, barely in their teens, who had been taken on to do much of the menial work. They were also the ones sent to do the highest work, up among the small sails at the top of the mast, more than a hundred feet above the deck. The sails above the topgallant level were called the royals, and the boys were often hired on as "royal boys."

With frequent shouts from above and below, those aloft and those working lines on deck coordinated their actions. The calls and commands were terse and short, words developed over the centuries to be easily communicated over howling winds in rough seas.

"Ease the sheet!"

"Haul!"

"Clew the yard!"

Mary lowered her gaze from the rigging and saw two men approaching. One was a large, barrel-chested man of swarthy complexion. Joshua made introductions.

"Mary, I would like you to meet Mr. William Keeler, first mate. Mr. Keeler, I present my wife, Mary Patten."

Keeler removed his hat. Bowing politely, he said, "Ma'am."

Mary nodded and said, "Pleased to meet you, Mr. Keeler. It is very fortunate that you are available to join my husband on such short notice."

"The pleasure, Mrs. Patten, is mine. Both in the opportunity to serve on this fine ship and in the opportunity to meet you." Keeler offered a stiff smile, which Mary recognized to be an effort to be on best behavior in the company of a woman. His efforts to be polite were inadvertently contradicted by the up-and-down look he gave Mary. She recognized it as the one loutish men use to appraise women, whether they mean to do so or not.

In return, Mary took a few seconds to size up Keeler. He was difficult to read, his face showing little emotion. His eyes were dark, deep, and serious, qualities that enhanced the appearance of many men but with Keeler seemed only to contradict his smile. His skin, Mary noted, was dark and oily, much more so than normal for a white man, and she wondered if he had some mix of foreign blood in him. His dark hair was combed back from a wide, protruding forehead that seemed too high for his face, which further emphasized the impression of the depth of his eyes. Keeler's nose, too, was wide and flat, and appeared to have been broken at least once.

Joshua had warned her that he did not present himself as overly friendly, but like Joshua, she had predetermined to give the man the benefit of doubt. Perhaps he was nice enough, but was just unable to show it. Still, her first impression was that she did not particularly like him, but she smiled back and said, "You are very kind."

Keeler said nothing else, and for a moment an awkward silence ensued. The first mate seemed to know it was his turn to speak but, not knowing what to say, said nothing.

Relieving the moment, Joshua turned to the young man standing beside Keeler. Youthful and slender, second mate Timothy Hare was dwarfed by the second mate's bulk.

Joshua said, "You remember Mr. Hare, don't you, Mary?"

Mary looked toward the slightly built mate, two years older than her nineteen years, and could not help but have a bright smile come to her face. During the previous trip around the world, she had found Hare to be a very likable young man. His blue eyes were always shining; his face held an open expression. Entirely honest and dependable, she thought. His only flaws seemed to be a lack of education and an apparent inability to always think for himself. By hard work he had risen above the position of able seaman, but would likely never make first mate. Mary felt a little sorry for him, but he appeared content. He seemed to know his limitations and was at ease with them.

"Yes, of course. I remember Mr. Hare," she said, "and I am very pleased to see that he is to be with us again."

Holding his cap in both hands before his chest, Hare grinned but said nothing.

To Keeler, Joshua asked, "How are things on board?"

Polite formalities over, the conversation turned to business, and Hare melted away to resume his duties. Keeler began catching Joshua up on the morning's progress, with Joshua asking a dozen questions about one thing or another. Invariably, Keeler was able to answer in the affirmative. Preparations were almost complete. The bending of the sails was not yet finished, but by the time the ship was out of the harbor, every yardarm would be dressed for duty.

"Good," said Joshua. "Continue on, Mr. Keeler. I'll be getting Mrs. Patten settled in."

"Aye, sir."

Keeler turned and started forward toward the bow.

Mary watched him walk away, his gray work shirt pulled tight over his broad shoulders. At her side, Joshua said, "Well, what do you think?"

Mary thought for a second and said, "I do not know. I can see why you are not fully comfortable with him. I am just not sure why."

"I told you he didn't seem all that friendly."

"It's not that," she said. "He just seems to have a darker side."

"Not exactly happy-go-lucky."

Mary gave a short laugh. "Not even close. But you think him competent?"

"I have no reason to think otherwise."

"I'm sure he will do fine. He just doesn't seem to know how to make a sincere first impression."

"I don't believe that being sincere is required for the position," Joshua said. "Let's go below and make sure all our luggage is on board."

By "going below," Joshua meant getting to the captain's cabin, which was not actually below the main deck, but rather on it, in a rectangular cabin that occupied the deck aft of the main mast and extended under the raised quarterdeck. Entering the door on the forward end of this after house put Joshua and Mary in the saloon, a large room richly paneled in the finest woods and dominated by a large dining table.

Every part of the saloon was finished with the best rosewood and mahogany laid with a careful eye to the details. In the ceiling over the table was a skylight of delicate stained glass rising into the deck above like a long rectangular cupola. Other parts of the ship might be rough and functional, but this room was appointed with fine wood and quality ironwork. The table, set with the best crystal and china, was intended to provide a touch of class for the captain and any guests he might entertain.

On either side of the room were the living quarters of the junior officers. On the port side stood the cabin of the first mate, just large enough for a bed, with a storage locker below it, and a small desk mounted to the wall. Immediately aft of the mate's quarters was a room for the steward, who served the meals and kept house. On the opposite side of the saloon similar quarters housed the second mate and in a second room slept the cabin boy, if there was one, or other passengers or guests who might be on board. On *Neptune's Car* the steward doubled as cabin boy, and there were to be no other passengers, so the spare room would be used for storage.

At the rear of the cabin, beyond the dining table, was a larger room belonging to the captain. As deluxe accommodations, they would scarcely rival the Ritz, but for life on board a ship at sea—and a cargo ship at that—the captain's stateroom on *Neptune's Car* was as good as on any ship. Occupying a third of the after cabin, it served as the sleeping quarters and sitting room for the captain and his wife. It was also his office.

To this cabin Joshua led Mary.

The Pattens' baggage had been delivered and left stacked by the door. With the aid of the steward, who had been hovering nearby, it was moved into the cabin. Mary directed some of the packages to be stored away in the spare cabin. The rest, including the large trunk, stayed in the middle of their cabin. Later, when the excitement of getting under way was past, she would unpack and arrange her clothes in the built-in wardrobe and chest of drawers, the better to lead a civilized life.

Joshua stood in the doorway of the cabin, as there was scarcely room to enter once the luggage filled the floor space. His hand rested lightly on the small of Mary's back. "Home, sweet home," he said.

Mary glanced at her husband, noting the apology in his voice. "It will be fine. I have learned to make do quite well with limited space."

"Just the same, you know how small a ship can become after a few months at sea. To say nothing of a small room."

"I prefer to think of this as cozy." Mary smiled coyly and wrapped her arm around Joshua's waist.

"Mary!" Joshua said. "We have company."

Mary turned. She had forgotten that the steward still waited behind them, and immediately regretted acting that way with him watching. Joshua's feelings for her in the bedroom were not shown as easily on the ship, especially with an audience. The steward, to his credit, had looked away, pretending not to have seen the flirtation. It was a mature reaction considering his youth. His name, Mary recalled from the last trip, was Henry. At seventeen, he was one of the few on board younger than she.

Slim and fresh-faced, as if he had just stepped off a prep school lawn, Henry had joined the crew in San Francisco the year before and had earned the steward's position by his capable handling of those necessary domestic duties. Like many, he had gone to California seeking fortune but had found mostly hardship, and he had signed on to the crew of *Neptune's Car* as a way back home from that land of elusive dreams. He had never been to sea before, but he took to the life well, and Joshua was pleased to have him return for this voyage. Mary was also pleased. She liked his charming boyish personality, which was well, considering the close confines of the after cabin.

Mary removed her arm from Joshua's waist, acting once again with proper manners, and separated herself from him. She entered the cabin, stepping around her valise, and said, "I'll just put some of this away before we sail. I know you have things to do."

Joshua seemed glad for the opportunity to get out of the cabin. The preparations on deck and ashore required a captain's attention, and Mary seemed quite capable of taking care of herself.

"If you are sure you don't need me, then," he said, "I will go back out on deck."

Mary looked around the room, refamiliarizing herself with her surroundings. "I'll be fine, Joshua. You go ahead. I'm sure you are anxious to get under way, and I am as well."

"All right, then. Henry will be happy to assist you with anything you need, won't you, Henry?"

The boy smiled. "Yes, sir." To Mary he said, "At your service, madam."

Mary returned his smile and said, "Thank you, but I'm just going to stow a few things and rest for a while until we leave port."

Joshua departed for the quarterdeck and Henry withdrew to another part of the saloon, leaving Mary alone. She sat on the edge of the bed and looked around.

This cabin was considerably larger than the others, running the full width of the after house, some fifteen feet, and about ten feet from the doorway to the aft wall. At one end was the wardrobe and chest of drawers. In the corner was a tiny rosewood table with a recessed washbasin and a pitcher that sat in a little nook to secure it in place. A narrow door led to a small private water closet, which Mary considered a welcome convenience.

Against the back wall stood the bed. It was wider than most on the ship, another concession to the comfort of the captain and his wife, and quite comfortable, despite the six-inch-high preventer board often required to keep the occupants in place during rough seas.

A partition at the foot of the bed gave the captain's desk a private place of its own, where ship's work could be done. Here the captain kept his personal journal, as well as the ship's log, if not done by the first mate, and it was here that he would lay out the charts necessary to plot the vessel's course.

Above the desk, on a small shelf lipped by a carved oak strip to keep the books in place, was the library. There was a copy of Bowditch's *Practical Navigator*, Maury's wind and current charts with accompanying *Explanation and Sailing Directions*, and a volume of *Wood's Practice of Medicine*. Beside these useful volumes stood a copy of Cooper's *Last of the Mohicans*, a favorite of the captain's, a slim volume of Byron's poetry, and a Holy Bible. Mary's valise held other books, meant to keep her company during the long voyage, but as for the ship's library these half dozen volumes made up the entire complement. Any other books on the ship would be in the private possession of the foremast hands.

Stowed under the writing desk was a small wooden box containing vials of various medicines and a handful of instruments. Like most merchant ships, *Neptune's Car* did not carry a physician, and any doctoring to be done was usually performed by the captain or, often the case with minor ailments, done by the crewmen themselves.

The desk had a small wooden chair, and against the far wall was a wing-back chair covered in a pale green velvet. Those pieces of furniture effectively filled the remaining space in the cabin. Two small square windows on the back wall completed the entire inventory and description of her home for the near future, and Mary took it all in from her seat on the bed.

"Home, sweet home, indeed," she said to herself.

She ran her hand over the embroidered bedspread. Deciding it looked comfortable enough to lie down upon, she took off her hat and leaned over onto her side, resting her head on her arm. The stiff crinoline hoops of her skirt made any sort of lying or even sitting uncomfortable, and she looked forward to the pleasure of living aboard ship, where large skirts were unwieldy and common sense dictated leaving the hoops stashed away. Should such common sense prevail upon land, Mary reasoned, life would be much simpler. Perhaps, she thought, that is one reason she was back for another voyage—to wear comfortable clothes.

She rested on the bed. Looking up toward the ceiling, she watched the oil lantern above the desk swaying very gently on its hook. Even tied to the dock, the ship rolled slightly as men and gear moved back and forth and shifting wind blew through the rigging. By closing her eyes, Mary could feel the soft undulations. It was very peaceful and hypnotic, and she almost fell asleep. Only sounds of men working on the deck broke her reverie.

Some time had passed, perhaps a half hour, when a knock on the door frame announced someone's presence. A young boy, no older than twelve or thirteen, stood in the open doorway.

"Beg pardon, ma'am. The captain wishes you to know we are about to get under way."

Mary sat up. Knowing she would want to watch the ship leave the dock, Joshua had thought to send word. She knew it was a busy time for him and thought it very sweet that he remembered her.

"Thank you," she said. "I'll be right out."

The boy smiled and hurried away. He seemed eager to get back on deck. It might be, Mary suspected, his first time to be on a departing clipper, and he did not wish to miss anything. She put her hat back on, using the small mirror above the washstand. There might be a crowd, and she wanted to look nice.

Out in the sunshine of the deck, Mary was struck by the activity compared to the quiet of the cabin. All hands were topside, many still up on the yardarms working on the sails. Others on the deck grasped lines leading aloft, ready to haul them in when calls came from above. Other sailors cast off lines and fended the sides of the ship from the dock. Some manned a capstan, a large barrel-size winch mounted on deck to provide enough leverage to move heavy loads. Everyone was busy doing something, and all the activity was being directed by her husband. Mary thought Joshua, at his place on the quarterdeck, looked so handsome in his black coat and captain's hat.

At his side was Mr. Keeler, who took spoken orders from the captain and shouted them across the deck. Joshua had no need to raise his voice. Everyone knew who was in command. As Mary looked about the busy ship, her chest swelled with pride. For all the apparent commotion, every action had a purpose, producing a required result. Each movement was carefully orchestrated, and her husband controlled it all.

At the moment, a crew of eight men, two on each of four long wooden arms, strained to turn the bow capstan. A heavy line ran to a tall post on the far end of the dock. As the men rotated about the turning capstan, the line from the dock wrapped around the drum, slowly moving the huge ship away from the wharf. As they worked at their station, one sailor led the rest in a rhythmic chantey: "Sally Brown, of New York City, Sally Brown, she is so pretty. . . ." At the end of each line the men shoved anew, pulling the ship toward the end of the dock and the open East River. This warping of the ship away from shore began slowly, but once moving, the ship glided gracefully backwards, like a slow ballet movement, away from the crowd of workers and onlookers left on the dock. The only sounds were the melodic voices of the sailors with their chantey and the sharp cries of disturbed seagulls.

After three or four minutes, the full length of the hull slid clear of the end of the dock. Mary saw Joshua turn, his hands clasped behind his back, and say something to the helmsman, who spun the wheel hard. Slowly, so slowly that at first nothing seemed to be happening, the clipper ship *Neptune's Car* began to turn.

Clear of the dock, the momentum of the warping carried the ship into the wide river, where it coasted to a stop, its bow turned south toward the mouth of the harbor. For a few minutes the ship drifted with the tidal current as two small steam-powered tugs puffed into position. One at a time, the tugs maneuvered close by the bow, and lines were cleated to the bow deck. The tugs eased away, paying out line. When in position, the tow lines tightened, and with a renewed billow of smoke from their fat stacks the tugs strained to move the huge ship.

Two sailors with no immediate duties stood by the starboard rail watching the tugs pull. "Like shoving a fat lady," one said. "Push all you want, at first nothing happens." Both laughed, and as they did they happened to see Mary standing within earshot. The faces of both men fell at the thought of the captain's wife hearing their coarse joke. "Sorry, ma'am. We din't realize you was there."

Mary wanted to gracefully put the men at ease, so she just smiled and moved away. She decided to retreat to the quarterdeck. There she could better see the actions of the ship and tugs, as well as leave the rest of the deck to the crew. Joshua saw her coming up the steps and smiled at her. At his side, along with the first mate, was the harbor pilot, on board to see the ship out of port. She left her husband to his duties and went to the rail to watch the crowd on the wharf become smaller with distance. The faces were several hundred feet away now, and shrinking fast. The fat lady is moving, she thought to herself.

Neptune's Car was towed down the East River, passing another half mile of ships docked side by side. How, Mary wondered, can there be so many ships? This was only one port. A very large port, to be sure, but still one of many large ports. She wondered how many ships there were in the world.

The Battery, at the tip of Manhattan Island, slid aft, and the tightly packed buildings and crowded streets of New York were left behind. The ship followed the tugs through the channel between Governors Island and lower Brooklyn, passing into the wider expanse of the Upper Bay. Mary wondered if she was alone in feeling the excitement. The soft lapping of the bay's rippled surface against the hull was just a hint of the ocean to come. She was ready to see the sails dropped from their yards and feel the ship come alive.

She would have to wait a little longer. After a half hour or so, the shorelines of the Upper Bay drew close together and pinched the water into the mile-wide channel known as the Narrows, separating the end of Long Island from Staten Island. The tugs chugged through the Narrows and into the open waters of Lower New York Bay. Except for the thin New Jersey shoreline on the southern horizon, the bay looked as wide as the ocean itself, but Mary knew it was merely a placid backwater compared to the upcoming Atlantic.

In the middle of the bay, the course changed from southerly to almost east, following the hidden channel to the sea. Mary joined Joshua, who for the moment had little to do. The ship, until clear of the bay, was in the charge of the harbor pilot.

"Lovely day for a boat ride," she said, smiling in the midday sunshine.

"Certainly is," her husband agreed, looking up at a pennant on the mizzenmast. "A little more wind would be agreeable. What we have is off the bow and just not enough to efficiently sail out on our own. But it is a nice day. And the tug will get us to open water soon enough."

The helmsman, standing beside the wheel, made minor adjustments to keep *Neptune's Car* straight with the tugs. Except for the occasional small movements of the wheel, with its knobby spokes as tall as a man, he had little to do to command his attention, and he thus had time to look around. It was he, then, who happened to look astern and volunteer in a low voice, "Sir, we have company, sir."

Joshua turned to look, and Mary followed his gaze. Two or three miles behind, just emerging from the Narrows, was another ship, also under tow.

Joshua smiled. "The race is on. I suppose we couldn't ask for a more even start."

Mary remembered his desire to beat the other ships out of port. Knowing that *Romance of the Seas* had departed during the morning, she ventured a guess. "*Intrepid*?"

"It is. You remember Horatio Gardner, don't you, dear? You met him at Howland's party."

Mary remembered the party—it had been right after their return to New York from London—and recalled meeting the young Captain Gardner. He was about Joshua's age, and the two had formed a friendship.

"We spoke this morning. His *Intrepid* is not as large as the *Car*, but he thinks it will be as fast. We agreed to see who was waiting when the other arrived in San Francisco."

Mary knew what that meant. "And how much is the wager?"

Joshua dismissed the question with a wave of his hand. "Trifling sum. The importance is in the winning."

Mary knew that was so. No amount of money won on a wager could be as great a prize as simply winning the race. It might appear that wind and sails drove ships, but sometimes it was pride.

Joshua looked impatiently ahead. Coming into view was the light ship at Sandy Hook, a spit of land off the Jersey coast marking the end of the harbor. Beyond was the vast Atlantic.

Abeam Sandy Hook the tugs began to slow, and as the tow lines slacked, they were cast off. At the clipper's approach, a skiff had started out from Sandy Hook and oared its way out by the ship to take off the harbor pilot. The pilot shook hands with Joshua and Keeler, tipped his cap to Mary, and dropped over the side on a rope ladder. The oarsman in the skiff pulled away, taking the pilot to wait on any inbound vessel in need of his services.

Free of tugs and pilots, the ship and crew were on their own now and would be until arriving in California. The crew aloft was ready, and at the captain's word began hoisting the lower topsails. More sails quickly followed, filling with air and breathing life into the ship. *Neptune's Car* began to move on its own.

Mary watched from the quarterdeck as the crew swarmed over the ship. Everyone had work to do, and everyone was busy. At a word from the mate, the men hauled on the halyards, the heavy lines pulling the yardarms up the masts, opening the sails that hung below.

Just like turning the capstan, raising the yards required concerted effort, and again a chantey was employed, its rhythmic verse leading the men to pull: "A Yankee ship came down the river, blow, boys, blow!" At the second *blow*, the crew heaved hard. The iron collar attaching the yard to the mast moved up a few inches, raising the canvas with it. "Her masts and spars they shine like silver, blow, boys, blow!" A few verses later the yard was up, and with, "Belay the halyard!" the line was secured, looped back and forth around its belaying pin. Then: "Sheet home!" and the bottom of the sail was pulled down until tight against the wind. That line, too, was tied off at its pin.

Every line of rigging had a belaying pin dedicated to its use, either on the pin rails that ran below the side railings or on the fife rails, which boxed in three sides of the masts, leaving the forward side open. Along their lengths both pin and fife rails had holes, about two inches in diameter, spaced a foot or so apart. Into these holes fit the belaying pins, looking like nothing so much as kitchen rolling pins. Their knobby handles protruded above the rail and their slender shafts extended below, ready to accept the looped and crisscrossed lines, securing a tight hold but ready for quick and easy release.

As soon as the lower topsails were raised, luffing out to catch the wind, *Neptune's Car* began to move. As those sails were sheeted into place, the upper topsails were likewise released and set. Now each of the three masts had enough canvas spread before the wind to carry the ship forward in earnest. The other sails quickly followed.

Men clinging to the foot ropes leaned over the yards, unstrapping the fastening gaskets to allow the canvas to fall away. At the same instant, men on deck pulled lines attached to the lower corners of the sails, sheeting them home for maximum effect.

From the bare masts and yards, the tightly gathered canvas opened and spread before the wind. Mary watched this blossoming of the ship. After the topsails were set, the courses were unfurled. These largest and lowest sails, nearest the deck, were not only tall, but wide, stretching on their yardarms beyond the full width of the ship, extending out over the railings. These huge canvases were just overhead, so close that they seemed to fill the sky, and near enough that the wind could be heard humming its steady song as it spilled around their edges.

Finally the topgallants and royals were set, filling out nearly the full length of the masts. With each unfurled sail, the ship breathed a little more vigorously and moved a little more briskly across the water. Twenty minutes out of New York, the last of the royals was out. *Neptune's Car*, under full sail, cut cleanly through the sea.

In his log, Joshua wrote:

At 2 P.M. discharged the pilot at Sandy Hook and proceeded to sea. Fine weather, winds light from the south. Made all sails to the best advantage.

CHAPTER 5

Full Sail

Joshua stood by the helm, Mary at his side.

He said, "Good to be off, isn't it?" It was more a statement than a question.

Mary smiled. Her husband was in his element, now, and she was very pleased for him. "Yes. Very good. And the crew seems efficient at their work."

Joshua agreed. "We are off to a good start. I wouldn't mind a little more wind, but a light breeze is good for getting the men settled into their duties. They will have time enough in gales before we are through."

He turned to the helmsman. "Half a point to, young man."

Turning the wheel a little, the sailor said, "Aye, sir. Half a point to. And sir, the *Intrepid*?"

Joshua turned and looked. The shore was not much more than an indistinct rise on the horizon now, with a gap showing the entrance to the Lower Bay. In the middle of this gap were the unfurling sails of another ship. *Intrepid* was out of the harbor. Her captain no doubt saw *Neptune's Car* ahead and was setting sail to close the gap. Joshua Patten was just as intent upon widening it.

Looking up, he eyed the tops of the masts, above the royals, where a short space remained unused. There was room on each mast for one more small sail, normally used only during the lightest winds. Its name aptly described its location, at the very top.

"Mr. Keeler, have them put the moonrakers out."

Now the only sails left to be utilized were the studding sails, and Mary, knowing Joshua's desire for speed, was not at all surprised when he issued his next order. "Let's shake out the stuns'ls now. It will be a good time to see that all is in good working order."

He may have pretended to be interested in seeing that all sails and rigging were in order, but everyone on board knew that he was more interested in pulling away from the ship two miles behind.

The studding sails hung from extendable booms that increased the length of the horizontal yardarms, allowing sail far out over the sides, making the spread of canvas twice as wide as the ship itself. Under full sail the sky over the deck was filled with thirty thousand square feet of billowing white canvas making use of all the wind, however light, to push the heavily laden clipper across the water. And *Neptune's Car* was heavy. The holds were full of cargo, as well as water and provisions sufficient for the duration of the voyage. The hull was well down in the water, the sharp bow slicing through the oncoming swells.

Mary left Joshua by the helmsman and walked up to the starboard rail. Her walk was unsteady, her sense of balance unaccustomed to the slant of the deck. Her black leather boots, laced up over her ankles, were a carefully considered combination of fashion and practicality. They were fine enough for walking the streets of Manhattan but soled with a firm grip for wet, slanted decks. Now, trying them out on a moving ship for the first time, she was pleased with their purchase. Even the light breeze was enough to push the tall masts off the vertical and slope the deck, where upwind was always uphill. It would take a little time to regain what the sailors called sea legs, where the mind has adapted to the unusual pitching of the floor beneath the feet. Negotiating a tilted deck, usually slippery and wet as well, would be the norm for the months to come. She knew the adjustment would come, but these first few hours would require careful attention to do what on land was done without thinking.

Mary stood by the starboard rail, feeling the sea air on her face. The southern breeze was still warm, but not nearly so warm as the streets of New York, which, by the time of the midday walk to the ship, had become almost uncomfortable. The water of the ocean's surface, a deep indigo under an azure sky, cooled the breeze before it crossed the deck. The gentle wind blew across Mary's cheeks and ran its fingers through her hair, catching the wide brim of her hat and bending it up toward the rounded crown. Ingenious zephyrs reached under the hem of her dress and swirled around her petticoats, carrying away the heat trapped by the flounces of her skirts. The wind seemed to be a living thing, and not only was she feeling the wind, it was feeling her, caressing her.

Looking down over the side railing and forward toward the bow, she saw the black hull slide through the sea, a thin line of foam marking where the ship cut the water. Off the stern, the wake spread and weakened before diminishing back into the rippled ocean. Within the wake a smooth band of water showed where the ship had been, a long but temporary signature of its passage.

The vast ocean, save for the short choppy waves mottling the seascape, was otherwise unmarked. As far as the horizon, in every direction, the surface had a sameness, the only variations being shadows of drifting white clouds. For every lapping wave that broke the surface and disappeared, another took its place. Then it, too, slipped back into the sea. The ship ran across these waves, hardly noticing their tiny slaps against the hull. Under the waves ran long gentle swells—slow undulations that the bow of the ship rode over with barely perceptible rises and dips. The sea seemed to beckon, saying, Come out onto my gentle form and feel the pleasure of my rhythmic heartbeat.

The afternoon sun, making its slide down the sky, was shining off the glittering surface in a wide golden streak. Mary leaned on the rail, enjoying the warm sunny air. Once, perhaps twice, the ship slipped into a trough between swells hard enough to send a fine spray into the air. The nearly invisible mist rose to the railings, sending the taste of salt to her lips. With the taste came the smell of salt air, to be inhaled and savored after months of the dusty odor of land.

The ship and the men who ran it were settling into their routines. The sails were set and filled with air. The deck had been cleared of mooring gear and other accoutrements of land. The watch on deck was going about its duties. The rest of the crew were below, resting, awaiting their watch. Amidship Mary saw the bulky figure of the first mate, feet spread and hands on hips, issuing orders to men aloft. She turned and looked at her husband standing by the helmsman. Joshua, looking along the length of the long deck, seemed pleased with what he saw.

For the rest of the afternoon the sails of *Intrepid* followed the wake of *Neptune's Car*, not gaining but not falling behind, her sails becoming a fixture of the seascape. As the day ended and the sun slipped below the horizon, the distant sails remained in the light a moment longer than the sea itself, giving them a luminescent glow against the darkening water.

Mary watched this first day's sunset from the taffrail at the stern of the ship. Just as the red sun touched the water, Joshua came up beside her and placed his hand over hers as it rested on the rail.

"Pretty, isn't it?"

"Perfectly pretty," she said.

"I have no reason to believe that tomorrow will be any different. Smooth and easy sailing."

"I hope it lasts."

"I hope it doesn't."

Mary knew what he meant. Sailing along at five or six knots was fine for someone in no particular hurry, but that was seldom the case with any ship, and especially for a merchant clipper that advertised quick delivery.

She smiled. "I am sure you will get your wind. Speaking for myself, I am thankful for the easy start. I wasn't looking forward to seasickness again."

Now it was Joshua's turn to smile. "It isn't likely you would go through that again. You are an experienced traveler now. You can handle anything."

"I hope so. I doubt the entire trip will be this easy."

"I suppose you are right." Joshua leaned out over the rail and looked down at the swirls of water closing to meet in around the stern. Below the rail, carved into the back of the ship, was a bas-relief of Neptune, sitting in a chariot, his long hair flowing wildly. In one hand he held a trident, ready to rule the seas. "But not to worry," Joshua said. "You are riding in the car of a god."

CHAPTER 6

Storm Clouds

When day broke the next morning, the sea behind *Neptune's Car* was empty. During the night the sails of *Intrepid* had disappeared over the horizon. Joshua had risen early, his movements in the cabin stirring Mary from her slumber. She dressed in the pale light of morning and joined her captain on deck for a look at the dawning day. He was standing by the quarterdeck rail, head tilted back to look up into the high rigging.

"Anything, Mr. Hare?"

High in the trucks of the mainmast was the second mate with a short brass telescope.

"No, sir, Captain. No sail in sight."

Either *Intrepid* had fallen behind or the ships had diverged in their courses, each captain choosing a slightly different path across the open ocean.

Joining Joshua, Mary said, "Do you suppose it passed us during the night?"

Joshua scoffed at the possibility that *Neptune's Car* was not the faster of the two ships, but then he said, "I hope not."

Mary looked forward along the deck. Just off the port bow and barely above the horizon was the orange morning sun, framed by the masts and lower edge of the sails. Its rays cast their light across the deck, wet from its morning scrubbing. From the coop near the kitchen, a cock crowed.

The ship was heading almost directly toward the sun, and Mary stepped to Joshua's side and discreetly whispered, "You are going the wrong way, again."

Joshua laughed.

On Mary's first voyage, she had emerged from the cabin weak from seasickness to find the ship on an easterly course when she had expected it to be going south. Her first words to Joshua had been to inform him of his error in navigation. After a night of intestinal misery, she wanted the trip to be over as quickly as possible, and saw no advantage in taking the long way around.

Unfortunately, for the sick at heart and sick at stomach, the way to the far end of South America, six thousand miles almost directly south of New York, is to sail not south, but east. Not only does the coast of Brazil protrude far into the middle of the Atlantic, requiring an easterly deviation of more than two thousand miles, but ocean currents in the North Atlantic rotate in a huge clockwise pattern. To take advantage of the current's gentle push, ship captains usually sailed easterly toward Europe before turning south in midocean. This route also positioned the ship, once the equator was crossed, to better take advantage of the southeast trade winds. This roundabout way of going down ocean adds a thousand or more miles to the trip, but saves weeks at sea.

"The long way around is the shortest way to go, you know," Joshua said.

Mary knew that, but she still did not like it. She looked again at the sun. In the few minutes she had been on deck it had climbed noticeably farther above the bow.

"If this is the way to go, why don't we see your friend Captain Gardner going the same way?"

Joshua took an involuntary glance around the sea, as if he hoped *Intrepid* would suddenly reappear. "He is no doubt somewhere not far over the horizon. It is a big ocean, though, with plenty of room for differences in opinion."

By the third day out the ship curved its course slightly south, so that the rising sun appeared a little more to port. The wind also steadily

increased, and the vessel skated across the sea in a fashion more befitting a full rigged clipper. The sails filled with the power of the
wind, straining the rigging and leaning the masts far off the vertical.
With the deck's tilt, the lee rail rode only a few feet above the
choppy surface, while the weather side rode high above all but the
strongest bursts of sea spray. Throwing the chip, a triangular board
attached to a marked line, showed *Neptune's Car* to be making at least
ten and sometimes fourteen knots, very good speed for the North
Atlantic. Any time Joshua could log three hundred miles in a day,
he was pleased. Four hundred, of course, would be even better.

During the late afternoon the increased wind brought increasing
clouds. They were still high and thin, but anyone who watched the
weather as much as did men of the sea knew that these stratified
bands were portents of changes to come.

The next morning the eastern sky dawned a burning red that in
the weather lore only confirmed the message of the cirrus seen the
day before. Throughout the day the clouds thickened, turning from
white to a darkening gray, their bases leaden with suspended rain.
With the clouds came even more wind, the placid seascape of the
first few days replaced by whitecapping waves that rode on the
backs of long, deep swells. The ship, too, rode the swells, rising on
the crests and dropping into the troughs, the bow meeting the sea by
punching into the oncoming ridge of water. The ocean expressed its
displeasure at the assault by breaking over the bow, drenching those
on the forward deck and raining a heavy mist as far aft as the
mizzenmast. Indeed, no part of the deck was immune.

Mary had spent the previous days strolling about the sunny deck,
watching the blue of the sea from the quarterdeck. Now she
watched the change in the weather.

"I am sorry to see the nice weather end," she said to Joshua.

"This is nothing compared to what can be expected later," he answered, "when we encounter the storms of the southern ocean. Still,
it is a rude end to those first fair days."

"Perhaps it will not last long," she ventured.

Joshua looked up at the sky. "I would not be too hopeful of that.
This will not be a summer shower."

Mary knew he was right. Yesterday's high clouds had foretold the arrival of a tropical storm and perhaps, though still early in the season, of a hurricane.

"It seems, though," he added, "that the heavy weather may stay south of us. Perhaps we will see only the edge of the storm."

Far forward, Joshua saw men climb the foremast rigging and work their way out to the ends of the yardarm, where they went to work on the studding sail booms. He turned to find his first mate.

"Mr. Keeler," he shouted across the width of the quarterdeck. "What are those men doing?"

"Bringing in the fore stuns'ls, sir. The bow is near pushing under."

Joshua looked toward the bow and watched as it punched into the oncoming swells, studying its ability to ride over the waves.

"Let's wait, Mr. Keeler. She will take a bit more than that."

Keeler looked as if he disagreed, but he called out orders to leave the booms extended and their sails out. The men aloft secured any line loosened and retreated to the deck.

Neptune's Car pushed toward the southeast, spray flying over the bow.

That night, periods of heavy rain lashed the ship. Passing squalls, spinning off what Joshua suspected to be a large storm somewhere beyond the southern horizon, dampened the crew's celebration of Independence Day. One of the foremast hands had brought aboard two rockets, which he tried to fire off the bow, but the damp air had penetrated to the powder, leaving them useless.

The festivities over, the crew went back to work.

The storm might be a hundred miles away, but even at that considerable distance was strong enough to make life less than comfortable. Dinner was served as usual, but eaten quickly and without ceremony, before the plates had time to slide over the fiddles around the edge of the table and onto the floor. Mary retired early to read, but the motion of the ship and the swinging of the lantern made it impossible to give proper attention to the book. She finally turned out the lamp and lay in bed, waiting for Joshua to join her, but she eventually fell asleep without him.

All the next day the weather remained unpleasant. By evening everyone on the ship was thoroughly soaked by the hard slanting rain and breaking seas. Mary remained in the cabin most of the day, venturing out during lulls in the rain. Even these brief forays onto the deck left her wet from spray, despite the oilcloth raincoat Joshua gave her. The night brought some relief as the wind eased and the ship took on more benign characteristics. Dinner was served without incident, and afterwards Joshua made only a brief tour topside before leaving the ship with Mr. Keeler for the night watch.

He and Mary lay in bed, talking softly and listening to the sounds of the ship rising and falling to the rhythm of the sea.

"Welcome back to the seafaring life," he said, pulling her back against his chest. He rubbed her neck and then moved down between her shoulders, willing away the stiffness of her muscles.

"Pleased to be here," she said. "It's everything I imagined."

"I'm glad you are enjoying yourself. Perhaps tomorrow I can arrange for you to see a waterspout."

"No need to trouble yourself on my account." Mary flexed her back to better receive the massage. "That feels good."

"Anything for my lady."

"Anything?"

Mary turned to face her husband, and he kissed her. In the dark cabin, with no light to see the other's face, they explored by feel alone, lips touching lips, cheek grazing softly against cheek, one inhaling the other's warm breath. Around them, the ship creaked ever so slightly from the strain of the waves, and any noise they made while making love was masked by the music of the wind.

Joshua rose early the next morning, and after a moment spent stretching under the covers, Mary also got up. She was beginning to enjoy going out with him to see the day begin. The deck was always clean, freshly scrubbed by the morning watch, and the air of the new day always seemed particularly fresh as well. On clear days, she delighted in seeing what the sunrise looked like. Even with the never-varying horizon of sea and sky, each day was different. The surface of the ocean, for its vast monotonous expanse, was never exactly the same. The size of the waves, the strength of the endless swells, the very color of the water—it all changed from day to day and even moment to moment.

The sky, too, was never the same. Some mornings the sun stepped up from its place beneath the sea in full brightness, its blinding white instantly dominating, claiming the sphere of the sky for its own. Other times it rose big and orange, gathering its intensity as it climbed away from the horizon, only gradually taking its place of command for the day. Sometimes it slipped into the sky behind broad smears of color, unlimited shades of red and orange that were sometimes fiery bright, sometimes soft pastels, colors from the Artist's palette.

Joshua said to her, on one of those mornings, "I believe that God created sunsets only as a consolation for those who never get out of bed in time to see the sunrise."

When he said things like that, Mary loved him all the more.

There would be no pretty sunrise today. The light through the tiny windows was dim and gray, giving a clue to the kind of day Mary would find when they went out. Dressed and ready to go, Joshua waited while Mary finished fastening the long row of buttons along the front of her dress, which she had hemmed up several inches to keep it off the wet deck. Once her boots were on and laced, she tied a scarf around her head, checking her appearance in the mirror. All that remained was to don her oilcloth from the hook where it had dripped dry.

Ready for the elements, she said, "Thanks for waiting, dear," taking Joshua's offered arm. "It's nice to have an escort."

As promised by the window light, the day dawned with the metal gray of low clouds. The rain had stopped, though, and the wind had slackened considerably. The sea was not whitecapping nearly as much, but the deep swells endured, telling of still heavy weather not too many miles distant.

Mary looked about at the sea, but Joshua's attention was immediately directed up into the sails high above the ship. He looked around the deck and found the second mate by the far rail.

"Mr. Hare!"

Mary noted a sudden displeasure in his voice.

The mate spun around and did not delay in stepping quickly across to the captain.

"Yes, sir," he said, removing his hat.

"Mr. Hare, the royals are struck."

"Yes, sir."

"Can you tell me why that is?"

"Mr. Keeler ordered it so, sir."

Joshua looked up into the yards again, gauging the strain on the masts. "He is below?"

"Aye, sir. I believe he is in the forecastle, sir."

"The forecastle?"

Mary shared Joshua's question. Keeler's cabin was aft.

"Aye, sir."

"I see," said Joshua. "Would you be so kind as to send someone down and ask him to come see me?"

"I'll go myself, sir."

Hare took a step, but Joshua stopped him.

"Mr. Hare, as second mate, your duties do not include being a messenger."

Timothy Hare looked thoughtful, as if considering the meaning of the captain's words. "Of course. I'll send someone for him."

Hare went to the quarterdeck rail and called down to the main deck. A seaman dropped what he was doing and headed forward, disappearing down the companionway to the forecastle.

Joshua watched the second mate executing the order. He had worked to cultivate the young man, to make him into a capable officer. It was, ironically, his willingness to work that was sometimes detrimental to his progress.

Hare turned back to his captain, who said, "Have the royals unfurled, Mr. Hare."

"Aye, sir. Right away, sir."

Hare scampered forward to put the captain's wishes into effect, and Joshua turned his attention back to his wife, standing unobtrusively off to the side.

"I'm sorry, Mary," he said. "Not the cheeriest way to greet the day, is it?"

Mary gave him an understanding smile. "A captain's work is never done."

"Nice day though," Joshua said, putting on a smile.

"Yes," Mary said. "Should be a nice day."

"But as the ship stands now," Joshua said, "we could use some more wind. I don't understand why . . ." He let the words hang.

The storms had abated and the seas had calmed, although the ship still rose and fell with the crests of the swells. The wind, now from the northeast, was not nearly as strong as it had been. Joshua was clearly irritated, not by the lack of wind, Mary knew, but by the lack of sail.

She said nothing more, but waited to see what Joshua had to say to the first mate. While waiting for him, they watched the boys climb the standing rigging toward the tops of the masts.

Keeler came up from the forecastle companionway and made his way aft, walking with the wide step and rolling gait of a sailor, arms bowed out at his side. He reached the quarterdeck steps and came up to meet the captain. His swarthy face was clouded with a frown.

Joshua returned the favor. Mary stepped off to the port rail and looked out over the ocean while she listened to their conversation.

"You sent for me, sir?"

"Yes, Mr. Keeler. I was wondering, why we are running under reduced sail."

"I felt the wind to be too strong, sir, so I took in the royals."

"When was this wind too strong?"

"During the night, sir," Keeler said.

"And is the wind too strong now?"

Keeler looked aloft, although he had to know the answer Joshua expected, merely by having been asked the question. The royal boys were at work up on the yards. "Apparently not, sir."

"*Neptune's Car* is heavily sparred, Mr. Keeler. She can withstand considerably more wind under full sail than we have experienced thus far." Joshua left unsaid what he really meant: The ship is not timid about the weather, so let us not be either.

Keeler stood his ground. "I judged the wind too strong and acted accordingly."

"You judged wrongly."

Keeler's face reddened, with the effect of making his dark features darker. "Yes, sir." He stood, waiting for more.

Joshua apparently decided enough had been said. "That will be all, Mr. Keeler."

Keeler turned to depart the quarterdeck, and as he reached the steps Joshua decided to try to soothe his feelings a little.

"Mr. Keeler," he said. "No lasting harm has been done, but the ship is like a fine thoroughbred. She likes to run, and we should let her."

Keeler, looking somewhat assuaged, said, "Yes, sir, I'll do that," and disappeared down the steps.

With Keeler gone, Mary moved back over to her husband's side. Joshua let out a deep breath, as if expelling the bad air of the conversation. "Well, perhaps we have just seen an example of the trouble others have had with our Mr. Keeler."

Mary offered hope. "Perhaps it was just a one-time occurrence."

"I do not think so. In the last couple of days I have seen hints that suggest otherwise."

"Oh?"

"He seems quite willing to work the crew hard, which is good, of course, but I have noticed that he is not as forceful with the ship itself. Twice, not counting when you have been present, he has reduced sail when it was not warranted."

"Have you said anything else to him?"

"On each occasion. And on each occasion he says that he understands my desires, only to contradict them again."

"Do you think him unfit?"

"I'm not sure. Running short sail could be a sign that he is not comfortable pushing the ship hard, but there could be other reasons."

"Such as?"

Joshua shrugged. "I don't know. It's easier to lay off the wind a bit. It's less work, and you don't have to pay as much attention."

He lightened his tone and smiled. "But enough of that. Let's go see what Henry has for breakfast." To the second mate, who had returned to his post by the helm, he said, "Mr. Hare, carry on, and make best speed."

Timothy Hare, apparently recognizing the crisis with the royals to be over, was safely back to his happy and pleasant demeanor. He smiled and said, "Aye, aye, sir."

As the Pattens went below, he called out commands to the crew to brace the yards a little more tightly to the wind. By the time

Joshua and Mary were seated at their table, the ship was heeled noticeably more than it had been, and the sounds of the sea against the hull told of faster speed through the water.

Joshua was satisfied that all was going well, and the events that had begun the morning were forgotten. The eggs and ham were cooked just right, the coffee was hot, and he sat back to enjoy breakfast with his wife.

CHAPTER 7

Down Ocean

It is difficult to get a good night's sleep on a ship. The pitching and rolling tugs one to and fro in the bed, it is often too cold or too hot, and there are constant sounds from both within and without the ship to stir the slumbering. The wind, depending upon its strength, either whispers or roars, and the waves can tap gently on the side of the hull or crash against it. From above comes the sound of footsteps and shouted orders, chanteys sung while men work, and the sound of gear being dragged across the deck. Nevertheless, those on board become accustomed to these external noises.

A new tack can be taken to turn the ship across the wind, with multiple commands and much hauling of lines and scuffling about, while those sleeping below are no more aware than as if the commotion was part of a restless dream.

More disruptive are sounds from within the after house itself. For better ventilation, the doors of the individual cabins, including the rear cabin of the captain and his wife, are louvered, admitting not only air but also sound. Every four hours the watch changes, one mate coming in and the other going out, with the accompanying moving about and opening and closing of doors. There is usually some talk, though kept low, and the other inevitable sounds of getting up and going to bed. At other times the steward moves about, clinking and tinkling his utensils, making coffee and cleaning his station.

Mary learned to ignore most of the sounds. Just as those living by the tracks come to never hear the train, the normal sounds of the ship were tucked away in some alcove of the mind. It was only the unusual, a sharp word or slammed door, that tended to disturb her. The noise did not have to be loud, just out of the ordinary.

It was for that reason, Mary supposed, that a faint, barely audible sound caught her attention and stirred her from sleep.

What had awakened her? She lay quietly in the bed and listened. A moment later she heard a muted pop, like that made when a housewife shakes out a rug. Was that a slack sail? Sails in proper trim were always taut, with never any looseness to rob a ship of power and subject the canvas to undue wear.

Joshua must have heard it, too, and he stirred beside her.

He slipped out of bed and pulled on his pants and coat. He felt for his boots in the dark cabin, slipped them on, and quietly opened the door. Mary did not say anything, but watched as he stepped out into the saloon, his form silhouetted in the doorway. She wondered why a sail would be out of trim and allowed to be left that way long enough to draw the captain from his bed. She had the feeling that Keeler was somehow involved, despite no further problems since Joshua had chastised him for furling the royals. In the several days since that incident, she had come to the conclusion that her initial discomfort with the man was warranted.

Joshua crossed the length of the saloon, rubbing his face to clear the interrupted sleep from his mind. He was not sure what was happening on deck, but it could not be good. There was no reason not to have a taut ship. He stepped onto the deck and pulled the door closed behind him. The sky was dark and starless, the air cool with the peculiar dampness of night. It was too dark to see the clouds, the only light coming from the single lantern hanging from the spanker boom over the stern, but Joshua sensed that the weather had lifted. Clouds that had been hanging low and ragged above the masts, almost within reach, were now higher, hidden somewhere up in the darkness.

The quarterdeck was empty except for the solitary helmsman. He was resting in a half-sitting position on the long wheel box containing the worm gear between the wheel and the shaft to the rudder, holding the wheel with one hand. When Joshua appeared on the steps he rose guiltily to his feet and grasped the wheel with renewed authority. Joshua joined him by the helm, ignoring the slack behavior.

"Henson, isn't it?"

"Aye, sir."

Overhead, on the mizzenmast, the errant sail rippled again, the wind running uncontrolled across its span and spilling out, leaving the canvas free to work against the lines. The helmsman winced, turning the wheel slightly in an attempt to put the sail back into trim without throwing the others out. Joshua gave him a sideways glance. The young crewman seemed cowed by the captain's presence.

"We are still on Mr. Keeler's watch, are we not?"

"Aye, sir."

"But he is not on the quarterdeck. Is he elsewhere topside?"

"I suppose so, sir."

"You have seen him of late?"

"Not for some minutes, sir."

"Some minutes?"

"Aye, sir."

Looking up at the sails, Joshua took several steps toward the quarterdeck rail. "How long do you mean, Mr. Henson, by 'some minutes'?" He had raised his voice to be heard clearly over the wind. "I should like to speak with Mr. Keeler."

The nervous seaman holding the wheel did not answer right away, and did not have to, as Joshua's loud voice had the desired effect. Almost immediately, the heavy step of boots sounded on the stairs coming up from the starboard side of the main deck.

Keeler stepped up onto the quarterdeck and approached the captain. On his face was a mixture of puzzlement and scowl. He seemed surprised to see the captain and was doubtless bothered by it. This was not a midnight social call.

"You wanted to see me, sir?"

"Yes, Mr. Keeler, I do."

Keeler waited. His face was blank. He doesn't know why I am on deck, Joshua thought. The sail, as if on cue, popped again. Keeler's eyes snapped upward, and then at the captain.

Joshua's voice was icy. "Shall I instruct the crew, Mr. Keeler, or will you?"

Keeler's dark eyes blazed, and he turned to the rail overlooking the main deck. "Starboard watch, to the mizzen lower topsail sheets!"

A crew of men materialized from the dark forward deck and took their stations by the pin rails.

"Haul starboard sheets, ease the tacks!"

The work of a moment put the loose topsail back into trim, the ease with which the work was done underscoring the ineptitude that had allowed it to become out in the first place.

"Belay those lines," Keeler called out, "and tie them off proper this time."

Joshua noted a sharp glance from one or two of the crewmen toward the first mate before they melted back into the darkness. He had also noted that even before Keeler ordered the sheets hauled in the men were already in their motions to do just that. They had known, as had he, that the sail needed to be tightened. Why had not Keeler?

Any change in performance could be debated, but the ship seemed to breathe easier with all sails properly set. The hard driving might be for more speed, but Joshua also took great pleasure in the feel of a ship running in good form. He stood in silence, his thoughts divided between the sensory pleasure of a fast ship heeled over, plowing across a dark ocean, and his growing concern about the man at his side. He needed to trust his first mate, and it was beginning to appear that he could not.

Keeler interrupted his thoughts. "I'll work the men about how to properly belay a line, sir."

"That might be well," Joshua said, "but I am more concerned with the delay in correcting the problem."

"Sir?"

Joshua looked over at Keeler, amazed that he did not seem to have been aware of the slack canvas.

"Mr. Keeler, where were you when I came on deck?"

"I was by the main shrouds, sir, inspecting the seizing."

Joshua raised his eyebrow. "In the dark?"

"There was light enough, sir, to check for tightness."

"You must have been considerably occupied, not to notice a luffing sail."

"I did notice, sir, and was on my way aft when you called."

Joshua was not appeased. "You could not call foredeck hands from where you were?" He did not mention the length of time he had lain in his bunk, listening to the popping sail.

Keeler opened his mouth to offer an excuse, or perhaps to protest, but then he paused and said only, "Yes, sir, I should have, sir."

Joshua leaned over the binnacle housing the compass and checked the course. Straightening up, he said, "I'm returning to bed, Mr. Keeler. Carry on."

On most days, Mary spent a part of each morning strolling forward to midship, where she fed the livestock. *Neptune's Car* had left New York with a portion of the main deck looking more like a barnyard than a ship. There were four sheep, three hogs, and a coop full of chickens intended to provide fresh meat and eggs for at least a part of the long trip around Cape Horn. Periodically, an animal was taken and slaughtered, and before the Horn was rounded the large stock would be gone, as well as most of the chickens. The deck would be cleared of the pens before the onset of the cape's heavy weather, their wood fed to the cook's fire.

Mary found the daily feeding a pleasant diversion from normal shipboard life of reading and sewing or simply watching the ship and sea. When visiting the animals she felt like a farmer's wife going out to do the chores, and it felt good to be doing something, anything, besides being the proper example of a captain's wife, standing idle about the ship. The activity felt liberating, and she enjoyed having an excuse to wander forward of the quarterdeck rail.

Joshua, from his place near the helm, often watched her as she made the rounds, visiting each pen in turn, doling out kitchen scraps to the pigs in their sty, twists of dried grass to the sheep, and scattering handfuls of cracked corn to the hens. Mary, as she moved about the ship, made for an attractive sight on an otherwise drab deck. He was pleased that she was on board, and that she seemed to be enjoying the voyage.

He saw that the crew was glad to have her on board, too. They gave her all the respect she deserved as captain's wife, and not the least bit grudgingly, it seemed. He also noticed the sideways glances that went her way, despite the men's best efforts to hide them. He could have admonished them, but did not. They were young men, the voyage was long, and they restrained themselves to only looks, not leers.

On the morning after Joshua's midnight visit to the deck, Mary completed her feeding foray by lingering at the sheep pen, watching the woolly animals eat, and then started back aft. Joshua smiled. The wide, rolling gait required on a leaning, pitching deck seemed perfectly normal when affected by an able seamen, but seemed out of place in her long pale blue dress with matching bonnet. She reached the steps, and he met her at the rail, taking her hand as she came up onto the quarterdeck.

"I was watching you with the sheep," he said. "Which one do you have picked out?"

Mary pretended not to know what he meant. "Whatever are you talking about?"

"You recall the anguish you suffered last time. At the fate of Bo Peep's Sheep."

Mary remembered. Bo Peep's Sheep was the name she had given a particularly cute little ewe on the last voyage. Against her better judgment, she became attached to the animal, and had been quite distressed when its turn came to be served for dinner.

"I'll not let that happen again."

"No, of course you won't," Joshua said, knowing that she already had.

Mary changed the subject. "It is certainly a beautiful day."

"More wind would be nice."

"You always wish for more wind."

"I much prefer the challenge of too much sail to not having enough. This constant working to adjust for light winds is tiresome.

Even now," he said, looking up into the yards, "there are sails not earning their keep. Mr. Hare, have the foresails braced up sharp. There is no need to allow such slackness."

The second mate looked abashed at having the captain correct his rigging and set to work issuing commands. Far forward, the watch went to work, adjusting the trim by sheeting home the sails a little more tightly and cleating off the lines anew at the belaying pins. Other men went up the shrouds to attend to work required aloft.

Joshua watched the men for a moment, and then returned to the conversation started by his wife. "The weather is indeed warming. We are turned almost south, now, and during the night we crossed the Tropic of Cancer. We are in the tropics now and headed for the line. If the wind holds, we shall be in the Southern Hemisphere before the week is out."

CHAPTER 8

Crossing the Line

The wind did not hold. Mary had been following the progress plotted on the chart, watching as the ship's distance north of the equator counted down from forty degrees north, the latitude of New York. Slowly at first, as the ship worked its way southeast, and then more quickly as the course curved southward, the degrees of latitude recorded on the log began to decrease. The ship was nearing latitude twenty now, halfway to the zero degree line of the equator.

She knew that the rapid progress would soon come to an end. As is common in the equatorial regions, the northeast trades that powered the ship in its turn to the south eased in strength over a period of days until they died away almost completely. The ship entered the doldrums, a wide band of light and varying winds that had plagued mariners since the days of Henry the Navigator and Sir Francis Drake. Joshua had the heavy sails, in use for the two weeks of the easterly crossing of the Atlantic, taken down and replaced with ones of a lighter weight, saving the good canvas for later trials.

It was just as the ship began to be steered in its turn toward the south that the trades died away, leaving *Neptune's Car* just when the ship could have benefited most from the following winds. After days of making ten knots or better, it now rocked along at three or four knots, the speed of a man walking. Sometimes less. Joshua was on deck a great deal of the time, watching the sea and the sails for the slightest shifts in the wind, ready to take any advantage that presented itself.

The sails, while not quite hanging limp, were soft, filled with just enough air to keep their shape. The lines and spars supporting the canvas, designed to withstand gales and storms, merely did holding duty, like a groom handling the slack reins of a standing racehorse. A sail that might take a half dozen men to furl in a fresh breeze was easily gathered by two. Not only was the canvas easier to grasp and pull up to the yard, where it could be gasketed in place, but in a light wind the ship heeled over less, leaving the masts more upright and the yards more horizontal, greatly reducing the difficulty of the work by those aloft.

The sailing might be easier, but the crew had no less to do. The slack time was spent doing a hundred other duties. Some were repairs necessarily neglected during busier times, some were just busy-work, performed to keep all hands doing something. By shipboard rules, the Sabbath was a day of rest, but at all other times there was to be no idleness. If that meant putting hands to scraping rust from the anchor chain, so be it.

Some days were fair, with sunshine basking the ship all day long. More often, tropical showers developed during the afternoon watch, wetting the ship and crew, but the rain was not resented. It filled the rain barrels with good-tasting water, and the dry times in between allowed for laying wet clothing and gear out to dry.

Mary spent much of these idyllic days watching flying fish flee before the ship and dolphins playing in the bow wave. To her, the voyage was proving to be most pleasurable. Joshua might have agreed had he not been so immersed in the quest for speed. Easy sailing brought no pleasure to a clipper captain.

It was also during these easy days that Mary began to have a rekindling of her interest in navigation, brought on by watching the southward progress on the charts and by the onset of boredom. She started by watching Joshua, looking over his shoulder as he recorded his observations. Soon she was nudging him aside, doing the work for him and reacquainting herself with the many steps of correlating the positions of the sun and stars with the position of the ship. For each observation there were tables in the almanac dedicated to a particular declination or azimuth at a particular hour. Within these tables, after necessary corrections, resided the information needed to plot lines of position on the chart. Each observation resulted in a line, and two crossing lines resulted in a fix. Each day at noon the fix was plotted, and the position compared to the previous day.

Sometimes the new position was many miles from the last. On other days, particularly as the ship became mired in the equatorial calms, the mark on the chart hardly moved. Joshua, ever diligent, kept working the ship in a tireless search for the errant breeze.

The men serving before the mast felt the brunt of this quest. No sooner did they have the sails set for a particular wind but the captain decided a change was necessary, and they were called up again to haul this line or belay that one. There were almost constant adjustments, with no delay permitted in making them, lest the advantage of the moment be lost. From the quarterdeck came the commands, and it fell to the common and able seamen to put them into effect. When the weather was fair, it was only hard work. When the weather was stormy, with gales and rain and spray, the work was both hard and dangerous.

At the center of these efforts, the root of all orders to the crew and the cause of all their work, was the captain. It had taken Mary some time to adjust her perceptions of her husband from the kind and loving man she had met and married to the no-nonsense taskmaster he became on his ship. She had not entered into matrimony blindly. Her father was a shipbuilder, and she had been around ships and the men who sailed them all her life. She knew the duties of a sea captain and what those duties required. A clipper ship's reputation, its very existence, was predicated on speed, and its captain had to push the ship hard. And to push a ship hard required pushing the crew hard.

Hard driving aboard a sailing vessel was not endemic only to the clippers. Since the beginning of travel across the seas, and in the centuries since, the goal was to make best speed, and captains had long been given free reign to do whatever was necessary to make that happen. The common seaman had little say in matters, short of general mutiny, although since the days of galley slaves chained to their oars their situation had improved considerably. Richard Henry Dana, beginning with publication of *Two Years Before the Mast* and its detail of abuses in the merchant shipping business, had championed many reforms to make the life of forecastle hands more bearable.

Still, maritime law greatly favored the captain. He was responsible for all aspects of the ship and crew, and final accountability of every action and every consequence fell to him, regardless of who was officer of the watch or who was at fault. Along with the responsibility came the freedom to do whatever he required to ensure a successful completion of the voyage.

Maritime law also dealt harshly with any seaman who failed to do the captain's bidding. Shipboard punishment was solely at his discretion, although the lash had recently fallen out of favor among most forward-thinking captains. Beyond that, the laws were very specific concerning the disposition of any crew brought up on charges once back in port, and almost without fail favored the captain or ship owners. Any sailor who jumped ship before his agreed upon time was up, for instance, was required by law to be held by authorities, at the sailor's expense, wherever he was caught until the captain or his representative came for him. And a conviction of mutiny was punishable by death.

Even kind and benevolent masters, then, ruled with an iron hand, and it was up to the individual captain's methods whether the men were led willingly or driven by fear. There were abundant examples of each. Each method had its successes, and each had its failures.

Some ships' masters drove their ship and its cargo to the very edge of disaster, sometimes crossing over that fine line. Ruthless in their ambitions, they sometimes exceeded the limits of their crew, earning reputations as slave drivers, with no regard for the health and safety of those signed on to carry out their wishes. Mary knew of such men, who built their careers upon the broken backs of nameless sailors, but her polite sensibilities prevented her admiration of them. Other captains earned their success by carefully pushing crew and ship to their limits, but knowing when to back away from the dangers of mutinous men and bending masts. Even before observing him aboard ship, Mary felt certain that Joshua Patten belonged to this group. Early in their courtship, he spoke of his philosophy of ships and men.

"There is a difference," he had said, "between being put in command of men and being able to command them."

Mary, seeing him now at his duties, was proud of her husband. He worked his men hard but was fair in his treatment. In exchange, the men were willing to work hard without complaint.

"These are not beasts of burden," Joshua said one evening during the second dog watch, when all hands were on deck. He was looking out over the ship, resting his elbows on the quarterdeck rail, hands clasped in front of him. "They are men. Each has some dream, some goal, if only to reach the next port and its row of taverns."

In the evening the normal four-hour watch was divided into two short watches of two hours each. The arrangement of these dog watches, the first from four in the afternoon to six and the other from six to eight, enabled the crew to shift their turns at any particular watch so that the same men were not forever keeping the midnight-to-4:00-A.M. watch, for example. This time of the evening, after supper but before night fell, was often a time of relaxation and personal time for many of the crew, as all were normally topside but not all were engaged in duties of the watch. Some of the men worked in small clusters, mending worn line and overhauling gear, making casual conversation. One or two were by the bow, snatching a few puffs from their pipes, ending their labors for the day. Some captains allowed no such conversations or idleness, but Joshua saw no harm in minor leniencies during quiet times.

"They will earn their pay in due time. The leisure of the tropics will be longed for when we reach the Horn. Let them enjoy their pipes while they are able."

Joshua noticed that his first mate was likewise looking out over the ship, from the far end of the rail. Keeler had avoided his captain since last night's incident of the out-of-trim sail, but Joshua decided it was time to break the silence.

"Easy sailing this evening, Mr. Keeler."

Keeler looked his way, unsure of the overture. "Aye, sir. Light wind, but steady and true."

"The men seem to be enjoying it as well."

"I can change that, sir."

Joshua glanced at Mary. She was forming a dislike for Keeler, and he knew she did not like the mate's gruff attitude, especially after her husband had just been humanizing the crew.

"I meant no disparagement of your management of the watch, Mr. Keeler. I merely observed that the men seem as content with the state of things as do we."

Keeler had seen Joshua's glance to Mary, and he visibly stiffened. Mary felt that the first mate did not share Joshua's appreciation of her presence on board.

"They were not signed on to be content, sir."

"Nor necessarily malcontent, Mr. Keeler. Their lot is hard enough without our efforts at excess."

Keeler said nothing.

On the afternoon of the following day, the quiet of the ship was broken by a shout from the foretop truck.

"Sail ho!"

All hands looked up from their work, and Mary, on the poop of the quarterdeck with Joshua, quickly scanned the horizon. At first she saw nothing. Then, dead ahead, a tiny peak of white appeared for just a second before disappearing again behind a low swell. A moment later it reappeared, staying in view a little longer. Mary felt a surge of excitement. This was the first vessel sighted since New York, proof that they were not, after all, alone in the world. She looked at Joshua for his reaction. He maintained his captain air, but she was not fooled. He was excited as well.

From a small locker by the rail he took his spyglass and held it before his eye. He watched through two or three oscillations, examining the sails each time they appeared. Without taking his eye away from the telescope, he said, "She's bark-rigged, tacking to our starboard."

He watched a minute longer and lowered the glass. Looking up at his own sails and checking the wind pennant, he turned his head back toward the helmsman. "Fall off a little, if you please. Two points for now."

"Two points off, sir." The sailor at the helm turned the wheel to steer *Neptune's Car* a little more to the west. The new course would come closer to intercepting the track of the oncoming vessel.

A few minutes later, the bark's sails likewise changed course, presenting less profile as its captain turned toward *Neptune's Car*. It took an hour in the light winds to bring the two together, but finally the other vessel was near enough to make out figures on the deck. Other men were on the rigging, furling some of the sails, slowing forward progress. When two hundred yards separated the two ships, a voice came across the water.

"Ahoy! Greetings from *Susan Walker*, of Norfolk."

The words floated across the water, the voice made thin by the distance but still clear and easily heard, aided by the use of a speaking tube. Mary was glad to hear it. She thought of the letters she had written. Perhaps they would be delivered after all. As though reading her mind about a meeting, Joshua said, "We may as well invite them over. We are making precious little headway in this calm."

Mary was familiar with the custom. Meeting another vessel on the vast ocean was a rare occurrence, and even when the wind was allowing good progress it was common practice to at least hail one another and if possible heave to long enough to exchange mail and news. At times of slow going, as in tropical calms such as they were in now, it broke up the monotony to have company.

Joshua took up his own trumpet and called back. "*Neptune's Car*, New York. Would the captain like to come aboard?"

"I would be pleased to. We will come about."

Mary saw the man doing the speaking lower his trumpet and address his crew, and presently the bow of the *Susan Walker* started a slow swing toward the larger clipper.

At the same time, Joshua issued commands of his own. "Heave to, Mr. Keeler." He looked again at the wind pennant. The winds were very light. "I believe that striking all but the spanker and dropping a sea anchor should do us nicely."

Thus held steady, *Neptune's Car* waited for the *Susan Walker* to close the distance between the two. Joshua watched the captain's handling of the bark, and was pleased to see the maneuver done skillfully, with the result placing the two vessels side by side eighty or a hundred yards apart. He spoke again through his trumpet.

"Captain, you are invited to stay for dinner." Glancing at Mary, he added, "And of course, any other guest is welcomed."

After a pause, there came the reply. "Thank you, Captain. There will be two of us."

A short time later a boat was lowered over the side of the *Susan Walker*, and four men boarded, two as passengers and two men on the oars.

Mary was disappointed. She had hoped there might be another captain's wife to join her.

The two men climbed aboard using the ladder dropped over the side, and the boat returned to the bark. The visiting captain was a balding middle-aged man with the extra heft around the waistline common to older men. His first mate was tall and slender, with serious dark eyes. It struck Mary that the two were polite to each other, but no more. Very much the same as Joshua and Keeler.

They came bearing gifts. The captain carried a bottle of port, and the mate a box of pineapples, brought from the Sandwich Islands. Mary had had pineapple before, and her mouth watered at the thought of the sweet yet tart taste of the strange fruit.

Greetings and introductions were made all around, and Captain Cleary of Virginia and Captain Patten of Boston went below, joined by Mary, for a glass of wine before dinner. Cleary's mate, whose name was Hardy, stayed on deck with Keeler.

There was the usual stiff politeness of new acquaintances, but after a short time the conversation slipped into the easy tone of men having made quick assessments and deciding that the other was worthy of friendship. Mary was sure the wine helped.

Cleary shared the Pattens' frustration with the light winds. "But what can we do?" he asked with a smile of resignation. "One cannot go from the south half of the world to the north half without crossing the middle."

Dinner was served after the third glass of wine. Mary thought it was quite admirable of the cook to so quickly adjust his menu to the extra guests. Keeler and Hardy joined them for the meal, which was served by the steward with as much flair as he could muster. Mary was sure that Joshua appreciated the efforts that Henry and the cook made to impress the visitors. The dinner of potato soup, baked lamb, sweet potatoes, steamed carrots, and fresh bread, with mince pie for desert, left the round middle of Captain Cleary a little more round than before.

"My compliments to the chef," he said, patting his belly. "We are nearing the end of a long passage, and are a little less varied in our diet."

Joshua understood. "We shall no doubt be in your same situation by the time we reach the Pacific side. By then you will be safely in port, free to visit the finest restaurants."

Cleary laughed. "By then I hope to be in my own kitchen, watching my little Gretchen making sausage gravy. You, Captain, are fortunate to have your bride to join you. Mine tried the sea only once, and never again."

Mary, who had said little while the men talked, said, "It does require some adjustment."

"You have the Horn ahead. That will require all the adjustment you can muster."

Mary smoothed a wrinkle in the tablecloth. "Perhaps the weather will have pity on us and not be too difficult."

Cleary glanced toward Joshua, as if wondering how much he should say.

Joshua said, "Mary has seen plenty of weather."

The visiting first mate, who had been eating in silence, said, "She will be seeing plenty more soon enough."

Joshua looked at Cleary. "Is that right?"

Cleary hesitated. "I've been around a half dozen times, and I believe the weather this year to be the worst I have seen. And it is not just my opinion.

"Oh?"

"It was the main topic of crews arriving on Oahu while we were there. Two or three ships told of a bad ride around, and there we were, getting ready to go ourselves. Ha!" He laughed, as if questioning his own wisdom.

"At least you were going easterly," said Joshua.

"And I'm glad of it. I have bucked those winds, and they are not always kind. This time, especially. As we were heading into the start of the weather, we met a clipper just making the turn into the Pacific. I guess they had a rough time of it."

Joshua, whose attention had been commanded by an errant slice of carrot, looked up with new interest. "What ship was that, do you know?"

"Yes. It was the *Competitor*, under Captain Holmes. We spoke and replenished some of their supplies. They were a worn-out bunch, I'll say."

Mary looked at Joshua, judging his concern.

Cleary took a sip of wine and looked at Mary briefly before turning back to Joshua. "The captain told me they were eighty days beating their way around. Eighty days."

Mary glanced again at Joshua, to find him looking at her. She knew that eighty days was much too long for a normal passage of the cape. The clipper *Flying Cloud* had made the entire New York to San Francisco run in only eighty-nine days, and last year Joshua had made it with *Neptune's Car* in an even hundred. The winds of the place some called "Cape Stiff" must be particularly stiff this year.

Joshua looked back to Cleary. "Was she whole?"

"She was. She had lost some sails, I guess, but the masts had held. Perhaps that is what took so long. Not enough drive."

"Yes," Joshua said pensively. "Perhaps that was it."

Mary knew that was not enough to explain eighty days around Cape Horn. A man did not become a clipper captain unless he knew how to drive a ship. She wondered what they were getting into.

She turned the conversation toward lighter subjects, and the dinner ended pleasantly. After the captains had cigars on deck, courtesy of Captain Cleary, the meeting ended with an exchange of mail and a trading of supplies. Joshua gave away two hens and got more pineapples in return, and both captains went away pleased with the trade. As darkness fell, the two vessels hoisted sails and drifted apart.

Mary watched the visiting ship grow small, pleased that her letters would be delivered within a few weeks. Joshua joined her by the rail. "Seemed like a nice man," she said.

"I think so. I hope he has a successful run home. He has had some trouble with his mate, apparently."

"Really?"

"I'm afraid so. I believe it was a near mutiny at one point. I think that is why the first mate came to dinner. I do not think Cleary trusted him with the ship."

Well, thought Mary, at least our man Keeler is not that bad.

The last day in the Northern Hemisphere was spent in an almost dead calm, the sails holding barely any air at all. Joshua took his noon sight and calculated the position as being less than a half degree north, close enough that allowing for errors might already put them in the South Atlantic.

"Tomorrow, for certain," he said to Mary, "will find us over the line. It will be cause for celebration among the crew, and I am of a mind to announce crossing this afternoon."

Mary suspected what he was thinking. "Today is Sunday after all, isn't it?"

"Yes, it is. An ideal day to allow the crew some extra leisure." Glancing up at the slack sails, hanging almost completely limp from their yards, he said, "There is certainly no wind to hinder them. Perhaps tomorrow we will get a breeze, and they can get back to work."

At four in the afternoon, when the entire crew would be coming on deck for the first dog watch, Joshua called all hands to the quarterdeck rail. He announced with great fanfare that the line was at that moment being crossed. A cheer went up from the assembled men. After it quieted, Joshua thanked them for their efforts thus far.

"We are halfway down the Atlantic, and you have made a solid crew. Ahead lies stiffer weather and much more difficult days. But having seen you at your duties, I have no doubt that you will stand against the coming storms. And I do assure you that there are storms coming. These calm days will not last, but I have no fear that you men can handle all that King Neptune will throw at you."

At the mention of Neptune, there was a roar from the bow of the ship, a monstrous bellow that seemed to rise from the ocean itself. On cue, the second mate shouted, "Look!" All hands turned to see, climbing over the bowsprit, a fearsome apparition from the deep, a manlike specter dressed in hides of seals and swathed in garlands of seaweed. On the figure's head was a crumpled hat, clamped tightly down over a wild tangled mane of hair. A tattered beard of kelp covered the face almost to the eyes, which blazed with anger. The creature climbed upon the railing and leaped upon the deck, dripping seawater onto the boards.

"Who," it screamed, "dares tempt the sea? The sea is mine! No one crosses its waters without answering to the god of the waves!"

The crew roared with delight. Except for those few making their first equatorial crossing, this demon of the deep had been seen by them all, in one form or another. It was for the neophytes that he had appeared.

"Bring me the virgins!" the sea demon shouted. "Bring them to me!"

There were a half dozen among the crew who, having never before crossed into the Southern Hemisphere, qualified for the summons. The rest grabbed them and roughly shoved them forward toward the man at the bow, whom Mary now recognized as the ship's cook.

"Give me the tar!"

A willing sailor took a bucket of tar thinned with linseed oil, used to coat the shrouds, and carried it to the demon. While others held them, each novice seaman was smeared with the foul substance until all bare skin was covered. When all were suitably coated, the wild-eyed cook, obviously delighted at the opportunity to rough up those who cursed his cooking, bellowed at the top of his lungs.

"Overboard! Be rid of them. I want no more to do with their scabbie hides! Overboard, I say!"

The rest of the crew roared again, happy to do the bidding. The poor targets of the game had no choice but to go along and allow themselves to be tossed over the rail and down into the sea. They fell with a shout and a splash, one at a time, until all six were in the salty water. Some were better swimmers than others, but all flailed about, trying to keep their heads above water. From the rail came shouts of laughter and warnings of sharks.

Mary watched the proceedings by Joshua's side, sharing in the humor of the scene but concerned for the men's safety. Even though there was little wind, the ship was drifting away from the heads bobbing in the sea, and she was worried they might fall too far behind and miss the trailing lifeline. Joshua let the fun last as long as he dared, and then he turned to his second mate.

"Mr. Hare, have additional lines thrown out, and be ready with a boat. I may have a need of those men later."

"Aye, sir."

To his first mate, watching the activities from near the helm, he said, "Mr. Keeler, let me know when everyone is safely back aboard. And have the cook make up something for an extra dessert for the men."

Keeler smiled, and Mary realized he rarely did that. "Aye, aye, sir. Consider it done, sir."

"And then let's set all sails. Somewhere there is a breeze, and I wish to catch it."

CHAPTER 9

South Atlantic

Neptune's Car was five weeks out of New York when it crossed the equator.

The first airs of the Southern Hemisphere were of the same character as the last of the Northern, and the ship merely coasted before the lightest zephyrs. The wind stirred the flat surface of the sea no more than the gentle swirls of a cat's paw in a goldfish pond.

Two days south of the line the flat calms of the doldrums were left behind. A storm came brewing out of the east, its dark countenance casting a shadow over the sea, blotting out the bright sun. With the clouds came the wind. The hands jumped into action, setting all sails to catch its power. *Neptune's Car* leaped forward, as if eager to resume the race down the Atlantic. The ship ran before the wind, fleeing the coming storm. All on board relished the fresh breeze, weary of the warm and still equatorial air.

With the flying spray the smell of salt returned to the air, and Mary inhaled deeply, enjoying the feeling of the sea air filling her lungs. Soon enough she would tire of the chapped skin, but for now she enjoyed the taste of salt.

Joshua saw her licking the spray off her lips. "Now you see how an old salt gets that way," he said. "It begins with just a mist of spray in the face, and soon enough it is in the blood."

"It is a refreshing feeling," Mary admitted. "And a refreshing sight to see the ship under strong sail again."

"Spoken like a true salt."

Mary ignored his comment, continuing her musings. "It is almost like being back at sea anew, beginning an entirely new voyage."

"And a romantic salt, at that."

She smiled and reached over to touch his sleeve, resting her fingers there a few seconds before letting them fall away. Romantic, indeed.

The captain ordered the studding sails left out, and all others up to the skysails, taking advantage of the long-awaited wind. The ship heeled over until the studding booms were almost touching the white tops of the waves. It seemed to Mary that the running sea slid past only inches below the lee rail.

Ecstatic to be moving again, Joshua said, "Now, we'll make some time, by God!"

Mary understood. The past days of inactivity had been maddening for her husband, and she shared his irritation. The rocks of Saint Paul, just north of the equator, had been in sight for a day and a half, providing ample visual evidence of the incremental progress of *Neptune's Car*. Now these tiny protrusions of land fell behind and disappeared below the horizon. All around was only sea. The nearest land was the coast of Brazil, a hundred miles to the west and out of sight over the horizon.

Using the wind and current charts recently developed by Lt. Matthew Maury of the United States Navy, Joshua chose a course he thought to give the best advantage. Too near the coast might put the ship in an area of diminished wind. Too far east could take them out of the Brazil Current, a southward flowing stream that helped carry vessels down the western Atlantic. Fifty miles either way could have a marked effect upon their progress, but there was no way to know with certainty which route was best at any particular time.

While Joshua worked to find the fastest route, Mary often took his sextant and practiced taking her own observations, comparing her numbers with his, and taking her own look at Maury's charts. In nearly every case, she reached the same conclusion as her husband.

She was proud of her results and felt that Joshua was pleased as well.

Intrepid had not been seen since leaving New York, and Joshua wondered whether the route its captain was taking was proving to be the better choice. Captain Cleary, of the bark *Susan Walker*, had seen neither *Intrepid* nor *Romance of the Seas*, but that did not mean that those two ships were not ahead of *Neptune's Car*. From the deck of a clipper on the open ocean the horizon was only ten or twelve miles away. Any vessel much farther away would remain out of sight, its sails disappearing below the edge of the sea. *Neptune's Car's* competitors could easily have passed Cleary's ship unseen. Which captain was making the best decisions would not be known until reaching San Francisco. Joshua could only make all possible speed and hope for the best.

To that end he kept all sails set, pushing his long ship through the deepening swells. As the afternoon wore on, the wind steadily increased, stiffening the sails against their sheets and punching the sharp bow into the rising sea.

Mary stayed on deck for the first hour or two after the wind came up, reveling in the renewed sensation of fast travel, not retreating to the cabin until increasing amounts of sea spray began to break over the ship. Joshua remained topside. Mary was not surprised. Although it was Hare's watch, she knew it was unlikely that her husband would leave him the ship during the first significant breeze in a week. Joshua felt that Timothy Hare, while dedicated and willing, and perfectly capable of handling the ship, did not necessarily have the nerve to drive the ship as hard as he would. If the wind presented any advantage, Joshua wanted to be there to take it.

As the wind increased, even Joshua was obliged to order the studs pulled in, but did so only when it became apparent that their booms were on the verge of departing the ship. With the studding sails and their extended yards pulled in, he turned his attention to the tops, gauging the strain on the highest masts, up by the royals. He also watched Hare and studied his second mate's assessment of the wind. Hare had become much more at ease with hard sailing as his experience increased, but he was still too quick to err on the side of caution. The strengthening winds pushed on the high sails, and the tops of the masts showed the strain, visibly bending forward. As the masts bowed, Hare looked anxious.

"Steady, Mr. Hare," Joshua said in an even voice. "She's not there yet."

Hare nodded, but stayed close to hear the next order when it came.

The storm that bore the wind closed in upon the ship. Overhead, the clouds darkened and grew more turbulent. The wind played its tune through the tight rigging, the lines and shrouds no less an orchestra than one found in a symphony hall. The gentle whisper of the new wind's first breezes became a heavy sigh, spilling from around the canvas, and then deepened into a moan, the sails lamenting the strain to come.

The sky grew darker. The waves became higher, smashing against the hull. The ship took the higher seas just as it was designed, its sharp bow cutting into the swells, lessening the oscillations of crest and trough, keeping forward momentum. This riding through the sea rather than over it brought the waves higher, their foamy tops breaking over the rails and cascading onto the deck. The men before the mast donned oilskin coats and stayed at their duties, the easier days of sailing already fading into memories.

Those on the quarterdeck were not immune to the water, and were nearly as wet as those forward, but Joshua's spirits were far from dampened.

"This is very fine, Mr. Hare." He had to raise his voice to be heard above the wind. Both men watched a larger than average swell approach the bow. Joshua planted his feet in a wide stance to brace for the coming roll of the deck. The ship met the swell, cutting into its face. *Neptune's Car* rode over the crest and dropped with a shudder into the following trough. Joshua lurched, regained his footing, and glanced over at Hare, who kept a grip on the quarterdeck rail.

"Good sailing, is it not?"

Timothy Hare liked a good wind, as long as the ship was handling it, as much as any sailor, and agreed with his captain. "Aye, sir. Good sailing."

Joshua, mindful of his second mate's still conservative sail use, said, "Not too much wind, though?"

Hare smiled. "No, sir, not yet."

For another hour, *Neptune's Car* worked its way through the increasingly heavy sea. The storm precipitating this abrupt change in the weather continued to darken the eastern sky and eventually darkened the sky in all quadrants. As fast as the clipper was moving, the coming rain was moving faster, and it became apparent that the rain-laden clouds would overtake the tall white sails of the ship.

The rain was soon close enough to see, its steel gray mass obscuring the distant horizon, when a strong gust front came across the waves, blowing the froth off the choppy wave tops. Anticipating the wind, Joshua turned to the helm.

"Two points off, and quickly now."

The helmsman, also eyeing the gust, wasted no time in spinning the wheel. Even with the ship turning away, the wind hit the sails and heeled it over hard to starboard.

"And Mr. Hare, let's get the royals in."

Even as he gave the order, Joshua knew there was not time for the crew even to start up the standing rigging, but after the gust passed, they would be on their way. There was a tense moment as the lee rail dipped dangerously close to the waterline, but the ship stopped its roll with some freeboard to spare and slowly righted itself.

High on the royal yards of all three masts, 130 feet above the deck, the crew gathered the canvas as the sheets were loosened at the pin rails, working quickly to complete the work before the next gust. Joshua looked up at them, tiny figures clinging to handfuls of canvas as they pulled it up, the soles of their boots working along the thin footropes. As soon the last gaskets securing the sails were fastened to the jackstays, he delivered his next order.

"Standby the men to the topgallants, Mr. Hare. Another gust like that, and they'll be next."

"Aye, sir."

Hare had been promoted to second mate during Joshua Patten's first voyage on *Neptune's Car*. He was still gaining experience, but Joshua saw in him good possibilities, and looked forward to bringing the young man along. Hare became mate upon leaving London for the short homeward passage to New York, and was still feeling his way into the position. He seemed to have confidence in his own abilities, but at the same time was perfectly content to have Joshua on deck. He clearly enjoyed the thrill of a clipper at the maximum of its performance, and Joshua was sure that in time he would keep as tight a ship as anyone. For now, he might not have the nerve to keep the topgallants out in this wind, but he was willing to stand by Joshua's side and learn. Joshua was just as willing to teach.

"Have you much experience with racehorses, Mr. Hare?"

"No, sir. None at all." Hare's words were nearly whisked away by the wind.

Joshua smiled. "I don't either. But I think I'd like to. I understand that if you just let them go, they love to run."

Hare looked at his captain, absorbing the meaning. "I think I understand."

"I'm sure you do, Mr. Hare."

Joshua knew how the young mate felt. He, too, had once been in the position of experiencing the excitement of a hard-driven ship without having the responsibility for it. It was a free and unfettered existence, and it certainly had its merits. There was merit, too, in the feeling of command. To take a ship and crew into a storm with wind and rain and waves as high as the topsail yards and then back out again gave a captain a feeling within himself that he could master any adversity. For the chance to experience that feeling, Joshua Patten was eternally grateful.

There were no more sudden strong gusts, but the wind rose to near gale force. The waves increased from two or three feet to ten feet, the repeating pattern of underlying swells obscured and lost beneath the jumbled sea. As each wave peaked, its top blew off, with frothy foam scattering before the wind. Overhead, the high masts bent under the strain. Joshua waited, allowing a few more knots of wind to build. The rain fell over the ocean, its gray curtain advancing across the waves. The leading edge of the precipitation was a few hundred yards away and getting closer.

"The topgallants, now, Mr. Hare."

Hare used the speaking trumpet to be heard above the wind, sending men aloft for the third time in less than a quarter hour. Fully aware of the impending weather, they made quick work of furling the topgallant sails, but despite their haste the full force of the rain and wind caught them up on the yards. The ship rolled before the gust, the masts leaning well off the vertical, the downpour sudden and heavy. The men tightened their grips and doggedly stuck to their tasks.

The storm enveloped the ship, with rain coming from all sides and all directions. The swells and waves no longer marched in orderly rows, but met and crashed together at all angles. The surface of the ocean, only a few hours ago a flat and tranquil blue, became a churned and convoluted mass of crests and troughs. What was a dip in the sea one moment became in the next a sharp-peaked mountain of water. These cold, green peaks stood only until the next wave shouldered into them, the mass and strength of one merging into the other in confrontations of spray and froth.

The wind was no less confused than the sea, shifting in force and direction as the storm overtook the ship. *Neptune's Car* was caught between the opposing forces of wind and sea and took a battering from both. This storm was easily the strongest encountered since leaving New York, but even as the weather surrounded him, Joshua remained confident that the ship could handle everything offered on this day. He looked over at his second mate, steady at his position by the rail.

"Still fine sailing, Mr. Hare?"

At that moment a well-timed wave broke over the port side and cascaded over the deck. Freshly soaked, Hare answered, "Aye, sir," and offered a thin smile. "But not nearly as fine as it was."

Joshua Patten laughed, the rain running down his face. He loved running a ship at full speed and facing the exhilarating challenges of the weather. That being so, he suspected that he would love the coming weeks as the ship approached Cape Horn.

CHAPTER 10

Chain of Command

Joshua may have been eager to face the coming challenges of Cape Horn, but Mary felt that he must have harbored certain reservations as well. No one approached the weather of the cape without them. And as captain, he had more concerns than anyone else on board.

In many ways, the day-to-day duties of a clipper captain were not difficult. The captain had ultimate authority and absolute command. He was required to take no watch of his own, leaving them to the mates. He was free to come and go as he pleased, but when he was on deck, the mate on duty deferred to his wishes. A mate might be in control of the ship and crew, but at all times it was the captain's ship, and his word was law. Rank definitely had its privileges.

Rank also had its responsibilities, and in no profession were they so singularly great as in that of a ship captain. How well a captain balanced these privileges and responsibilities determined his skill and his standing among his peers and crew. As a captain's wife, Mary knew these things. She had become quite familiar with the chain of command during her first voyage. Having seen Joshua command, Mary knew that he preferred giving the mates a free hand in running the ship, though in the interest of a fast passage he was quick to offer suggestions for better speed, suggestions expected to be taken.

It was an order in the guise of a suggestion Joshua made a day or so after the first storm of the South Atlantic. He came up with Mary from his afternoon tea and found the sails up to the topgallants full and taut before the wind. The smaller royal sails, high on the masts, however, were furled against their yards. Looking around, he found Keeler up on the poop of the quarterdeck. The first mate was leaning easily against the stern's taffrail, watching the wake spread behind the ship. Joshua frowned. Sensing a confrontation, Mary followed her husband up to the higher deck but moved over to the port railing and pretended to be interested in the seascape as she eavesdropped on their conversation.

The wind was fresh abeam port, making for fast sailing. Joshua said as much to Keeler.

"Aye, sir," Keeler replied, straightening up stiffly but still looking aft. "Good sailing."

"Has the wind been steady?"

Keeler spoke slowly. "Fairly dependable, yes."

Mary, listening from by the rail, could tell that the mate was on his guard, as if he knew Joshua was not pleased with him. And he probably knew why. This would not be the first time, or even the second, that Joshua questioned his mate's sail settings.

"Would it not be better," Joshua said with a forced measure of patience, "to utilize the royals?"

The answer was the same as Keeler had given before. "I judged the strain to be too great, sir."

"I see. I thought that we had agreed that *Neptune's Car* was heavily sparred and would stand a good deal more weather than this."

"It is not the spars, sir, but the sails I am concerned about. I'll not be wanting to blow out a sail on my watch, not in as moderate a wind as this."

Joshua looked at him, as if not comprehending his logic.

"What I mean, sir," Keeler went on, "is that if a sail goes in a gale, well, that sometimes can't be helped. But for it to go here would be my own fault, and I can't abide by that."

"Your concern for the ship is admirable, Mr. Keeler, but if the sails cannot stand this wind they deserve to rip. We have no use for weak canvas."

"You want the royals out, then?"

Joshua drew in a deep breath. Mary admired his patience. Even she was amazed by Keeler's lack of comprehension.

"Yes, Mr. Keeler, I do."

Again Keeler frowned, but said nothing, except to issue orders to the crew. Joshua started to leave him to stew, but turned to make one more comment. "If it is tearing a sail you are worried about, you should have reefed the courses. Those larger sails are the more likely to blow out."

Mary had rejoined Joshua, thinking the conversation over, and was by his side when Keeler was handed this last rebuke. Although Keeler was probably aware of her listening from across the deck, she did not deign to embarrass him by her close presence. It had not been her intention to provide an audience, but it was too late to discreetly move away.

Keeler glanced toward her, and his face clouded even more than it already was. "It is your ship, sir, and I shan't dispute you, especially before your wife."

"Anything you have to say, Mr. Keeler, may be said freely, even in Mrs. Patten's presence."

Mary was pleased that Joshua had affirmed her right to be there, but Keeler said nothing else.

The days that passed as *Neptune's Car* tacked down the South Atlantic got no easier. One storm followed quickly upon the heels of another with scarcely enough time for the ship and crew to dry out from one before the next came along. During one of the storms, with plenty of rain and contrary winds, Mary remarked upon the hindered progress.

"I expect nothing less of the weather," said Joshua.

It was hard sailing, with every opportunity for speed requiring careful setting of the sails. *Neptune's Car* was spending more time getting down the Atlantic than Joshua would have liked, and as the days passed, he became anxious. He was too good a captain to allow his frustrations to be openly displayed, but Mary recognized a gradual change in his humor. He tried to act philosophical about it, but she could see that, despite what he said, he did expect more of the weather and more of his crew. Especially of his recalcitrant first mate. By the day, it seemed, William Keeler became more of an aggravation.

"It's hard to put my finger on it," Joshua said, "but he seldom seems to have the best interest of the ship at heart. And sometimes he seems diametrically opposed."

Mary saw that he was troubled. "I know you have talked to him. Has it not helped?"

"Not as much as I had hoped. I keep finding him with shortened sails."

Mary knew that to reduce sail when the ship was still able to take the wind was not something a hard-driving captain could allow. "Why does he do that? You have told him repeatedly how you want the ship run."

"To little avail, it seems. If I didn't know better, I'd think he was sleeping on duty or some such."

"Oh?" Mary knew that for the officer of the deck to sleep on duty was a grievous sin and a nearly unpardonable breach of conduct.

"Shortened sails require a little less diligence. Allows for a little nap once in a while."

"And you think Mr. Keeler is guilty of that?"

Joshua hesitated. "I shouldn't say so. I have no proof. But should I find any, heaven help him."

Eight weeks out of New York, as *Neptune's Car* plowed down the South Atlantic, the weather turned worse. At first it seemed no different than the storms of the previous days, but there was an underlying feel to the air, a feeling of change. Two or three days at a time might pass without sun or stars to fix the ship's position, and Joshua relied upon dead reckoning to plot his progress. This method of deducing position, based upon estimated distance and direction traveled since a last known point, was a rather vague navigational technique but quite sufficient on the open ocean. Joshua only desired a more exact sun fix before the ship approached Cape Horn.

At the rate of progress thus far, that was still a fortnight away. As the ship pressed on through the increasingly higher seas, the wind continued to blow, and not always from a direction beneficial to the ship's progress.

During the first week of September, with increasingly cold temperatures, the first snow fell. It stung the eyes of those on duty and coated the deck with a thin layer of white. Mary thought it pretty, and she was reminded of the first snowfalls of her New England home. She also knew that soon enough she would despise the sight.

"This is just the first taste," Joshua reminded her. "We'll be rounding the Horn in the early spring of the Southern Hemisphere, but if what Captain Cleary of the *Susan Walker* said is true, it might as well still be winter."

In addition to the chilling weather, Joshua became ever more disturbed by Keeler's work. Every effort to speed *Neptune's Car* along seemed to be countered by his efforts to slow the ship down.

With the advent of colder weather, Mary spent less time on deck and more time in the cabin, so she was not often present when Joshua and Keeler had their almost daily confrontations. She saw the expressions upon Joshua's face, though, when he came below. It seemed that every time he left the deck during Keeler's watch, he wore a look of indignation. Indignation mixed with aggravation.

Most of the time he said nothing, but Mary saw the frustration building up. When she saw them together, whether on deck or at meals, they were civil to each other but nothing more, extending politeness only as far as the rules of manners required. If Joshua was cold to Keeler, Keeler was even more icy to Joshua, becoming almost surly to his captain, which alone was enough to tax Joshua's patience.

Mary watched the situation deteriorate, wishing it would improve, fearing it would not, and knowing there was little she could do about it but offer herself to her husband as someone he could talk to and get things off his chest. Joshua allowed himself some of her comforting but mostly kept his concerns to himself. When Mary encouraged him to discuss the matter with her, he deferred.

"I do not wish to spoil your day," he said.

Despite his desire to separate her from the conflicts, he said enough and Mary saw enough to know all she needed to know. Keeler was obviously more trouble than he was worth, and she regretted that Joshua had been obliged to sail with him. Still, before they had left New York, Joshua had been confident that he could handle any problems the mate presented, and Mary was still confident that he could do so.

Every day brought more cold rain and, increasingly, sleet or snow. The working conditions on the deck and in the rigging were becoming more difficult as the surfaces became slippery and the lines sometimes had a thin film of ice coating them. Work that was strenuous even in warm climes was now much harder, and simple tasks became complex as hands and fingers became stiff from the cold.

Those were the crew's problems, of course. The problem for the officers was less intimately painful. They were not the ones clinging to icy shrouds sixty or seventy feet off the deck, but their work, too, was made more disagreeable by the weather. Long periods spent standing in the wind-driven sleet, with no vigorous activity to warm them, left Joshua and his mates chilled to the core.

During one of these bone-chilling watches, Joshua decided to once again make a conciliatory overture to his first mate. It was not because he wanted Keeler's friendship. He had no interest at all in that, but he did need Keeler's cooperation and support in the coming weeks. He opened the conversation, as is often done when conversation is difficult, with a comment upon the weather.

"Cold air, Mr. Keeler."

"Aye, sir."

"More to come."

"Aye, sir."

"Hopefully it will not be too bad down by the Horn."

Silence.

"Last year," Joshua said, "we went around in March, when the southern winter was just coming on. I thought that weather to be generally bad enough."

"It's often worse in the spring, I've always heard."

Joshua was pleased to get more than a simple *aye, sir* out of Keeler. "Very true. Not to mention the ice hazard. There will be a winter's worth of ice drifting around in the Drake Passage."

Keeler said nothing but looked subdued.

The two men stood side by side for several minutes, watching the sea and sky. Perhaps each was contemplating the storms that would surely be waiting in the wide passage between Cape Horn and the mysterious Antarctic land mass to the south. Joshua considered what he could say to Keeler to improve the first mate's willingness to properly handle the ship.

After some thought, he said, "Mr. Keeler, I can fully appreciate your concerns with regard to strong running, and I do not wish to force you to do things you consider unsafe. On the other hand, few things about the sea are without some element of danger. Call them calculated risks, but we must take them in order to arrive at our destinations in a timely manner. It is time, after all, that we are selling here."

He looked over at Keeler, judging his reaction. The mate stood looking toward the bow, expressionless.

"I am only saying," Joshua went on, "that there are certain things that I require, and one thing I require is that we move the ship forward as best we can without undue danger to the crew. And I emphasize *undue* danger."

Again Keeler said nothing, his face still masking what he was thinking. Perhaps, thought Joshua, he is not thinking at all.

"I am not saying anything, Mr. Keeler, that you do not already know. You have been around the Horn, and you have served enough time at sea to know what it is that these fast merchant ships do, and what is needed for them to do it.

"It is your experience that makes me question your actions. If I find Mr. Hare sailing under conservative rigging, I understand that he is less than sure of himself. He will learn in time. You, sir, should by now have already learned."

He turned and looked directly at Keeler. "You do know how to run a ship, don't you?"

Keeler's face flexed, as if some hidden emotion was trying to surface, but he said simply, "I believe I do, sir."

"Then I trust that you will demonstrate that to me. More so than you have thus far."

Keeler's eyes flashed. He opened his mouth to retort, but then closed it. After several seconds, he spoke with forced calm. "I have done my duty as I saw fit, sir, and will continue to do so. I will, however, try to do things in a fashion more to your liking."

"I would appreciate that."

"Antagonizing you has not been my intent, sir. I desire that you be satisfied with my performance. If you have not . . ."

Joshua waited for him to finish, but no more came. He supposed that Keeler was trying to work up a defense but was unable to do so. In a perverse way, Joshua, who was saying that he wanted Keeler to do well, enjoyed watching him struggle.

"Your performance, Mr. Keeler, has been less than what I had hoped for. But it will not take a great deal of change on your part to alter my opinion. We are not that far apart."

Keeler stood silently at the rail, looking down at the main deck, and then said, "Yes, sir."

Joshua wondered if this conversation would have any effect. Keeler seemed penitent, but he was also strong-willed. There had been plenty of signs of that since leaving New York. It should have been a simple matter for a first mate to learn the ways and wants of his captain. Once a captain's methods were known, it was the duty of the second officer to conform to those methods. That continuity was best for the ship and best for the crew.

Joshua decided that his point had been made. Further discussion was not likely to produce any more result and would only serve to berate the first mate. Not that Keeler did not deserve berating. He decided to end with a last strong statement. A final volley.

"I do not expect to have this conversation again, Mr. Keeler. You are doubtless intelligent, and knowledgeable in your duties. Otherwise you would still be in the forecastle. You know what I want, and you know how to give it to me. Are we clear on these points?"

"Aye, sir. Perfectly."

Joshua eyed him coldly. He did not like the contemptuous tone in Keeler's voice. Still, enough had been said.

"I'm going below, Mr. Keeler. Keep her steady and at best speed."

"Aye, sir."

Joshua left the quarterdeck by the port stairs and entered the after house. The air outside had not seemed cold, but now that he was out of the wind, he found himself enjoying the relative warmth of the still inside air of the saloon.

The steward, hearing him come in, emerged from his tiny cabin along the port wall and offered to go forward to the kitchen to get Joshua some tea.

"It will only take a minute, if Cook has it ready."

Joshua declined the offer. "I think I will just rest in my cabin awhile. I believe Mr. Keeler has things well in hand above."

At the aft end of the saloon, he knocked once on the door to their cabin and went in. Mary was at the desk, writing. When he entered she replaced the pen in its stand and rose to greet him.

They kissed and he held her against him, feeling the movement of the ship through her. He was pleased that she was on board. Her soft form and pleasing face were a welcome diversion after dealing with Keeler. They stood together, swaying with the ship, and kissed again, longer this time. They could have released each other and moved apart, but did not. It seemed perfectly normal and natural to stay in each other's arms.

It seemed just as natural, while still in the embrace, to move over to the bed. Joshua eased Mary down, first to sit on the edge, and then to slowly fall back across the neatly tucked quilt. Mary had bought it from a boat vendor in Macao, and it had become a favorite piece of the cabin's furnishings. She thought its colorful embroidered patterns gave the otherwise austere cabin a personal, lived-in look. Whenever Joshua saw it he was reminded of Mary. And both were pleased.

Now they lay across it, gently touching each other. She felt the coarseness of Joshua's coat. He felt the woven texture of Mary's woolen smock, and the hints of smooth skin beneath. Joshua brushed a strand of hair from Mary's face.

"The better to see you, my dear," he said.

Mary smiled. "And what big teeth you have, Grandma."

"The better to eat you with, my dear."

She laughed. Joshua did not pursue the role of the wolf any further, but simply lay by Mary's side, looking at her face.

"Is everything all right?" she asked.

"Everything is fine."

Joshua told Mary of his talk with the first mate and of his hopes that Keeler might yet come around.

"Do you really think he will?"

"Realistically? Probably not. But at least he listened. I think I'll not expect much, and then perhaps be pleasantly surprised."

Mary touched his cheek with her finger, tracing a line past his ear to the back of his neck, where she rubbed the tight muscles. "Here is another pleasant surprise," she said, leaning over to follow the finger with her lips. Joshua turned his head, joining his mouth to hers, opening the lips and tasting her tongue with his. She slid her hand inside his jacket, feeling his warmth through his shirt.

Joshua responded in kind, but went a step further, loosening buttons to slip inside and cup a breast in his hand.

Mary laughed playfully as he rolled toward her, and she said nothing else for quite some time.

CHAPTER 11

In the Kitchen

Mary dreamed that she was back in Maine, lying in the bow of Joshua's fourteen-foot single-masted sloop, feeling the gentle rocking of the boat as he held the tiller, steering it across the harbor. The sun fell across her face, and she soaked up the warmth. It seemed that she had not been warm for some time, and she basked in its rays.

Joshua had taken her to his home in Rockland to meet his parents, Abel and Sarah, and to see the place he had come from. Now he was showing her how he had grown up, gliding small boats out of the tight harbor and across Penobscot Bay. The tiny wavelets of the harbor slapped against the bow, a gentle percussion beat to the music of the water as it whispered by the hull. It was all so relaxing. So peaceful. A person could almost fall asleep.

The dream was jolted to an end by the slamming of the cabin door. It took Mary a second to leave the warm sun of Rockland harbor and return to the dim cabin of *Neptune's Car*.

"Blast him." Joshua dropped into his wing-backed chair, visibly disgusted.

Mary realized that she was still struggling with sleep. "Who?"

"Who do you think?" Joshua looked at his wife. "Oh, I'm sorry. Were you asleep?"

"Just a little catnap," Mary said, becoming more fully awake. "What has happened now?"

"I suppose he wanted to show me that he could push a ship as hard as anyone. I guess the winds of hell could have come across the ocean and he would not have brought in any sail, just to prove me wrong."

Mary did not say anything, but sat up in the bed to listen.

"I can say, though, that we have some good canvas. The sails never blew out. Not that he didn't give them the chance."

Joshua paused, looking around the room, forcing himself to calm down.

"There was some trouble with the lines just as a strong gust hit, and the foremast brace was carried away. The yard came hard against the lee backstays, nearly taking away those lines. All in all, things became quite a mess. But even with the gear failure, it should not have been much of a problem—things like that happen some-times—had Keeler responded promptly."

"So what did he do?"

"Nothing. That is what's so exasperating. Of course, we had to fall off the wind to ease the strain. That was bad enough, but neces-sary. Then by the time he called for corrective measures, everything was fouled. It took three times as much work to put everything back in trim."

"Everything is back together now?"

"Yes. Finally." Joshua leaned back and looked at the ceiling. "I think he let it go just to show me that I was insisting upon too much sail. He is probably pretty pleased with himself right now."

From the deck there suddenly came a call for all hands.

Joshua looked at Mary. "What now?" He stood up and started for the door.

Mary slipped out from under the covers and smoothed her dress, which she had not taken off when she lay down for her nap, and stepped quickly into her boots.

"Wait," she said. "I'll go with you." But Joshua was already out the door. She hurried after, certain that this, in some way, involved Keeler.

Outside the sky was the color of slate, with smooth gray cloud bases stretching to the horizon in all directions. The air was cold and smelled like snow, but Mary could see no obvious reason that all hands were required. The ship seemed to be sailing smoothly and on course. The wind was still strong, but without hazard, and the spray breaking over the rails was nothing more than the usual dampening inconvenience. The only unusual sight was the gathering of the crew amidships. Joshua stopped outside the cabin, sizing up the situation, and then hurried toward them.

"What in blazes?" he said.

Mary followed, but at a distance. As Joshua neared the cluster of men, a path parted and she saw, in the center, a man tied spread-eagled to the standing rigging. A few feet away was Keeler, holding a knotted rope end.

She gasped involuntarily. Flogging, once common on ships, was now used only in the most severe of cases, and she wondered what the man had done to deserve the punishment. Joshua, apparently, wondered the same thing.

"What have we here, Mr. Keeler?"

Mary recognized in his voice an urgency tempered by a desire to not sound anxious.

Keeler turned to the captain. "This man's laggard pace is what caused all the trouble with the rigging. Had he jumped to it, things would have held together just fine."

Joshua looked at the sailor, helpless on the thick ropes of the rigging. His face was filled with terror and dread.

"What have you to say about this?"

"I had the line in my hand, sir, but no way could I hold it."

Keeler jumped back in. "He could have if he had wanted to. His slovenly work made more work for the rest. Any man here could see that, and no one will argue that he deserves what he gets."

Joshua looked at a few of the faces in the circle of men called to witness the beating. Most were expressionless, some wore pity, some even looked afraid. None looked ready to condemn anyone.

"And what is it that he is getting, Mr. Keeler?"

"I thought ten would suffice."

Joshua looked hard at him, and then at the sentenced man, already bare of shirt in the cold wind. He knew that Keeler, besides demonstrating an ability to run a tight ship to his captain, was also exhibiting his authority to the crew. And as long as Keeler was serving as first mate, it was to Joshua's benefit that the crew respect that.

He doubted the man deserved what he was about to receive. If he did deserve it, the crew would learn a hard but necessary lesson of discipline, courtesy of the hapless man's back.

"Ten lashes it is, then," he said, turning away. "Wait until Mrs. Patten is below."

Later, when the lashes had been laid on and the sailor was cut down and sent to have his wounds dressed, Joshua had Keeler meet him by the stern rail.

As Keeler approached, Joshua was looking aft, over the stern rail. Without looking away from the spreading wake, he said, "As a rule, I do not approve of the cat, Mr. Keeler. Of course, I will make exceptions, but when exceptions are made on my ship, I wish to know of them beforehand."

Keeler said, "Yes, sir. I did not intend to undermine your authority."

"If the punishment was deserved, no one's authority was undermined. Indeed, you will find your standing among the men increased. I allowed the lashing, Mr. Keeler, in order not to undermine you." He looked over at his first mate. "If you have erred in your actions, the crew knows it, and you know it, too. And I will know the truth soon enough."

Keeler swallowed. Much of the forceful character he had displayed with the lashing rope in his hand was now absent. "Yes, sir."

After the incident with the flogging, Joshua paid more attention to the crew's attitude toward Keeler. With the officers on the quarterdeck and the men forward, close contact was rare, but the looks cast aft from before the mast could tell Joshua what he needed to know.

Before, he had noticed nothing more than the usual hard glances from men sent up to undo what they had done only a half hour before. Now, he was seeing more. It seemed the men were a little slower to react when Keeler called out an order, and performed their work with less ardor than might be expected. Keeping an often motley group of sailors working was somewhat of an art, and Keeler seemed to be losing his touch.

The sailors were not the only ones whose work suffered. Keeler himself went about his duties with less diligence than his position called for, giving Joshua all the more reason not to trust him.

"He just does not care," he said to Mary. "I have half a mind to bust him down to able seaman and take his watches myself. Let the justice of the forecastle court straighten him out."

"Let the crew take care of him as one of their own?"

"If they will have him."

Mary remained hopeful that it would not come to that. Perhaps, she thought, after a few days the crew would get over their recent dissatisfaction with Keeler and resume the steady work habits they had exhibited before. Joshua was not as optimistic, but delayed any decision, partly in mind of Mary's hopes. Eventually, action from the crew hastened the next inevitable confrontation.

A few days later Joshua was finishing a last cup of tea after breakfast when Henry, the young steward, said, "Beg pardon, sir, but may I speak?"

Mary was still asleep, and Joshua was alone at the saloon's dining table.

"Of course. Speak freely."

Given permission, Henry did not say anything right away. He seemed uncomfortable, and instead began clearing dishes off the table. Joshua pushed his chair back and half turned toward him.

"Well?"

"Sir, I . . . Let me put these away." Joshua watched, puzzled and concerned as Henry carried the plates to a sideboard.

"Would you like more tea, sir?"

"I would like you to say what is on your mind."

"Yes, sir. Actually, I am forwarding a desire upon the part of Mr. Erwin to speak with you."

"Mr. Erwin?"

"Yes, sir."

George Erwin was the ship's cook, the same who had served as the apparition of King Neptune during the crossing of the equator.

He had been with *Neptune's Car* when Joshua Patten had taken command two years earlier. Joshua thought highly of the man and considered their relationship to be sound.

"I see. Why did Mr. Erwin not come to see me directly?"

Henry glanced toward the door, as if afraid someone might come in to interrupt. "I think, sir, that he would consider it a kindness if you would visit him in the kitchen."

Joshua thoughtfully considered what he was hearing. "A private meeting, so to speak."

"Yes, sir."

"Are you at liberty to say what this is about?"

"I could, sir, but I'd rather Cook to tell you."

"Very well. I'll go see him."

"Thank you, sir." Henry moved away, tending to his duties.

Joshua watched him work. "Is there anything that you would like to say about the matter?"

Henry thought, but said, "No, sir, but I thank you for asking."

Joshua wondered what George Erwin had to say that required a visit to the galley. The cook could easily have come to see him. Unless he wanted the visit to be kept quiet.

He finished his tea and went on deck. After a cursory tour of the quarterdeck, satisfying himself that all was well with the watch, he made a nonchalant stroll forward along the main deck. Several of the men glanced his way, unused to seeing the captain in their midst. He made a point to offer each a polite nod.

He carried his cup, and when he reached the forward deck house, the aft part of which held the galley, he ducked through the partially open portside doorway. Inside, perched on a stool by his worktable, was the stoop-shouldered form of George Erwin, dicing potatoes with a long knife. Around him were the tools and utensils of his trade. From heavy hooks hung a variety of pots and pans. In a block of wood fastened to the wall were the blades of a half dozen knives, the wood of their handles darkened from years of use. Scattered about, in seemingly haphazard but organized arrangements, were sundry other wares, including a blackened tin pot resting on the recessed top of the cast-iron cookstove.

"Good morning, Mr. Erwin. Do we have anything left in that pot?"

"Aye, sir, coffee. Always. Or would you have tea? Just take a minute."

"No. Coffee sounds fine."

The cook put down his knife and reached for the pot, holding its warm handle with a piece of rag. Joshua held out the cup, watching the thick black liquid pour from the pointed spout. He blew across the cup, cooling it, and took a sip.

"Good and strong. As usual."

"Aye, sir."

Joshua had closed the door to the weather, and the stove was already overheating the closed room. "I see now why you had the door ajar," he said, cracking it again. The cold air immediately accepted the invitation and swept in, mixing with the warm.

The cook resumed chopping potatoes, and Joshua peered through the small glass window in the door, pretending to be interested in the lines tied off on the port rail a few feet away. There were faint clinkings of cookware rocking with the ship, and for a time that was the only sound, as neither man spoke. Joshua waited, supposing the cook would talk when he was ready. Two or three minutes passed, and the potatoes went into a kettle of water. The knife was wiped off and put back in its place in the block.

"Warm-up?" the cook asked.

Joshua looked into the cup and said, "Please."

The cook poured and looked up at Joshua, his hazel eyes studying his captain's face. He had once been a tall man, but age had bent him. He looked nothing like the monstrous god of the sea he had so ably portrayed only two weeks earlier.

"Henry ask you to come?"

"Yes, he did."

"He's a good boy. Would make a good cook."

"He is also a good steward."

"Aye, that he is."

"But we are not here to talk about Henry." Joshua could tell that the cook was not comfortable. "You have been a valuable man to me for two years, now. If you have something to say, I am interested in hearing it."

The cook said, "I appreciate them words, Captain. Makes it easier to talk free."

Joshua was tired of all the hem-hawing around, but remained outwardly patient. "Please, speak your mind."

"Like you say, Captain, you have knowed me awhile. You know I ain't a complainer. And I ain't complainin' now. Not for myself, anyway. It's for the other men."

"Go on."

"You know, sir, that some of the men don't have much in the way of smarts. And even if they have smarts, they never got the learnin' to use them. Especially the Arabs."

Erwin was referring to the half dozen or so Malay and Calcutta Indians on board. They, along with several more, had been picked up during last year's departure from San Francisco, after most of the original crew from the New York passage had defected to the goldfields. They had signed on to get back to their native lands. Most had jumped ship in Singapore, but these few had stayed on. Some were good sailors, notably one who called himself Sinbad, but they did have some strange habits and odd notions.

Joshua nodded.

"Well, sir, that Mr. Keeler has been sort of rough on some of them. The Arabs especially, but some of the others, too. Now, don't get me wrong. They expect some of that. They know their lot. They know they are on a merchantman, and that the work is hard. And it ain't the work itself, it's the way the mate goes about it. He ain't always doin' what we expect to be done. Has the men doin' things what ain't logical. It's not like regular busywork. We know that when we see it. And he's mean about the way he goes about it. That's one reason I decided to talk to you. Some of the fellas are startin' to talk among themselves of doing somethin' about it."

"You mean like mutiny."

"Mutiny is a strong word, sir. It ain't to that yet, but it could be, if he keeps up."

"Keeps what up? The men would mutiny over illogical work?"

"Not just that. Like that man what was flogged, there was nothin' he done wrong, and the men are afraid of who might be next."

"Afraid enough to mutiny?"

"Maybe. But let me say, sir, it ain't against you. It's him."

"I have spoken with Mr. Keeler. There should not be a next time unless I say so."

The cook, who had sat back down on his stool, said, "Beg pardon, sir, but there already has been."

Joshua started. "What?"

"Oh, not a floggin', sir. But a beatin', just the same. Down in the forecastle. Because a man wouldn't give Mr. Keeler any tobacco. We was told to keep it quiet, or there'd be more."

So, thought Joshua, Keeler is also a bully.

"And there is talk of rebelling against Keeler?"

"Aye, sir, by some of the men. Not all."

Joshua shook his head. As much as he disliked Keeler, such actions by the crew were unacceptable. "I cannot have that, Mr. Erwin. To mutiny against my officers is to mutiny against me. Tell the men that. Unless you would have me bring this into the open, in which case I'll tell them myself."

"It's a little more complicated than that." The cook had an unpleasant look on his face, as if he were eating something distasteful. "Here is the main reason I thought I should talk to you. I am pleased to serve under you, and you have earned my respect. I'm just a cook, but if I may have the liberty of sayin', I feel I'm more than just another foremast hand." He smiled at himself. "It's one of the privileges of bein' the cook, I guess."

Joshua waited. Surely what the cook had to say would be worth the wait.

"The talk against Mr. Keeler ain't the only talk of its kind." The cook looked at Joshua, as if to say, Do you want to hear more?

He did. Impatiently, he said, "Go on, man."

"I believe there has been some roundabout talk against you, sir. Tryin' to win support should a move be made."

"Has there been support?" Joshua had never been faced with a truly mutinous crew before, and his mind was already working on a course of action.

"Not much, but a crew is a fickle thing. There are some who could be easily swayed, with a promise of power."

Joshua considered what he was hearing. One mutiny was trouble enough, but for two different plots to be floating around at the same time was just too much. "This is against me, is that right?"

"Aye, sir."

"But not well developed as yet?"

"No, sir, it's not. It's more just ideas. Talk put out to see how it floats."

"Can you tell me who is circulating this talk?"

"If you don't say where it came from."

"I'll keep your confidence."

"All right. It is your first mate, Mr. Keeler."

Joshua shook his head. He had hoped Keeler would not be one to go so far. At the same time, he was not surprised. He worked to keep his composure before his cook.

"I see."

"Now, sir, he may be just talk. He likes to talk. Likes to brag. But I hear enough to make me think that he may have intentions."

"You have heard this yourself?"

"No, sir. Not directly. But the men, they talk."

"Yes. Men do. Women have no monopoly when it comes to gossip."

"I was afraid this was more than gossip, sir."

Joshua's head was full of thoughts, already running through different scenarios and different outcomes.

"I do not mean to imply otherwise, Mr. Erwin. And I certainly appreciate your bringing this to my attention. Addressed early, it may not have a chance to grow."

The cook shrugged. "It may not even be anything. But I wanted you to know."

Joshua filled his cup again and held his hand over the heat coming off the stove. He hoped a change to a neutral topic would give him time to plan his next action. "As we get into the colder latitudes, it seems that a cook's duties have certain advantages."

"Aye, sir, but I pay in the tropics."

Joshua smiled. "I suppose it all evens out." He looked out the window at the sky. "I should get back to my business. But there has been a certain pleasure in visiting with you. And Mr. Erwin," he said, turning back as he opened the door. "For now, while I keep your confidence, I'll ask you to keep mine. Let's keep this conversation to ourselves."

The cook nodded. "Consider it done, sir."

"And Mr. Erwin, feel free to send for me anytime."

"Aye, sir."

Back out on the deck, the wind seemed especially biting, and Joshua pulled his collar up as he made his way aft. The deck, wet with spray, had slippery patches on it. Must be freezing again, he thought. When he reached the quarterdeck, he did not go up onto the poop, but went back into the after house. Keeler was on watch, and Joshua did not wish to talk to him right then.

As he went below, he glanced up to the rail and saw Keeler standing in the cold wind. The first mate's face was hard, with a stern set to his jaw. His expression may have been due to the weather, but Joshua felt that the mate was staring hard, directly at him.

CHAPTER 12

All Hands

Joshua may have been concerned about his first mate, but Mary could see no discernible difference in the way her husband ran his ship or treated the men. His methods had seemed right before, and they still seemed right.

"All I can do," he told Mary, "is keep an even keel. If my second in command is to be the source of trouble, he will show his colors in due time."

Day by day, the weather turned colder and Keeler turned more surly. Despite his promise to keep his watch more in the manner Joshua wanted, he seemed all the more determined to do things his way. He began avoiding Joshua, even to the point of walking away when he saw his captain come on deck.

"This dealing with Keeler," Joshua said one evening, "is wearing upon my nerves." He rubbed the back of his neck, twisting his head stiffly.

"Are you all right?"

"I have a bit of a headache."

Mary moved to the back of his chair to massage his neck, working her way down to knead his tense shoulders. She wished there were more she could do, both about his tight muscles and about the mate.

It was clear that Joshua was finding it increasingly difficult to tolerate Keeler. To have his first mate avoid him was infuriating. At the same time, Joshua had no desire to see him.

"Even seeing him on deck makes me want to go below," Joshua said. "Or more correctly, it makes me want to send him below. Having no first mate at all may be preferable to having one of Keeler's caliber."

Joshua saw the look of worry on Mary's face and said, "I'm sorry, dear. You should not have to hear this, but again and again I find myself confiding in you."

Mary took his hand and gave it a sympathetic squeeze. "I am pleased to be your confidante. If my presence and support makes it easier, by all means, I am willing to listen."

Joshua lifted her hand, his fingers intertwined with hers, and kissed it. "Your presence and support makes it much easier."

A few days earlier, when Joshua first mentioned that he had half a mind to take Keeler down to seaman, Mary had hoped it would not come to that. Now she was beginning to think otherwise. She watched her husband struggle with the problem of maintaining order aboard his ship, and it was becoming increasingly evident that there was only one cure. The cancer eating away at the crew's morale and the captain's peace of mind was affecting the ship itself. Like any cancer, it would have to be cut away before it spread.

As in any surgery, however, there was danger in the operation. Simply removing Keeler would not ensure complete health to the ship. It must be shown that he was clearly in the wrong. This was especially true if Keeler had indeed been recruiting others in any mutiny plans.

"I could act against Keeler without regard to the opinions of the men," Joshua said, "and many sea captains would do just that."

They were sitting in their cabin having tea, Mary in the wing-back easy chair and Joshua at the desk, his chair turned toward her. Mary studied her husband's expression. He appeared concerned, his face serious, but there was a confident look about him. "But you will not," she said, following his line of thought.

"I prefer having a crew that is behind me, as well as under me."

Mary nodded, understanding her husband's desire for a willing crew.

"Keeler's days are numbered, I'm sure," he said. "He is not fit to be an officer. Soon enough, his actions will put him back among his true peers under the forecastle deck, if not worse."

Mary agreed that it would be best to wait for the proper time, but found herself wishing for a quick resolution to the problem of William Keeler. She wanted Joshua to again enjoy complete command of a well-run ship. He could worry about being shorthanded when the time came.

She did not expect it to be a long wait.

Fifty-five days out of New York, and about three-quarters of the way down the Atlantic, the crew of *Neptune's Car* experienced how quickly the weather could change. The day began bright and cold, but by midmorning a long, thin line of clouds appeared on the distant horizon. Within an hour the thin line became a looming gray mass, obliterating the sun. By the end of the morning watch, when Hare relieved Keeler, all blue sky was gone, replaced by clouds the color of gunmetal, their bases stirred into ragged swirls.

The wind blowing across the surface of the sea was steady at about fifteen knots, but the turbulent appearance of the clouds told of shifting, conflicting winds aloft—the swirling winds that created storms. As he often did when Hare had the watch, Joshua came up on deck, with Mary at his side. He looked at the thickening clouds.

"It will be a blow, I'm sure," he said. "And it will be a good one."

Mary had seen enough weather to know he was surely correct. The storm was coming quickly. "No midday sights today, I'm afraid," she said, referring to the customary position check made with the sextant and the sun.

"And maybe none tonight," Joshua added.

"You think this will last?"

Joshua shrugged. "No way to know."

The second mate, as steady at his post as the first mate was unpredictable, stood nearby.

"Mr. Hare, have the men secure all gear and ready for weather."

"Already done, sir," Hare answered.

Joshua smiled. Of course. He was not the only one who could see the coming storm.

"Shall I have them double-check their work?"

"No, not if you are satisfied with it."

"I believe I am, sir."

Joshua looked out along the deck. The watch was scattered along the ship, the men near their stations. Clearly, Hare had things under control.

From high aloft and forward, somewhere on the foremast, came a call. "Gust to starboard!"

Joshua and Mary looked to the west. Coming across the sea was a strong gust of wind, its presence announced by the shearing of the wave tops as the leading edge of wind advanced. Joshua started to make a suggestion to Hare, but the mate issued the order before he could speak.

"Helm, heave to."

"Heave to, sir," the helmsman said, repeating the order.

He grasped the heavy oak spokes and spun the wheel to starboard, directing the long ship to turn into the coming wind.

"Take her four points to and hold her there," Hare said.

"Four points to, sir." The helmsman gave the wheel several pulls and then stopped, holding his full weight against it to keep it where he wanted.

Hare's next order was shouted to the crew on the foremast lines. "Furl the fore royal and topgallant." The men, far away on the forward deck, went quickly to work, loosening lines on the pin rails and hauling the highest sails on the foremast up against their yards.

"Upper staysails. Ease the halyard, tend the sheet!" Hare's orders came quickly now, with pauses just long enough for the men to keep up.

Joshua was pleased with Hare's actions. They were made swiftly and without hesitation. The bringing in of the forward mast's high sails would lessen the ship's tendency to plow its bow under the swells. The only thing that he would do differently, Joshua thought, would be to possibly shorten the next sail down the mast as well, in case the wind proved especially strong.

As he was thinking that, Hare spoke again.

"The upper topsail, now. Bring it in quick!"

Hare had waited the few seconds to get the first sails loose and moving before ordering the next furled.

"Very fine, Mr. Hare."

"Thank you, sir." The mate's modest reply was nearly lost to the wind, which suddenly and without preamble struck the ship a hard blow from the port side. The bow, far forward of the commanding rudder, had been slow to react, and was only partly into the turn. The ship shuddered and rolled before the gust, but took the change well, and after a moment righted itself.

Joshua turned to Mary but found that she was no longer by his side. His momentary concern for her safety was allayed when he saw her reappear from the cabin, carrying the oilskin coats needed to shed wet weather. A wide band of rain followed on the heels of the wind gust, and Mary had seen it coming. She handed him the long coat just as the first large drops of rain fell to mix with the heavy spray.

As the storm enveloped the ship, Joshua refrained from offering suggestions to Hare, letting the young man handle the weather as he saw fit. In short order, royals and topgallants from the mainmast and mizzenmast were also taken up to their yards as Hare reduced sail commensurate to the weather. To Joshua's satisfaction, there was little he would have done differently.

As the gale intensified, with winds of forty knots sending water over the deck and spray to the mast tops, the forces against the lines became more than the crew on watch could adequately handle. Joshua saw the need for all hands on deck but let Hare decide for himself.

Soon after, Hare put out the call.

From below spilled the off-duty watch. Each man, feeling the weather from his hammock or bunk, had known the all hands call was imminent. With the ship under a full complement, work went easier for all concerned. The yards for the courses were quickly lowered to spill the air, and the large canvases were gathered into their gaskets.

Within a short time, half the canvas on the ship was furled and the ship turned back to a more on-course heading. The storm still

battered the vessel, with waves breaking over the rails and spray flying over the deck, but *Neptune's Car* was under good control and
standing to the weather nicely. As the ship ran before the wind,
Hare began to have the men bring out some of the canvas so hur-
riedly furled. The treacherous gusts were past, and it was time to
again make best speed forward.

"Well done, Mr. Hare," Joshua said, across the wind.

Timothy Hare allowed himself to beam, despite standing
drenched in freezing rain in his soaked oilskin coat, water dripping
from his hat.

Joshua was pleased with his second mate's performance, but his
pleasure was dampened by the absence of his first mate.

The call for all hands should have brought Keeler from his cabin,
but it had not. Joshua did not mention his absence, but he was
keenly aware of it and was sure that Hare was aware of it also. Blast
him, thought Joshua. He was tiring of confronting his first mate,
but Keeler gave him little choice.

Mary, who had stayed on deck throughout the approach and en-
velopment of the storm, had also noticed the lack of Keeler's presence. When Joshua said, "Carry on, Mr. Hare. I am going below for
a bit," she knew he was going to find Keeler.

He got as far as the top of the steps leading down off the quarterdeck poop when the subject of his irritation came hurrying
around the corner of the after house, holding his hat against the
wind. He looked up to see Joshua on the steps and faltered for a half
second before proceeding. Joshua waited on the stairs. Keeler
reached the steps and paused for Joshua to make way for him. A
burst of spray rained down, wetting both men. Keeler waited, water
dripping from his face, but it became apparent that Joshua did not
intend to vacate the steps.

Forced to face his captain, Keeler tipped his hat and said, "Sir."

Joshua looked down at him and said, "There was a call for all
hands, Mr. Keeler."

"Aye, sir."

"You heard the call?"

"Aye, sir."

Joshua looked coldly at Keeler but said nothing.

Keeler's eyes shifted about, looking around the deck. "I was in my cabin, sir. I confess that I did not hear the call at first. I must have been sleeping especially soundly."

"Sleeping through a call for all hands is no excuse," said Joshua. "You know that as well as I. And to sleep through the weather of the past hour is almost unfathomable to me. How could anyone in an officer's position sleep as soundly as that?"

Keeler looked blank. He said nothing and waited for Joshua to continue.

Finally, Joshua gave Keeler an exit, although not a gracious one. "Why don't you return to your cabin, Mr. Keeler. The need for extra hands is well past, and Mr. Hare has the situation firmly in hand. We have no need of you here."

Keeler's eyes blazed, and Joshua noticed the mate's hand forming a fist.

"If you mean to use that fist, Mr. Keeler, you had better make it count."

Keeler glanced down at his hand as if he were unaware of its actions, and relaxed his grip.

"You may return to your cabin, Mr. Keeler."

Keeler stood fixed in place, his face clouded.

Joshua kept his voice even. "You are dismissed."

Keeler glared, saying nothing, before turning on his heel to head back toward the doorway of the cabin. He stopped once, looking back at Joshua, before finally disappearing around the corner.

Letting out a long breath, Joshua became aware that two seamen, working nearby, had stopped to listen. He looked toward them and they quickly looked away, busying themselves with coiling line that had already been coiled. Above him, at the quarterdeck rail, he saw that Hare and Mary had also been watching, her face still showing alarm. Trying to ease her, Joshua smiled and shook his head with wonder, as if to say, What next?

When Hare's watch ended, Keeler took his turn as usual. Joshua considered taking the watch himself and leaving Keeler to stew in his cabin, but he seemed inordinately tired. The intensity of the storm and the incident with Keeler had left him fatigued of mind as well as body.

In their cabin, he told Mary that he had made a decision. "To-morrow I will deal with Keeler once and for all. I'll not have him countering me on a daily basis. If he wishes to earn his keep, he may do it from a bunk in the forecastle."

"Having Keeler off the quarterdeck will make me much happier," Mary said, "but won't that make for more work for you?"

"That can't be helped. I've kept watches before. I can do it again."

"But you spend so much time on deck when Mr. Hare is up, checking on him and helping him."

"Mr. Hare will have to do more of it on his own," Joshua said. "He is coming along well. He will do fine."

Mary was doubtful. Not about Hare's abilities, but about Joshua's ability to let him go. "You really think you can leave the ship to Hare that much?"

Joshua smiled. "I will just have to rest when I can. For instance, I think I'll lie down right now for a while. I could use a nap."

Mary studied her husband as he stretched out across the bed. He had often seemed tired lately. It was not like him. It was not the work, she decided, but the worry that was wearing him down. Having Keeler off the quarterdeck might result in longer hours, but Joshua would be resting better.

Pleased with her husband's decision to remove the first mate, she took up her book and returned to *Wuthering Heights*.

Chapter 13

Keeler

Joshua slept through most of Keeler's afternoon watch and did not return to the deck until the evening's dogwatches. Keeler acted as if he were above any fault, his nose up and chin jutted out as he stood by the helm. With the coming of darkness, now falling well before the dinner hour, the storm abated somewhat, and the ship was steady on its course to the south. Joshua offered only the most perfunctory of greetings, equally returned, and only the briefest of instructions before leaving with a curt, "Carry on, Mr. Keeler," and returning with Mary to the warmth of their cabin. As he went down the steps to the main deck, Joshua felt Keeler's eyes on the back of his neck but did not turn to look back.

Mary went to bed early, as had become her custom to better pass the long winter nights, and after a time Joshua slipped quietly in beside her, allowing her warmth to soak away the cold.

He enjoyed lying with Mary, warm and comfortable, but on this night he slept fitfully. He dreamed he was in a small room, with moonlight coming in through a window. Then there were shadowy images moving around him on a dark deck, or perhaps it was not a deck at all. What were the menacing forms? He shook his head, trying to clear away the dream.

When he awoke, he was beside Mary, hearing her gentle breathing. The dream, so vivid only a moment before, was gone. The only remnant was the moon, shining through one of the small windows on the stern of the ship. Just as in the dream, the moon's light peeked in and out of breaks in the clouds. It must be clearing up. Joshua lay awake, listening to the sounds of the ship. There was the faint but steady rush of water by the hull, the creak of timbers as the ship rose and fell with the waves, the occasional footfall or muffled voice on deck.

All seemed well, but sleep did not return. Finally, he decided to slip out of bed as quietly as he had slipped into it and take a turn about the quarterdeck. He put on his boots and coat and took his hat off its hook, going out into the saloon. He pulled the door closed behind him, careful not to wake Mary.

Outside, the deck was dark save for a weak light cast by the lantern hanging near the stern. The blackness of the sky overhead was fragmented by occasional beams of moonlight shining down through ragged holes in the cloud layers. *Neptune's Car*, it appeared, had outrun the weather, leaving the storm's fury in its wake. The moon went behind the clouds, and the sky and the sea became equally black, the only visible form being the spectral white of the waves as they broke over the deck.

The ship was quiet. Sails were trimmed for maximum speed, but in the blackness of night other work was kept to a minimum. The crew was relieved of most caretaking duties, the night too dark and the deck too often awash to do more. The air felt close to freezing, and Joshua looked for signs of ice on the rigging.

The moon reappeared, revealing the seas to be running at five or six feet, calm for the season at this southern latitude.

The sails were full, taut panels of white billowed against the night, and the ship was heeled over nicely, the wind whispering through the rigging and around the sails. He walked up to the weather rail and wrapped his hand around the smooth handle of a belaying pin. Looking like a slender rolling pin, it stood its post in a long row of pins, holding secure its particular line that ran to places high in the mast tops and yards. The line was tied off about the pin, the excess line in a neat knot below the rail.

Joshua inhaled deeply, and the salty air of the sea filled his lungs. With the smell of salt came the scent of the linseed oil and tar on the rigging, reminding Joshua of his youth in Rockland Harbor, readying his sloop for the summer season. Of all the senses, he thought, the sense of smell was the one most able to alert the mind to things familiar.

The familiar smells of tar and damp hemp, so fleeting before the wind, blended with the ever-present fresh aroma of the sea. He never tired of the smell of sea air and had learned its nuances, minor variations that changed with the strength of the wind and warmth of the day, and whether a storm was brewing or not.

The ship rocked over a random large swell, and Joshua gripped the belaying pin to steady himself as the spray of the rushing sea wet his face. He felt the texture of the individual strands of rope, wound tightly about each other to make the line thick and strong, and then coated with tar to protect the fibers from the weather. As captain, he seldom had occasion to handle the rigging, but it still felt familiar from his days before the mast. It struck him as odd that he missed the pleasure of working the lines himself, since he had strived so hard to become an officer and get away from that very work.

Perhaps, he thought, that was why old sea captains, in their retirement, so often had little sailboats, like the one he once had, to scoot about the bays and harbors of their old age. He smiled to himself at the thought of growing old and doing the same thing.

The smile tightened the stiff muscles of Joshua's cheeks, reminding him of the cold, reminding him of his inspection of the deck. He could see nothing that would give cause to his restless inability to sleep. All seemed shipshape. "Shipshape and Bristol fashion," as the old saying went.

Tightening his coat against the wind, he went up the steps to the poop of the quarterdeck. By the tall oak wheel he found the solitary figure of the helmsman, a young man of perhaps twenty. He was alert at his post, cognizant of his responsibilities.

Keeler was not present.

Joshua approached the helm and checked the binnacled compass. Straightening up from the compass, he turned toward the cold-stiffened sailor.

"Greene, isn't it?"

The helmsman answered, "Aye, sir."

Joshua stood with his hands clasped behind his back and looked about the ship for a moment. "Is Mr. Keeler about?"

"He has gone forward, sir." The helmsman's words came stiffly, the muscles of his jaw tight from the cold.

Joshua looked down the length of the ship. The moon had retreated again behind the cover of clouds, and darkness obscured the foredeck.

"Do you know where?"

"No, sir."

Joshua pondered this. "Has he been forward long?"

The young sailor gripping the spokes of the wheel hesitated a few seconds and then said, "It's hard to say, sir. Twenty minutes, perhaps."

Joshua, acting upon suspicion, said, "Perhaps longer?"

"Perhaps."

"Perhaps an hour?"

"Oh, no, sir, not that long." Then, after a second, he qualified that with a tentative, "I don't think."

Outwardly, Joshua remained calm, but inside he seethed. As he stood on the quarterdeck looking forward, Joshua saw no unusual activity that would give reason for Keeler to go forward. Indeed, in the darkness, he could see no activity at all.

"Hold her steady, Mr. Greene," he said, and left the poop by the same weather stairs he had come up.

The wet deck sloped down toward the lee rail, but Joshua's boots held a firm footing as he walked forward. He looked around. There was no sign of the first mate. He walked through the darkness past the rectangular forward house, with its galley and cook's stores and quarters. Forward of the cabin, he reached the forecastle deck, raised much like the quarterdeck, with steps leading up to it. Below was the forecastle, a lingering remnant of the days of men-of-war ships of the line, when a high bow structure gave a height advantage in close deck-to-deck fighting. Now the forecastle, still home to the sailors, was almost completely below deck, with only a few feet still rising above the main deck. The area of the forward deck was lighted by a dim lantern hung from a staysail shroud.

Near the steps, Joshua found a group of the men on watch, clustered by the windbreak of the short wall of the forecastle. Some were working at minor tasks. Others were simply standing their watch, waiting for the bells to sound the hours. All jumped to alertness at the sudden appearance of their captain. Save for one's greeting of "Sir," the men, uneasy at the captain's close presence, said nothing. There was no good to come of having the captain be forward, especially in the dead of night.

Joshua wished he could put them at ease. "Fair winds, gentlemen. Good time being made."

With questioning looks in their eyes, the cluster of men studied him for motive. Several were foreigners, mostly shanghaied Indians and Arabs.

Finally, a young Englishman said, "Aye, captain. Fair winds."

Joshua looked them over. "Your work during the squall was admirable. Good effort."

"Thank'ee, sir." It was the Englishman again.

The men relaxed a little. It was apparent that the captain was not there to vent his wrath, at least upon them.

Enough time spent on polite niceties, Joshua got to the heart of his mission. "Can anyone tell me where I might find Mr. Keeler?"

The men shifted about, glancing at each other.

Joshua waited.

"Well?"

The question was met with silence. If anyone knew of Keeler's whereabouts, they were not telling.

He prodded the men. "Out with it, now."

One man, until now silent, stepped up and said, "Perhaps some of us could go have a look around, sir. Find him for you."

"And where would you look?" Joshua asked.

"I honestly don't know, sir. Just look, is all."

Joshua considered this. It was possible that the men were truthful, that Keeler had slipped away from their sight as well. "Very well. A couple of you look below. If he is in the forecastle, tell him I wish to see him. You two," he said, motioning to the English boy and to a strong-looking Arab, "come with me. And bring that lantern."

With the two sailors following behind, Joshua started back aft,

intending to check Keeler's berth in the after house. In the alley between the forward house and the starboard rail he pulled up short.
Beside him was the door of the galley, where, three days earlier, he'd
had the insightful conversation with the cook. The door was recessed slightly into the white painted siding of the cabin wall, leaving it hidden by shadow. The dark rectangle had caught Joshua's
eye. He had not thought of the galley before, but now it seemed to
be the obvious place to look.

He turned and looked at the men behind him. If they knew
Keeler was inside, their faces did not show it.

"Where is the cook?" he asked softly.

"In his bunk, I believe, sir."

"In his cabin?"

"Aye, sir."

"Not in the galley?"

"No, sir. No bunk in there."

Joshua nodded. The cook's cabin, shared with the ship's carpenter and two others, was in the forward part of the deck house, separated from the galley by a storeroom. He took the lantern from the
Englishman. Its wick was short and its light feeble, but it would suffice to see inside once he opened the door.

"You men stay close by me," he said.

He had no idea why he was so certain that Keeler was inside, but
certain he was. He carefully moved the handle of the latch, hoping
the sound would be lost in the creaking of the ship.

Once the door started moving, he pushed it open quickly. As it
opened to its full travel, the door struck the work counter, and the
sound of the bump was the first noise made. Joshua stepped briskly
into the room, leading with the lantern. The light penetrated the
darkness, casting its yellow glow onto the floor and walls, adding to
the faint moonlight coming through a window. The implements and
tools of the cook's craft hung from the walls, the pots and skillets
and long-handled ladles and spoons making long shadows of surreal
shapes in the light of the lantern.

The yellow light and bizarre shadows lent the galley a haunted
look, made all the more eerie by the dim human form hidden low in
the darkness on the far side of the room. The mate was sitting

against the lee wall, taking advantage of the heel of the ship to lean comfortably back. His knees were drawn up to his chest, arms folded across them. His head, hidden by his hat, had been resting on his forearms.

At the sound of the door opening, Keeler jerked up in surprise, revealing wide eyes illuminated by the lantern. For a second, he did not move, but he then lumbered to his feet with a muttered, "What—"

Joshua interrupted. "Mr. Keeler, you are on watch."

"Yes, sir."

"But you are here, asleep."

"No, sir."

"No, sir?"

"I was—"

"Enough, Keeler. I've heard quite enough from you to last me."

This was the moment Joshua had been waiting for. Cross words, scowls, even half-disregarded orders—any of those things could have been used to depose Keeler from duty, but catching him in the act of sleeping on duty, with two witnesses, sealed his fate. Joshua turned to his men.

"Did Mr. Keeler appear to be asleep when we entered this room?"

The men's reaction to finding Keeler removed any suspicions Joshua had about allegiances. Both had poorly contained smiles on their faces.

"Sound asleep, sir."

"Yes, sir. Dead to the world."

"Blast you!" Keeler said, moving forward a step.

Joshua ignored his advance. "Mr. Keeler, you are relieved of duty. You are to go to your cabin and stay there until reaching San Francisco, at which time—"

Joshua could not finish his sentence. At that moment, Keeler exploded into a rage. "Damn you, Captain. Damn you!" He lunged his massive body forward and plowed into Joshua, knocking him against the two crewmen crowding the doorway. The lantern flew from Joshua's hand as the four of them tumbled out into the alley. He heard it hit the deck and the sound of its glass breaking. Joshua fell to the deck, its wet boards hard under his shoulder. Keeler fell on top of him.

Joshua was momentarily pinned beneath Keeler's bulk, the mate grappling for a better hold. Then Keeler was lifted away by one or both of the crewmen, and Joshua scrambled to his feet. He had barely straightened up, however, when Keeler shook free and attacked again. This time Joshua was more prepared and kept his footing. The other men moved back in. Keeler was outnumbered, but his strong upper body, supplemented by his blazing anger, kept the fight on nearly equal terms. In a mass the four men fell against the bulwark of the ship. Joshua tried to get back up, but Keeler got him by the shoulders and slammed his head against the deck.

For a second or two the night got even darker, and a black tunnel formed around his field of vision. Joshua felt that he was passing out. The ship seemed to spin around him, and through the tunnel he saw the same shadowy forms moving about him that he had seen in his dream.

The struggle went on, with the crewmen and Keeler wrestling and punching each other. Any advantage gained by one was soon lost to the other as the first mate, with the rage of a trapped bear, refused to succumb. One sailor was slammed against the rail, slumping to the deck, and for the moment did not get up. The remaining crewman was locked in a tight hold with Keeler, both with arms around the other. Joshua thought it was the Arab, although in the black night he could not be sure. The two men struggled, closely matched in size and strength. Keeler was forced down to the deck, but within a few seconds reared back up, lifting his adversary and shoving him against the cabin wall. The Arab grunted but did not ease his grip, and he pushed off the wall to force Keeler back into the open.

The fuzziness in Joshua's head cleared away, and he stood up. Seeing him on his feet again, Keeler roared and broke free, pushing the other man away. Joshua realized that he had pulled himself up by an unused belaying pin, and as Keeler came at him it seemed the most natural thing in the world to pull the pin out of its hole and bring it down against the side of the mate's head. The blow was well placed. Keeler stopped in midstep and dropped to the deck.

A crowd, led by the cook and carpenter, who had heard the altercation outside their cabin, gathered to find Keeler sprawled across the deck boards. Joshua, still breathing hard, was astounded that even Keeler would assault his captain, and he had not anticipated a brawl. He had a fleeting thought that he was glad that he had not relieved his first mate during the confrontation at the quarterdeck steps. Keeler very likely would have attacked then, and Mary would have been there to see it.

He was just catching his breath when he heard her familiar voice. "Joshua!"

He looked up to see his wife rushing forward, a horrified look upon her face.

He took her into his arms and held her. "I'm fine. It's all over now."

"What happened?" In Mary's voice was a mix of bewilderment and terror.

"I'll tell you all about it later."

To the men gathered in a circle around the scene, he said, "Gentlemen, as of this moment, Mr. Keeler is no longer acting as first mate." Looking down at the prostrate form, he added, "Nor will he serve in any other capacity."

The men lingered silently, absorbing the import of what had just happened. Sensing that they were unsure whether to stay or go back to what they had been doing, Joshua said, "Everyone may return to their duties or to their beds, as the case may be."

The crew began to move away, and Keeler began to stir. To a few men standing nearby, Joshua said, "Take this man into the hold and lock him there. I want nothing more to do with him."

CHAPTER 14

Double Duty

With Keeler stowed away below deck in an emptied storeroom off the cook's larder, the tensions of the past weeks instantly evaporated from the quarterdeck. Timothy Hare seemed more at ease, as did the rest of the ship. Any allies the first mate might have had among the crew either switched their allegiance back to the captain or were lying low. While watching for further signs of discontent, Joshua saw only a crew that seemed more willing, the chanteys sung with a little more cheer.

"That man," Joshua said to Mary, "has been like an albatross around my neck. I'm glad, if not to be completely rid of him, at least to have him out of sight."

Mary could only agree.

Neptune's Car continued down the southern Atlantic, drawing ever closer to Cape Horn. There were occasional days of fair weather, but most days the weather was most foul. Each new storm seemed worse than the last. The gale that came on the day of Keeler's removal was the first to be delivered from the west since soon after their departure from New York, marking a distinct change in the weather. Leaving the northeast trades that had pushed the ship since passing the equatorial calms, they now began encountering the strong westerlies that constantly roared around the southern end of the world.

"They circle the globe," Joshua told Mary. "Almost as dependable as day, always there to help a ship going east and hinder one going west."

"And we, of course," said Mary, "are to be going west."

Joshua smiled ruefully. "Not only are we westing, but we will be doing so in the place where the winds are strongest."

"But why Cape Horn?" Mary asked. "Why are the winds so strong here? Why must it be our route that is so plagued?"

"Who knows for sure. Perhaps it is God's way of saying he does not want us to have an easy time in life. Perhaps it is just coincidence. Perhaps," he said, "it is the mountains."

"The mountains?"

Joshua took a rolled-up map of the world from a shelf and spread it across his writing desk. Mary moved over to his side. As they bent over the map, she noticed the familiar smell of her husband, recognized whenever she awoke and he was beside her in the dark. It was instantly identifiable and pleasantly familiar. It was the fragrance of her man—his hair, his skin, his clothes, the faint odor of the pipe he sometimes smoked. She leaned into him, feeling the coarseness of his jacket sleeve as the side of her breast pressed against his arm. She was most interested in him, but diligently studied the map.

Unlike his sea charts, this one was of landforms. He pointed to South America. The margins of the continent were well drawn and detailed, with cities such as Rio de Janeiro and Buenos Aires marked in their places along the eastern coastline. Except for thin lines marking major rivers, the largely unexplored interior of the continent was mostly blank.

"Look," he said. He ran his finger down the long range of mountains that formed the spine of the continent. "The Andes extend all the way to the tip, right down to the Straits of Magellan. The islands of Cape Horn itself are the last visible remains before they disappear in the sea.

"Now, the winds of the Southern Oceans blow in a wide band, all the way around the world, with hardly any obstruction to block them. Until they get here. Then they strike the Andes. Most of the wind, I suppose, is forced up and over the mountains. Some, though, is funneled down to the south and around the end."

"At Cape Horn."

"Yes. Adding to the wind already there."

"And with the wind comes the waves."

"Exactly. But there is more. The sea is not deep around the cape. It is plenty deep enough for ships, of course, but not as deep as the open ocean. And I believe that affects the waves."

"Shallow water makes larger waves?"

"In a manner of speaking. Consider breakers on the coast of New England. What begin as gentle swells on the open ocean rise up as they reach the shallows of the beach until they spill over and break upon themselves even before they get to the rocks.

"So it is around Cape Horn. The water rises to spill about the surface and the wind whips it all about. Wind and currents have traveled unimpeded around the globe to come together between Cape Horn and the frozen land of Antarctica to the south."

"Like a funnel, as you say."

Joshua nodded. "And here we go, right through the middle of it."

Mary tried to remain lighthearted. "Sounds like a lovely cruise."

Joshua smiled. "Throw in a few icebergs and a hailstorm or two, and you have quite a mix. Sir Francis Drake had something to say about it, you know. He wrote that Cape Horn was home to 'most mad seas and most intolerable winds.'"

Mary smiled back. "I have no doubt, my captain, that you will steer us through."

"No doubt."

Mary thought about the *Competitor*, which Cleary of the *Susan Walker* said had such a rough time. "And hopefully in less than eighty days."

Joshua looked thoughtful. "Yes, let's hope. A week would be long enough."

The water encompassing Cape Horn was generally described by sailing men as that which lay beyond fifty degrees south of the equator. The distance between that latitude in the Atlantic and the same latitude in the Pacific was about twelve hundred miles. Such a distance, at a clipper's best speed, could be covered in three or four days, should conditions be favorable.

Around Cape Horn, conditions were never favorable.

A call from above summoned him to the deck. Alone in the cabin, Mary studied the map, familiarizing herself with the lands about Cape Horn. South America ended in a jumble of tiny islands with narrow passages winding around and between them. It was through these channels that Magellan had navigated, becoming the first European to find his way into the Pacific from the east. In the centuries since, the route through the Straits of Magellan had been discarded in favor of navigating the open water of the Drake Passage around the end of what he named Tierra del Fuego, and its extreme tip, the island of Cape Horn.

As inhospitable as the waters of the Horn were, Mary saw by the map that life on land was not likely any better. Across South America's southern end, in the blank region known as Patagonia, the mapmaker had written, in an arc of block print, LARGE BANDS OF ROVING INDIANS.

Hardly a hospitable invitation, she thought.

With Keeler no longer of use, Joshua took the first mate's turns on watch while Hare continued keeping his own. At first glance, the arrangement seemed satisfactory. Joshua was simply taking Keeler's watch. Since the captain had never been required to keep a watch of his own, it meant that he was now on duty for four hours followed by four off, just as Keeler had done.

Had Joshua been able to keep that schedule, Mary reflected later, the voyage might have turned out differently.

As it was, however, Joshua spent a great deal of his off-duty time on deck, lending advice and assistance to his young second mate. Storms of wind and rain mixed with snow and sleet battered the ship almost constantly, trying Hare's level of experience and Joshua's ability to rest easy. Even in the best weather the ship labored under strained sail and rigging that was more and more often coated with layers of ice. There were frequent calls for all hands on deck. Until the Horn was rounded and *Neptune's Car* was safely in the calmer waters of the Pacific, no one on board would be getting enough sleep.

Of all those keeping long hours, none were on deck more than Joshua, who was determined that the loss of a mate would not delay the progress of the ship. Of the three captains who sailed from New York on July 1, one would have the pleasure of being in San Francisco when the other two arrived, and Joshua wanted to be that captain.

Mary did not share his consuming passion. "Pride goeth before a fall," she quoted from the book of Proverbs, but not aloud to him. To Joshua, she kept her enthusiasm for a fast trip. To herself, she kept reservations.

She also began to worry about her husband's health. Joshua often stayed on deck into the night, and she found herself going to bed alone. She just as often awakened to find herself alone again. She sometimes wondered if he had even been to bed. The headaches and stiff neck he had been complaining about continued, becoming more frequent with the lack of sleep.

Joshua's well-being, it turned out, was not the only health concern Mary had. After nearly seven weeks at sea, in all varieties of weather, she suddenly found herself afflicted by recurring seasickness. It usually did not last long, and then only early in the day, soon after rising. Some days she did not feel like rising at all until well after breakfast, which she did not feel up to eating anyway. Not wishing to worry Joshua, so busy on deck, she did not mention her seasickness to him.

With Joshua so often at his post, Mary spent considerable time alone in their cabin. It was relatively warm and cozy, and much more comfortable than the winter weather outside, but she found the room confining without Joshua. Frequently, then, she put on her coat and bonnet to join him on the quarterdeck.

"It's surprising," she said, "how small the cabin seems when I sit in it alone, but how adequate it becomes when you are there to help fill the space."

Joshua smiled. "And it is better up here on deck?"

The wind pulled at her coat and whipped her skirt, and a fine spray stung her cheeks.

"Much better."

They stood for a while, watching the ship plow through the waves, the deck rhythmically rising and falling across the swells.

"It is cold, though," she admitted.

"I've noticed."

The sky was the color of lead, with the bases of the clouds scalloped by the turbulent winds.

"Looks like rain again," she said.

"Or sleet."

"The cabin may be more inviting than I thought."

"I would love to join you."

Mary saw the strain of the voyage on Joshua's face. He seemed to have aged a year in the last week. It had been nearly a week since Keeler's arrest, and during that time she was certain he had slept no more than an hour or two at a time.

"You should. You need to rest."

"Perhaps rest is not what I have in mind."

"Joshua!" Mary nudged him playfully. "You are incorrigible."

Joshua offered a sly smile. "I try to be. And it has been some days since I have had the chance to be alone with you."

"And whose fault is that? When you do come to bed, you are so tired."

Joshua frowned. "I'm sorry. I'll try to rectify that. It's just this damnable weather. Once we are around the Horn, I will feel better about our young second mate."

"He is doing fine."

"I know. But there is still much for him to learn."

"There always will be. You just have to let him go."

Joshua frowned. "I don't think you know all that is involved."

"I do not mean to say that I do. I just wish you could get some rest."

"I will rest in the Pacific."

Mary said nothing.

Joshua looked at her and spoke more softly. "I'm sorry, Mary. I don't mean to be short, but I expect the weather of the next week or two to deserve my every consideration."

Mary smiled wanly. "Of course, dear. I understand."

But she was not sure she did. For a captain to depose his mate was a relatively rare occurrence, though by no means unheard of in the driven world of clipper sailing. For it to happen at this point in the voyage, though, where every hand was needed to negotiate the coming weather, seemed very hazardous.

Mary wished Joshua could get more sleep, and worried about his long hours, but she had seen him go without sleep before, especially during stretches of adversarial weather. Perhaps, she told herself, she was overreacting.

A few days after the midnight altercation with Keeler she found Joshua by the starboard rail, gazing out over the sea. The swells were long, with a half a minute or more between crests, the up-and-down oscillations providing a hypnotic effect. Joshua seemed caught up in their motion, and for a moment he did not notice her presence.

"Oh, Mary," he said, coming out of his reverie. "I did not see you come up."

"The motion of the swells can have that effect," she said.

"Swells? Oh, yes, the swells. I hadn't noticed."

Mary dismissed the incident until she noticed a similar occurrence the next morning, when he again seemed to be in a world of his own. It was not like her husband to daydream. She began to watch him carefully and often noted lapses in attention. They were brief, to be sure, but so uncharacteristic that her concern increased. She knew Joshua usually to be cognizant of situations around him, but suddenly that did not always seem to be the case.

A day or two later, after her almost daily bout of seasickness had subsided, Mary went up on deck. There was a lull in the storms, when the waves were only ten feet high rather than twenty, and she found Joshua standing near the helm. As she approached, nothing seemed amiss, but the helmsman was looking at his captain with a questioning look. He glanced uneasily at Mary.

From high in the rigging she heard the soft pop of a luffing sail, with wind spilling around to its front. In effect, the wind was being wasted. She looked toward Joshua. He appeared not to have noticed.

Mary moved to his side. He seemed distant, and his eyes seemed dull. "Joshua?"

For a moment he did not answer. Then his eyes focused on her. "Oh, darling, there you are. Sleeping late today?"

"I've been reading. Joshua, are you feeling well?"

"Of course. Why do you ask?"

The wind providentially chose that moment to roll across the loose out-of-trim sail. Mary watched for Joshua's reaction and was relieved to see him look up at the source of the sound. He then called forward to the crewmen amidship.

"You men, there! Ready to brace the mizzen topgallant."

The crew moved quickly to loosen lines from their pins and stood ready for the order.

"Tend the tacks and sheets. Ease starboard. Haul port braces."

The men up on the starboard pin rail eased line while those on the lee side hauled, pulling the yardarm of the mizzenmast topgallant around to the wind. With the yard now canted more across the deck, the upwind side well forward of the lee, the sail was now better able to catch the west wind coming from almost directly abeam the ship. Once the topgallant yard was belayed into its new position, Joshua ordered the royal yard likewise braced more sharply. Satisfied with the new arrangement, he called out, "That's well, men," and the crew, after securing the excess line, went back to other duties.

The yard braced up and the sail back in trim, Joshua turned back to Mary. "I'm sorry. What was it we were talking about?"

Now that he was behaving normally, Mary hesitated to mention her concerns. "Nothing, dear," she said, but added, "I am worried that you are tired."

"Of course I'm tired. Keeler has left me in a difficult position."

"I am concerned about your health."

"Don't be."

Mary thought his voice was unduly sharp and told him so.

"I said not to worry. Perhaps you should go back to your book. Let me do my work."

Mary was caught off guard by Joshua's pointed remarks. She started to say more but stopped herself, deciding that now was not the time. Turning away, she said, "I'll be below," and retreated off the quarterdeck.

She had not intended her visit topside to be so brief, but she was unnerved by Joshua's behavior. She was not accustomed to seeing him in less than total command of his faculties and was certainly not accustomed to having him be curt with her.

Back in their cabin, Mary sat in what had become her favorite reading and sewing chair, the pale green wing back by the bed in their cabin, and wondered what—if anything—she should do. Something was bothering Joshua, leaving him preoccupied. He was clearly not devoting himself fully to matters at hand. She wondered what the distraction could be. Keeler, who had proved to be no good, was locked away below deck and was no longer a threat. Surely Joshua was not concerned about further trouble with him. Without outside aid from the crew, Keeler was almost certainly secure in the hold's storeroom, and the crew seemed as pleased to be rid of him as Joshua was. The absence of the first mate's services, of course, was unfortunate, but certainly no worse than his presence. There was no other problem confronting her husband, at least that Mary was aware of.

As Mary thought of these things, she found herself worried nearly to the point of tears, and then to the point of nausea. She felt the queasy feeling of seasickness return, leaving her weak in the stomach. She sat still in her chair, feeling that if she moved, she would surely throw up, but at the same time needing to go over to the washbasin for when she did. It was a sorry state she was in, she thought. Eventually she gave in to the unavoidable, reasoning that it was best to get it over with. As she hovered over the basin, she cursed the motion of the ship and the swells and waves that caused it.

Or was it the motion of the ship? Despite her best efforts to ignore the signs, Mary knew that there was another reason for her to feel sick in the mornings. As the lone woman on the ship, she had no one to turn to for advice, but she was acutely aware that she had missed her last period, and she knew what that might mean. Her suspicions left her emotionally torn. She had always been eager to have a family, having babies and children playing at her feet, but not now. Not while journeying through the weather of Cape Horn, and not while she was troubled over the health of her husband. She found herself hoping all the symptoms would go away, at least for now.

After a time, the feelings of nausea passed and she was able to turn away from the basin stand and return to her chair. Thinking again about the problem with Joshua, she reached no clearer conclusion than before. She decided that when his watch ended and he came below, she would talk to him and see if she could discern what was troubling him.

Unfortunately, when the eight bells announcing the watch change rang, Joshua did not come down. Hare went up—Mary heard him leaving the saloon—but Joshua stayed on deck.

The day passed, and then another. Joshua continued to spend hours at a time on deck, despite the cold. It had to be a lack of sleep, she decided.

She supposed that could also explain the headaches. Those had started a few days before the bout with Keeler, but had since become more frequent. They were now coming about almost daily, sometimes twice a day. Joshua would not admit it, but Mary suspected that on some days they never left, that a headache complained of in the forenoon and one of the afternoon were one and the same.

If a lack of sleep was the problem, Mary hoped that the symptoms would be transitory. It became apparent that they were not. Day by day his condition deteriorated. With each day the headaches seemed worse, although he ceased to complain.

The bright light of day seemed to aggravate the pain. Joshua took to wearing his hat pulled down low over his eyes, which he kept closed a good part of the time. When he needed to see, he squinted through eyelids barely open, grimacing as he did so. Young Hare, aware of the problem, began taking odd watches, coming on deck when the sun was out or the sky was otherwise unduly bright, allowing Joshua more of the nighttime watches.

It was these retreats from the light of day that finally enabled Joshua to get some bed rest, although the increasingly persistent headaches often prevented sleep. When sleep did come it seemed fitful and fleeting, as if accompanied by unpleasant dreams. Seeing him lying restless in the bed worried Mary as much as when he was never in bed at all.

There were other symptoms as well. He became ever more listless, and his appetite all but disappeared. His thirst, however, was unquenchable. Mary grew more and more worried, but she did not know what to do about it, short of encouraging him to rest.

Outside, the weather became more disagreeable. The sun, to the benefit of Joshua's sensitive eyes, made only brief appearances through the clouds, which blanketed the sky in thick layers of gray. Rain fell often, and frequently turned to sleet, stinging the skin and making the deck hazardous even to stand on. To move about and work on the ship was more treacherous still, both on the slippery deck and aloft, where a coating of ice on the rigging became almost ever present. Even when there was no rain or sleet, the constant spray from breaking waves misted the ship all the way up to the royal yards, depositing yet more ice.

More often now the royals, and sometimes the topgallants, were kept furled, the wind too strong to carry all sail. Still, *Neptune's Car* plowed on. Even under reduced sail, the big clipper carried more than enough canvas to make good headway. It was designed for speed in all weather, and as it neared the turbulence of the Cape Horn winter, it continued to prove the worthiness of its design.

On Joshua's charts Mary saw Staten Island, a spot of land off Patagonia that bore the same name as the island in New York Harbor. This Staten Island was the first land the ship would come near since passing the rocks of Saint Paul near the equator, and they marked the entrance to the Straits of Le Maire, the ambiguous entrance to the waters of the Horn. She could see by Joshua's markings on the charts that these straits lay just ahead, probably not far over the misty gray horizon. She had been awaiting the Horn, and now it was almost before them.

The weather was cold and miserable, nothing like the September days of early autumn in New England. She cocooned herself in the warmth of the cabin, having no desire to see the outside world. She thought often of Joshua out on the deck, in all the elements that Nature could hurl at him, and wished he were in the cabin staying warm with her. The afternoon watch would be ending soon. She hoped, as she always did when the watch changed, that he would come below for a while.

As she was thinking this, she heard the outer door of the after cabin bang open and voices in the saloon. There seemed to be a commotion, and she rose to open the door to their cabin. She was not prepared for what she saw.

Two sailors, water dripping from their soaked coats, were struggling to get the limp body of a third person past the large dining table that filled the middle of the room. Mary's heart jumped when she saw that the sagging form hanging between them was Joshua. His face, eyes closed, was half hidden by his coat, which had pulled up over his shoulders as he was dragged inside, his legs and feet trailing behind.

Seeing Mary in the open doorway, one of the sailors said, "We're sorry, ma'am. He collapsed on the deck."

Mary, terrified, said, "Collapsed?"

"Yes, ma'am. Just fell over."

The other man spoke. "We thought we should get him inside."

"Yes, of course." Mary thought quickly. "Bring him to the bed."

She stepped out of the way, and the two men dragged Joshua into the tiny room.

"Let's get his wet things off," she said, and stood helplessly by, hands fearfully over her mouth. The sailors struggled with the wet coat, then outer clothes. With the four of them inside, the cabin seemed very small, and the smell of wet clothes filled the air.

Finally, they had Joshua down to his underwear, and they piled him into the bed. For the first time, Mary got a good look at his face. It seemed unnaturally pale, almost white. For a moment, she feared he was dead. She fell to her knees beside him and heard him breathe. Then a low moan passed his lips. Filled with fear, she turned back to the crewmen.

"What happened?"

"We don't know, ma'am. He just fell out. One minute, he was standing by the rail, the next we found him on the boards."

"What should we do?"

The men stood helpless.

Mary's heart was racing. "What should we do? What?"

She looked around the room. She had to do something. But what? "Is Mr. Hare on deck?"

"Yes, ma'am."

"Fetch him, please. Please fetch him."

CHAPTER 15

Affliction

For the rest of that day and all of the next, Mary stayed by Joshua's side nursing him, although she hardly knew what to do. She also prayed for him. Occasionally he stirred, and once even attempted to get out of bed, but never was he truly conscious, seemingly never aware of his surroundings. When he spoke, his words came in fragments—broken sentences of murmurs and mutterings.

Mary was at a loss. That her husband, the captain of the ship, was unconscious in the bed presented a considerable dilemma. Foremost in her mind was Joshua's welfare. It was clear now, and should have been clear before, she decided, that his behavior and actions of the last few days were not simply matters of a lack of sleep, but of a much more serious problem. It was now obvious that Joshua was suffering from some affliction, an affliction that required medical care that she did not know how to give.

Beyond Mary's concern for Joshua as her beloved husband, there was also the matter of his position as captain. *Neptune's Car* was a large and complex ship, requiring constant attention. Keeler's removal from the post of first mate had already left the quarterdeck short one officer. As long as Joshua remained ill, second mate Timothy Hare was faced with being the only officer on deck.

The problem of command, for now, was not high on Mary's list. Her principal concern, indeed, her only concern during those first heart-wrenching hours after Joshua's collapse, was what to do for him. If she could nurse him through whatever had stricken him and get him back on his feet, the problems of the deck would take care of themselves. During that first day and night she was never away from his side, ready to render whatever aid he might need. If she only knew what to do.

She consulted the medical book from the small library above Joshua's desk, but it was of little use. It was a massive volume, with thirty or forty pages devoted to symptoms similar to what Joshua exhibited. She read in great detail of the various forms of meningitis, the different tubercular diseases, and other inflammations and tumors. After reading the pages dealing with fevers of the brain, she still did not know what to do. The text, for all its verbosity, gave her little practical instruction. Some of the symptoms described were similar to what Joshua was experiencing, but none matched perfectly. The book presented itself as a compendium of medical knowledge, but to Mary it revealed far too little of the arts of the physician.

Closest to describing Joshua's state was the section concerning the onset and treatment of meningitis, which turned out to be a broad and all-encompassing term. There were several types of the disease, but after looking through the various causes and effects, it seemed to Mary that there were scant differences, as far as either symptoms or treatment, between them. The book described headaches and dullness of thought, and progressive worsening of insensible talk, fever, blindness, and eventual unconsciousness. Joshua had never engaged in insensible talk, at least until after his collapse, and while sensitive to bright light he was certainly not blind, but his headaches and wandering concentration caused Mary to watch fearfully for the rest of the symptoms.

She also wondered about another cause, which might have at least contributed to the illness. Had the blow of Joshua's head against the deck, delivered by Keeler during the midnight fight, played a role? The headaches had begun before, but quickly worsened after that night. Mary felt certain that either an injury from the bout with

Keeler or the excess hours on the freezing deck had played a great role in Joshua's condition. Perhaps both were to blame.

Most worrisome, even terrifying, was the prognosis of the acute form of meningitis, particularly the paragraph concerning its duration:

> Death sometimes takes place within the first twenty-four hours, often between the fourth and seventh days, but still more frequently within a period of one to three weeks.

That a person could go from health and vigor to death in a matter of days was not a new thing to Mary. There was much that medicine did not know how to cure, even diseases beginning with the most benign of symptoms. But for this to happen now, to Joshua, was almost unfathomable. And unbearable. In wild despair, she read for a treatment.

There seemed to be only two. One was to induce bleeding to relieve the pulse, should it seem too strong, as well as to carry away the bad blood. Mary was not ready to do that, yet. The other was to keep the head cool, using bladders of crushed ice or compresses of cold water. That she could do, and she began immediately.

Joshua did have a fever, which she had not been aware of before. He had never mentioned feeling feverish and had not seemed unduly warm whenever he was close to her in bed. When he was carried in from the deck, however, he had seemed warm, despite having been in the freezing outside air, and had become warmer as the hours passed.

The fever, of course, alarmed Mary greatly. She kept a cool cloth on Joshua's forehead, changing it every few minutes. When she took away the warm compress, replacing it with a cool one, she felt that she must be doing some good, that each time she was removing some of the fever. No matter how often it was changed, though, the cloth soaked in cool water soon warmed again against Joshua's skin. There was always more feverish heat.

As she changed Joshua's compresses, Mary spoke softly to her sleeping husband, offering soothing words of comfort, hoping he could hear. She also spoke to him of her concerns about the ship.

"I am wondering, Joshua, about how things are going up on the deck. Mr. Hare, you know, is the only officer, now that you are ill, and I wonder how he is faring without you." She gently felt along Joshua's pale cheek. "I do not wish to concern you, but if you can offer any suggestions as to how he is to manage the handling of the ship without you, I would love to hear them."

Joshua, in response, lay silent.

Timothy Hare, apparently, was wondering the same thing. The next morning, he came below.

He said he was there to check up on the captain. Mary was sure that was part of the reason, but as he lingered in the cabin, she could tell that he had more he wanted to say. She watched him worry the brim of his hat as he held it in his hands, and she waited for him to bring up what he was surely thinking. He could not seem to find the place to start.

Finally, she said, "Joshua's sudden illness puts you in a rather difficult situation, Mr. Hare."

"Yes, ma'am, it does."

"Have you been on the quarterdeck all night?"

"Yes, ma'am."

"You must be exhausted."

"That should not be your worry, ma'am. Your concern lies here."

"I suppose you are right. I'm sure that I'm worried enough about Joshua for both of us."

"Yes, ma'am."

Mary looked at the young second mate. He was not much older than she was, barely into his twenties, and had little experience with command. His role as second mate had always left him answering to someone else, with someone else to go to for advice, should he need it. The tight expression on his face showed the strain that he no doubt felt.

"Hopefully," she said, "this . . . this, whatever it is that has afflicted the captain will be of short duration, and . . ." Mary suddenly felt that if she said another word, she would burst into tears.

She took one of the washcloths she had been using on Joshua's forehead and wiped her own face. She was sure it was streaked from tears already shed, and the wet rag felt refreshing, cooling. She dabbed emerging tears from her eyes. She breathed deeply, composing herself.

"In any event, Mr. Hare, we must consider our situation."

"Yes, ma'am."

"Until he recovers, you are in command."

"Yes, ma'am." Hare looked tentative.

Mary said, "Is there something you wish to say? Please speak freely. We are in no position not to be completely open with each other. If you have suggestions, Mr. Hare, I would like to hear them."

Timothy Hare forced a smile. "It is not a suggestion, ma'am, but a concern. I am willing to run the ship, and I think I can, but I will be needing some help."

Mary thought he was broaching the subject of Keeler. As far as operation of the vessel, to release the first mate might be a prudent thing to do. But to simply absolve him of his transgressions was not something she desired. Still, she thought of the long hours Hare would be putting in, just as Joshua had. Deferring any mention of Keeler, for the moment, she said, "Is there any among the crew who can assist in taking a watch, or part of one?"

"There are one or two that I think can be trusted to keep the ship on course. And maybe even make some changes in the sails. As long as the weather does not become more than I know what to do with, I think we'll be all right. As far as the actual sailing is concerned." He paused and then said, "There is one problem."

While he had been talking, Mary rinsed the cloth she had used on her face in a basin of cool water. She squeezed out the excess and carefully placed it on Joshua's forehead, exchanging it for the warm one now removed. While gently feeling Joshua's skin, gauging his temperature, she asked, "What problem is that, Mr. Hare?"

"I don't know how to navigate."

Mary suddenly realized that she had never seen Hare with a sextant in his hands, but had thought nothing of it. She turned toward him. "You don't?"

"No, ma'am. I never had the chance."

"Joshua has never instructed you in the sextant? Nor did Mr. Keeler?"

Hare looked downcast. "No."

Mary started to say something, but Hare spoke quickly. "I knew I should learn. The captain has asked me, on occasion, if I wished to work a sight, but I always . . . I always came up with a reason to be busy."

"Did you not want to learn?"

"Oh, yes. I wanted terribly to learn, but that would mean admitting to the captain something that would hinder my being an officer."

Puzzled, Mary asked, "What was that?"

"I don't know how to read. Or write."

"Oh." She bit her lip thoughtfully. "You could not expect to keep that a secret for long."

"I know. I hoped to learn. The steward, Henry, has been helping me some. We work sometimes when no one is around."

"I see."

Mary looked at Joshua, for the moment peacefully sleeping, with no tossing and muttering through what must be delusional dreams. If only she could ask his advice and get some guidance from him about what to do. What of Mr. Keeler? What would Joshua do about him? She voiced her thoughts to Hare.

"Suppose we release the first mate," she said. "That would relieve you of a great deal of responsibility."

"Aye, ma'am, it would do that."

She studied his face. "Would that please you, Mr. Hare?"

Hare inhaled, delaying his answer. "No, ma'am. I mean, yes, it would ease the hours of duty, but I'm not so sure it would help, all in all."

"All in all?"

"Aye, ma'am. Things might not—they might not go as well, sometimes."

"His presence would be disruptive?"

"Aye, ma'am."

"More harm than good."

"Could be. Or not. I just don't know."

Mary was pleased that Hare did not want Keeler back on deck. Nor did she. At least not until it was proved that he was indispensable.

"Do you think, Mr. Hare, that if navigation were not a problem, that you could get *Neptune's Car* around Cape Horn and up to San Francisco?"

"Yes," he said hesitantly. "Like I say, if the weather is not too bad."

"How bad is too bad?"

"I could stand some worse than what we have had so far."

"What other choice do we have? Besides bringing Mr. Keeler out? Should we turn back?"

Hare thought for a moment. "I guess we could go back up to Rio. I have thought about that some. Long hours on deck last night gave me time to think."

"Is that what you decided?"

"To be honest, during the night I thought it best. No one would blame us if we did. But this morning, in the light of day, I feel differently. I think we can go on. If you want. But there may be a doctor in Rio who can help."

"Do you think so?"

Again, Hare did not answer immediately. "I think better care will be found in San Francisco. But it is much farther away."

"Yes," Mary said simply. Her stomach was very unsettled. The morning sickness, as she was now sure it was, had been less distressing the last day or two, but now her insides were twisted up by the stress of these decisions.

"There is still the matter of navigation," said Hare.

Mary knew that Hare was asking her if she could do it. He had seen her work the sextant and knew that she had at least a rudimentary knowledge. She wondered if she dared trust the ship to her skills. With Joshua's calculations to double-check her own, she had full confidence in her ability to take a sight and plot a course. On her own, she had much less. She thought for a minute and said, "I can plot the course, Mr. Hare, if you can make the ship follow it."

"I can do that."

"And what of the crew? Will they follow, knowing that I am leading?"

Hare shrugged. "All you can do is ask."

Chapter 16

A Pledge of Support

Mary leaned over the unconscious form of her husband, wetting his face with the cloth. She stroked his hair, damp from the compresses and the fever, caressing it with her fingers. He lay still, not responding. It struck Mary that, although he lay quietly, he did not seem peaceful. His face did not wear the contented look of an easy sleep, but had a tenseness, as if showing the strain of turmoil within. Mary felt that he was fighting his illness, trying to defeat whatever demons were residing in him. She wanted him to rest, to gain strength, but she needed him. She needed his advice.

"Joshua," she whispered. "I need you to tell me what to do. I need to know which way to go."

Joshua did not respond.

Timothy Hare had gone back up on deck to check the progress of the ship, to make sure that, for now at least, good speed was being made toward the cape. Mary felt blessed to have him aboard. Hare's friendly face and easy demeanor were proving to be a great comfort to her. Many men, she felt, would not be nearly so willing to come to her and offer to work with her the way he had just done. Many would have simply taken the ship as their own and made decisions without regard to her wishes. Many would not have considered asking for her help, whether they knew how to navigate or not.

After the second mate left the cabin, she had spent an hour, and then another hour, in deep thought. Occasionally she spoke to Joshua, asking his advice, voicing her options. Hearing them out loud helped her to study them, to clarify what she was thinking.

"There are many things to consider," she said to the silent Joshua, "but it all comes down to only two choices. I can have Hare turn the ship around and run for Rio de Janeiro, or I can have him press on, toward Cape Horn, toward San Francisco. Which would you have me do?"

Going back to Rio was the prudent thing to do. The weather around Cape Horn, she had heard from the captain of the *Susan Walker*, was as bad as anyone had ever seen. The first mate was under arrest, and the captain was incapacitated, leaving only an illiterate second mate to run the ship. All navigation duties would be left to her, a nineteen-year-old girl. Certainly, she knew how to work the sextant, and she knew how to work up a position and plot it on the charts.

"But what if I make an error?" she said aloud, both to Joshua and to herself. "If a calculation is wrong, what then?"

What would happen if a simple mathematical mistake cost the loss of the ship and cargo? What if it meant the loss of the crew? If a mistake on her part caused *Neptune's Car* to be lost at sea, no one would ever know the cause of the wreck. Joshua, she was sure, would be blamed for the loss. Joshua's reputation as a skilled and masterful captain would be ruined even as he lay incoherent in the bed.

But what if she did turn back? The ship had been commissioned to deliver a cargo to California in the least time possible, and to retreat to Brazil, a thousand miles behind them, would do nothing toward fulfilling that contract. It had been done before—any number of clippers had met with misfortune and had put into Rio for repairs or remanning. Still, Mary did not want a ship under Joshua's command to do so.

And what if Joshua's illness were only a temporary condition?

"What if," she asked him, "a day or two from now, you wake up, to recover and regain your health, only to learn that your wife and your trusted second mate had cost the ship days of progress by needlessly running away before the wind?"

To all these questions, Joshua lay silent. The decisions would have to be made by her. By her and her ally, Timothy Hare. Hare, the only one left on board who could aid her in whatever direction she decided to go.

She decided to go forward.

"When you wake up, dear," she said, "I want you to see that we are on course and still bound for San Francisco. You will see that the time you spent teaching me the sextant was time well spent."

Now all she had to do was convince the crew to go along with her. The crew. A rough and not necessarily trustworthy collection. Some were coarse and salty sailors, spending their lives at sea. Others were merely working their way to the goldfields, filling the role of common seaman, providing strong backs for the tasks of putting up and taking in sails. There were also the Asians and the Arabs, working their way back around the world. Then there were the boys, young apprentices who viewed a life at sea with the excitement and romance that only the young can have.

What did she say to this diverse lot of men? By now they all knew of Joshua's collapse. They had seen him fall and had carried him below. They knew that Hare was the only officer left to guide the ship and probably knew that Hare, not so long removed from before the mast himself, knew nothing of navigation.

What did they need to hear from her, a woman they knew only from the distance of the quarterdeck? Mary thought of how she might appear to the crew. She would not project a commanding presence, given her slender size and youth. How would she give them the confidence that she could steer them through the storms and into a safe harbor? Even if Hare were the one giving the orders and running the ship, what if they refused to serve on a ship being directed in its courses by a woman?

Mary had another thought. Suppose they knew that this woman was with child. What then?

She lay down next to Joshua, arm across his chest, her head nestled against his shoulder. She was exhausted from a night of worry and a day of attention and care to a feverish disease that she did not know how to treat. If she were this tired already, she wondered, how would she keep going? That she was carrying a child, a condition that she only now accepted as fact, could only tire her even more. Did she have the strength to care for Joshua in a pitching and rolling cabin and at the same time help Hare steer the ship through the dangerous waters ahead? Was she putting the ship and all on board at too great a risk?

"What do I do, Joshua? What do I do?"

Joshua lay beside her, his chest moving up and down under her arm in steady breathing. Mary held tight to him, as if seeking to absorb from him the courage and determination to do what she must. She thought hard, trying to consider all sides of her dilemma, weighing the possible consequences of her actions. And she prayed, asking for divine guidance and strength.

The afternoon passed with no discernible change in Joshua's condition. She knew that she had to decide upon a course of action. The storms of Cape Horn were too near to delay. The crew needed and deserved guidance if they were to confront the weather with a clear purpose. There was no time to be tentative.

A little before four o'clock, she summoned the young steward from the outer room.

"Henry," she said from the open doorway of their cabin, "I need to speak with Mr. Hare. Will you ask him to come down, please?"

The steward looked past her shoulder at the figure of the captain on the bed, the concern showing on his face. Even so, he tried to smile cheerfully, saying, "Yes, ma'am, I'll do that right away."

Hare soon arrived, wet and dripping, and stopped in the doorway of Joshua and Mary's cabin.

"I won't come in, Mrs. Patten, until I dry some."

"That is considerate of you," Mary said. "Is it raining?"

"Only blowing, ma'am, but there is a good bit of spray in the air."

"I can see that. Mr. Hare, I asked you down to see if you were still of the same mind. Shall we continue on?"

"I think we can." He looked into the room at Joshua. "Any better?"

"No."

"I'm sorry."

"Yes, well," Mary said, thinking of no better response. "I suppose it will be up to us." She felt a sudden lump in her throat. It took an effort to speak. "At least for now."

Hare said nothing, waiting for Mary to compose herself. After a moment, he said, "I should show you this," holding out a small sheet of paper.

Mary took the paper. It was damp from sea spray. "What is it?"

"It came to me, to give to you. It's from Mr. Keeler."

"Keeler?" Mary felt a tightness in her stomach. She recognized the feeling. It was fear. How, she wondered, could she feel fear from him? He was securely locked away, whiling away his time in a small room lined with empty cupboards. Nevertheless, the feeling was there, and it was very real.

She looked at the note, quickly digesting its content. "Do you know what this says?"

Hare admitted that he did. "It was delivered to the cook unsealed. It was too convenient, I guess, and he took a peek at it."

"And Mr. Irwin read it to you?"

"Aye, ma'am," Hare said. "I'm sorry."

Mary waved away his concern. "I'm sure it was hard for the cook to resist." She looked down at the message. "Well, knowing what Mr. Keeler has to say, what do you think?"

Hare smiled. "I think he is fine where he is."

Mary smiled, too, and it occurred to her that it was the first time she done so since Joshua was carried to his bed. "I think we agree upon that point."

"I think we agree on several."

"Do you think it will work, us sharing the command? That is what it will be, you know."

"Aye, I know."

"Will you be comfortable with the arrangement? You will have command of the ship and crew, but I will be involved in many of the decisions that may, in fact, be the most important decisions of all."

"I'm in no position to argue," said Hare.

It struck Mary that he was fairly articulate for someone with no education, and she remarked upon it.

Hare looked sheepish. "I've spent a lot of time listening to people talk. Especially you and Captain Patten."

The answer was a logical one, but it surprised Mary, and she felt a slight blush. "I am flattered, Mr. Hare."

She glanced down at the note she held in her hand. "It would appear that our friend Keeler feels that he is in a good position."

"There is no doubt," Hare said thoughtfully, "that he could take command. The only question is, do we want him to?"

"Do you?"

"No."

Mary smiled. "I like your assurance. We will leave Mr. Keeler where he is, for now. I am curious, Mr. Hare. You have made it clear that you have little use for Mr. Keeler. Is that opinion based upon purely personal feelings toward him, or is it something in the way he handles the ship?"

"I don't trust—I don't think he handles the crew well, ma'am."

"Meaning?"

Hare hesitated. "I think the crew is working well right now. That was not always so on his watches."

"I see," Mary said, thinking. There was something about Keeler that Hare did not trust, but he was compelled not to say it aloud to her. She wondered what that was, but did not press the issue.

She moved over to the writing desk and took a sheet of paper from a drawer. She thought for a moment and started writing. "I sent for you, Mr. Hare, to have you gather the crew at the watch change. I suppose I should go up and speak to them. They are no doubt wondering what we intend to do. In the meantime," she said, folding the paper and handing it to Hare, "take this to Mr. Keeler."

Hare took the note and fingered it.

"You may read it if you wish," Mary said.

Hare opened the single fold and looked at the writing. "I would if I could, ma'am."

Mary felt instant regret. "I'm sorry. I wasn't thinking."

"That's all right, ma'am," he said. "I'll deliver this right away."

Hare turned and left through the saloon. Mary watched him go, and then she turned back to Joshua. Wringing out a fresh cloth, she folded it and placed it on his forehead. The cloth she removed was, again, warm from absorbed fever. She swirled it around in the basin, rinsing it out, stirring the water, thinking many things.

❖   ❖   ❖

Mary had not been up on deck since the previous morning, and the cold air startled her. The weather seemed colder and more windy than ever, the air damp and heavy, and she pulled the collar of her coat more tightly against her throat. She wondered if it was really that much colder, or if she was chilled from within by worries about Joshua and nervous thoughts about her plan to speak before the men. She had given considerable thought to what she would say and still was not sure.

Hare saw her come up on the poop of the quarterdeck, pulling the hood of her coat tight around her face, and met her at the top of the steps.

"It's awful cold today, ma'am."

"Yes, it is, Mr. Hare."

"Probably much more pleasant below."

"Hardly pleasant down there, Mr. Hare."

Hare seemed embarrassed. "I'm sorry, ma'am."

Mary gave a tight smile. "Think nothing of it."

She stood by the rail above the lower deck and looked along the length of the ship. It had always seemed huge, its long deck stretching away into the bursts of spray that came over the bow rails, but now it seemed even larger. The deck seemed longer, the masts taller, the sails more massive. The men seemed smaller, like worker ants clinging to the only thing solid in their world, braving the broad hand of weather's wrath.

Before, Mary had been a passive passenger. Now, she was preparing to step up into a role of responsibility. In the comfortable confines of the cabin, sitting by Joshua's side, she had convinced herself that she was up to the task. Here on the wet and windswept deck she was not so sure. The ship dropped into a trough and started its climb back up the next swell. She felt the mass of the vessel under her and also, suddenly, a feeling of great weight upon her shoulders.

The ship's bell sounded the end of the afternoon watch and the beginning of the dog watches. Hare, who had moved away during her contemplations, appeared back at her side.

"Ready to call the men together, ma'am?"

Mary looked at him. He was looking back, his eyes studying her face. She hoped he could not see the fear she felt.

"Yes, Mr. Hare, I am." She forced a weak smile. "I'm not sure what I will say, though."

Hare said, "Would you want me to talk to them?"

"You might do a better job of it. But I think I have to do this. I have to convince them . . ." Mary searched for the right words. She wondered how she was to speak to the entire crew if she could not convey her thoughts to her ally. "I have to convince them that we can take this ship to San Francisco."

"You can do it, ma'am. They respect you."

"Do you know that?"

"Yes, ma'am. They have seen you using the sextant and have seen you on the deck in all sorts of weather. And many of these men were in the crew last year, when you were first aboard *Neptune's Car*. They know you."

"Thank you, Mr. Hare. You don't know how much your confidence means to me."

Hare smiled. "I'll muster the men."

He took a small whistle from his pocket, gave a shrill call, and shouted an order for all hands to gather at the quarterdeck rail. All along the ship, the men stopped what they were doing and looked up. They were clearly puzzled by the unusual order, but when they saw Mary standing there, they secured whatever they were doing and started moving aft. Thirty-five men and boys, coming from all points of the ship, converged on the deck below the railing. Mary waited while they all clustered before her, their upturned faces regarding her with some curiosity.

Despite the fact that she was standing above them, she felt very small. She wondered where to begin.

"I had Mr. Hare call you together," she said, but then stopped. Her words had been snatched by the wind and flung away, lost to the sea. Her voice seemed thin and weak against the wind rushing through the sails and rigging, and she wondered how she was going to make herself heard. She held tightly with both hands to the rail at her waist, and began again, forcing the words from deep within, using her diaphragm to push them out into the wind. The crew, doing its part, moved in closer.

"I had Mr. Hare call you so I could tell you of the captain's condition, and of our plans for the voyage. I am sure you have been wondering."

Again she paused, both to take a deep breath and to plan her next words. "You know that Captain Patten has taken ill. I don't know the exact cause, or what his symptoms are telling us, but I believe his illness was brought on by overwork after First Mate Keeler was relieved of duty. I have hope that a few days' rest will lead to a recovery and a resumption of his presence on deck.

"I will not mislead you. The captain appears to be very ill and has been resting in bed since he was taken below yesterday afternoon. I confess that I am not certain what is needed to improve his situation, nor do I know how long it will be before he recovers.

"In the meantime, Mr. Hare and I have decided that the best thing we can do is keep the ship on course and proceed toward San Francisco. To do so will require, of course, your cooperation. You know that the captain is ill. You know that Mr. Keeler has been placed under arrest. You know that Mr. Hare is the only officer able to perform his duties, at least for now.

"He will be calling upon some of you to assist him in taking watches. If any of you have had a desire to progress from the forecastle to a position as an officer, such as was done only last spring by Mr. Hare and was once done by the captain himself, now is an opportunity for you. The move may not be permanent, but it will give you some experience on the quarterdeck and will give you good standing when future positions become available, whether on this ship or some other.

"And for all of you, even if you do no more than keep to your duties, your standing among seamen will be increased. This will not be an easy passage. Cape Horn is before us, and without the experience of the captain to rely upon the weather will surely test us. But should Joshua— But should Captain Patten not recover during our time at sea, this will prove your mettle as men of the sea. When we get to San Francisco and word of our endeavor becomes known, you will never have difficulty in finding a berth on any ship. And a good berth at that. You will be known as men of perseverance in the face of adversity, as men to be trusted, and any master of any ship will know that to sign one of you on will be to sign the best man available."

Mary was somewhat surprised by the ease with which her words were coming. It was as though, once she got started, she knew exactly what she needed to say and what the men needed to hear. The crew seemed to be giving her their complete attention, which pleased her greatly. She hoped their attitude would not change as she went into the details of the new command.

"As I said, it has not been so long ago that Mr. Hare was one of you, living and working in the forecastle, and many of you have worked with him and know what a skilled handler of ships he has become. I have often been on deck with the captain, and I have seen the confidence that he has in Mr. Hare. There is no doubt in my mind that he is fully capable of taking *Neptune's Car* to the completion of this voyage.

"And then there is the matter of myself.

"I will, of course, be spending a great deal of my time caring for the captain until he recovers. As his wife, I do not wish even to leave his side. Those of you who were on board during the passage from London last spring will recall the storm which we encountered during the crossing. Lightning struck the mainmast, sending debris and men crashing to the deck, causing injury to several of the crew. You will recall that I was able to render aid and to nurse the injured until we arrived in New York. Now I find myself again in the position of nurse and doctor, and I assure you that no patient will receive more devoted care than my own husband."

Now Mary came to what was a very delicate point. If the men did not already know that Hare was unable to navigate, they soon would, and she had to make sure that they trusted her.

Some sailors, she knew, were absolutely without any of the social graces, and were not only the roughest, coarsest men on the planet, but also considered women the more inferior of the species, giving them no respect beyond objects of sex. To her good fortune, Joshua's crew was a relatively civilized one, with at least some manners and morals. Otherwise she was not sure she would have been able to stand before them as she did.

"In addition to caring for Captain Patten, I will also be assisting Mr. Hare in certain aspects of his duties. He will have more to do, of course, than one man should have to do, and so I will aid him in matters of navigation. As many of you have seen, the captain has showed me the workings of the sextant, and I am well versed in its use. I have also been instructed in the proper way to use the fixes that the sextant gives to plot positions on the charts and how to determine the desired course to follow. I learned these skill as a pastime, to while away the hours on board.

"Now I will use them to further the completion of my husband's charge. I will be using my experience to aid Mr. Hare, relieving him of those duties of navigation of which, to be honest, I am more knowledgeable than he. It is together, with Mr. Hare commanding the ship, I assisting with the navigation, and you as the able crew, that we will take *Neptune's Car* to its destination of San Francisco."

To Mary's surprise, from within the cluster of men came an unsolicited, "And we will, too, ma'am!" From others came murmurs of what to Mary sounded like agreement.

Mary found that she could not repress a smile. "Thank you," she said to the crowd.

She stopped and rested her voice. Despite her confidence in herself and Mr. Hare, she had feared the men would not be receptive to her, that at least a few would raise concerns of safety without more experienced leadership. Most, if not all, certainly had qualms about serving under any command even nominally shared by a woman.

She had also supposed that Keeler, even though he was locked away, had at least a few allies in the crew, and she had been expecting some opposition from them. So far they had not spoken up, and she decided that now was the time to bring up the matter before they had a chance to challenge her.

"I am almost finished here. There are matters that require our attentions. I desire to return to the side of Captain Patten, who is below and in need of my care. There are duties out there," she said, gesturing over their heads, "on the deck and aloft, that need your care. Even as I have been speaking, the helmsman has been steering us on toward our destination. We will, with your support, proceed apace, keeping to our original goal of bringing our cargo to port with all due speed. But before I dismiss you, there is one matter that I must address. It concerns our first mate, William Keeler.

"Mr. Keeler has been relieved of duty. He was not only relieved, but forcibly so, after physically attacking the captain. Despite our shortage of trained officers, his reinstatement is out of the question. Some of you may be inclined to disagree with that decision. I know that before his arrest he had certain contrary opinions regarding the operation of the ship, and that he may have had support among some of the crew. There was no place for that then, and there is no place for it now.

"Word of Captain Patten's debilitation has reached Mr. Keeler. He has sent a message to me insisting that he be freed to assume command, saying that should any misfortune befall the ship while he remains imprisoned, I will be held responsible. Mr. Keeler is correct. I will be responsible. But he will not be released.

"I have sent Mr. Keeler a written reply. I have informed him that since Captain Patten considered him unworthy to command while he was well, I consider him unworthy to command while the captain is ill. And that is the end of the matter."

Mary paused and realized she had nothing more to say. Whatever the crew decided was out of her hands now. Should they decide to resist her, there was nothing she could do, short of retrieving Joshua's pistol that he kept in the cabin, and she had no desire to do that.

She stood before the men, quietly studying their expressions, trying to gauge their opinions. She saw no signs of hostility. They mostly looked expectant, as if they were waiting for more. Finally, she remembered her conversation in the cabin with Hare. She had asked him if he thought the crew would follow her, and he had said, "All you can do is ask." So she did.

She raised her voice to battle the wind, which had, within the last few moments, begun blowing harder. She felt it whipping the skirt of her spray-soaked dress against her legs, and she felt its sting against her cold cheeks.

The ship heeled over before the gusts, needing adjustments to the sails.

"Do Mr. Hare and I have your support?"

For a second, there was no response, and then came a firm, "Aye, ma'am." Then another, "Aye!" and another, and another. Then a chorus. "Aye! Aye!"

"Cheers for Mrs. Patten!"

"Hurrah! Hurrah! Hurrah!"

The reaction of the men was far beyond anything she had hoped. If there were any sympathizers for Keeler among the crowd, they did not voice that support, and indeed were swept up in the cheers. That the entire crew was shouting support overwhelmed Mary.

Suddenly, she felt totally spent. Worry over the outcome of meeting with the crew, she realized, had kept her tied up with tension, and in the space of seconds, in hearing the cheers, the tension drained away. She could return to caring for Joshua and not worry about the ship. It was in good hands.

Throughout the speech to the crew, she had remained firmly in control of her feelings, channeling all her thoughts to making the proper impression upon the men. Now, their support won, she relaxed. The heavy weight of worry over the ship and crew was lifted away, and she felt emotions flood her. Tears, without warning, filled her eyes and threatened to run down her cheeks. She turned to Hare.

"Carry on, Mr. Hare," she said to her new first mate. "I'll be below." She was struck by the thought: her first mate. *Her* first mate.

Hare was grinning. "Aye, aye, ma'am."

She gathered her skirt to descend the steps, and the men stepped aside as she made her way to the door of the aft cabin, where Joshua lay waiting. As she went inside, she heard Hare shout orders in preparation for retrimming the yards for the increasing wind, and the men went back to work.

CHAPTER 17

Sun Sight

The wind that increased as Mary ended her speech to the crewmen rose in strength during the evening. With the wind came the waves. The ship repeatedly pitched up and then dropped with a shudder into the next trough, laboring its progress. Mary, in the cabin with Joshua, secured all loose objects from rolling to and fro with the motions of the ship. This included the unconscious Joshua. She put the six-inch-high preventer board up to keep him in the bed, and then was obliged to wedge in extra pillows to keep him from rolling against the board.

She could hear Hare's frequent orders, though too muffled for the words to be understood, through the timbers of the deck. He no doubt was trying different combinations of sails and headings, trying to find what worked best for the conditions of the moment.

That was all she knew of the outside world. As the wind rose and darkness fell, she stayed in the cabin. The light of the oil lamp, fastened to the bulkhead above the desk, illuminated the room, casting long shadows on the far wall as Mary moved about, tending to her husband. Most of the time she simply sat at his side, waiting for something to happen, watching for some small sign of improvement.

Sometime after dark the storm arrived. It had been promised by the wind, and the promise was fulfilled. Mary felt that she and

Joshua were cocooned in a tiny world of their own, a world that in the weak light of the lamp was smaller than she had ever realized.

More light would have helped, but the only other source was a lantern hanging from a hook near the door. Its light, swinging by its bail, gave inanimate objects life, their elongated spectral images dancing on the walls, so Mary left it dark. She preferred the dim light of the single lamp to the company of shadow demons.

In that private chamber of wait and worry within a tossing, shuddering vessel, Mary spent her second sleepless night at Joshua's side. Once or twice she climbed over the preventer board to lie down beside him, but it seemed that every time she did, something caused her to have to climb back out. Once, she had just slipped into a much-needed sleep when motion in the covers awakened her. Joshua was stirring and attempting to get out of bed, but he was not lucid enough to negotiate his way over the board. He had one leg out of bed, but it was still wrapped in the blanket, impeding his progress. Trying to get loose, he kicked at the cover, which served only to tighten its hold upon his leg and further frustrate his efforts. Mary crawled quickly around him and stepped down, feeling the cold floor through her stockings.

"What is it, Joshua?" She kept her voice soft. "What do you need?"

Joshua answered groggily. "Nothing. I can't get my leg out."

"Why don't you lie back down, dear?"

"I need to get up."

"But then we can untangle your covers."

"I suppose," he said, dropping backwards onto the bed.

Mary lifted his errant leg back over the side of the bed and worked it free from its entanglement with the blanket. "There," she said, "isn't that better?"

Joshua's only answer was a sound very close to a snore.

With a mixture of relief and disappointment, Mary sat down in her chair. Perhaps, she thought, it would be easier just to sleep there.

She had almost dozed off when the ship pitched heavily through a swell, waking her up. She remembered Joshua's fever and found the washcloth from his forehead among the folds of the bedding.

The exaggerated motions of the ship were such that water would not stay in the washbasin, so she had resorted to using a tall pitcher with a narrow neck. Reaching in to wet the cloth, she placed it again on his forehead. Before she did, she leaned over him and kissed him there, feeling his warmth through her lips.

What, she wondered, was going to come of this? Then she sat back in her chair and pulled a blanket around her. From the deck came a ringing of the ship's bell. She counted as each toll sounded until the bell had rung six times. Three o'clock in the morning. It was no wonder the night seemed so long. Quiet returned to the ship, and within a few minutes she was asleep.

The knock upon the door awakened her, but only gradually. At first it seemed to come from far away, as if someone were knocking on a door at the far end of a house. Another knock, and the sound was much nearer, as though in the next room. Mary stirred, reluctant to leave her dreams. Then a voice called her by name.

"Mrs. Patten?"

She opened her eyes and looked around. She was not in a house at all. There was just the cabin of the ship. On the bed, unmoved since she had last looked his way, was Joshua. A faint light came through the window. It was morning.

Another knock. "Mrs. Patten?"

"Yes," she answered. "Just a moment."

She took her boots from by her chair and slipped them onto her feet. Thus dressed, she stood up, leaving the warm blanket on the chair. "Come in."

The door opened slowly, as though the visitor, for all his knocking, was hesitant to come in. In the doorway was one of the crewmen, his oilskin coat and hat wet from sea spray, his face red from the cold.

"Beg pardon, ma'am. Compliments from Mr. Hare. He wishes me to tell you that there is clearing."

Mary, still half asleep, said, "Clearing?"

"Aye, ma'am."

She stood blankly, trying to comprehend what *clearing* meant.

"He also mentioned bringing the sextant, ma'am."

"Oh." Mary understood perfectly now. "Yes. Please tell Mr. Hare that I will be right up."

The crewman departed, and Mary turned to check on Joshua. He remained asleep, and his fever seemed unabated. She changed his compress, which elicited a soft sigh but no other response. Pouring a little of the cold water from the pitcher into the basin to wash her face, she noted that the water was staying in the bowl now. It seemed the seas had calmed somewhat since the previous evening. Perhaps today would be a better day. Perhaps today would be the day that Joshua began his recovery.

Hopeful, she washed her face, letting the cold water invigorate her skin.

Refreshed, she took the sextant from its case near the desk and checked it over carefully. For the first time her use of it carried importance. A compact instrument, it was some eight or nine inches across, small enough to hold in one hand while using the other to set its readings. For its apparent complexity, the sextant was a fairly simple design. Mounted to the side of its triangular frame was the six-inch-long sight tube, an empty barrel when sighting the sun or holding a small telescope to sight stars. The small mirrors to direct the object of the observation into line with the horizon, sun filters, and the pointer arm that moved the index mark along the curved scale made up the rest of the moving parts. All appeared to be in order.

The instrument itself weighed two or three pounds, but as Mary prepared to leave the cabin and go on deck to use it alone, for the first time, she felt a tremendous weight of responsibility. All her previous work with the sextant was done as a pastime, with Joshua at hand to catch any mistakes. Now each angle she calculated and each mark she made on the chart was to be made in earnest, with the fate of the ship riding on her accuracy. And there was no open ocean to provide room for error. Somewhere very near were the islands and shoals of Cape Horn, and it was up to her to ensure that the ship steered clear. The thought nearly made her sick to her stomach. Or was it morning sickness again?

Lord, help me, she prayed silently. She wound Joshua's pocket watch, purchased that spring in Boston, and checked it against the ship's chronometer in the cabin. The two timepieces were within a minute of each other, attesting to either their accuracy or their conspiracy. She reset Joshua's watch to match and, satisfied that she knew the time as well as she could, left the cabin. The ship, as she walked unsteadily around the long table of the saloon, seemed to increase its rolling. She choked down a feeling of rising nausea. Fresh outside air would do her good, she thought.

She stepped out to a mostly gray world. The water beyond the high side rails rose and fell in long gray green swells. *Neptune's Car*, in the trough between crests, was dwarfed by these smooth hills of water looming beyond the railings. As the ship rode up the crests, the water fell away, replaced by unobstructed sky. For a few seconds the ship rode above the sea, dizzily high to Mary, and then down the smooth slope of water into the next trough. The entire cycle took fifteen or twenty seconds, the up and down of which seemed to directly contradict the desires of Mary's stomach. The fresh air felt good and helped clear her mind, but the nausea subsided little. She stood for a moment, willing herself to adapt to the motion of the deck, but whenever the ship dropped into a trough her stomach seemed to stay on the crest.

Above the slate sea, the gray of the sky was a lighter hue. Lighter, certainly, than the sea, and lighter than the clouds of the day before. They were not the dark clouds of an approaching storm, laden with rain, but the color of a storm just passed. To the east, the clouds had moved out completely, leaving a swath of sky painted the pale azure of a coming day. Looking in that direction, Mary saw the orange glow announcing that the sun was just below the horizon, like the star performer waiting in the wings, stage right.

She took several deep breaths, forcing air into her lungs and forcing the taste of rising bile back down her throat. Despite the cold wind, she felt a sweat break out on her forehead. Gathering her resolve, she cradled the sextant in her arm and climbed the steps to the high quarterdeck.

Hare, watching from the rail, greeted her. "Good morning, ma'am."

"Good morning, Mr. Hare." Mary tried to put some strength in her voice, to deny nausea the pleasure of winning.

"I didn't want to wake you but was afraid the clearing would not last."

Mary looked toward the glow in the east. She knew how quickly the weather could reverse itself. "Yes, Mr. Hare. I think you are right. We should take whatever opportunity we have. Although I would much prefer a higher sun."

The effect of refraction in the atmosphere, she knew, affected the apparent position of the sun as much as a full diameter when low to the horizon. The effect diminished as the sun rose, and largely ceased to be a factor after the sun was halfway up the sky. For ease of calculation, the best time to take a reading was exactly at noon, but Mary would take advantage of the morning clearing to make whatever observation she could.

She took the sextant in her right hand and sighted through the tube at the distant horizon and made small movements of the pointer arm to check the calibration of the instrument. Satisfied that it was accurate to within a few minutes of arc, she noted the error and waited for the sun.

"How goes it here on the deck, Mr. Hare?" she asked.

"Very well, ma'am. It was not an easy night, but the men worked through the storm without hesitation. I believe your speech to be very successful. We have their support."

"At least for now."

"You are fearful that it might not last?"

"I am fearful of what our friend Mr. Keeler might try to stir up should our passage of the Horn not go smoothly."

Hare smiled, his lips weathered with tiny cracks. "Then we shall make it go smoothly."

Mary returned his smile, but her heart was not in it. More correctly, her stomach was not. Looking through the sextant tube had intensified her nausea. She knew she should eat something, but was not sure she would be able to do so.

The eastern sky became brighter, and the orange curve of the top of the sun appeared, rising out of the sea. A minute later the full sun was in view, its orange disk just touching the waves. Mary checked Joshua's watch and noted the time. She did not need a sextant to know that angle. The sun, zero degrees above the horizon, was telling her where they were, or would be, once she made a few more observations and consulted the almanac.

The sun climbed quickly, and Mary anxiously waited to take another sight. The higher it rose, the better, but she knew that fast-moving clouds could move back in almost without warning.

She went below once to check on Joshua and change his cloth, to make certain that her charge was not in immediate need of her presence. Joshua seemed to be resting comfortably, and she went back up on deck.

The clouds held off, leaving the eastern third of the sky clear for observations. Mary waited an hour, giving the sun time to rise above the distorting atmosphere. In the meantime she ate some bread. It was dry and tasteless in her mouth, so she spread a small amount of butter across it. That helped her force the bread down, but once it was in her stomach, she was not sure the butter was a good idea.

Finally, she decided she had waited long enough and prepared to take her first sight. Her preparations, beyond looking again over the readiness of the instrument, consisted mainly of willing herself not to get sick.

Steadying herself against the quarterdeck rail, she raised the sextant to her eye and waited for the ship to ride to the top of the next swell. From that highest vantage point, she sighted the horizon through the tube. Two or three inches beyond the end of the tube was the small square of glass, clear on its left half and a mirror on the right. She had done this many times, she told herself, and now must simply do it again. Ignoring the new importance of her measurements, Mary put the horizon in the middle of the clear side of this horizon glass and moved the pointer to bring the sun's reflected image into the mirror.

The ship slid back into the trough before Mary could make an accurate measurement, but the pointer was close to where it should be. A few more seconds on the next swell, and she would be able to make the needed fine adjustments. The ship rose, sliding up the smooth face of the sloping water. Mary felt her stomach rise with it and felt as though she were about to throw up. She tried to will away the feeling. Let me do this first, she thought.

As the ship reached the crest, she raised the tube to her eye.

Looking through the sight, holding it on the horizon, intensified the feelings in her stomach. In the space of a second, her ability to control the rising nausea was gone. There was no stopping it now. The observation would have to wait.

Dropping the sextant to hold it at her side, she rushed to the port rail, reaching it just as the contents of her stomach surged up into her throat. Throwing her head out over the side, she vomited into the sea.

The waves quickly carried away the evidence of the act, but nothing could relieve Mary of the ignoble feelings that came with it. Half the crew was no doubt watching her and was fully aware that their fate was in her hands. Far beyond the distaste of the moment, she was even more sorry that it had been witnessed by the very men she needed to convince of her competence. As she spit the last of the burning vomit from her mouth and ungraciously wiped her lips with the sleeve of her coat, she resolved to turn away from the rail with all the dignity she could muster. She had gotten sick, and everyone knew it, but she was determined that she would regain control of the situation.

She tilted her head back and looked to the horizon, ignoring the turbulent water rushing past. A deep breath, and then another. The air smelled good, as sea air should, and for the moment, at least, she felt better. She decided that she should take advantage of what was certain to be a brief respite. "Now," she said to herself.

She straightened up and turned back to the waiting Timothy Hare. He tried, without success, to pretend he had not seen what happened.

Mary spoke first. "I seem to be unaccustomed to the deck, Mr. Hare. Too much time in the cabin, I suppose."

"I suppose so, ma'am." Hare was quiet for a moment and seemed to be searching for the right thing to say. Finally, he said, "Is there anything I can get you?"

Mary made it a point to smile. "No, Mr. Hare. I just want to get this observation made."

Without looking back along the deck to see if the crew was watching, she again took up her braced position against the quarterdeck rail. She raised the sextant to her eye to see the horizon through the horizon glass, and waited for the ship to ride up a swell. The sun's image, captured by the shaded mirror at the top of the sextant, near the pivot point of the pointer arm, was reflected to the mirror half of the horizon glass. At the moment she felt the ship reach the crest, Mary moved the pointer to bring the sun into line with the horizon, adjusting the mirror until the lower edge of the sun's disk was exactly even with the horizon. She deftly tightened the clamp, locking the pointer into place against the scale, and pulled out Joshua's watch to check the time.

"There," she said, taking out a pencil and marking the time and angle on a small piece of paper. "One more will do us well."

Hare congratulated Mary upon her success, and Mary glanced over at him. The earnest look on his face showed that he was as pleased as she was. Well, she thought, almost as pleased.

"In five minutes, I'll take another. Perhaps one more after that. Counting the sunrise, that should give us a good plot."

"I hope so," said Hare. "I think it will cloud up again before long."

Mary, busy with the sextant, had not noticed, but a look at the sky proved the mate to be right. The sky directly overhead was still obscured, and now a new line of clouds was advancing from the east. The window of blue was starting to close.

Over the next ten minutes, she took two more observations, each time forcing herself to ignore the queasy stirring in her stomach. Noting the times of the observations and the angles of the sun, she left the deck to return to the cabin. As she started down the steps off the poop, a single cloud scudded in front of the sun, briefly casting a shadow across the ship. The sun just as quickly reappeared, but Mary could see that the sunshine was to be a temporary phenomenon. The clouds were about to reclaim the sky, just as they had for days.

Down in the cabin, she checked on Joshua, still unconscious on the bed, and went to work at the desk. By comparing the time on Joshua's watch with the time in Greenwich, England, and the declination, or angle, of the sun with that published in the almanac, she was able to perform the calculations required to fix the position of *Neptune's Car*. She wished she could have the luxury of a noon sight.

It would have made the calculations much simpler and the fix more accurate. Still, the early morning sights, provided she carefully corrected the inherent errors, would fix their position within two or three miles. She had to be careful, though. Even tiny errors in angle and time, when advanced across the charts, could magnify into large differences.

She figured altitudes and angles of the sun to plot each of the four timed sights and made a mark on the chart for each. One mark was out of line with the others, and she dismissed it as an erroneous observation. Using her ruler, she drew a straight line to pass, as closely as possible, through the other three. Somewhere on that line was *Neptune's Car*. Using the noted time and tables from the almanac, she then determined a second line, intersecting the first. Now she knew where on the first line they were, and drew a small circle where the lines crossed. She had her position.

She noted the last mark that Joshua had plotted, dated three days earlier. For three days the compass and estimated speed had been their only means of navigation.

Using the parallel rulers, she measured the distance between her mark and Joshua's. Four hundred and ninety miles. She had hoped for better, but could not be disappointed, either, considering the weather. It was also encouraging that they had remained almost perfectly on course.

Her plot showed the ship to be only a few miles north of the islands marking the entrance to the Straits of Le Maire, the beginning of the Drake Passage around the cape. The sun had shown its face just in time. Realizing how close they had come to land without knowing it, Mary chastised herself for not keeping up with their position from Joshua's last fix. She had been preoccupied with caring for him, but all the care she had to give would be futile if they ran up on the reefs and shoals waiting not so very far ahead.

As it was, her calculations showed the ship to be nearly in line with the entrance to the narrow strait, requiring only a slight turn to port to sail down the middle of the passage. She was extremely pleased by the good position, and felt that God must be with them, after all.

Not wishing to leave the warmth of the cabin, she sent for Hare.

"Continue for an hour on this course," she said, "then steer two points to the east. And Mr. Hare, watch for shallows. We are at Le Maire, and the channel may not always be wide."

The rounding of Cape Horn, long anticipated and long dreaded, was beginning.

CHAPTER 18

Command

The clouds did return, making the sun's appearance all too brief, and with the clouds came the storms.

Mary was not surprised. To enter the waters of Cape Horn and not have storms would be the surprise. Neither she nor anyone else on board *Neptune's Car* expected any semblance of fair weather to last. She was pleased merely to have had a chance to take a good sight. Having a firm position fix was a great comfort. Still, worried that she may have erred, she instructed Hare to make frequent soundings with the lead line as they slid through the Straits of Le Maire.

"Once clear of those shoals and back into open water," she said, "I will regain my confidence. Until then, keep an eye on the water's depth."

After the brief morning clearing, the rest of that day had seen thickening clouds that foretold of weather to come. The winds had remained steady, though, and when Mary felt safe from hidden shallows, Hare set the sails to take full advantage of them.

Night fell, black and clouded. With no moon to silhouette the sea against the sky, the long clipper pushed on into the invisible sea. Sure of the position Mary had plotted and secure in the knowledge that there were no land masses lying in wait, Hare left the sails set for best speed. Wary of other ships, a watch was kept from the fore-mast trucks, for this passage was, for its apparent expanse, narrow compared to the open ocean. Should a ship approach, a lookout might see its light, feeble though it might be, just as *Neptune's Car* carried its own beacon.

Storms carry their own light, in lightning that announces their procession. But not always. A storm, if it chooses, can come up unseen, like a predator. This night's storm approached in just such a way.

Its arrival, during the early hours after midnight, was announced by a sudden rising wind, followed immediately by stronger gusts. Without warning, high winds and massive waves slammed the vessel from the starboard side, rolling the ship hard to port. The sails, set for the much more moderate prevailing wind, took the full brunt of the gust.

In the cabin, Mary had awakened from a snatched bit of sleep in her chair and was leaning over Joshua when the sudden roll pitched her forward into the bed. Her legs slammed against the narrow top of the retaining board, and she cried out in pain as she sprawled across her husband.

She lay there for a moment, rubbing the bruising pain in her legs, and waited for the ship to right itself. It seemed to take an interminably long time. She could imagine the activity on deck. It was almost certain, judging by the amount of roll, that the crew had not expected whatever weather had struck the ship.

After a few minutes, Mary lifted herself off the bed and regained the floor, adapting her footing to the extreme angle of the deck. After seeing to it that Joshua had not slipped into some uncomfortable position, she went to the pitcher of water, literally pulling herself up the sloped floor to the basin stand, to wet the cloth for what seemed to be the ten thousandth time. She placed it on his forehead and then went around the room picking up items that had fallen from their places.

In a corner, against the wall, she found her silver-plated hand mirror.

"Oh," she said to herself, seeing that it was cracked, a distorting line running diagonally across the glass. She saw the reflection looking back at her from either side of the break, and wondered if she really looked that tired and haggard. Surely she could blame the light, she hoped, and the lateness of the hour.

The ship slowly regained its keel, but standing was still difficult. To lie down was much easier, and the bed inviting, so she crawled in and lay with Joshua. He had slept soundly for most of the night, and perhaps would sleep soundly still. Mary ached to get a good sleep. She slid up against Joshua, finding solace in the familiar feel of his body, but wished he could find solace as well.

There were small signs of improvement. During the evening just past he had even stirred enough to have some soup, only the second time he had taken nourishment since his collapse. Several times before she had placed small amounts of broth in his mouth, hoping he could swallow it, but more often than not it only choked him as it ran down his throat or spilled from his lips onto the pillow and bedclothes. It had greatly encouraged her to see him eat. Now he was quiet and seemed to be sleeping peacefully.

Perhaps this nightmare will soon be over, she thought.

Overhead, she heard the muffled shouts and sounds of activity on the deck, and wondered how Hare was doing. She knew enough about the sailing of the ship to know that such a sudden shift of the deck meant unexpected strong winds. She hoped he was not having too much trouble.

The first light of dawn came a few hours later. Mary had slept some but was often awake, listening to the ship. The hurried sounds of the deck had returned to a normal pace, but there were still more than the usual number of orders being shouted out. She suspected that there had been some damage from the wind.

There was also an odd scraping sound that lasted for a few seconds, was silent for a moment, and then began again. The sound seemed vaguely familiar, but she could not quite place it.

Slipping away from Joshua, she quietly dressed for the outside. The air seemed more frigid than before. She wondered if it was really colder, or if she had just become accustomed to Joshua's warm body. Her coat and boots on, hood tied close around her face, she opened the door from the saloon to step out on deck. A cold blast of air almost sent her back into the relative warmth of the cabin.

The world outside was vastly different from the cloudy but dry day she had left the afternoon before. Everything had turned white. A layer of snow blanketed the deck and covered the windward sides of the sails. Ice and snow coated the rigging and clung to the masts, leaving the bare lee sides as the only places on the ship not coated in white. The air itself was white, filled with still falling snow. The wind-driven flakes swirled across the deck, adding to the accumulation and pelting Mary's face.

Men worked to clear the snow from the deck, their shovels making the mysterious sound she had heard from below. Each scoopful was carried over to the side and heaved over the high railing into the sea, and the shovel brought back for more. The men trudged back and forth, weary from their labors.

Mary climbed the steps, cleared but still slippery, to the poop deck. There she found Hare, looking exhausted, his face drawn and red from the cold.

He worked his cheeks into a smile. "Morning, ma'am. Wintertime out here."

Mary could see the weariness in his eyes. "Indeed, Mr. Hare. What a difference a night has made."

"It was quite a night."

"I suspected as much when I found myself unable to stand up."

"I'm sorry for that. Weather caught me off guard."

Mary studied his face. He looked as though he was ashamed to have let her down. "I'm sure it was unavoidable, Mr. Hare." She looked about at the men working to clear snow off the deck. "It appears that you are dealing with the situation."

"The men have worked hard."

"Joshua has always said that we must deal with the adversities as they arrive."

Hare smiled again. This time it seemed to come with a little less effort, as if talking had loosened his facial muscles. "Adversity we have had."

Mary looked along the length of the ship and saw the men working to repair torn sails and broken rigging. "I can see the evidence of that."

"Most of the trouble has been taken care of," Hare said. "Another hour and she will be as good as new."

"What happened? A sudden storm?"

"Very sudden. We never saw it coming. I called for shortened sail, but there was no time. Lucky to still have all our spars. She's a strong ship, ma'am. The first gust pushed the lee rail underwater."

Mary formed a picture in her mind of the ship rolling far over to its side, the tips of the yardarms brushing the waves, and tons of ice-cold seawater flooding over the deck and all who were on it. "I suppose we are fortunate we are still upright."

"Indeed, ma'am. She would not have taken much more. As it was, the water on the deck left the ship terribly top-heavy. The recovery was awful slow."

Mary listened while he described the events of the last few hours. The force of the wind had ripped the main topgallant to shreds and carried away a large part of the foremast's rigging. Two of the triangular fore staysails were torn from the ship and lost to the froth of the sea. With his rigging torn away, the foremast lookout could only wrap his arms and legs around the thick mast, itself bending under the strain, and hold on for his life. The loose sails stood away from the leaning foremast like huge wind-whipped pennants, defying the crew to come and get them.

But get them they did. Even while *Neptune's Car* was still righting itself, the men had started into the rigging, climbing aloft into the fierce gale. They ignored the cold numbness of their fingers as they fought to hang on, holding fast to the ratlines that were their only connection to the ship — indeed, to life, for to fall into the waves was certain death.

Despite the danger, there was advantage to going aloft. Those left on deck sloshed through ice-cold water, knee deep at times, as they struggled to bring the ship back into trim. As they worked, more water broke over the starboard rail, high up the tilted deck, falling on them in heavy sheets of drenching cold.

Those aloft, at least, suffered only the sting of wind-flung shards of icy water. They held to the wet and frozen rigging, difficult enough when the ship was whole, and stuck to the task at hand. They had no choice. The tossing, sea-swept ship below them was the only firm thing in their world, the only refuge from the watery void that was all encompassing, all surrounding. There was nowhere to go for safety but the ship itself, and now that the ship had suffered damage, there was nothing to do but repair it.

All about the foremast and its yards were men clinging to the ship as they toiled away at their repairs. Mary saw that the shredded main topgallant had been replaced by one slightly more gray in color and showing more wear. The replacement was an older sail, intended for use in lighter winds.

"It hasn't been easy," Hare said. "The darkness, the wind, the ice—there has been much effort to make small progress. At least the snow has almost stopped. A little while ago I could not see the bow."

Mary looked around and saw that the visibility across the sea was perhaps a half mile, but no more. "Hopefully the worst is over," she said.

"Yes, I hope. It comes and goes, though."

The pair stood by the rail, looking out over the main deck, and were silent for a minute. Then Hare said, "The men have served well."

Mary's simple, "Good," did not begin to show her gratitude.

Hare waited another minute and then said, "Ma'am, would you mind if I went below for a bit? Warm up, maybe have some tea?"

Mary was surprised that he was asking her. She did not think it her place to approve his actions. Nevertheless, she answered him. "Of course, Mr. Hare. Please go rest."

"Thank you ma'am. I won't be long."

"Take whatever time you need. The men seem to have things in hand."

A smile slowly spread over Hare's face. "You have the ship, Captain Mary."

Before Mary could respond, he turned and went down the steps. A few seconds later he disappeared into the cabin.

She was aghast. Surely he did not mean that she was in charge of the ship. She looked back at the helmsman, standing in the cold wind by the wheel. He seemed unconcerned that there was no officer on deck and no one from the crew standing in.

She stepped back toward him and tried to act nonchalant as she wiped a thin layer of snow off the binnacle. She looked at the compass and then casually said, "Who has been taking the watch when Mr. Hare leaves the deck?"

"Mr. Irwin, most often."

"The cook?"

"Aye, ma'am."

"Should we have him here, now, do you think?"

"I think that now he is cooking breakfast, ma'am."

"I see. I was just wondering if Mr. Hare had intended to leave the deck unattended."

"I believe, ma'am, that I heard him leave it with you."

CHAPTER 19

Storm Damage

Mary's turn at command of the watch passed uneventfully. Hare came back on deck after only a little more than a half hour and apologized for being gone as long as he was.

"I found myself dozed off," he said.

"You should have stayed longer. I'm sure you needed the rest."

Hare shrugged. "I'll catch up on my sleep later. I will say, though, storms two nights in a row have been trying."

Mary looked up at the lightening sky. "Maybe we will get a break."

"That would be good. Give us time to get the rigging back in order."

Mary had been watching the crew working at the foremast lines. Their work was hampered by the ice and wind, and they had yet to get everything back to where it belonged. Several lines, normally tight and secure, still hung limp and useless, swaying in the wind. "I'm sorry I missed all the excitement."

Hare said, "It was exciting all right. We were within a hair of losing the fore topmast altogether. And the mainmast was pretty strained."

"You seem to have handled it well."

"I was scared as hell." Hare caught himself. "Sorry, ma'am."

Mary smiled at this glimpse into Hare's personality.

Their conversation stopped as Hare studied the sea. The snow had stopped, but that was the only improvement. As they talked, the wind started to increase again, *Neptune's Car* riding into markedly higher and rougher waves. At first, Mary thought it only a passing gust, but the gust did not die away. Mary felt sea spray, where before she had stayed mostly dry.

Hare shouted an order to a man standing midship. "Mr. Greene, ready the men to bring in the main course."

Greene's reply was lost to the sound of the wind, but his arm waved in acknowledgment, and he turned and called out orders to others. Within minutes men on the deck had eased the main sheets and tacks and hauled up on the clew lines and buntlines, pulling the mainsail up to its yard. As the wind spilled from the huge sail, others aloft fought the gale to gather the sail as it came up to them. The thin crust of ice coated the foot ropes, and the men had to pay close attention to their footing as they leaned over the thick yard to gather an arm's reach of canvas at a time and pull it against the yard to gasket it into place.

With over two-thirds of the canvas furled against the yards, *Neptune's Car* was largely bare of sail, but those remaining in place held enough wind to put a definite bend in the masts. Hare studied them, judging the strain.

"Helm," he called back toward the wheel, "come a point to."

The helmsman responded. "One point to. Aye, sir."

The bow turned slightly upwind, effectively reducing the side load against the ship. The turn also changed the angle of the sails relative to the wind, and Hare called out another order.

"Mr. Greene," he shouted to his man down on the main deck, who at the moment was not far from the railing, "let's get braced up another point to the wind. I think it is here for a while."

"Aye, sir. I believe you are right."

Mary watched the men loosen the lines to the upwind side of the yardarms and haul on the lee lines, bracing to a sharp angle, with the starboard tips of the long yards some forty feet ahead of the port ends. The sails now faced more directly to the wind, the better to move the ship.

Along with the sharp bracing, yards were cockbilled, with the windward ends pulled down and the lee side raised, keeping them level with the sea rather than perpendicular to the tilted masts, to keep the wind from being lost over the top of the sails.

From her viewpoint by the stern, seeing the yards braced and tilted into the wind reminded Mary of a drunken man stumbling down the street, pitched forward and at the same time falling sideways.

As the wind increased, Hare had more sails taken in, until each mast was down to one square sail. The staysails and jibs, small triangular fore and aft rigs between the masts and the bow, were left in place, as was the spanker, straining between its gaff and boom that extended out over the stern from the mizzenmast.

The seas became rougher, with waves of fifteen feet, and sometimes twenty, smashing together from all different directions, their tops exploding from the impacts. Long beards of frothy spray tore off the crests, shearing in the wind. The heavy hull of *Neptune's Car* bulled its way through, taking part in the melee, and the sea fought back, hurling itself at the sides of the ship, breaking its waves over the deck.

Mary decided she had seen enough. She would leave the weather to Mr. Hare. Any good she could do would be below, in the cabin tending Joshua. She had just reached the door to the cabin when a rogue wave, thirty feet high, assailed the starboard bow, its mass as great as the ship's. The two forces met, and neither wanted to yield. *Neptune's Car* blocked the path of the wave, stopping the mountain of water in its tracks, and the wave did the same to the ship.

The water disintegrated into a hundred million particles of spray, its energy bursting over the railings, the decks, the masts. The ship, with most of its motive force furled against the yards, slammed against the hard wall of water and shuddered to a stop. Mary lost her grip on the door latch and was thrown down onto the deck boards. She tried to catch herself, but her knees absorbed most of the fall. A second later she was covered with ice-cold water. Shockingly cold. It washed over her with enough volume to lift her off the deck and float her several feet toward the lee side. She thought for a moment she was being washed overboard until the water receded and she felt the deck boards under her knees again.

Getting her bearings, she stood up, being careful not to fall again. She felt a hand grip her arm.

"Are you all right, ma'am?"

The anxious voice belonged to Timothy Hare. He had seen her fall and hastened to her side.

She pushed her wet hair out of her face, taking stock of herself. "Yes, Mr. Hare, I think so."

Hare eyed her, as if to make sure, and turned his attention back to the ship. Looking aft, he shouted, "Helm, heave to!" To the bow, he called out, "You men, there, sheet home tight that jib! Mr. Greene! Mr. Greene!"

Mary had seen Greene at the helm during the voyage, and he and the cook were apparently Hare's choices as interim officers. Hare was looking about the deck for him when his calls were answered from above. Looking up, Mary and Hare saw Greene in the mizzen rigging. A line had become entangled with another, and he was working at separating the two.

Hare called up to him. "Good, there. Have them check all the rigging, Mr. Greene. And let's be ready to fall off, if need be."

"Aye, sir, aye. Might you call all hands for me?"

"Of course." Cupping a hand by his mouth to be heard toward the bow, Hare called for all hands. The order was promptly relayed to the forecastle and quickly answered.

Mary waited until he had the crew back at their tasks, and then gently said, "I'm all right, Mr. Hare."

Hare looked at her questioningly.

"My arm?" she said.

Hare glanced down and saw that he was still gripping her tightly. "Oh," he said, quickly letting go. "I'm sorry, ma'am."

Mary smiled. "I appreciate your concern."

"It frightened me when I saw you get washed over."

"It was a little disconcerting for me as well."

Another large wave rocked them. This time the ship took the brunt of the water without incident, but the entire vessel, all 216 feet of it, was continuously tossed about. There was no moment that any sort of steady heading was being held. *Neptune's Car* appeared to be in the hands of the weather.

Standing in the midst of the fury, Hare said, "I thought for a minute I had lost you, ma'am."

"I was not so sure, myself, of my fate."

They braced each other through another roll of the ship, and then Hare said, "I don't think I could stand it if something happened to you."

The concern in Hare's voice caused Mary to stop and take a good look at his face. His expression was one of tender caring, as if she meant more to him than he dared admit. That realization came to her as a completely unexpected revelation, yet it did not seem out of place. For a moment she only looked blankly at him, unable to absorb her own thoughts. The sound of the storm left her, and for a few seconds the scene around her was quiet and still. For that instant the import of Hare's concern seemed perfectly expected, and perfectly right. That it seemed so right was disquieting, and Mary did not know what to say.

In the next instant, the roar of the storm returned to her ears, and she forced any thoughts but those of the present situation from her mind. The ship, she thought, I must keep my thoughts on the ship.

"What next, Mr. Hare?" she asked as the deck fell into yet another trough. "Will the masts stand this weather?"

Hare offered a little shrug. "We'll see. We were dead stopped there for a minute, and I thought we were going aback, but we have some wind in our sails now. If we can keep any headway at all, we should be all right. I'd rather not have to fall off."

Falling off, Mary knew, meant turning and running before the wind. Not only would that send *Neptune's Car* in the wrong direction, it also presented some danger in water this rough. Should following seas overrun the stern, the ship could be placed in mortal danger. She understood Hare's concerns.

By the lee rail a seaman was struggling to haul in a line. He pulled with all his weight, but the wind was pulling with its own, and the wind was stronger than the man. No other crewman was nearby, and Hare left Mary's side to aid him. Together, the two men worked to restore the line to its rightful place.

The sea was a jumbled mess, moving all around and in all directions. The water seemed intent upon breaking away from the surface of the ocean, building into sharp waves that leaped up into the air, into the wind, shearing off into long strands of foam. Water rose up and smashed against the interloping hull of the ship, a wall of dark green that poised for half a second before cascading over the rails and onto the deck. Heavy spray rose to the highest tops of the masts, its mist clinging to the rigging and adding to the layers of ice.

Mary again decided to return to the cabin, and she started back across the pitching deck. Again she was stopped.

A call from the aft end of the ship made her look up, and she saw the helmsman fighting to hold the wheel. He was hanging by the spokes, the entire weight of his body applied to the task. Holding ropes, used to tie the wheel in place, lay near his feet, but the frequent adjustments needed in the storm precluded their use. It was a time when the wheel had to be manhandled, and one man was not enough. She looked around, and saw no one who was not already occupied. Hare was still at the stubborn line and had not heard the helmsman call.

Mary considered her place. Did she dare? Another gust, and the ship lurched sideways among the waves. The helmsman was barely holding course, and she knew the importance of keeping the bow into the wind. She hurried up the tilted stairs, holding tight to the hand rail, and crossed the quarterdeck to the wheel.

Pulling to starboard with all his might, the seaman strained to hold the wheel. Mary took up a position on the other side of the wheel and grasped one of the spokes. Its smooth round wood seemed foreign to her hands. This was the domain of the sailors. Bracing herself with a firm footing, she pushed up, hoping her slender weight would relieve some the effort of the exhausted young man on the far side of the wheel.

Through the wheel, Mary felt the weight of the rudder, far below the deck, its long length straining to hold the hull against the will of the wind.

"Thanks, ma'am," said the sailor on the far side of the wheel. He spoke through clenched teeth, still straining to hold the ship.

He looked frightened. He was young, only twenty or so, and very fair. Probably Scandinavian. "I'm not much, but I'll try to help until someone else gets here," she said.

Together, they held the ship steady. Sometimes they eased the wheel. A moment later they would be working with all their might to hold it against the wind. Mary was amused by the helmsman's politeness. When a strong gust of wind or heavy wave rocked the ship, requiring instant adjustment, he would say, in his Nordic accent, "If you please, ma'am, let's ease off a bit."

All along the ship, from mizzen to bowsprit, the crew worked to keep the remaining sail in trim. It was constant work, due both to the changing conditions and to the continuing efforts to repair the gear failures. There was a fine line between heading too much into the wind and being caught too much across it. Throughout was the danger of having sails blow out or having the masts becoming sprung.

It was in the midst of this balancing act that a voice high in the yards cried out, most unexpectedly, "Sail ho!"

Mary looked around the horizon. At first she saw nothing. Then the crest of a swell lifted *Neptune's Car*, and from the better vantage point she saw the ship.

It was a mile or so away, off the starboard bow, heading the opposite direction. It disappeared behind the seas for a moment then popped back into view. Its long dark hull identified it almost certainly as another clipper ship, but without the tall masts of a clipper. The foremast was stubby and short, and the mainmast was shorter by a third than usual. It was several seconds before Mary realized that the ship had been severely demasted. The top two-thirds of the foremast had been carried away. The only foremast yard left was the lowest, and it was without sail. The only canvas on the forward portion of the ship was a single jib rigged from the top of the broken foremast to the bowsprit. The mainmast had lost the topgallant mast and its yards. Just as *Neptune's Car* was doing now, the ship had battled the storms, but the storms had won.

Hare came up from the main deck. At his side was another crewman. "Here, ma'am. Let this man take over for you."

Relieved, Mary said, "Most gladly, Mr. Hare." Surrendering her post, she turned her attention to the other ship. "Do you see that ship, Mr. Hare? Look at those masts."

"I see them, ma'am. And we need to decide what we should do."

"Do?"

"Aye, ma'am. Do you see that flag on its mizzen?"

The ship was nearer now, and would soon be abeam the starboard rail. Mary saw that it was carrying the stars and stripes, but in a most peculiar way. The flag, blown forward by the wind, was upside down.

"What in the world—" Mary stopped in midsentence, and answered her own question. "That's a distress flag."

"Yes, ma'am."

"What do we do about it?"

"By fair sense of duty and nautical law," Hare said, "we are bound to respond. Which puts us in a bit of a dilemma. If we attempt to turn now, we might be in more distress than they."

A wave broke over the railing, casting a new spray of icy water over them. The deck heaved under their feet, and Mary grasped the gear housing for support. Hare looked as if he was waiting for a response.

"It is up to you, Mr. Hare," she said, shouting to be heard over the wind. "You know our limitations, both of this ship and ourselves, better than I."

Hare looked indecisive. Seconds went by.

"What do you think, Mr. Hare?" The wind snatched Mary's words and flung them into the gale. "Can we assist them?"

Hare studied the passing ship, now abeam, and said, "If we are to assist, we must do it now."

The crippled ship had closed to within about a half mile, near enough to reveal the damage done to its masts. What was left of the fore topmast ended in splinters just above the fore course yard, now seen to be hanging at a useless angle. On top of the forward deck cabin was a section of mast and a tangle of rigging. Mary realized it was wreckage that had been cut away and left where it had fallen.

The mizzenmast was still whole, but above a single topsail held only tattered white streamers, shredded remains of blown-out sails. She looked for signs of the crew, but at first saw no one. Finally, she saw movement on the quarterdeck, and saw three or four tiny figures seeming to be looking toward them. She supposed the distant crew were anxiously watching for *Neptune's Car* to turn their way.

Hare was watching Mary. She felt that he knew what needed to be done and was waiting for her approval. "I agree, Mr. Hare. If we are to help, now is the time."

Hare immediately ordered all hands to their stations for a tack to starboard. "This is risky, turning across into this wind, but to wear ship around the other way under this amount of sail would take an hour. And almost surely take us too far away from them."

To wear ship, Mary knew, meant to turn downwind and around to reverse course. To tack across the wind was less time consuming, but was far more hazardous in strong winds. If successful, though, tacking would also position *Neptune's Car* closer to the other ship at the end of the maneuver.

The problem in tacking a square-rigged ship in high winds was that in midturn, as the bow faced directly to windward, the sails would be taken aback, blowing aft rather than forward. With rigging designed to support the sails before wind from the aft or side, wind from the bow put stress on lines intended to do little more than holding duty. With the roles of the rigging reversed, the result could be as simple as ripped sails and damaged rigging or as disastrous as demasting.

Mary, well aware of the danger, said, "Mr. Hare, will the wind allow us to do this?" She did not wish to voice doubt over his decision to tack, but fear of the consequences prompted her to speak.

"I hope. There is advantage to not having much sail out. Less to be taken aback against the masts. And I'll aim to turn between gusts. If we can catch the wind in a little lull as we come about, we will be all right. It is only the gusts that will do us in."

Mary did not like the phrase "do us in," but said only, "I have every confidence in you, Mr. Hare."

Hare smiled weakly, the wet spray dripping off his chin. "Let's just pray that it works out."

Mary looked at the passing ship, now off the stern quarter and beginning to move away. "I'm praying now, Mr. Hare."

Hare had the helmsman sail as close to the wind as he could without luffing the sail. The cockbill of the yards, so arduously performed only an hour ago, was taken out, and lines were loosened and readied. As soon as all was ready, Hare climbed a few feet up the mizzen ratlines for a longer view of the coming wind. Wrapping his arms in the rigging to hold himself in place, he studied the waves to windward, watching for the telltale signs of a break in the wind. Meanwhile, the passing ship was off the stern quarter and moving away.

With no time to spare, Hare took the first lull to come toward the ship, its approach foretold by wave tops that were not being sheared away into foam.

Just before the lull arrived, with wind of only twenty knots rather than forty, Hare shouted to be heard by the men waiting at the pin rails. "Haul the spanker amidship!" At the command, the spanker boom was pulled to a neutral position along the centerline of the ship. At the same time, Hare ordered the helm to put in right rudder, and the long bow of *Neptune's Car* began its swing into the wind. The fore staysail and jibs began to luff, losing their wind. A moment later the square sails did the same. Soon after losing their lift, the square sails began to back, blowing against the rigging and masts. Hare ordered the spanker brought hard to starboard to aid in the turn and called for the main yards to be hauled around into the new tack.

Timing was critical. If the yards were turned too soon, the sails would be faced too long into the wind and act as a brake, stopping the ship. Too late, and the amount of sail taken aback would be so large that the men would have great difficulty overcoming the wind to brace the yards into position. Either way, there was danger of losing all forward speed.

The ship was over halfway through the tack, making slow but steady progress, when the wind dealt a harsh and unexpected blow. The lull Hare counted on to enable a tack across the wind ended abruptly. The gale returned, not only stronger than before, but from a new direction, more from the west. It was now again off the starboard bow, in effect putting the ship in the position of being back at the beginning of the tack, but with no speed to give the rudder authority over the ship. In the space of a few seconds, Hare's carefully orchestrated tack degraded into a ship taken completely aback, with all yards braced for the wrong direction.

The ship's forward momentum stopped in an instant. All sails backed against their masts. The stays, forced into the unaccustomed role of supporting the masts, strained against the stress. Hare issued hurried commands.

Mary, watching from the deck, saw the panic on his face.

Fearing imminent failure of the stays as the ship began moving backward, making sternway, Hare shouted back to the helm, "Rudder hard to starboard! Spanker, haul to port, brace her up sharp!" Shouting toward the bow, he ordered the foremast yards braced to catch the wind and hopefully force the bow back to port before damage was done to the rigging. Once the commands were delivered, he could do nothing but await the result.

Mary felt her insides churn as she realized that the ship was in considerable danger of being overrun by the seas.

Until then Hare had remained up in the mizzen rigging. Now he climbed down to take a place near Mary, who had watched the aborted turn from the quarterdeck rail, to which she held tightly in an attempt to keep her footing on the deck. A wave bearing down from the port side beat against the ship. A second later another wave, just as big and powerful, slammed from starboard, rocking the ship in the opposite direction. With no forward speed the ship wallowed in the swells, for the moment at the full mercy of the sea.

On the main deck the men fought in knee-deep water to bring the ship off the wind, bracing tight the starboard sheets while belaying the port side, knowing that as soon as the ship fell off before the wind all the work would have to be undone and reversed.

Hare, soaked by the icy water, took stock of the situation. "Helm," he called back to the two men manhandling the wheel. "As we gather sternway, hold the rudder to bring us around to port."

To Mary, he said, "Sorry, ma'am. The wind shift got us." His face was red from the cold, his breathing hard from the exertion and excitement. "It was not a good tack to begin with. Not enough sail out to steer right."

Mary knew Hare had done his best. "The wind is not cooperative," she said, her voice raised against the howl of the gale. "Tell me, Mr. Hare, what we can do now?"

"Once we get a little wind back in the sails, we can wear ship around. Like I suppose we should have done in the first place."

Mary looked around for the other ship and found that during the tack it had moved nearly a mile to the stern, and was receding quickly. "Do we have time to do that?"

"And keep the other ship in sight? I don't know. Right now we are adrift. She doesn't seem to want to fall off."

"The waves are shifting us around so much," Mary said. "First one way, then the other." As if to illustrate the point, at that moment a cascade of water broached the deck, washing over both her and Hare, forcing them to kneel at the rail and hold tight with both arms.

As the water receded, Mary stood back up, aided by Hare. Water had penetrated her clothing, and she felt the cold rivulets trickling between her breasts and into her undergarments. Shivering, she took a long look at the departing ship, now just a black outline on the gray horizon. A clear decision formed in her mind.

"Mr. Hare, we must abandon our efforts to gain the other ship. Once turned around, I fear we will not be able to find it, and if we do, not be able to safely approach it."

Hare appeared to be relieved. "You wish to resume course, then?"

"I am afraid so. We must trust them to do without our aid. Do you think them able?"

"Depends." Hare said. Another wave splashed over the rail. "They are not yet adrift. I mean, they seem to have helm control, and some sail. We have been in the heavy weather for what, an hour? They should be out of it soon. We haven't gone very far."

Mary agreed. "Not far at all."

"And you are right. It would be difficult to bring the ships together in these seas. Still, I wish we could offer aid."

Hare seemed torn. He clearly felt it was his duty to assist the passing ship, but he had not been able to make the turn. Mary reminded herself that he was, after all, inexperienced. Until a few months ago he had been one of the foremast hands. To command the ship through the storm was no doubt trying to him. She attempted to ease his mind.

"The decision is mine, Mr. Hare. My goal is to get my husband to San Francisco and medical help. I believe we should proceed to that end. We know what the captain of that other ship does not, that he can expect fairer weather within the hour. I think we should trust he will soon find it."

Neptune's Car drifted among the shearing waves for several more minutes before finally regaining use of the sails. By then the other vessel was but a ragged mark on the distant sea. Watching it fade from sight, Mary said, "What ship was that, do we know?"

"I don't know," Hare said. "I didn't recognize her."

Mary wondered if the captain was anyone she or Joshua knew.

With the distressed ship out of sight, *Neptune's Car* continued its struggle against the wind and water. Neither Hare nor Mary mentioned it again. Hare resumed issuing commands to the men, and Mary went back down to Joshua.

It was some time before she did not dwell upon the fact that the ship had passed by, torn and battered by the dark weather, needing aid and receiving none.

CHAPTER 20

Against the Wind

Under the best of conditions, the fastest clippers could sometimes sail four hundred miles in a twenty-four-hour period. To do so was a rare accomplishment, having been done less than a dozen times. That it had been done, though, set a standard for which to strive. Any day over three hundred miles was considered quite successful, although most captains would never let their satisfaction show as they continued their hard driving.

It was those days when scarcely fifty miles were made that infuriated them.

A week had passed since Mary's morning sight at the entrance to the Straits of Le Maire. The sun had just made its first appearance since, allowing her to take a midday sight and get a firm fix on their position. Her calculations complete, she stood over the chart on Joshua's desk contemplating the new lines drawn to plot their position. She was relieved to find the ship to still be more or less on course. Not as far along as she had hoped, but on course. Hare was doing an excellent job of keeping them on her dead-reckoning course.

In the eight days since Joshua's last sight, before his incapacitation left Mary and Timothy Hare in command, *Neptune's Car* had progressed fewer than five hundred miles. The week had been spent in almost constant storm. Some days had been better than others, but none were good. The ship continuously pitched and rolled, heaving in the jumbled seas, and the men fought the elements on an icy deck and frozen rigging. Still headed more south than west, they were not yet far enough along to make the turn for a run past the cape. Until then, until they headed west and attacked the wind head on, the worst part of Cape Horn was still ahead.

The only good thing was that Mary's morning sickness had abated to only a mild queasiness.

Joshua, if anything, was worse.

He had periods of wakefulness, but they were seldom coherent. When he spoke, his words were slurred and disjointed, and Mary rarely had any idea of what he was trying to say. Still, she tried to carry on conversations, speaking to him in normal tones of normal things.

"I think," she might say, "that today we should have better weather."

His reply usually consisted of syllables that never seemed to belong together.

Mary wondered if, in his mind, he was making any sense.

He subsisted almost exclusively on liquids, with only mush and the occasional bit of bread to supplement the broth he was sometimes able to eat and sometimes only let run down his chin. Mary wiped the mess off his face, off his neck, off his chest, and, as best she could, off his bedding.

More difficult to contend with were the discharged urine, which without warning flooded the sheets, and the thin, runny diarrhea that filled the air with a sickening stench. Mary, her stomach just past the worst of the morning sickness, was barely able to stay in the cabin with the smell.

The wet weather made cleaning the bedclothes almost impossible. They could be washed, but would not dry unless hung for hours by the small stove in the saloon, and even then retained a dampness from the humid air. Eventually she all but abandoned efforts to keep Joshua's sheets clean. There was only one spare set, and he soiled them faster than she could wash. To control the mess, she had a ripped sail cut into three-foot squares and used them as pads under his midsection.

Despite the unpleasant airs of the cabin, Mary usually stayed at Joshua's side and left the running of the ship to Timothy Hare, going topside only to offer the young mate some time below. Even though Hare had selected the cook, Irwin, and the sailor named Greene to aid him in commanding the crew, he was reluctant to leave his post. The constant demands of the weather made him worry that if he were not on deck, timely decisions might not be made.

Mary, who knew less about handling a ship than almost anyone on board, found that she was the only one who could order him to rest, and she began making it a point to go up and relieve him. She found that she enjoyed the time spent on deck, despite the cold, and the length of her stays gradually increased. She needed the break from the confines of the cabin, and started to enjoy the feel of command, even if she rarely did anything but stand and watch the crew work. At least on deck there was some activity, some movement, some visible progress. In the cabin, there was none.

Joshua sometimes stirred and spoke his monosyllable words, sometimes ate, sometimes even appeared to be lucid for a few minutes at a time, but for the most part he simply lay delirious or unconscious, under the spell of the fever that gripped him.

Mary never ceased to speak to him, in case he was hearing and understanding. Often, having nothing else to say, she read to him. Seeking comfort for both him and herself, she read long passages from the Bible. Those, she found, sometimes comforted her and sometimes only troubled her more. The time she spent in prayer, and there was a good deal of it, offered her hope but thus far no relief. Sometimes she read aloud from the medical book. Like prayer, the book was proving to be of little benefit, but it gave her words for Joshua to hear.

In the volume of Lord Byron's poetry, she found a marked page, and read it to him often.

Roll on, thou deep and dark blue Ocean—roll!
Ten thousand fleets sweep over thee in vain;

Man marks the earth with ruin—his control
Stops with the shore—upon the watery plain
The wrecks are all thy deed, nor doth remain
A shadow of man's ravage, save his own,
When for a moment, like a drop of rain,
He sinks into thy depths with bubbling groan—
Without a grave, unknelled, uncoffined, and unknown.

As often as she read that verse, Mary could never quell her fear that it might come to pass, that Joshua's unknelled, uncoffined body might end up being slipped into those deep and dark blue depths. Reading on, though, she was always lifted by the final stanza, and saw in the poet's words what drew Joshua to the sea.

And I have loved thee, Ocean! and my joy
Of youthful sports was on thy breast to be
Borne, like thy bubbles, onward; from a boy
I wantoned with thy breakers—they to me
Were a delight; and if the freshening sea
Made them a terror—'twas a pleasing fear,
For I was as it were a child of thee,
And trusted to thy billows far and near,
And laid my hand upon thy mane—as I do here.

Venturing out upon the world's oceans, Mary knew, involved certain risks. For those drawn to the sea, they were risks worth taking. With the pleasures of sailing, the feel of wind on the face and the flying spray, came dangers and challenges, but even those brought the satisfaction of facing a storm and prevailing over it.

Another risk, one not part of the sailing mystique and therefore not part of the lore, was the danger now facing Joshua. To become ill at sea, far from medical help, was a very real and constant possibility. Like the dangers of storms, it was a risk men of the sea considered worth taking. As she sat by Joshua's bed, though, Mary only despised the fates that had put her there.

If only Joshua were not sick, she thought, how much better things would be. She, too, could face the rounding of the cape with the eager anticipation of Byron's "pleasing fear." Instead, she was just afraid.

Her fear, which swelled in her heart and threatened to explode out of her chest, sometimes very nearly consumed her.

She longed to be back in Boston, within reach of her father's strong and loving arms, where her mother could advise her about carrying a child, where a physician could be summoned to administer healing to Joshua. She longed to be free of the damp and putrid air of the tiny cabin. She longed to be off this wretched, rolling ship. She wished to be in sunny climes, not the soaking, freezing ocean at the bottom of the world, thousands of miles from anything familiar.

She wished for anything besides what she had.

The next afternoon, or perhaps it was the day after that, Timothy Hare came down to the cabin and asked Mary if perhaps she thought they might have progressed far enough to start a turn to the west.

"We have kept careful track when throwing the chip," he said, "and I believe we may be far enough south."

He and Mary leaned over the chart. Her most recent fix had been plotted and marked by a tiny circle with the date noted beside it. Since then she had again been relying upon dead reckoning to keep up with their position.

She hesitated and said, "Tell me, Mr. Hare, do you know if today is the third of October, or is it the fourth?"

"Why, I think it is the third, ma'am."

Mary smiled. "I am very embarrassed, since I have been keeping the log, to have lost track of the days."

Hare glanced at the captain, lying silently on the bed. "It is understandable, ma'am. There is much on your mind."

"Nevertheless, I should be able to keep up with the date." She stood for a second, feeling subdued, and shook off the thought. "How far do you figure we have come in the last two days?"

"Well, we have been making four knots, and often five. Two days, that's forty-eight hours. That makes about two hundred miles, is that right?"

Mary worked the math in her head. "Yes. Two hundred, or perhaps more."

Hare nodded and turned to the chart. "Show me, then, where that would put us."

Mary took the ruler and asked, "You have been sailing south, still?"

"South by southwest."

She drew on the chart with a light pencil line. "Here," she said. "We should be about here, depending upon how much error we allow for."

The point she marked was well south of the Straits of Le Maire, which guarded the tip of the South American mainland where it hooked into the Atlantic. Or was it the Southern Ocean, circling the Antarctic? In the frigid seas approaching the cape, the distinction was blurred, where the name of the ocean lost its importance in the icy-cold waters.

"Then we should be able to turn."

Together, they examined the chart, its soundings marked in fathoms. *Neptune's Car* appeared to be safe from the shoals and shallows that extended beyond the tip of the continent.

"Yes," Mary agreed. "I think we should."

"I'll do it then," Hare said. "We'll set course to the southwest, even southwest by west, tomorrow morning. Maybe we will get around the cape in quick fashion."

"Could we be so fortunate?"

"I doubt it," said Hare.

As the ensuing days unfolded, Hare's doubt was proved correct. There was no good fortune in the rounding of Cape Horn. *Neptune's Car* made the turn to the west and immediately came face-to-face with gale-force winds. Hare tacked south, then north as far as he dared, then south again, tediously wearing ship for each course change. Even without having the sun for a good fix he could tell the ship was making little westward progress.

"I feel as though we are pacing back and forth on the same piece of ocean," he lamented.

Mary, with nothing of encouragement to say, remained silent.

On subsequent tacks Hare went farther south, sometimes for a half a day at a time, until concerns about ice drifting in otherwise open ocean compelled him to come about. Should *Neptune's Car* meet with one of these mostly submerged floes, damage to the hull could easily result. With the pounding of the sea alone enough to work loose the seams of the hull, forcing the caulk out and allowing the water in, it was easy to see how even a relatively small floe of ice could do the hull severe harm. A true iceberg, or even a smaller imitation, could do irreparable harm, to the point of caving in the hull. A wary watch was kept from the foremast truck, and often warned of danger ahead.

"Ice to port!" would be the call from above. The helm would steer clear of the obstruction and then, if no more ice accompanied the first, turn back on course.

Keeping watch was hard duty, requiring constant vigilance. From the platform a third of the way up the forward mast, high enough to be buffeted by the winds but not high enough to avoid the spray rising from the breaking waves, at least one man and sometimes two kept careful watch for hazards ahead.

An hour or two at a time on watch was enough, and other seamen then climbed the ratlines and took their turn. It was never long before their coats and hats were frozen stiff from the sea spray and rain. Hoary white frost accumulated on their eyebrows, and the exposed skin of their faces became numb from the cold. Finally, the next replacement arrived, allowing them to descend to the deck, where they spent some minutes pacing vigorously back and forth, trying to renew their circulation and return feeling to frozen feet.

Those on deck fared better only in that they were able to move about and let activity warm them, and sometimes manage to work in the lee of the gunwale or wall of the forward cabin, where the biting wind was at least partially blocked. They were, however, always wet. Oilcloth coats and hats pulled low only lessened the immediate impact of the incessant waves that reared up and over the ship.

The foremast hands fared the worst, but in seas rising to twenty, thirty, or even fifty feet, no part of the deck was immune from the water. The quarterdeck, domain of the ship's master, his officers, and passengers, was no less wet than the foredeck. As large as a clipper ship might be, it was but a chip of wood to the wrath of the ocean.

The ship was alternately assailed by freezing rain, snow whipping across the deck, and sleet storms heavy enough to blind the crew. Despite the wet and cold, Mary continued to venture out at least once a day from her watch over her husband. Hare would greet her on the quarterdeck and invariably admonish her for being out.

"You should stay below, ma'am. This is no weather to be out in."

"I needed to take some fresh air, Mr. Hare."

Timothy Hare smiled, his lips thin and blue. "Fresh air we have aplenty, ma'am. Take all you want."

Mary ignored his insistence that she stay below out of the weather and felt sure that Hare enjoyed having her on deck. Her presence broke the monotony of the watch, made all the more tedious by the lack of other officers with which to converse. Likewise, Mary enjoyed the time she spent with the young mate. After long hours of silence from Joshua, she needed time to talk with someone who could speak back, if only to exchange comments about the weather. Hare gladly filled the role, and a true friendship began to develop, although neither talked about it.

One noon she came up, hoping to find a sun to sight for navigation but finding only heavy gray clouds. Mary felt no hurry to leave the fresh air, and she spent a little time watching the crew at work. Some were aloft, chipping ice off the rigging and spars. It fell to the deck in slivers and shards, keeping those below wary of falling missiles.

"Cold and bitter work," she observed.

"Aye, ma'am, and never ending."

"Always more ice."

"Always more."

"And the men? Are they staying of good cheer?"

"I'm not sure I could call it good cheer."

A shower of ice fell from the mizzen rigging, twenty feet from where Mary and Hare stood. It crashed onto the deck and skittered in all directions. Mary looked up to see men pounding the stiff shrouds. "Perhaps *cheer* was a poor choice of word."

Hare, also watching the men, said, "I suppose they are grumbling no more than any crew would. Even less, I think. We are lucky to have a good lot."

"What of those whom Mr. Keeler claimed as allies?" Mary said. "Any stirring from them?"

"No, ma'am. If they still support Mr. Keeler, they are keeping pretty quiet about it."

"Do you suppose we have anything to worry about with them?"

"Who knows?" Hare turned stiffly toward Mary, the cold having pierced him to the core. "My feeling? I don't think we have any problem."

"Just the same, let's stay alert."

"Of course, ma'am."

Mary watched the crew work a little longer and said, "I may be worried for nothing. Joshua selected this crew, and he prides himself in picking good men."

"Aye, ma'am, I suppose he does."

Mary thought briefly about William Keeler, being held below deck. The one failure to choose well was not all Joshua's doing. But he had allowed himself to be swayed against his better judgment. Thinking of Keeler troubled her, and she forced the thought from her mind.

She lightly touched Hare's sleeve with a gloved hand. "He picked you as a suitable mate, did he not?"

"Yes, he did. I hope to not disappoint him."

"I don't think you will."

Mary saw in Hare's eyes a flicker of appreciation. For several seconds her thoughts lingered as she looked into the young man's face. His eyes were warm, by far the warmest thing she had seen of late. She found herself considering the contrast between Hare and Keeler, whose cold stares she had not missed at all.

The thought of Keeler, her first in several days, made her shudder. Her desire to forget ever knowing the man was strong, and she consciously pushed him out of her mind. Timothy Hare was a different story. She felt a sudden closeness to him, and wanted to touch his sleeve again. To touch his arm.

"You are my lifeline, Mr. Hare. I will be forever indebted to you."

Hare looked at her, his eyes soft. "And I you."

His hand raised toward her arm, wavered, and then dropped back to his side. Mary felt that he had the same thought as she had but dared not show it.

"Let's see if I get us around the Horn, first," he said. "Then you can be in my debt. Besides, perhaps I should be in yours. I can only sail the ship. You are steering it."

Mary smiled and withdrew a step, putting a little distance between them. "Very well. We are a team. But I am doing very little steering these days. I should certainly like to take another sight."

"The sun has been reluctant to show its face, hasn't it?" Hare paused and said, "I'm afraid that if you were to plot our position you would be disappointed."

"Difficult winds, still?" Mary asked the question already knowing the answer.

"Hard out of the west. But it shifts around. Seems when we tack south the wind turns to blow against us. If we turn north, the wind comes from the north. I can't seem to outsmart it."

Mary pulled her coat more closely against her. The cold seemed to soak all the way through her. She thought of the new life stirring inside her, and wondered if it, too, could feel the chill. "Sounds frustrating."

"Very."

"I am cold, Mr. Hare. I believe I have had all the fresh air I want. If you need me, I'll be below with Joshua."

"Yes, ma'am. I'll call you at the first glimmer of a sun."

Mary started toward the steps, but Hare called after her.

"Dare I ask, ma'am? Has there been any change?"

Mary knew he was referring to her husband, now into his second week of fevered and delirious illness.

"No, Mr. Hare. No change."

CHAPTER 21

Cape Horn

Winter was on its way out and the days of spring were coming on, but the deeper *Neptune's Car* went into the southern latitudes the shorter the days seemed to be. The night was six hours longer than the day, and when the sun did show, between belts of cloud, its trek across the sky was made in a shallow arc, its high point at noon still oddly low above the northern horizon. Mary worked through the narrow scale of differences of angle and made her plot.

Just as Hare suspected, she determined that they had made little westward progress. *Neptune's Car*, for all the miles traveled on back-and-forth tacks, was only marginally closer to the Pacific. She was beginning to wonder if they would ever get to San Francisco.

"Do you have any suggestions, Mr. Hare?"

She had ventured out to deliver the results of her fix to the second mate. The break that had permitted the view of the sun had already closed back up, the clouds blanketing the sky in thick wind-driven layers.

"I'm not sure, ma'am, what we can do." Hare's voice had a tone of frustration to it, even helplessness. "All I know is to keep up on tacking. Eventually we will get through."

"We hope."

"Aye. We hope. I've tried different angles to the wind, coming into it and falling off. Neither gets us any more west. I have tried more sail, and then have to take them back in before long."

"Too much wind, I suppose."

"Aye, ma'am. In normal times, maybe not. But all that ice aloft makes us more top-heavy. Crew can't bust it off fast enough. Causes the ship to heel over too much. So I must reduce sail."

"I see," Mary said, finding another reason to despise the cold.

Conversation lulled, and the two stood on the quarterdeck, watching the ship pounding through the waves. After several minutes, Hare said, "I believe it is time to start a tack back to the north. I hate to do it, though. The wind for this south tack has been better for the last hour or so."

Mary was puzzled. "Then, why are you turning?"

"I'm afraid that farther south will put us too deep into the ice."

"Oh." Mary thought hard before she spoke again. She normally refrained from questioning Hare's decisions, but felt compelled to ask, "Has there been a lot of drifting ice lately?"

"No. We have been lucky. Only isolated floes. But, I have no doubt that more is out there."

"I am sure you are right, Mr. Hare. But—and please forgive me for asking—if the winds are favorable right now and the ice is scarce, why not press on a little longer?"

Hare looked thoughtful, as if suddenly considering a new option. "I don't know. I suppose we could."

"We are making good speed now?"

"Fairly good, yes, ma'am."

"It is your business, Mr. Hare, not mine, to know these things, but is there any reason that we could not continue this course for another hour, or at least a half hour?"

"I . . . I guess not. I'll leave things as they are, and we will see what happens."

Mary felt that she was on the verge of usurping Hare's authority. She was sorry she had said anything, and said so.

Hare's smile seemed sincere. "Think nothing of it, ma'am. I am open for suggestions."

❧   ❧   ❧

Neptune's Car kept its south by southwest tack, with no significant ice seen for the remainder of the day. Hare stayed the course until coming darkness made a turn back north seem prudent.

The next morning, with the wind still favoring a southerly run, the ship was again turned that direction. During the afternoon, Mary went on deck. Hare met her with a smile.

"I am happy to say, ma'am, that venturing farther south seems to have benefited our progress. I must admit that my fears of ice have been unfounded."

"Hardly unfounded, Mr. Hare," Mary answered. "But I am pleased that a clear path presented itself. Let's hope our good fortune continues."

"Just the same, I have you to thank. Without your urging, I doubt I would have come this far south."

"I am sure the idea was already in your mind, Mr. Hare. You just had not acted upon it yet."

"Maybe so. But I had not the—what's the phrase?"

"The courage of your convictions?"

"Aye, ma'am, that's it."

Mary reflected for a moment, and then said, "My father once told me that courage of that nature is often the hardest to find. He also said it could be the most rewarding. I have tried to remember that."

Hare looked at her with a measuring eye and said, "I think you have learned well."

"Thank you, Mr. Hare."

As the ship struggled against the wind, Mary learned that the conflicts on board could not be fully dismissed. Mr. Irwin, the cook, returned to his galley from a turn of relieving Hare on the quarterdeck to find two of the foremast hands in his larder, huddled against the door of the room holding Keeler. They beat a hasty retreat, but not before the cook saw that they were communicating with the imprisoned mate through the door.

Irwin reported the incident to Hare, who questioned the men. They insisted they were simply checking up on Keeler, with no ill intent, but Hare was not so sure. The rounding of the cape was taking a long time, at the expense of a great deal of work from the crew.

It was easy to imagine that some of the men might think Keeler able to do a better job getting the ship around.

"Keep an eye on things," Hare said to the cook, "and let me know if we have any more visitors to your cupboard. To the crew, he issued a reminder that Keeler and his cell were off limits.

To Mary, he said, "It seems I may have been wrong when I thought there were no problems with the crew."

With the ship deep into the Southern Ocean, it was colder than ever, the temperatures well below freezing, but over a period of days it became apparent that the difference of a degree or two of latitude was having a positive effect upon progress. There was sea ice to be dealt with, but nothing that could not be circumvented, and the vessel was making noticeable gains against the wind.

Still, there were setbacks. As Hare sailed up and down the Drake Passage, beating his way westward, gains made over two full days were sometimes lost in the space of two hours. A vulnerable weakness may have been found in the strength of the weather, but Cape Horn was not giving up easily.

Ice on the ship became more of a problem. The crew worked constantly to clear the rigging and spars, beating, chipping, and chopping the ice away, using axes, knives, and bare hands to break away the accumulation. The deck, too, had its own layer of ice, as did the rails and every other surface. Each day's dawning revealed fresh layers of glazed coatings over the entire ship. Clearing away the ice was not just for safety when walking and working. Ice aloft on the spars and rigging made the ship top heavy, increasing roll and wallowing in the swells.

Only once did the drifting ice nearly prove a true and deadly danger. "Ice, ho!" came the excited cry, and a dozen faces turned to look, Mary's included, on deck to check the speed.

"Where?" Irwin was by the helm, and his voice had an impatient edge to it. "Which way?" From the lookout: "It's off the port bow. The port bow! Start a turn, by God!"

"Hard to starboard, boy," Irwin ordered, and the helmsman threw the wheel. The cook strained to see the ice for himself, more than a little irritated by the late warning. Tossing the chip forgotten for now, Mary leaned over the rail to see the ice floe, a large flat cake a hundred yards across, one edge marked by a sharp edge rising at a sharp angle. It was almost at the slowly turning bow, its mostly submerged bulk hidden by the waves. For a moment it appeared that the ship would not avoid at least a brushing collision, and Mary held her breath in anticipation of the impact.

The edge of the ice went out of sight beneath the lee rail, so near it was to the ship, and those near the rail peered over to watch it slide silently by. Its surface of pale white was veined with numerous gray cracks, stresses from long ocean travel. The edge, almost near enough to touch over the low lee rail, was rounded by wave action, except for the one sharp area, the fractured ice pushed up like a dagger by a recent collision with other ice.

Hare, having heard the lookout's call from inside the cabin, rushed out the door and up the quarterdeck steps. He found Irwin leaning over the side, watching the ice pass.

"Are we clearing it?" he asked.

"So far. What I can see of it above the water."

Hare looked forward and saw that the bow was now clear, the far edge of the ice about amidship. The dagger of ice was sliding within a foot of the top rail of the main deck, and several of the crew reached out to touch it as it passed. The only danger now was to the stern. The turn, once beneficial, was now swinging the aft end of the hull into the ice's path.

"Hard back, now," Hare shouted over his shoulder. "Hard back to port!"

"Aye, sir, hard to port," and the helmsman reversed his spin of the wheel.

Hare knew that the order was too late to do any good. If the ice was going to strike the ship, there was nothing he could do about it now.

Neptune's Car slid by the ice untouched, although Hare could not be certain of that until the ice had passed completely astern.

He straightened back up, relieved. "That was close enough, wouldn't you say?"

Irwin looked chagrined. "I'm sorry, sir. We didn't see it coming."

"Don't fret about it, Mr. Irwin. All's well that ends well."

Irwin relaxed. "Thank you, sir." He smiled. "All's well that ends well, you say? I didn't know you knew Shakespeare."

"Shakespeare? Oh, yes, of course." Hare coughed. "Yes, well, carry on. I'll be below. And have them double up the lookout. No more surprises."

While Hare worked the ship toward the open Pacific, Mary worked to give Joshua comfort. She felt that she was no more successful at providing that than she was at providing healing. Whether she attempted to try yet another remedy from the medical book or simply tried to keep him comfortable, he seldom seemed to have any response to her at all.

Not to say that he was completely inert. Though unconscious of the world around him, Joshua often stirred in the bed, the demons of his delirium besieging his mind. Mary could only watch as he fought unknown conflicts within that caused great turmoil without. The battles Joshua imagined frequently caused him to thrash about in the covers and sometimes compelled him to attempt to rise from the bed altogether. Fearing his actions and the motions of the ship would pitch him out onto the floor, Mary was obliged to restrain him with rope tied across the bed.

The strain began to wear on her, and she despaired of ever getting Joshua well. There was so little to encourage her. She was at the bottom of the world with a husband who seemed much nearer to death than to life and showed nothing to indicate that he might recover. The warm and romantic days in New York now seemed so long ago. How could the voyage have gone so wrong?

She could not help but blame Keeler, and she cursed the day he had appeared in their lives. Throughout the days since Joshua had fallen ill, the imprisoned first mate had made frequent demands to be released, citing the welfare of the ship and crew. Mary had never considered doing so. She had ceased even responding to his notes, making her last reply as clear and blunt as she could.

"Should the ship founder," she wrote back, "and be in danger of sinking below the waves, I still will not release you until the end is imminent, and then only so that your drowning will be, ultimately, in God's hands."

Hare continued at his post, striving to run the ship as Captain Patten would do were he able, and Mary continued at hers. They were well into their second week of beating their way against the wind when the next opportunity to sight the sun presented itself. The fix, made with a dull sun hiding behind a thin veil of clouds, showed that *Neptune's Car* was approaching Diego Ramírez Island, some hundred miles south and west of Cape Horn itself, and would pass it to the north. Diego Ramírez was the last significant point of land before reaching the Pacific, and once the ship was clear of that obstacle, nothing but open ocean stood between it and San Francisco. Cape Horn, the bane of their existence for the last weeks, was now passing behind them.

Mary was ecstatic. Not only did they have a firm landmark pass behind them, and not some mere point penciled onto a chart of empty ocean, but it was the single most significant landmark of the entire voyage. She felt as though she had climbed the highest of mountains, as if the Matterhorn itself was now behind them, and mere foothills spread below.

"I finally feel," she said to Timothy Hare upon reporting her results, "that progress is being made. We are practically in the Pacific, soon to leave the horrible cold behind."

Hare, stalwart as ever throughout the ordeal, had been long hours standing by the helm, and his red face showed the effects of the wind and weather.

"It will be a relief, ma'am."

"Especially for you," Mary said. "I have been concerned for your health. You spend far too many hours on deck, and I can ill afford to have you follow the path of my husband."

"I have had the same thoughts ma'am. But don't worry. I go below more than you might think. You do not see it because you are so often closed up in your cabin."

Mary gave him a sharp look. "I usually know when you go below. And it is not often enough. Not to mention the fact that every time I come up on deck, you seem to be here."

Hare smiled. "Coincidence, ma'am."

"I'm sure it is."

A wave broke over the railing, and Mary stepped back to dodge a tide of water that ran across the deck boards. "You are quite correct, though," she continued, "It will be a relief. Each day of late has seemed to last forever, and the nights are longer still. And the captain has been even more restless these last days."

"He has been awake, then?"

"No, not awake. Active, but not awake."

Hare stood silent, looking thoughtful. Then he said, "Hopefully, warmer weather will improve his state."

"It is certain to improve mine. I'll be below, Mr. Hare."

Eighteen days were spent rounding Cape Horn. Eighteen days that each seemed to last a week. The storms were reluctant to release them. *Neptune's Car* turned northwest and into much more favorable winds, but the storms remained, following them into the South Pacific. Still, Mary could see the end now and no longer felt daunted by their fury. Like a March snowfall, shouting winter's last hurrah, she knew the weather that made Cape Horn so feared and respected was simply loath to be left behind.

The final leg of their journey to San Francisco was ahead, and she and Hare had hopes of fair trades sweeping up the wide open ocean to propel them quickly onward. The day of Mary's first sight with the sextant, putting them near the entrance of the Straits of Le Maire and the beginning of the passage, seemed so very long ago.

Finally, they reached the long awaited Pacific Ocean. Two days after passing Diego Ramírez Island, *Neptune's Car* burst from the gray world of rain and sleet and into bright sunshine. The sky regained its unclouded blue, the sea absorbing its light and taking up its colors. The water ceased its tumult, and the waves again became friendly. Spray flew, and beneath the bow dolphins surged ahead, leaping with playful exuberance.

That night, Mary knelt beside Joshua's bed and lovingly caressed his pale face. "Take heart, my sweet. We have bested all that nature has put before us, and are again making good time toward California."

Joshua was quiet and made no response, giving no indication that he had heard her.

She lay her head on his chest, feeling the rise and fall of his breathing and the warmth of his fevered body. She felt certain that Joshua's only hope lay in getting him to medical help, and fervently hoped they would not be too late.

CHAPTER 22

Respite

"Tell me, Mary, all about it. Tell me how the ship fared while I was asleep. I feel like Rip Van Winkle."

As *Neptune's Car* had started its run up the Pacific, leaving the misery of Cape Horn in its wake, Joshua began a slow recovery. At first Mary thought it a temporary respite, like others that had come and gone. Now, three days into this latest improvement, he was alert and sitting up in the wing-back chair in the corner of the cabin. His curiosity was also aroused, and he asked Mary about all he had missed.

"I would be awake, at times," he said of his long stupor, "but be only vaguely aware of my surroundings. I would hear you speaking and understand what you were saying, but was unable to make sense of it."

"That might not have been all your fault," Mary said. "Sometimes I talked just to be talking, and not making much sense to me either."

Joshua smiled, his face still wan. "Thanks, but I don't think that was the problem. I was just out of my head."

"Well, let's hope that is all over with. I need you back with the living."

"With the living is where I truly want to be. I'm ready to get up on deck."

"Do you think? It was all I could do to help you over to that chair."

Joshua sat forward and tried to stand, but had not the strength to push himself out of the chair. Slumping back, he said, "I may not have my sea legs, yet."

Mary, at his side, brushed her hand across his hair, combing it into place. "It will take some time. You have been gravely ill. And judging by the warmth of your skin, I would say that you are still far from well. Going up top can wait."

"Perhaps tomorrow."

"Perhaps."

"Has there been any sign of *Intrepid*, or *Romance of the Seas*?"

Mary smiled. Even in illness her husband had not forgotten his race with other ships. "No. No sign of either."

"Then we may be ahead. Or not."

"I suppose we will learn soon enough."

"That is true. One of us will be in San Francisco to welcome the others." Joshua was quiet for a moment, with a thoughtful look on his face. Finally, he said, "Mary, during the time that I was sleeping, I often heard you speaking, but you sounded distant, as if far across the room."

Mary considered what he said. "You were ill, hearing me through a fever."

"Yes, but now I am awake, and I still hear you in the same way."

Mary waited for Joshua to continue. "What is it you are saying?"

"I'm afraid to say."

"Please."

"I fear the fever has affected my hearing."

Mary swallowed. She had hoped to tell her husband about her pregnancy, but now decided to wait. He had enough to worry about.

"Well, let's be optimistic. Surely it will not last, now that you are recovering."

"Let's hope," Joshua said.

Despite Joshua's improvement, Mary was still very concerned. This revelation about a hearing loss reminded her that he was not yet well. He had been too ill for too long to expect a full recovery very soon.

Still, she had renewed hope. If only his health could continue to improve, she told herself, the trip may turn out successfully, after all. As Mary told of all the ship had been through in getting around the end of South America, she began to marvel that she and Hare had been able to do it. Joshua, too, was amazed.

"And Keeler? You did not use him?"

"Would you have wanted us to?"

"It would have made things easier for you."

"I'm not so sure."

Joshua looked thoughtful and said, "I'm not sure either."

Mary told him of her navigation, and how days went by without sun or stars, and of meeting with the unknown ship, nearly derelict but beyond their help. She told of days and nights of storm, of rain and snow and hail, and ice to the mast tops. She told of the wind, and of venturing deep into the passage to defeat it, and the ice that drifted in their path.

"Most were flat," she said. "Like big cakes of soap, but two or three times we saw tremendous mountains of ice, majestic and beautiful, but at the same time terrifying. We steered around the ice, though, and eventually we got around the Horn. I must tell you, Joshua, that it was quite exhilarating to realize that we had made it into the Pacific."

Joshua smiled. "I understand," he said. "That is what makes a challenge such a pleasure."

" 'And if the freshening sea made them a terror, 'twas a pleasing fear.' "

Joshua nodded, recognizing the verse. "I heard you reading Lord Byron to me."

Mary, taking advantage of Joshua's sitting in the chair, was stripping the bed and putting on a fresh sheet. "I had plenty of time."

Joshua frowned and a sadness filled his eyes. "Oh, Mary, I would do anything to take away what you have been through. As I lay there on the bed, I could sometimes sense your fear, your uncertainties. That made my infirmities all the more unbearable, that you needed my help and I was not able to provide it."

He sat in the chair awhile longer, talking to Mary, hearing her speak of the ship and gallant crew, until he began to tire. To talk required unaccustomed effort, and conversation dwindled to a stop. Finally he said, "I believe I have been up long enough for my first day," and Mary helped him back to the bed. He promptly fell asleep, exhausted.

An hour later he awakened and said he was thirsty. Mary brought him water, and he took a long drink, unaided.

Laying his head back on the pillow, he said, "I have been thinking. You have done a wonderful thing, taking care of me and navigating the ship. Hare, it seems has done yeoman service and beyond. You mentioned your fears of him being overwrought by work. I share those concerns. You both need some help, and I cannot give it. At least not yet." Joshua closed his eyes and rested for a minute. When he spoke again, he said, "Have someone get Mr. Keeler, and bring him to me."

Mary flinched. "Are you sure?"

"I'm sure. I have thought hard, and even with my weakened mind I think it is the only thing to do."

Mary hesitated a second and opened the cabin door. "Henry," she called to the steward, who was lingering by the stove. "Please have Mr. Keeler brought up from below. The captain wishes to see him."

The young steward looked surprised but said, "Yes, ma'am, right away."

As an afterthought, she said, "And Mr. Hare. Have him come also."

Mary did not ask Joshua what it was he had in mind. She was afraid she already knew.

Joshua sat up in bed. "Help me back into the chair."

"Are you not too tired?"

"Yes. But I would rather deal with our friendly first mate sitting up. I look infirm enough as it is."

Mary understood, and she offered her shoulder for Joshua to lean on. Together, they left the bed and crossed to the chair. Joshua's entire weight seemed to hang on her, and Mary struggled under the load. He was much less able to help than he had been earlier. His show of strength would be just that.

He was settled into the chair when there was a knock upon the door. Mary steeled herself for seeing Keeler again. Joshua, forcing his voice to be strong, said, "Come in."

The door opened, and its frame was filled with the hulking form of William Keeler. Mary stiffened, and despite a desire to be strong she felt herself recoil. Keeler's appearance frightened her. It had been nearly a month since she had last seen him, and his days locked away had served to make him look, at least to Mary, more sinister. He seemed thinner, but his gauntness served to accent his still barrel chest. His skin, still dark and olive, nevertheless had the pale sallowness of one locked away out of the light. His black hair was unkempt, as was his beard. Most disconcerting, though, were his eyes, hard and black. They had never been friendly, but now they stared out of his face with a burning look that she could only believe to be despising hatred.

Keeler stepped into the room. Behind him, nearly a head shorter and in contrast almost inconsequential, was Timothy Hare.

"Captain," Keeler said simply, with a nod. His deep voice carried none of the humility of one who had been imprisoned for his transgressions.

"Come in, Mr. Keeler. And Mr. Hare, make room for yourself. This will concern you as well."

Hare slid from behind Keeler and stood beside him, clearly trying to appear as his equal but not so clearly succeeding. Keeler, by his bulk and personality, dominated the tiny cabin.

"Mr. Keeler, a lot has happened since that dark night when I last saw you, when your weeks of less than admirable service ended in a brawl with your superior officer. Is that the way you were trained to serve as first mate?"

Keeler, expressionless, said nothing.

Joshua ignored his lack of response. "I can see now why you had so much trouble staying on other ships.

"Mr. Keeler, much of what has happened since that night has taken place without either of us being present. While you were doing penance I, as you know, suffered a particularly debilitating illness, of which I am only now beginning to recover. In the meanwhile, young Mr. Hare here has run the ship as well as either of us could have hoped to do. It has, however, been a considerable strain upon both him and my wife."

"I offered my services," said Keeler. "More than once I offered to assist them, but they chose not to take advantage of my help. They made it hard upon themselves."

The expression on Joshua's face, already hard, changed to one of contempt. "They did not make it hard upon themselves. The origin of their hardship, Mr. Keeler, came at the hands of a treacherous first mate. A first mate who I hoped would have had time over the last month to see the error of his ways.

"Mr. Hare has been considerably overworked, and if I thought I could trust you to do your duties without further trouble, I would free you to do so. You do not, however, seem very penitent."

Mary, observing from the corner near the washbasin, saw Keeler immediately change his expression. It appeared to be a conscious effort, but his face softened, and he somehow took some of the hardness out of his eyes.

"You can believe me, sir, that a month locked in the hold through the storms that we have been through will cause a person to rethink his position. I will promise you whatever I must to keep from going back."

Joshua looked critically at him. "But will you keep your promises?"

Keeler did not hesitate. "Absolutely."

"Yes. Well, we'll see," Joshua said. "Have you had any contact with any other members of the crew?"

At first Keeler said no, that his time spent locked away had been in complete isolation, save for the delivery of his meals and change of his pot. Then Joshua asked about the men outside the storeroom door. Keeler admitted that, yes, he had had a few of the men venture in to ask of his health.

"But there was no plotting to gain your release?"

"No, sir. None whatsoever."

Joshua eyed Keeler coldly. "I find myself unable to put much trust in you, Mr. Keeler, but I will tell you why I had you brought in to me. I am not yet able to resume my duties. And I think your services, properly tendered, might give Mr. Hare some welcome relief. Am I correct in that, Mr. Hare?"

Hare, until now just an observer, had not expected to be brought into the conversation. He stammered but then collected his thoughts.

"Aye, sir—I—yes, some relief." He took a breath and said, "Sir, another officer would indeed be welcomed. If you are ready to return Mr. Keeler to duty, I am ready to hand over any command I have had. But if you please, sir, I will say this. Mrs. Patten and I took this ship around the Horn, and if need be we can take it to the Golden Gate. If you are doing this just for my benefit, it is not necessary."

Joshua looked at him for several seconds, as if analyzing the young mate's newfound strength. "I have no doubt, Mr. Hare, that you are up to the job." Then, with a flicker of a glance toward Mary, he said, "But it is not solely for your benefit."

To Keeler, he said, "You are paroled, sir, but do not think it is due to any goodwill I have toward you. I have not forgotten, and will not forget, the mutinous behavior you have exhibited. At the first hint of trouble with you, if I learn of any collusion between you and any members of the crew, you will find yourself back in your cell. If you will perform your duties properly, though, I will take that into account when we reach San Francisco."

Keeler nodded. "Thank you, sir. I am ready to begin immediately."

Joshua gave Hare a little smile. "I think young Hare is ready for you to begin, as well. Share this watch with him, to reacquaint yourself with the situation, and then take the next to allow him a rest. He has earned it."

"Aye, sir," said Keeler, turning to leave.

"And, Mr. Keeler. Don't disappoint me."

Keeler stopped in the doorway. "I will do my duty."

Joshua watched the two men leave. Calling Hare back into the room, he said, "Keep an eye on him."

Hare nodded. "Aye, sir. I certainly will."

Mary, from her post in the corner, hoped that Joshua was not making a mistake.

CHAPTER 23

Course Deviation

After the exertions of his interview with Keeler, Joshua's strength was so depleted that he returned to the bed and did not get up again that day, or the next. He was alert, though, and talking, and Mary felt that he was still on the way to recovery. She would just have to make sure he did not overextend himself again. His hearing, too, had not improved, but it did not seem to become any worse.

Having Keeler back on deck left her with mixed emotions. While it was good to have someone to alleviate some of the strain on Timothy Hare, as well as relieving her of the navigation duties, she did not enjoy seeing the first mate's brutish form brooding over the quarterdeck. And *brooding* seemed to be just the word to describe his demeanor. He stood near the helm, legs apart, his arms often folded across his thick chest. He said little, except to issue orders, which came forth in a deep voice gruff with impatience: "You there! Why isn't that main sheet taut? Haul it in, and be lively about it."

"It almost appears," Mary said to Hare, "as if he is not enjoying his newfound freedom."

They were standing on deck, just outside the door of the after cabin. Joshua was asleep, and Keeler was up on the poop of the quarterdeck. He was pretending to be watching the ship, but Mary felt certain she could feel his glare.

"I don't think it is in him to enjoy anything," Hare replied. "In a way, I almost feel sorry for him. I think he just lives a miserable life. Of his own doing."

Mary felt no such sympathy. "I do not care what sort of life he chooses to live. He has no right to impress his misery upon others. And if he wants misery, he may find it in the courts of San Francisco, when Joshua presses charges against him."

Hare bit his lip and said, "He may be thinking about that. It would make me pretty sullen."

"Let him think. Let him stew." Mary took a deep breath and exhaled, as if to clean her thoughts of Keeler. "The air is warming up, a little more each day."

"It is good to leave the cold behind us," Hare said. "In a week it will be hot again."

"That will be a welcome change, Mr. Hare." Mary turned toward the cabin door. "I'm going back inside. Hopefully the captain will awaken soon."

As she spoke, the ship's bell rang out the noon hour, and the watch changed. Hare went to relieve Keeler, who she saw had the sextant out to make the noon sight. While glad to be free of the burden, she felt a twinge of regret that it was no longer her job to work the sextant and figure their position. It was work to do so, but Mary had come to enjoy the challenge. Now that the ship was actually making progress again, she also missed seeing her marks on the chart and seeing the distance traveled in tangible form. The satisfaction of measuring the plots and saying, "Today we have traveled two hundred miles," or, even better, "Today we have traveled three hundred," was no longer hers.

Oh, well, she thought as she went back to her husband. It is also no longer my worry.

The next morning, after being awakened by a restless Joshua, Mary went out on deck to see the sunrise. After the weeks of gray skies it was a sensory pleasure to see the reds and oranges of the eastern sky at the break of day. She said good morning to Timothy Hare, on duty by the helm, and went over to the starboard rail.

Since turning away from Cape Horn and sailing back toward the equator, the sun was rising earlier each day, and gradually moving back to a more accustomed position as it traversed the sky. The days of sixteen hours of darkness and only eight of light were ending, and Mary was glad to see them go. Each day, as the sun stepped up out of the ocean horizon, it appeared a little farther south on the horizon, and a little more aft of the bow of the ship. Mary was encouraged by this physical evidence of their northward movement, and waited to see what change another day of sailing would bring. Since Keeler had assumed the navigation duties, it was her only evidence that they were progressing toward San Francisco.

The sun's incipient appearance was announced by the predawn glow of color, always a stirring sight at sea. For some minutes Mary leaned on the rail, watching the sky brighten, thinking how it was to be a beautiful morning. As she watched, however, she developed a nagging feeling that something was amiss. Despite possible variations in the track of the ship due to changes in the wind, she felt a certain disorientation. The sun, she thought, was rising too far forward in relation to the ship.

Surely she was somehow confused, and she tried to reason out her thinking. Every logical explanation, however, fell short, save one. The ship was on a different tack than she would have expected.

"Mr. Hare," she called, turning in the direction of the helm, "is our course more easterly than usual?"

Hare crossed the deck to where she was standing. "More easterly, ma'am?"

"Yes. We seem to be heading more toward the rising sun than we were."

"Aye, ma'am. That is true. By the compass we are going almost due north."

"Why is that, Mr. Hare?"

"That is the course Mr. Keeler has given me to steer."

Mary tried to visualize the charts in her mind, and how the winds and currents should best be utilized. "I would have thought we would be on a more northwest by north course."

"It is almost eight. Mr. Keeler will be up for his watch in a few minutes. Shall I ask him about it?"

As Hare was speaking, Keeler appeared from around the corner of the after cabin and was striding toward the steps leading up to the poop. Mary thought quickly. If she were to question Keeler's navigation, she wanted to be more sure of herself.

"No, Mr. Hare. Say nothing at all. Just sail as he says, for now."

Before she could say more, Keeler was within earshot. With a half smile, he said, "Morning, ma'am."

Mary nodded with a purposely stiff politeness. Keeler, she was still convinced, was the prime cause of her husband's illness, and she saw no reason to pretend any friendliness.

Keeler tried again. "You're out early. In time to see a nice sunrise."

Mary answered, being certain to keep her voice cold. "Yes, Mr. Keeler, it is." At the last second, she could not keep from offering a hint of her thinking. "And an interesting sunrise, too, don't you think?"

"Is it?" Keeler asked, looking out over the rail.

She felt a sudden nervousness. Time spent in Keeler's presence made her uncomfortable, and she decided to leave the deck. "Good day, gentlemen," she said. "I'm returning to the cabin."

A few minutes later, when Hare had left the ship with Keeler and departed his watch for the cabin, Mary was waiting for him at the dining table in the saloon.

"Mr. Hare, when the first mate takes his noon sight, let me know as soon as he returns the instrument to its case. I would like to see for myself exactly where we are."

Once the ship had been turned over to Keeler, he had taken possession of both the sextant and the charts, so Mary was not certain how to best gain access to the instrument. As it turned out, Keeler himself afforded her just the opportunity she needed. After taking his noon sight, the first mate returned to his cabin to work up the position on his small writing desk. Whether it was his own carelessness or a lack of work space, Keeler left the wooden case containing the sextant unattended on the saloon table. While he was bent over the chart and almanac, Mary had simply to slip past his open door, spirit the sextant from its resting place in the cushioned box, and step outside.

In a matter of minutes, she was back in the saloon, returning it to its place. She was only a few seconds from a completely unnoticed operation when Keeler abruptly turned around, catching her in the process of closing the lid. Startled, she involuntarily slapped the box closed. She was certain she looked as guilty as she felt.

Keeler studied her for several seconds, his eyes narrowing with suspicion. "Can I do something for you?"

Mary quickly composed herself. "No, Mr. Keeler. Please, continue what you were doing. I was just taking a look at the sextant."

"Was everything satisfactory?"

Mary saw what Keeler was thinking. "Oh, yes. I was not inspecting, Mr. Keeler. I was just admiring it. We have become well acquainted over the last weeks."

Keeler was clearly not placated. "I see. I should put it away. It should not have been left out on the table. We would hate for it to be damaged, wouldn't we?" He fastened the hasp and took up the case, tucking it under his arm. As he turned, he said, "I'm sorry. Were you finished admiring it?" He put emphasis on the word *admiring,* and Mary felt her face redden.

As much as she hated to see him carry it into his cabin, she could only say, "Yes, of course. I was finished."

She was certain he would not be so careless with its placement again.

It did not matter. She had her own set of numbers for a sight, taken only a few minutes past the noon hour. Using an old chart from Joshua's desk she was able to plot her own position. Once that was done, careful tracking of the compass would tell her all she needed to know about their course. What she learned shocked her. At the same time, she was not surprised.

Joshua was sound asleep, and had been most of the morning. His strength was returning, but it was proving to be a slow process. She did not want to awaken him but felt she needed to share her findings with someone. Saying the numbers out loud, she thought, might help her to make sense of them. With the chart under her arm, she went out on deck, finding Hare at his post.

"Look at this," she said, dispensing with any preliminary conversation. She spread the chart out on top of the wheel's gearing house. "My last fix, before Keeler had been given command of the ship and possession of the sextant, had us seventy-four degrees west of the prime meridian and tracking northwesterly." With her finger she tapped at the wind-rippled paper. "This is where we are today."

Hare leaned over and examined the map, but said, "Pardon me, ma'am, but you know this means little to me."

"I'm sorry, Mr. Hare. I'm just very perturbed by this. But you can see the picture, can you not? Look. This new fix indicates that we are at seventy-two degrees. That is two degrees east of where we were the day before yesterday. East when we should be more west. Tell me. Are we still sailing north?"

"Aye, ma'am. Directly north."

"If my figures are correct, Keeler is not only steering north, as he is having you do, but even back toward the east. But why?"

Hare could only look perplexed. "I haven't a clue, ma'am."

"Look at this chart," she said. "We cleared Cape Horn and turned northwest at about seventy degrees west. Right here. The western bulge of South America, up by the equator, is at eighty degrees. Each degree near the equator is sixty miles. That means that any ship sailing from the Horn and intending to clear South America must travel at least ten degrees of longitude to the west. That is six hundred miles. Why is Keeler sailing north?"

Hare began to understand. "He should not be."

"No, Mr. Hare. He should not. And there is more."

Showing her results to Hare was having the desired effect. Mary was becoming sure of herself, and she was certain there was nothing wrong with her numbers. She unfolded the chart to show the entire eastern Pacific, all the way to California. The cartographer's lines of latitude and longitude showed that San Francisco lay at nearly 123 degrees west.

"Putting pencil to paper, quick math tells me that our destination is forty-eight hundred miles north and three thousand miles west of where we are now. We should be steering northwest. That makes me ask two questions: Where is Keeler going, and what does he know that we do not?"

Hare straightened up from the chart and looked forward over the bow, as if looking ahead at the open ocean would offer a clue. "I don't know, ma'am. I don't know."

CHAPTER 24

Keeler

Joshua lay on the bed, looking up at the ceiling. His eyes were glancing about the cabin, but Mary could tell he was not really looking at anything. She waited for him to say something.

After he had awakened and had a cup of tea, shaking off the sluggish feeling of one coming out of a deep sleep, she had presented to him what she had determined about Keeler's apparently errant course. She hoped that he would have an explanation for it, something she had missed.

"I do not think you missed anything, dear. And there is only one person who can provide an explanation." Joshua sighed. "Damn him. Bring him to me."

Keeler was summoned from his sleep, and Mary could hear him muttering to himself as he emerged from his cabin on the side of the saloon and rounded the dining table. He appeared not to be fully awake when he knocked at the open doorway.

"You wanted me, Captain?"

"Yes, Mr. Keeler, come in." Joshua had elected to conduct this interview from the comfort of his bed. Mary had offered to get him up, but he either did not feel up to it or was less concerned about a strong image than he had been before. Mary took the chair for herself. She wanted to stay out of the conversation, but she wanted to be in the room to hear it.

"I don't wish to second-guess your course," Joshua continued, "but please indulge me. It has occurred to me that we seem to be sailing farther east than we should be. Of course, you may have a reason." Joshua paused, giving Keeler a chance to answer. The mate's only response, at first, was a narrowing of his eyes and a slight darkening of his face. It looked to Mary as if he was wondering what role she played in this.

"Do you?" Joshua asked.

"Do I have a reason?" Keeler blinked. "Reason for what? That we are where we should be?"

"Are we?"

"I believe so, sir."

"The compass tells otherwise."

Keeler flicked a glance toward Mary, but went quickly back to the captain. "You have seen the compass, sir?"

"I have been kept apprised of its readings. A tack to the north might be understandable, but we seem to have north as a primary course."

"I have kept a mostly northerly tack, sir, to the advantage of the winds. They are of the southwest, sir."

"You expect to turn back west, eventually?"

"Of course, sir."

"Most ships get the best out the southwest trades by keeping west early, and turning north as they die out. They will die, you understand, toward the line of the equator."

Keeler seemed to puff up at being questioned. "Of course. I only know, sir, that I am making best speed to San Francisco."

Joshua smiled weakly. "I am sure that you are as impatient as the rest of us to make that port."

Mary saw Keeler bristle. She recognized Joshua's comment for the thinly veiled barb that it was. San Francisco, with its courts of maritime law, was probably the last place Keeler wanted to go.

It suddenly occurred to her what Keeler was doing. If he did not want to go to San Francisco, where would he choose to go? Was there somewhere on the west coast of South America he could be heading for? Mary realized she was squirming in her chair, and she forced herself to sit still. She wondered if this possibility had occurred to Joshua. When her thoughts returned to the conversation at hand, she found it was ending.

"I apologize for waking you early, Mr. Keeler," Joshua was saying. "I just wanted to be sure we were both clear upon the desired course."

"Were I not clear before, sir, I am now. I'll take your advice about that wind. Rest easy, sir, and we'll get you to a doctor before you know it."

Keeler bowed out, and Mary waited until she was certain he had gone before sitting on the edge of the bed, where Joshua could hear her speaking softly. She laid out her suspicions and was surprised to learn that indeed Joshua had not already thought of it.

"I should have," he said. "It's perfectly obvious." He smiled. "In light of what I said to Keeler about San Francisco, he no doubt thinks I have. I may have accidentally said the right thing to get him back on course, if he thinks we are on to his plan."

"If that is his plan."

"Yes. Well, we will see."

Neptune's Car's turn back to the northwest lasted only for the rest of that day. Keeler took over the helm during the evening dogwatches, and it was not long after she had retired for the night when Mary felt the ship turn slightly toward the north. Her suspicions aroused, she was awake an hour or so later when she felt another course change, in the same direction as the first.

Slipping out of bed in the darkened cabin, she went out into the saloon, where a second compass, similar to the one binnacled on deck, was housed. A glance confirmed what she already knew. Keeler had shifted back to heading a full point east of north.

Mary considered waking Joshua to inform him but decided against it. She doubted the new course was proper, but did not want to rouse him from a sound sleep. She lay awake for some time, listening to the ship, alert for any changes that might tell her of a turn back to where they should be.

The ringing of eight bells stirred her, and told her that it was midnight. She was also aware of a different tone in the sound of the passing sea. She heard movement in the saloon and peeked out to see Hare preparing to go out for his turn at watch. Satisfied that Keeler would not be down until Hare went up, she stepped again out to the compass. It showed the ship to again be headed northwest.

"Mr. Hare, have you noticed a recent course change?" she asked.

"Aye, ma'am, I have. Not more than twenty minutes ago. A turn to port."

"I thought so. It would appear that our friend Mr. Keeler sails one direction for our benefit, and another for his. If we find him turning again later, when he goes back on watch, we will know that he is up to something."

"Such as?"

"That I do not know."

Hare looked thoughtful but had no theory. "I had better get out there."

"Yes," Mary said. "And I am going back to bed."

She crawled back in next to Joshua, trying not to wake him. It was in vain. "What is our course?" he asked quietly.

"We are going northwest by north," Mary answered.

"Good."

She hesitated. "But earlier we were not."

"Oh?"

"During most of Keeler's watch we were northeast, again."

"Damn." A long silence. "I will deal with him in the morning. My head hurts too much right now."

"You have a headache?"

"Terribly so."

"I'm sorry I woke you."

"You didn't. I was awake when you got out of bed."

The night passed restlessly. Neither Patten slept well; it seemed to Mary that whenever she did drift off, Joshua would stir, nudging her from sleep. Those interruptions, along with thoughts that dwelled upon Keeler's actions, caused her to awaken often. In the earliest dim light of the coming morning, when it was just light enough in the cabin to see forms take shape, she turned to Joshua. He had his eyes tightly closed, his face visibly tense.

"Are you all right?"

Joshua opened one eye halfway. "My head hurts."

Mary was concerned. It was with a headache that Joshua's illness had first presented itself, and she feared that this headache might be marking the end of his recovery.

She cupped his face with her hand. The skin was hot. The fever, which had never completely left, was making a return. Sliding over, she pressed her form against his. She wondered if he would notice the growing swell of her belly. She desperately wanted him to know she was carrying his child, but at the same time wanted to protect him from yet another worry. Compromising, she stayed against him but pulled away just enough to keep the small roundness from pushing too hard against him.

Gently, she kissed him, and his warm lips responded. She felt his tongue and opened her mouth for it to explore within. Tentative at first, and then more aggressively, Joshua searched her mouth, and she his, each tasting, for the first time in weeks, the physical love so long kept at bay. The pain in his head temporarily ignored, Joshua caressed her face, her neck, and down to the rise of her breasts. He worked two or three buttons loose at the top of her dress, and slipped his hand inside. Mary felt his fingers on a suddenly hard nipple, and she worked her own hand down into his underclothes to feel him. He was aroused, and he stiffened in her squeezing grasp.

Surprised by how quickly they had progressed from gentle comforting of the sick to these stirred emotions, Mary was afraid that they might fade just as suddenly. She worked Joshua's clothing down and pulled her dress up and she rolled over and slipped down upon him. She gasped. His breath came in short, heavy bursts. Together, for a few short minutes, they forgot the trials of the voyage and relished each other.

It lasted not nearly long enough. Passions ebbed, and Mary eased down upon Joshua's chest, each feeling the other's heartbeat. After a few minutes she moved off him and lay close beside him, basking in the moment. Whispered words of love passed back and forth. If he had noticed the change in her body, he did not mention it. She supposed he was still so ill, and the difference in her stomach so faint, that he was still unaware. That was probably best, she decided. After a while, she heard his steady breathing. With her hand on his chest, she felt the matching up-and-down rhythm and was soon asleep herself.

With the light of day came evidence, by way of the compass, that the ship was again headed northeast, even more so than the day before. Mary reported the compass reading to Joshua. He thought for a moment and said, "Bring me the chart."

He looked at it for several minutes, holding it close to better see the small print. Finally, he called Mary to read it with him. "I can't see in this poor light. This mark is our position as you took it yesterday. Correct?"

Mary nodded.

"And just guessing our way through the various turns that Keeler seems to have made, we might now be about here," he said, tracing his finger up the map. "Help me, dear. Along the coast of Chile. About here. Is that a port?"

Mary leaned over his shoulder. "That is Valparaiso."

"I thought so. Hard to read."

Mary thought that curious. Even with only the light from the window, she found the lettering easy to see. Joshua spoke again, interrupting her thought.

"Have Henry take the cot stored in the spare passenger cabin and place it in the saloon, by the compass. I think I'll lie out there awhile."

"I can read it for you," Mary said.

"I know. But I want to see for myself."

When Keeler came in from his watch, Joshua was sitting upright on the edge of the narrow cot in the saloon, waiting. Now Mary understood. Seeing Joshua by the compass took away Keeler's argument that Mary was misreading it or otherwise misinforming her husband.

Keeler was visibly disturbed at Joshua's presence by the telltale instrument, but it did not deter his story. He still would not admit to the course deviation.

"I am proceeding toward San Francisco," Keeler said forcefully. "You mistake a starboard tack for a steady course."

Joshua sighed and said, "Mr. Keeler, what do you take me for? Do you think that I am reading this compass only now? I have been watching it through the night. I am well aware of your track."

Keeler blinked. Mary knew that he did not believe Joshua had been up during the night, but he did not contradict his captain.

Instead, he questioned the accuracy of the compass itself. "By the compass on deck, sir, I am at this very moment steering northwest by north. Does that compass not show that?"

Joshua leaned forward and looked into the box at the glass-covered disk. He studied it in silence. Those in the room—Keeler, Mary, Hare, and Henry the steward—waited. Finally, Joshua leaned back and said, "No, Mr. Keeler, it does not."

"Then it is in error. What course does it show?"

"Look for yourself."

Keeler stepped forward and looked down at the compass card. "It is wrong, sir. There is something affecting its magnetic field. Perhaps it is the iron on your bed."

"It is not the bed," Joshua answered. "There is nothing wrong with the compass. What is wrong is your course. Perhaps, during your days locked below, you have forgotten some principle of navigation. Perhaps we should let my wife resume those duties."

Keeler's eyes flared. "There is nothing wrong with my navigation. I know exactly where I'm going."

Joshua closed his eyes and leaned his head back, weary of the conversation. "And would you be so kind, Mr. Keeler, as to tell the rest of us where that is?"

"San Francisco. Where else?"

Joshua opened his eyes and fixed them hard on his mate. "Valparaiso, perhaps?"

Keeler flinched. "Valparaiso? Why would you think that?"

"Because, sir, that is where the ship appears to be heading."

"Think what you wish. I am sailing for San Francisco, and that is all there is to it."

"I suspect," Joshua said, "that you would rather depart this vessel somewhere besides a United States port. Someplace where jurisdiction of the courts might not pose so much of a threat. Someplace such as Valparaiso."

"I have heard all I want of this. If you will excuse me, I am needed on deck."

He turned to leave. Joshua said, "Mr. Keeler, I am not through with you."

Keeler continued toward the door. "Someone has to run this ship."

"Mr. Keeler!"

Keeler stopped and turned around. "You want to go to San Francisco. That is where we are going. Unless you have something else to say, I am returning to my duties."

Joshua looked at him coldly. "For you to do your duties is all I have asked. But I warned you that should I see any evidence otherwise, you would find yourself damned to the hold again. I have no hesitation in doing so."

Keeler took a deep breath and came back toward the cot. His face fairly glowed with anger, and Mary felt herself shrinking away from him. Raising a thick hand, Keeler pointed at Joshua and then at her and Hare. "You should allow me to those duties, and you would do well not to listen so much to these two. They may think they know what is what, but they do not."

With that, he spun around and started for the door. In a few seconds he was at the far end of the cabin.

"Mr. Keeler!" Joshua shouted. "Stop right there!"

Keeler slowed for a half step, as if considering the consequences of his actions, and without looking back stepped out onto the deck.

Joshua stood up by the side of the cot. After ensuring his balance on unsteady legs, he started after Keeler.

Mary was aghast. "Joshua, where are you going?"

"Out to have that bastard put back in his place. Mr. Hare, come with me."

Hare, Mary, and the steward followed Joshua outside.

Out on the deck, Joshua blinked in the shining of the sun. It was the first time his eyes had been subjected to such brightness in weeks, and he was forced to cover them with his hand. Squinting, he moved across the deck to where he could see around the cabin toward the raised quarterdeck. Keeler was by the wheel, facing the helmsman, who at that very moment was turning the wheel. Joshua studied the movement and said, "Mr. Hare, are you with me?"

"Aye, sir. Right here."

"Do I see the helm making a turn to starboard? To the east?"

"Aye, sir, you do."

Joshua raised his voice, summoning all the strength he had. "Helmsman! Belay that order! Hold your course!"

The seaman at the wheel stopped the turn and stood with his mouth open at the sight of his long-absent captain standing coatless on the deck.

Joshua turned and looked forward toward the bow, still shading his eyes with a hand over his forehead. "All hands!" he called, mustering his strength. "All hands on the deck!"

The order was repeated down the length of the ship, and men materialized from all points, both aloft and below. To the first three or four to arrive before him, Joshua said, "You men, go up on the poop and take Mr. Keeler in hand." He turned toward Keeler, who was at the moment midway between the wheel and the quarterdeck rail and moving swiftly toward the stairs on the port side of the deck. Reaching the stairs he leaped over them, not using the steps, but landing in one jump on the main deck.

In an instant he was halfway down the deck to the mainmast fife rail. He climbed up on the U-shaped railing encircling the mast, one hand on a belayed line for support. The crew, still gathering from all parts of the ship, stopped their movement toward the quarterdeck to watch Keeler. It was to them that Keeler directed his words.

"This is the time, gentlemen!" Keeler shouted, making sure his voice reached everyone on the deck. "This is the time I warned you about! While in my captivity, some of you came to me, saying that you were not sure that the ship would survive under those in command. When I was released, I promised you that I would not let you be put under such inexperience again. I also warned you that the time would come when Hare and his sweetheart would twist facts to put me away again. This is that time!"

Some of the crew moved closer to Keeler, listening to what he had to say. Others stood rooted in place, displaying no allegiance to his rantings.

Joshua and Hare stepped toward the assembly. "Mr. Keeler," Joshua shouted. "Come down off that rail! Are you mad?"

"See? See?" Keeler said, his voice excited. "Now, men. Now is the time. Stand with me, and I will see you safe to California. The captain is sick. He is too sick to know. Stand with me. Together we will save the ship!"

Mary could hardly believe what she was hearing. Before her very eyes, Keeler was inciting the crew to mutiny. Did he have the support? Would Joshua be able to stop it? The next voice heard was her husband's.

"All hands, ignore that man. He is mad. He must be to act as he does. Follow him, and you will be following him to the noose."

As he spoke, Joshua's voice grew noticeably weaker. Mary feared that he would be unable to finish what he was saying. Hare, apparently sensing the same thing, stepped up to his captain's side, ready to take over.

Keeler stood his ground. For the moment he was silent. Taking advantage of his hesitation, Joshua said, "Mr. Keeler, you call your men, but I see no one taking your side." He turned to the crew. "So what is it? Are any of you ready to join this criminal act?"

No one moved. Joshua faltered and leaned on Hare. "You men there," he said, his voice lower, "take Mr. Keeler off that fife rail. Do it now, and end this matter."

Keeler glared down at the captain. "I'll be down, but only to keep the command you gave when of sound mind. Look at him, men. He is unable to even stand on his own. He is ill and has forgotten that he has entrusted me with the ship. Don't be swayed. Stand with me."

Joshua looked around at the crew. For a moment the ship was quiet. The only sound was the wind spilling around the mainsail stretched low overhead. "Does any man intend to join our friend on the rail? Go on, stand up there with him. You will get a feel of the view from the scaffold."

Mary watched carefully. One or two of the men seemed to start forward, but they stopped, unsure of themselves and unsure of other support. In the end it was Keeler, standing alone.

"It is as I suspected, Keeler," Joshua said, for the first time dropping the *Mr.* from before his name. "Any allies you have had followed only out of fear, and now fear to follow."

Turning again to the crew, Joshua said, "Bring him down. Use whatever force you need, but bring him down to the deck."

Three men stepped up to the rail and looked up at Keeler, who continued to glare down at the crowd around him. "Come on, mate," one said. "You'll do no good up there."

Surrounded and alone, Keeler said, "Damn you. Damn you all." Defeated, he slowly stepped down. Relieved, Mary moved to Joshua's side. She had expected Keeler to put up a fight, even against the odds.

"Take him below," Joshua said, his voice not much more than a whisper. "And shackle him this time. I don't want to see him again."

Keeler, without a word, shook loose the hands holding him and started off for his cell. His jailers followed closely, escorting him away.

Joshua looked around at the rest of the crew. He leaned against Mary, relieving Hare of the duty, and said, "Mr. Keeler's command of *Neptune's Car* is over. Mr. Hare, who served so well in the rounding of the Horn, is back in charge. I trust the respect you afforded him during that time will continue. I am on the mend, I think, but this excitement has sapped my strength. I need a few more days' rest, and until I am back on deck, Mr. Hare has the ship."

Mary felt the load on her shoulder get heavier. Joshua was exhausted. If he had intended to say more to the crew, he now cut it short.

"You are dismissed."

The men stood for a few seconds without moving as each took a look at their long-absent captain. Finally they started away.

Joshua stood watching them. "And men," he said suddenly, forcing his voice to find some strength. "Your service over these past weeks has been exemplary. I personally thank you."

Some of the crew smiled, and from within the ranks came several voices saying, "Thank you, sir."

Joshua smiled. As he turned toward the door of the cabin, he said, "Carry on."

With Mary's assistance, he went back inside.

CHAPTER 25

Pacific

Joshua fell across the bed after his excursion onto the deck, drained from the unaccustomed effort. He looked over at Mary, who had taken a seat in the chair.

"Well, so much for any change in Keeler's behavior. The man is more trouble than he is worth."

Mary scoffed. "He is worth absolutely nothing."

Joshua sighed. "Poor judgment, on my part, to take him on, I must admit."

"You had no way of knowing."

"It is my job to know."

"You mustn't blame yourself."

Joshua's face tightened. Mary recognized the look. "Pain?"

"Yes. I wish this headache would go away." After hesitating, he said, "And Mary, I may have another problem."

She waited.

"When I told Keeler to look at the compass for himself, it was because I could not see it well enough to read the course. I was bluffing about seeing that he was on the wrong course."

It dawned upon Mary what her husband was saying. No, she thought, not this, too. "What do you mean?"

"My eyes, Mary. I can hardly bring myself to say it out loud, but my sight is failing."

That explained his inability to read the small print on the chart, Mary thought. "How bad is it?" she dared herself to ask.

"Bad enough."

Mary tried to sound hopeful. "Maybe you are just showing your age. The eyes are the first to go, they say."

Joshua tried to laugh. "How old do you think I am?" he reached up and rubbed the back of his neck. "No, I don't think we can blame this on age."

Softly, Mary said, "I do not think so either." She wondered what else to say. She wanted to say how sorry she was. Instead, she said nothing.

Joshua reached out to her. She moved from the chair to the edge of the bed, taking his hand in hers, kneading his fingers. His hand felt warmer to the touch than it had the last time she held it. It was becoming apparent that his was to be a temporary recovery. She could see him slipping back into the delirious illness from which he had only so recently begun to emerge. She had the fleeting thought that she was glad to have made love to him when she did; it could prove to be her only opportunity. She admonished herself for thinking such base thoughts. Her husband lay ill, and she was thinking of carnal pleasures. She sent the thoughts from her mind.

"Perhaps you should rest. Get some sleep. That might help your headache, and the headache could have something to do with your eyes."

"You may be right." Joshua closed his eyes for a few seconds, and then opened them again. He glanced at her and then, avoiding the worried look she returned, looked away. "Oh, Mary, I so fear what is happening to me." As he said the words, lying on his back, she saw tears pool in his eyes. He blinked, and a drop ran down the side of his face.

Joshua had the cook identify the men he had caught outside Keeler's door before his release and had them brought before him. Mary recognized them as the same two who had almost joined Keeler at his stand on the fife rail. They were rough sailors, typical of slim pickings on an overharvested waterfront, the mean type of men that could be swayed into a mutiny, but they seemed cowed when called into the cabin. They were wide eyed at the fine accommodations after three months cramped into the dark forecastle. They would be certain to tell their mates of the disparity, but Joshua thought it worth allowing them inside in order to confront them. At the time, he felt unable to leave the cabin but had Mary help him to the chair.

He also felt little energy to engage in pleasantries. They stood beside his bed, hats removed, and he said, "Do you men know the penalty for mutiny? Or any action taken against authority on board a merchant vessel?"

The men fidgeted, working their hats in their hands. "It could be death, sir."

"No *could be* about it. It is death." He paused, taking one or two labored breaths. "You should think about that before making any plans through a locked door with a man already under arrest for treason."

"He told us it weren't mutiny if we just took over for a sick captain, unable to command."

"What of Mr. Hare, and my wife? Were they not in command?"

"He said they were doing it wrong. Putting the ship at risk."

"Did you feel at risk?"

"No, sir. But the weather around the Horn was awful."

"So you were not at risk. Just overworked. Not a good reason to mutiny."

Joshua rested. The silence was heavy in the cabin as the men waited for him to continue.

"Did Keeler tell you where he intended to take the ship, should he gain control?"

"Why, he said we'd go on to Frisco."

Mary, watching from her seat at the desk, saw nothing in the men's faces to doubt them. Perhaps Keeler had not told his co-conspirators of his full plans.

Joshua was not so secretive. Holding up a folded piece of paper from his bedcover, he said, "Can either of you read?"

One said, "Aye, sir, some."

Joshua handed him the sheet. Seeing him struggle with the words, Joshua paraphrased the contents. "It is a draft of a letter to the United States consul in Valparaiso, written by Mr. Keeler, pleading his case against prosecution in the charges of mutiny. Apparently, he was planning to hand-deliver it to the consul, in hopes of avoiding court."

The crewmen looked blank.

"You knew nothing about this?"

In unison, both said, "Oh, no, sir."

"Like we said, sir," said the one holding the letter, "we only knew of Frisco."

Joshua looked around at Mary, but she noticed that he did not focus on her. *He cannot see me clearly,* she thought.

The men waited.

"When Mr. Keeler was released to resume command, he began steering away from our intended destination and in the direction of Valparaiso, on the coast of Chile. When confronted, he insisted he was staying the course. This letter, found by the cook during a search of the storeroom serving as Keeler's cell, confirms what I suspected.

"You two took a terrible chance even conversing with him. Such actions could be construed as part of the conspiracy. As it is, I am prepared to assume you meant no ill will to me personally or to Mrs. Patten and Mr. Hare. In exchange, I want you to return to your mates and tell them what I have told you — that Mr. Keeler was putting the entire crew in danger of being charged with mutiny, should his plot have been realized."

"Aye, sir, we sure will, sir." The seamen seemed relieved that their call to the captain's quarters was leaving them unscathed.

"Very well," Joshua said, "back to your watches, then. Show me good work from here on out, and no more will be said of your visit to Keeler's door. Good day, gentlemen."

The men made a quick retreat, and Joshua said to Mary, "Well, you and Mr. Hare have the ship, again. I am tired, and think I will nap."

The return of Joshua's symptoms dulled what would have otherwise been a pleasant and satisfying run up the Pacific. Fair winds and good weather followed the ship and daily sights with the sextant showed the far south latitudes falling away in its swirling wake. From the freezing hell of fifty-eight degrees south of the equator, *Neptune's Car* sped before the southeast trade winds into the warmer climes of latitude forty, then thirty.

Two days after Keeler's reconfinement, Valparaiso passed several hundred miles to the east. Mary made note of its passage, pleased that his plan had been foiled. She was also pleased that he was back in his "out of sight, out of mind" quarters in the storeroom in the hold, where she did not have to look at his scowling face or see his bullying ways on the deck.

The weather may have been fair, but Mary was not able to enjoy it. She went up on deck at noon every day to take her sight and then returned to the cabin, where she pored over the chart and the almanac, carefully working up the ship's position. After another short visit out to inform Hare of their progress and discuss the course, she went back to Joshua.

Her dear, dear Joshua was slipping, just as she had feared, back into his private netherworld of fever and nightmarish dreams. In the space of only three or four days, after having the stamina to follow Keeler out on deck and remove him once again from command, his strength diminished until he was unable to help himself out of bed. His fever went up and his delirium returned, his speech again becoming nonsensical syllables.

By day his vision became worse, dimming until the world turned gray and shadowy. His hearing, too, was leaving him, but his sight worried him most.

"To be blind," he said in a lucid moment, "to be both helpless and dependent, is to be as good as dead."

It both depressed and angered him. The depression came first, and as his condition deteriorated, he became angry, sometimes violently so. Mary sat at his side, caring for him, nursing him, but ready to move quickly out of the way if he lashed out in wild frustration.

Mary herself was frightened. Not so much by the demon-spurred actions of her husband, although she was sometimes afraid he might strike her during some furious thrashing about, but more so by the deepening conviction that no good end could come of whatever illness gripped him.

She was seen less and less on deck. She busied herself caring for her husband. She worked to feed him. She urged him to drink. She fought his fever with endless changes of cool compresses. She washed him, and caressed him, and loved him with all her heart, but felt her heart was breaking.

Again and again her thoughts went back to home in Boston, where her mother could offer help, and to her father's strong shoulders. Here she was alone. Here she had only Timothy Hare to aid and counsel her, and even to him she must appear strong. She was not always successful.

A week after she and Hare resumed command, she was on deck to advise a slight turn to the east when she burst into tears. She hurried to the railing, hiding her emotions by pretending to look out across the sea, but with eyes closed. Hare quietly stepped over to her side.

Feeling his presence, Mary said, "The sea is pretty today." She wiped her hand across her cheek.

"Aye, ma'am. It's a beautiful day."

For a minute, neither spoke. Mary bit her lip, keeping her emotions in check.

Glancing sideways, Hare said, "It's been difficult, hasn't it, ma'am?"

"Yes, Mr. Hare. It has been." Suddenly, Mary felt the dam give way. She released an audible sob, and tears started anew. Again she wiped them away, but others followed. Involuntarily, she turned toward Hare and buried her face in his chest. Hare hesitated and then put his arms around her, lightly at first, and then a little more tightly. She fully acquiesced to his embrace, allowing herself to lean against him. His hands felt strong. She willingly accepted their touch, and she sobbed uncontrollably.

After several minutes, Mary lifted her face from his accommodating chest and choked back the next sob. She ran her finger over the lapel of his coat. It was wet with tears.

"I'm sorry. I don't know what's come over me."

"It's all right. You have been so strong. I'm surprised this hasn't happened sooner. The crying, I mean."

Mary smiled weakly. "Oh, it has. It has. Just not with an audience."

Hare gave her a last hug and said, "Anytime you need a shoulder to cry on, ma'am, I'm your man." Mary thought it had been intended as a brotherly hug, but she suddenly wondered if there was a hint of something more in his touch. Even more bewildering, she was not sure if, for that moment, she perhaps wanted something more.

He let go of her, and they separated.

Mary dried her face with her sleeve. "Thank you. Your support throughout has been invaluable."

She returned then to the care of her husband, back to the privacy of the cabin. The good cry she had with Hare had been a great release of pent-up emotions, but there were plenty more tears where those had come from. Alone with the unconscious Joshua, she did not have to be strong. She could be free to let the tears seep past eyes willed not to cry, or, when she felt like it, let the tears flow freely.

While Mary worried over Joshua, cloistered in the cabin with her hopes and fears, the clipper ship *Neptune's Car* continued up the Pacific. The line of the equator was recrossed, with little fanfare, on the seventeenth of October, 107 days out of New York.

As the weather warmed and the skies cleared, the crew wasted no time in laying out all their clothing and gear to dry. Everything outside the tightly battened holds, and probably some of the cargo inside, had been thoroughly drenched during the weeks of wet and cold weather. When the ship emerged into the sunshine, its deck was hung with all manner of shirts and breeches and pants, as well as underwear and overcoats. To Mary it looked like laundry day in the North End of Boston, where the week's clothes were hung on lines between the close-set tenements. Along with the crew's clothes were laid the spare sails, ropes, lines—anything that had been wet. It took several days to put the ship back into the dry, but the crew did not rest until it was done. The pleasure of dry socks was not taken lightly.

Mary followed the crew's lead, and as she peeled away her dress and skirts, to dry modestly by the stove in the saloon rather than out on deck for the men to see, she realized that it was the first time she had changed clothes since Joshua had fallen ill. She had been so preoccupied by his state that she had neglected to attend properly to her own. She was able to justify her lack of personal care easily enough, after thinking about it, with reasoning that anything she put on would soon be just as wet.

She also found, after changing into other clothes, that the new dresses were not as comfortable as the old, which happened to fit a little more loosely and had a little more room for the new fullness in her midsection. When she examined herself in the mirror, she found that the clean clothes revealed far too much evidence of her pregnancy, a fact she preferred to keep from the crew. As the days warmed toward the equator, she could hardly continue wearing her concealing coat, so after the wet dress was dry, she put it back on and continued to wear it.

Timothy Hare settled into his role as commander of the ship. Without the demands and dangers of the cape to concern him, he found it to be a very pleasurable experience. He could see the appeal of becoming a ship's master, of taking a vessel and crew and melding them together to form a tightly run machine. He expressed these thoughts to Mary during one of her times on deck, and she encouraged him to pursue the career.

"Joshua's misfortune could mean good fortune for you," she said. "I have no doubt that in due time you would be capable of moving beyond second mate, even without the experience of this voyage, but having brought *Neptune's Car* around the Horn will put you in good stead with other captains. I would not be surprised to see you as someone's first mate when you leave San Francisco."

Hare allowed himself a smile but shook his head. "All well and good, ma'am, but there is one thing you forget. Lack of education keeps me down. Your husband allowed me to be second mate, but only because he had no one else at the time. On most ships I'd be living yonder in the forecastle."

Mary thought back to the previous voyage and the trip home from London. "I believe, if I remember correctly, that Joshua offered the second mate position to you because he saw a potential. On this trip, you have proved him correct."

"Still, ma'am, I am but an ignorant sailor, and that I'll always be."

Mary looked forward along the deck, now cleared of drying gear and back in its best seagoing form. Overhead, the sails were set for best speed, straining tightly against the wind.

"Do you suppose, Mr. Hare, that this ship sails itself?"

"What do you mean?"

"I mean, do you suppose that, left to its own, the crew would have the ship running in such a shipshape fashion?"

Hare shrugged slightly. "I'm sure they would do their best."

"That may be, Mr. Hare. But their best would be sorely lacking. Someone would have to know how to best set the sails, someone with the authority to make it happen, without dissension. Do you agree?"

"Yes, of course."

"Well, that someone is you. You are hardly an ignorant sailor."

Hare looked at her. "You know what I mean, ma'am."

"Yes, Mr. Hare, I do. And I do not mean to say it will be easy. Your future as a ship's officer will not be handed to you on a platter. But with work, you will rise to the occasion."

"How?"

"You will learn to read and write."

"You make it sound simple."

"You can do it."

"If that were so, I would have done it long ago."

"You said once that Henry was teaching you."

"That was when I had more time."

"Later, when this voyage is over, you will have more time, and I am certain that, having had this taste of command, you will not be content to go back forever before the mast. It will not be easy, but I believe you will make time to learn to read. It is inevitable. You handle a ship too well to remain an ordinary seaman."

Hare smiled at the compliment. "I appreciate your confidence, ma'am."

"It is not my confidence, Mr. Hare. It is yours."

CHAPTER 26

Calm

As much as Mary enjoyed the warmth of the tropics after the cold of the far southern latitudes, it was not many days before what had been pleasingly warm became unpleasantly hot. Topside was comfortable, where the movement of the ship sent a cool breeze across the deck, but in the confines of the captain's quarters, ventilated by only two small windows on the stern wall, it was soon stifling. Mary was sure it must have been just as warm in the equatorial Atlantic, but she recalled that as a much happier time, with more time spent on deck where the salt air was always cool and fresh.

Now, sequestered with Joshua in the cabin, she keenly felt the warm air of the tropics. It was thick and humid, holding in its volume the miasma of the enveloping sickness. At times Mary grew weary of breathing the stale air, but always, when she thought of Joshua's own state, hers did not seem so difficult.

And Joshua's state continued to worsen. Within days he declined so far that he was rarely conscious and never coherent. Mary saw so little to give her encouragement, and so much with which to be discouraged, that she felt herself sinking into a deep despair. She sometimes found herself sitting by Joshua for hours at a time, telling herself that she was caring for him, only to decide later that she was not caring at all. She was just waiting.

On those occasions, it took all her willpower to lift herself out of her despondency. She forced herself to rise and go out on the deck, to see that there was still viable life on the ship, that there was more than the sickened cell of the cabin. Hare offered kind words and expressed optimism for a fast passage up ocean, but to Mary his words rang hollow.

"We are making good time," he said, but she knew that near the equator the winds were light and progress was measured in much smaller quantities.

The southeast trades gradually lessened, but by good fortune the ship was spared the becalming doldrums experienced going down the Atlantic. The fifteen knots being made during the run up the South Pacific dropped to four or five, but it was still better than the painful slowness of beating around Cape Horn. Nevertheless, Mary found the slow-moving air and warm equatorial temperatures to exacerbate Joshua's fever.

With more fever came more delirium and more restless sleep. He also began experiencing convulsions. These periods of shaking and jerking, with agonizing stiffening of contracting muscles, alarmed Mary greatly. Sometimes as Joshua's body stretched out and became rigid he seemed to stop breathing, unable to take a breath until the episode passed.

As the convulsions worsened and became more frequent, Mary feared that a particularly violent one might end Joshua's life, that the breath taken and held might be his last.

"What happens," she asked her confidant, Hare, "when the seizure lasts longer than the air in his lungs?"

Hare had no answer, except perhaps the one she feared to hear.

"With these episodes he has been having," Mary said, "I have been wondering if we should try to hurry to a nearer port. Mr. Hare, do you know anything of San Diego or Santa Barbara?"

Hare shook his head. "Those places do not have near the shipping that San Francisco has. Or the population. San Diego probably has good doctors, but the whole place is in Spanish. Do you speak any Spanish?"

"Only a few words."

"I think it best we go on."

"I agree," Mary said. "If we were going to stop short, we should have done it a month ago, and gone back to Rio."

It was clear that neither wanted to go anywhere but San Francisco. Mary returned to the problem at hand.

"I feel the key is to reduce the fever," she said, "but no amount of cold compresses seem to do enough. I have even removed most of his clothes and often cover him not even with a thin sheet. I do not know what else to do."

Hare knitted his brow. "It is his head that is most affected, isn't it?"

"Yes."

"And his head that most needs relief?"

"Yes."

"Well," Hare said thoughtfully, "it might not help, but maybe we should cut his hair. I have noticed it is often damp with sweat anyway."

Mary suddenly felt foolish that she had not thought of that herself. "Of course. We should do that. We should do it right away."

Once the idea was presented, Mary carried it a step further. Throughout his illness, she had kept Joshua's face shaved. At first it had been at the hands of a skilled and willing crewman, but after closely observing the technique she had started shaving the light beard herself. Now she cropped his hair short and carefully took the razor to his scalp, shaving it bare. The pale, smooth skin where her husband's thick head of hair had been so greatly altered his appearance that at first it was hard for her to believe it was the same person. The bald, emaciated body now in her charge bore scant resemblance to the healthy, vibrant Joshua of the start of the voyage.

After the head shaving was complete, she cleaned and put away the razor and the strop. That done, and with nothing else to do, she sat back down at the side of the bed and wept, again.

North of the equator, sailing far off the coast of Central America, *Neptune's Car* came into winds that gradually increased again, but now out of the northeast, almost directly abeam to starboard. While not so fast as when running before the southeast trades of the Southern Hemisphere, reasonably good time was made, averaging better than ten knots. The crew seemed to sense that landfall was not many days away, and they went about their duties with good morale and diligence.

Once, while on deck, Mary noticed the spirit of the men and remarked upon it to Timothy Hare.

"The men seem to be going along quite well," she said.

"Aye, ma'am. They usually do when satisfied with their command. One ship is about the same as another. It is the master they serve that makes the difference."

"They must not mind serving under you, Mr. Hare."

Hare looked up into the mainmast rigging, watching the men bending a replacement topgallant. He did not look her way but said, "It is you they are proud to serve under, ma'am."

For all the success with the ship and crew, there was less success down below. As the changes of latitude distanced them from the equator and left ever more ocean behind, the temperatures moderated somewhat, and Mary watched Joshua closely. She hardly left his side in hopes of seeing that the cooler air would alleviate his fever. It did not.

The entire distance from the equator to the coast of California was traversed without a coherent word passing Joshua's lips.

Mary Patten, after a careful check of Maury's "Wind and Current Charts," had Timothy Hare follow a course that took *Neptune's Car* several hundred miles off California to avoid most of the south-flowing current that ran along the coast. Hare waited until nearly abeam the Golden Gate before turning northeast for the run into San Francisco Bay.

Thirty miles off the coast, the Farallon Islands stood like sentinels guarding the bay's entrance, the first land sighted by approaching ships. The appearance of the islands assured the crew of *Neptune's Car* that the long ocean passage would soon be over. Soon a harbor pilot would be coming aboard to guide the ship through the Golden Gate. In any time it was cause for joy, after months at sea and the trials of rounding the Horn, but on this particular ship each man knew the captain needed medical help, and that this was finally a place to get it.

They were no doubt also concerned for the captain's wife. The crew had to know that the long wait to reach land was a heavy burden for the young girl. She had been seen less and less on deck as the weeks had passed, withdrawing more and more into the small world of captain and cabin.

"The men offer you their sympathy," Hare reported once. "And I assure you it is most heartfelt."

"Tell the men I am very thankful," Mary said, her own heart swelling with emotion. "And that I will never forget their unwavering support."

Now, so near their destination, with the fruits of their labors nearly in hand, the occupants of the extreme clipper *Neptune's Car*— officers, crew, and lone female passenger—were confronted with yet another phenomenon of nature's weather. Much less dramatic than the ice and storms of the Horn, but no less a hindrance to their progress, was a loss of wind.

The northeast trades, which had blown steadily for the two and a half weeks since the ship passed through the light airs of the equator, began to die away. Over a period of forty-eight hours, the wind gradually diminished until, just as the welcome sight of the Farallons rose into view, the ever lessening breeze faded away completely. *Neptune's Car*, designed for speed and built for hard driving in heavy weather, coasted to a stop.

The Farallons, landmarks of the Golden Gate, slid to a position on the port horizon and stayed there.

Men working on the high masts reported that the headlands surrounding San Francisco Bay could be seen faintly breaking the flat line of the horizon. From her vantage point on the deck, Mary could not see these hills of the coast.

"It is just as well," she said to Hare. "If I could see the entrance to the harbor, but not get there, it might be more than I could stand." She looked at the surrounding flat sea. Overhead, the sails hung limp. "This is bad enough."

Hare tried to sound optimistic. "We may be seen by a pilot schooner. A pilot could arrange for a steam tug to come out and tow us in. Either way, it won't be long, now. We will be there soon."

But they were not there soon. A day passed, then another, with almost no movement. Mary waited, trying to be patient, but found it impossible to do so. To be so close but getting no closer made new demands upon her weary heart.

If anything, the ship drifted south with the ocean current, putting ever more distance between it and its destination. On the third day Hare had two boats lowered and teams of men oared for hours, towing the ship, trying to keep it from moving too much farther south. Their efforts seemed to have little effect. *Neptune's Car* was too heavy a ship, and too heavy with cargo.

"I have heard of captains moving their ships this way," Hare said, watching from the rail, "but I believe they must have been smaller ships."

Mary stood beside him. Her impatience to make port was causing her to come out on deck more often, hoping to see some luff in the sails. "It is not possible, then, to draw us closer to shore?"

"I know how much you want me to say yes. But I can't. It's too far, and the men couldn't take it. The best we can hope for is to row into a breeze. And that would just be a matter of luck."

"Luck is something we have been lacking, Mr. Hare."

The days passed. Each day Mary rose and went out on deck only to see the sails hanging limp from their yardarms. Ever mindful of the care of the ship, Hare had the crew replace the sails that had brought them up the Pacific with an older, more worn set to prevent the good from being damaged by slatting slackly against the rigging. Trying to gain every advantage, he put out all available sail, right up to the moonrakers, ready for any wayward breeze. He even had the men wet the sails, hoisting heavy buckets of sea water aloft to be poured over the canvas. The water was intended to close up the pores in the fabric, preventing the slightest air from slipping through.

For all Hare's efforts, and those of the crew, *Neptune's Car* sat, like the ship of Coleridge's Ancient Mariner, "as idle as a painted ship upon a painted ocean."

And so it was.

Lookouts watched for other ships, but no sailing ship could move any more than *Neptune's Car*, and if any steamer came or went out of the harbor it did not come near enough to be seen. Once or twice, men on the foretop truck reported a smudge of black smoke on the horizon, but not the ship or tug that produced it.

Joshua's fever finally seemed to ease somewhat, and although Mary did not know whether to attribute his relief to the cooler air of the more northerly latitude or the shaving of his head, she was deeply grateful. Temporarily, at least, the convulsions left him, and after a day or two of easier rest he even showed signs of regaining consciousness, drifting in and out of deep sleep. Vigilant for signs of recovery, Mary stayed close by his side, wanting to be there should he awake.

She had bathed his head with a cool cloth and was turned toward the basin when he said, "Mary."

His voice was weak and dry, but her heart leaped. In an instant, she was at his side, on her knees by the bed.

"Joshua?" She waited, afraid he would not say more.

His eyes flickered and opened, but as she leaned over his face she could tell that he could not see her.

"I'm here, darling," she said. "I'm right here."

"I cannot see."

"I know. But you are awake. And speaking. Which is more than you have done lately."

For a moment he was silent, as if considering his circumstances. "How long has it been?"

"Since you were last awake?" Mary realized she had no idea. It seemed like forever. "It has been many days. But that is past. Now you are with me again."

Joshua said, "I have always been with you."

For the rest of the day, Joshua lingered on the edge of sentience, sometimes drifting back into sleep, never becoming fully cognizant of his surroundings. Mary was afraid that at any moment he could slip back into unconsciousness.

In the afternoon he seemed to remember that he was the captain of the ship. He asked about their position, and was pleased to learn that San Francisco was near. "Your navigation skills have come into good use," he said.

"It is good that you showed me how."

"I recall that you insisted."

He was also not surprised to learn of the calm. "We are not the first ship trapped here," he said.

He asked about the crew, and after Mary reported their faithful service, he again gave her credit. "Your skills as navigator are surpassed only by your tact in handling men."

Mary passed the credit to Mr. Hare.

As night fell and darkness gathered in the tiny cabin, Mary broached the subject that she had not mentioned before for fear it would worry Joshua more than his weakened state could stand. During these last days of convulsive unconsciousness, however, she had decided that if he should awaken again, she would have to tell him, or she might not get another chance. What if he soon returned to his ethereal world, and did not come back out? Now, she knew, was the time to tell him that he was to be a father.

She slipped into bed, feeling Joshua's warmth under the covers. She touched him tenderly, running a finger over his cheek, around his lips, and a hand across his chest. He responded by raising a weak hand, taking her fingers in his.

"I have something to tell you," she said. "Something I have not mentioned before, for fear it would cause you worry."

Joshua frowned. "What is it, Mary? What's wrong?"

Mary squeezed his hand. "Nothing is wrong. In fact, it is something wonderful."

He turned his pale face toward her, straining his eyes to see her expression.

Mary was excited, but at the same time anxious. She had been wanting for so long to tell someone the news, and most of all she had wanted to tell her husband. "Please do not be angry with me for not telling you sooner."

"Then, please. Tell me now."

"Joshua, we are going to have a baby."

Joshua's face went blank. "A baby?"

"Yes." Mary felt herself beaming. She was so happy that Joshua finally knew.

"A baby." Joshua smiled, his face changing to one of amazement and then of joy. "Why didn't you tell me before?"

"I wanted to. So badly. But when I first became aware of it, you were so ill. I could not have told you if I wanted to. Then the weather turned so foul. I did not want to worry you."

"How could this worry me?"

Mary did not answer. She let him make the conclusion on his own.

"You did not want me to dwell upon the consequences, should I not recover."

Mary was silent, her agreement unspoken.

"Well," Joshua said. "I'll just have to. Recover, that is."

Mary pressed against him, no longer worried that he might feel her new shape. "And I know you will."

She kissed him and pulled his hand inside her cloak, placing it on her taut belly. "Feel," she said, and he rubbed about on the new roundness. His hand explored all about, feeling her new dimensions, and came to rest on top of her new and growing mound.

"You are eating well."

Mary laughed. Joshua's sense of humor remained intact.

"How soon, do you think?" he asked. "How far along are you?"

"I am not sure. Four and a half months, I think. It must have happened right before the voyage, or right after we left port. Perhaps during our stay at the hotel in New York. You were very loving then, you will recall."

Joshua smiled. "I recall."

"Ooh," Mary said suddenly. "Put your hand right here. Feel that?"

Joshua felt. Mary moved his hand an inch or two and pressed it against her. The movement was so slight, just a twitch, that she was afraid his fingers might not pick it up. After a minute, the tiny baby moved again, as if stretching its newly forming legs.

"I feel it!" The excitement in Joshua's voice, at the realization that he was feeling a child, his child, move in Mary's womb, was almost childlike itself.

The next hour, spent in playful cuddling, with kisses and touches and expressions of love, were heaven to Mary. The fears and perils of the last months were temporarily forgotten as she and Joshua reveled in their love and its coming legacy.

Finally, Joshua let his head sink back into the pillow. He closed his unseeing eyes and was soon on the verge of sleep.

In the dark of the cabin, Mary felt rather than saw that he had become very tired. "Rest, my darling," she said.

"I think I will. This excitement is too much for one day."

Reluctantly, Mary let him go.

The next morning, Joshua did not awaken, and during the course of the day his gentle sleep gradually became more restless. His fever returned, and by evening he was again enveloped in his own demonic world. To Mary's despair he had slipped away yet again, but she took some comfort in that he carried with him knowledge of his paternity.

Outside the quiet cabin, the ship waited on the quiet sea.

CHAPTER 27

Wind

On the morning of the tenth day becalmed, and the fifty-sixth day since Joshua became ill, Mary went on deck early. She found the daily housekeeping chores just completed, the deck still wet from the scrubbing with coarse holystones. The abrasive action of the stones kept the boards clean and new looking, rather than the darkened weathering that the elements would otherwise impose. It was a chore to rub the deck down every day, but even the most jaded sailor had to admit that a well-maintained deck was the single most important part of a good ship's appearance.

By tradition, all crews sailing the tall ships, and the proud clippers in particular, worked to make their vessel shipshape before entering port, and the delay forced upon *Neptune's Car* by the lack of wind gave its crew more than enough time to ready the ship for entry into San Francisco Bay. The decks were scrubbed. The seams between the boards were resealed, the oakum caulking that had worked loose in the strain of Cape Horn replaced. All woodwork was polished and varnished. Dull paint was covered by a new shiny gloss. The masts had been painted or whitewashed and newly "slushed" with grease from the kitchen for ease of raising and lowering the yardarms. The rigging, both standing and running, was coated anew with a slurry mix of linseed oil, lampblack, and tar. Besides making them weatherproof, the mixture blackened the lines so that they stood out sharply against the white of the sails. The only element lacking for a triumphant entry into the harbor was wind.

Mary surveyed the scene. The ship was sharp, the sails hung ready. All around was the flat, listless sea.

The ship had drifted south, and the southernmost Farallon, with the high peak called "Mast top" by the crew, had faded onto the faraway horizon. After weeks of getting closer to their destination, they were now farther away.

If Mary thought the sea looked listless, she reasoned, it was because she was looking at it through listless eyes.

The last days had been difficult. Joshua stirred often and was restless, but evermore unresponsive to Mary's touch. Nothing she did seemed to give him comfort, and she was weary of endless effort with no result. She was not sleeping well, and now, on deck, she hardly had the strength to climb the stairs to the poop. Beginning to visibly show her pregnancy, she was starting to feel the new weight, but as she went up the steps, slowly raising each foot to the next riser, it was the weight on her shoulders that she felt the most.

Timothy Hare, hands clasped over the port rail, forearms resting on the smooth round wood, looked tired, too. He did not move as Mary came up beside him.

"Morning, ma'am" he said.

"Good morning, Mr. Hare."

Both looked out across the smooth water.

After a time, Hare said, "Discouraging, isn't it?"

Mary wondered how long the calm could last. "I am not certain I can take much more of this waiting."

Hare half turned and studied her, but said nothing.

"This voyage has drained me," Mary said, "and I am about to worry myself to death."

Standing on the deck, with no other motion to obscure it, Mary felt the almost imperceptible sway of the ship as it rose and fell on long and nearly flat swells. Just as it had for ten days.

After a while, she said, "I guess I will return to the cabin. I see nothing out here to hold my interest."

She left Hare on the quarterdeck and was down the steps and almost to the cabin door when a voice from aloft shouted down to the deck.

"Breeze to starboard!"

Could it be? Mary felt hope. She looked to the south. At first the sea seemed unchanged, still mirror flat, but then came a movement, an approaching distortion of the surface that foretold a coming parcel of wind.

For a second no one moved. The score of men on watch, scattered about the ship, stopped whatever they were doing to look for the wind. Now, seeing the advancing front of the newly stirred water moving toward the ship, they sprang into action.

There was no need for Hare to order them to their stations. The breeze, however slight, was coming from the starboard quarter, and every man knew exactly what needed to be done to ready the sails for wind from that direction. Hare shouted instructions, but the men were already putting them into effect. Some lines were loosened. Others were hauled in tight and rewrapped around their belaying pins to hold the sails ready for the breath of air that promised to return life to the ship.

Seconds after the men went to work, the first puff reached *Neptune's Car*. It touched the high sails first, giving a gentle pop as the moonrakers and royals filled out. Then the topgallants rippled and likewise started to take shape. A half second later the topsails and courses waved, moving in a long slow billow.

As the leading edge of the breeze reached the deck, Mary felt the first tiny gust kiss her face. With renewed energy, she turned back for the stairs, hurrying up to the higher deck for a better view.

Hare was by the helm, watching for signs that this little wind was not a momentary pulse, but more lasting. It was not a strong wind, but the waiting sails took it in, filling their panels.

Just as the sails filled, the wind began to lessen, teasingly leaving the ship as quickly as it had arrived. The canvas sagged as the few seconds of new life slipped away. All on board stopped what they were doing, watching for more breeze to come, afraid that it would not. A minute later the sails swelled again, the breeze stronger now. This time the wind did last, giving purpose to the canvas that had hung useless for so many days.

Slowly, the ship began to move. At first the motion was so slight that Mary leaned out over the port rail to study the water where it met the hull. She could see the water begin to flow past the dark planks as the ship overcame the inertia of rest and slid forward before the wind. There was indeed movement. As the ship came to life, Mary's heart did also. What had been a dead weight in her chest suddenly beat with excitement. Perhaps all was not lost. Perhaps this voyage *would* end.

"We are moving, Mr. Hare!" She turned to make this report and saw Hare beaming back at her.

"Yes, ma'am, we are."

Mary felt the urge to spread the news. "I must go tell Joshua," she said, and hurried toward the steps and down to the cabin.

By the bed she knelt and took her husband's hand, gripping it tightly.

"There is wind, my love. There is wind. Listen. Hear the hull against the water? We are moving." She hoped he could hear and understand what she was saying, but just being able to say it helped her feel better.

She stayed with him for a while, nursing him once again with cool cloths and loving concern. For an hour she sat by Joshua's side, keeping an ear to the ship, afraid that at any moment the wind would die away.

But it did not. Instead, the ship moved faster, the floor of the cabin resuming its familiar tilt as the sails leaned the ship before the wind. With each passing minute, Mary's hope grew. Even a light wind, if it held, meant that sometime today *Neptune's Car* would be anchored in a safe harbor. In San Francisco Bay, with other ships moored nearby and a city of people just across the way. No more solitude, no more helplessness. There would be a hospital, with doctors who would know what to do.

Sure that making port was imminent, she decided to clean Joshua up for the arrival, bathing him with towels and a basin of water and shaving again, both his beard and his head.

The morning toilet complete, she kissed his smooth head and said, "Soon, dear, I will have you in the hands of the physicians you have needed for so long. Just a little longer."

Joshua, as usual, made no response.

*   *   *

After a hasty light breakfast, Mary returned to the quarterdeck. She was amazed at the change of scenery. The horizon, for so many weeks a uniform flat line in every direction, was filled for fully half its expanse with the hazy green hills of land. She looked back once at the wide ocean, and laughed out loud.

Hare looked curiously at her.

"We beat it, Mr. Hare. We forged on and we beat it. Cape Horn, the storms, the miles we have traveled. And now look. It is behind us. It is all behind us!"

Hare smiled, and his grin reminded Mary of the day they left New York. On that day, he had been standing next to Keeler, holding his hat in his hands, with a big smile on his face as if he were just as pleased as he could be. It struck Mary that she had not seen that particular smile in some time, perhaps since New York.

"It has been quite a trip, hasn't it, Mr. Hare?"

Hare basked with her in the light of their success. "Yes, ma'am, quite a trip."

Mary looked forward toward the hills. "Where are we? Where is the harbor?"

"I think it is right over there," Hare said. "If I remember right, that rise we see dead ahead shoulders the south side of the entrance, and that higher hill is on the north. I think I see an opening between the two."

"I see it, too. Oh, Timothy, I'm so excited."

Hare glanced over with an odd look, and it occurred to her that, for the first time, she had called him by his Christian name. She felt sheepish.

He said, "I think we are all excited."

As they neared the coast, the wind picked up even more, and one last throw of the chip showed *Neptune's Car* to be making ten knots.

"At this rate," said Hare, "we'll be in port in an hour."

Mary could hardly contain herself. She felt like a child at Christmas again, like a debutante getting ready for the ball. It was so good to feel young again. She hurried down to check on Joshua. He was missing all the excitement, and she told him so, rubbing his warm hand.

"The hills, Joshua. The hills are so green. Soon we will be safe in the harbor, and we will have you a doctor. We are going to make it, dear. We are going to make it."

Joshua was quiet, his unchanged expression giving no indication that he heard or understood. Mary stayed with him for a short while, then went back out to see their progress.

On deck, she said, "Should I bring up the charts, Mr. Hare, to help with finding the entrance?"

Hare was watching forward. "I don't think we'll need it. We will just follow that schooner."

Mary looked, and indeed there were sails a few miles ahead, likewise making for the bay. It was the first ship they had seen since the storm-damaged clipper that had signaled to them on the Atlantic side of Cape Horn.

"Why, yes," Mary agreed, thrilled at the sight of other sails. "We'll just follow them."

"Actually," said Hare. "Come to think of it, we may need the soundings for the bay."

Mary ran again to the cabin. Stopping only long enough to pat Joshua's hand and say, "Soon!" she returned with the chart of the bay, its depth marked in fathoms. Hare studied the numbers, and Mary watched him.

"Do you see what you need?" she asked.

Hare said, "Yes, I think so."

He seemed proud. During the last weeks, and during the ten days of calm especially, Mr. Irwin, the cook and old sage of the crew, had been working with him on writing and reading. Mary, too, had joined in his education and was proud for him.

"Call the men, Mr. Hare. I want to thank them for their support, and we may be too busy later."

Both watches were already on deck, as all hands were eager to see land, and within a matter of moments the crew was assembled below the quarterdeck rail, just as they had at the beginning of Joshua's illness. On that day, Mary had been forced to shout to be heard over the cold wind. Today the weather was much more pleasant, and the message was one of joy, but as she began, she realized she had little to say.

"Nearly two months ago this ship was put into unusual circumstances. At that time, you agreed to work with Mr. Hare and me in continuing the voyage. In those two months, which seemed to me more like two years, you have steadfastly served this ship. Today I wish to thank you."

Mary paused. To thank the crew was as far ahead as she had thought. The gathered men waited for her to continue.

"It was a difficult passage around Cape Horn, and you never wavered. You must have had uncertainties, knowing the amount of Mr. Hare's experience, and perhaps the first mate should have been allowed to take us around. But—"

"No."

The single word, coming from within the crowd, stopped Mary. A few of the men stirred, as if unsure of her reaction to the interjected word. She decided not to react at all. The voice of support was not loud, but it was definitive, and hearing it eased her nerves as she stood before the men.

She took a breath, and continued. "In the beginning, I had hopes the captain would recover from the fever that has gripped him, and that his absence from the deck would be short and temporary. As you know, that has not been the case. His illness has proved to be much longer lasting, and much more severe, than I had hoped. I remain hopeful . . ."

Mary felt an oncoming rush of tears. She fought them back, stopping again to compose herself. This farewell speech was proving to be more difficult than she expected. She decided to finish quickly.

"In a very short time, with the grace of God, we will be safely moored in San Francisco Bay. I will leave this ship with my husband and will likely never see any of you again. I assume a new master will take command of *Neptune's Car*, but I do not know how quickly that might happen. Should you wish to stay on as crew, I will speak well in your behalf. Your support, and the support and leadership of Mr. Hare, has been overwhelming."

She stopped, and wondered if there was anything more she should say. She felt her emotions crowding her again.

She turned to the mate, standing at her side throughout. In a low voice she said, "I'm finished, Mr. Hare. Dismiss the men."

Feeling tears in her eyes, she retreated to the stern rails, where she stood with her back to the ship, looking out over the ocean whence they had come, and wondered if the tears that flowed so freely now were from pent-up fears or if they were tears of joy.

Just as Hare had predicted, the next hour saw them passing the headlands of the Golden Gate, entrance to the wide San Francisco Bay. As the promontory of Point Bonita went by the port side, the limitless expanse of empty ocean was replaced by a harbor filled with boats and ships of all sizes engaged in all manner of activities. Scattered across the bay were countless small vessels, some anchored, some moving, many under black columns of smoke rising from steam boilers.

On the right side of the bay, coming gradually into view from around an obscuring point of land, was an enormous mass of ships. There must be hundreds of them, thought Mary, more than in the East River of New York, even. Unlike New York, these vessels were not parked in a neat row, but anchored wherever there was room. Among the active merchantmen were many others, ships that had been there for years, left derelict when entire crews had abandoned them for the goldfields.

Above this jam of ships, spread over the hills sloping up from the water, lay the city of San Francisco. Even at first glance, Mary could see that it had grown since she was last here. The gold rush was nearly over, but this city was still booming. She could hardly wait to be among its people.

Hare, concentrating on the course into the harbor, issued frequent commands, making small corrections to negotiate the channel and avoid other traffic. When well into the bay, and some mile or so abeam the city wharves, he called men to the anchor capstans. Others he sent to ready sails to be furled.

Approaching a jut of land labeled on the chart as North Point, he began, in rapid fashion, to order the sails taken, from top to bottom. The royals had been struck outside the bay, and now the topgallants: "Ease the sheets! Rise tacks and sheets! Upper topsails, now. Ease the halyard. Haul around the clew lines!"

One by one, with a half dozen commands for each, the square sails that had brought *Neptune's Car* around from New York were gathered in. Yardarms were lowered into their lifts, lines given their slack. High above the deck, feet on the foot ropes, rows of men leaned over the yards and grabbed handfuls of sail, pulling them up tight against the thick round spars. Working quickly, but careful to do a neat job for appearance' sake, as their work would be seen by all in the harbor, the crew lashed the sails in a tight, smooth bundle, fastening them with their gaskets to the yardarm jackstays. In ten minutes the work was done, and the clipper, losing its forward momentum, slowed noticeably.

Satisfied with their position, Hare said to the helm, "Hard to windward." The ship used the last of its speed to turn back toward the wind. In a voice loud enough to be clearly heard at the bow capstan, Hare said, "Let go the starboard anchor." Immediately, the heavy clatter of anchor chain running through the hawsepipe reverberated throughout the ship. After several seconds, the anchor found the ground. After paying out twice again as much line for proper scope, the men on the capstan stopped turning. All was quiet on board for a minute or two, and then came the call from the bow: "Anchor brought to and holding, sir."

The date was November 15, 1856. *Neptune's Car* was 138 days coming from New York. The time was well off the even one hundred days Joshua had made the year before, but the cargo was nevertheless at its destination.

Hare, his work of driving the ship done, looked over at Mary, who had been watching the proceeding from an out-of-the-way corner of the deck.

"We're here, ma'am."

CHAPTER 28

San Francisco

No sooner had *Neptune's Car* made its first swing on the anchor chain than it had its first visitors. From all directions came small boats, oared by frantic peddlers, each wanting to be the first to offer the ship fresh fruit, fresh meat, fresh bread, or anything else that the crew, after months at sea, would consider fresh.

Mary avoided listening to any conversations between men standing in the boats and the crew concerning fresh women.

Other boatmen arrived advertising boardinghouses, each being, by their word, the best place to stay. The old salts of the crew warned those making their first voyage to California to be wary.

"Those men are the pirates," they said through clenched teeth. "Some houses promise to supply crew to outbound ships. These pirates lure you there, just off a long sail, and the next thing you know you have been knocked on the head and wake up on your way to China. Shanghaied, they call it."

Finding no gullible takers, the boardinghouse men eventually rowed away. "Be careful ashore, too," the old heads said. "Those same bastards will be waiting in the taverns. Be wanting to buy you drinks."

Just behind the peddlers and the pirates came a small steam-driven boat, most of its tiny deck taken up by a small square wheelhouse. Smoke puffed from a short stack rising out of the engine compartment. From its deck came the hail of a harbor pilot, asking to be taken aboard. Mary thought it a little late for his services, but Hare called back, "Yes, please come aboard."

To Mary, standing at his side, Hare whispered, "There may be some cross words here, ma'am."

The pilot, dressed in a starched white military style uniform, complete with braid on the shoulders, was a squat, heavy man of Spanish extraction, his olive skin accenting the large white orbs of his eyes. His face was unsmiling, and he appeared to be on the verge of anger. He stepped aboard and said to Hare, "By whose authority was this vessel brought into port? And whose decision was it to anchor on this spot?"

Hare hesitated, and said, "I suppose it was mine, sir."

"You are the master of this ship?"

Hare glanced toward Mary and said, "No, sir. Second mate. Patten is master."

The pilot made a quick visual search of the deck. "I wish to speak to Captain Patten."

"The captain has taken ill these past months, sir, and is confined to bed."

"You are second mate, you say?"

"Aye, sir. Name is Hare." He offered his hand. The harbor pilot, still looking about the ship, took it for a brief, perfunctory second before unceremoniously dropping it.

"And the first mate?"

"The first mate is under arrest and is being kept below."

"Arrest?"

"Aye, sir."

"So the vessel is under your command?"

Hare looked toward Mary again. "I commanded the crew. But I was not in command of the ship."

"Then who was?"

"The captain's wife." Hare raised his arm toward her and said, "Mrs. Patten."

The pilot raised an eyebrow. Turning toward the young woman standing a few feet away, he said, "Is that true?"

While listening, Mary had formed a rather low opinion of the pilot. She had not planned to say anything, but his impertinence toward Hare prompted her to speak. "I played a small role in navigation. But it was Mr. Hare who ran the ship. And I must say, Mr.—I'm sorry. You never offered Mr. Hare your name."

As she spoke, the pilot turned fully her way. "Martino, Commodore Martino." He gave a toothy smile and extended a hand.

Mary took it and gave it the same half shake he had given Hare's. "Commodore Martino, *Neptune's Car* is in Mr. Hare's hands, and I would expect you to treat him with the respect he deserves."

The teeth disappeared, and some of the air that inflated the pilot's arrogance seemed to escape. "I see." He studied Mary for a second and said, "Please accept my apologies, madam."

Turning back to Hare, he said, "And I apologize to you, sir. I came aboard angry about your lack of procedure. Perhaps I was hasty in making judgments."

Hare offered a smile. "Perhaps your lack of civility and my lack of procedure balance each other out. No harm done, sir." He offered his hand again, and this time Martino took it and held it.

"As you say," he said, "no harm done."

The slate clean, Hare started the conversation anew. "Now I will apologize. I have never taken a ship into harbor before, but I think I knew I was supposed to wait outside the bay for you."

"So why did you not?"

Hare gave a brief smile. "Actually, we waited ten days, becalmed just outside the Farallons."

Martino nodded. This was not the first time a ship had suffered through those calms. "Still, next time you should wait. I could have found you a better place to anchor. But this will do. The tugs can move your ship to the docks from here, and I can help you negotiate the fee for a tug."

Hare said, "For a fee, of course."

"Of course."

Hare smiled, catching up to the local customs. Martino did not care that they had sailed in on their own, except that it took money out of his pocket. "Perhaps we can hire you to arrange contact with a doctor. It is for the captain that we did not want to stop, once we had a wind. He requires immediate attention."

"What is the nature of his illness?"

Hare deferred the question to Mary.

"I don't know," she said. "He is unconscious most of the time, delirious with fever."

Martino said, "May I see him?"

Mary took the pilot below, and he made a brief examination.

"We can send for a physician," he said, "but I think we should get him to the hospital."

Commodore Martino hurried back to the deck, shedding some of his haughty attitude. He looked out over the rail at the tiny boats clustered around the ship. One was manned by a young boy selling fruit. "You," he shouted, "apple boy. There's a dollar in it for you to go get a doctor."

"What about my fruit?" The boy had the high-pitched voice of youth.

"I will see that you get a good position to sell. Now go."

"Where? What do I tell him?"

Martino turned to Mary. "Madam, do you suppose the captain can be moved?"

"Moved?"

"Yes. Could we put him on my boat?"

Mary thought. Joshua would have to be carried off the ship, and Martino's boat was ready by the port rail. "Yes, I suppose."

To the fruit vendor, Martino called, "There is a doctor's office on Front Street, one block off California. Go there. Tell him the captain of this ship has a fever. Bring him to the docks. Meet us at the harbor master's."

"Yes, sir."

While Hare and a detachment of the crew lowered Joshua over the side to a makeshift cot on Martino's boat, the harbor pilot received from Mary some of the details of the voyage. As she told the story, his already large round eyes seemed to widen even more.

"You have had a truly trying experience, madam. Please forgive me for the way I came aboard. I deal so often with bully captains, I come ready to bully right back."

"Your assistance in getting my husband to medical care," Mary said, "will earn you complete forgiveness."

For the remainder of the day, Commodore Martino proved his sincerity and worth. At the dock he ushered the waiting physician to Joshua's cot and personally went out into the street to hire a passing wagon to take the patient to the Marine Hospital. He waited while Joshua was admitted and Mary reluctantly left him in care of others. After nearly two months, her husband's well-being was in someone else's hands. As they left the hospital, Mary silently prayed that they would have better results.

Martino showed her the way to the police station, where she reported Keeler's actions and arranged for him to be removed from the ship and placed in jail. The maritime court would no doubt be dealing harshly with him. Martino escorted her to the customs house, where he helped her begin the clearing process necessary to allow the ship to unload. After suggesting a hotel near the hospital, he offered to send for her luggage. Mary thanked him but declined the offer.

"There are things not yet packed," she said. "And I will need to oversee the removal of the captain's belongings." Mary swallowed hard and choked back a sudden surge of emotion. "We should not leave anything, as I don't suppose we'll be going back on board."

Martino patted her hand. "Very well, madam. We will take care of that later."

Mary took a breath, recovering her poise. "In the meanwhile, I would like to keep Mr. Hare apprised of my activities, if that would not be too much trouble."

Martino quickly dispatched a young boy to the docks with a note.

When Mary wished to go to the San Francisco offices of W. T. Coleman and Company, the consigners of the cargo in *Neptune's Car*'s hold, he showed her the way.

"Would this not be a duty of the second mate?" Martino asked.

Mary tactfully avoided telling him the reason Hare was not handling the clerical matters.

It was a walk of several blocks to the California Street address of Coleman and Company, part of which had a view of the harbor. The slender hull of the clipper, riding at her anchor, was visible across the way.

"You have a beautiful ship, madam. Well kept, it seems."

Mary offered a smile. "It has had a good crew. And they had ample time to make things neat during those ten days outside the bay."

"Still, I have seen many that were worse for the wear."

Mary thanked him for his comments. "It is a ship I have longed to be away from, but it is my husband's ship, and I do have a fondness for it. He had hoped to make a fast run of this passage."

She suddenly thought of the race that had started in New York. "Tell me, Mr. Martino. Do you know if the *Intrepid* has arrived in port?"

"*Intrepid*?" Martino's brow wrinkled. "I don't know the ship."

"It is a new one, on its maiden voyage. They left New York less than an hour behind us."

Martino smiled, his large teeth gleaming. "Ah, a race."

"It was to be. But we haven't seen it since the first day."

"I do not believe she has arrived, madam."

Mary was surprised. Without Joshua's drive for speed she had not entertained the notion of beating *Intrepid* to San Francisco. "And what of *Romance of the Seas*?"

"Now that," said Martino, "is a fine name for a clipper ship, is it not? Yes, *Romance of the Seas* has arrived. I piloted her in myself."

"When was that, sir? Has it been here long?"

Martino thought. "That ship arrived at least two weeks ago."

"I see," Mary said wistfully. So she and Hare had not done so well, after all. But *Intrepid* was late. She hoped it had not met with misfortune.

Informed of Joshua's illness, the agent of the Coleman Company assisted her in arranging the sending of messages to Stephen Wiley in the New York offices of Foster and Nickerson, the ship's owners. Arrangements would have to be made for the disposition of the vessel, and it would take two months for a response from New York.

Among all the uncertainties, the only thing certain was that Joshua would not be master of *Neptune's Car* whenever it left San Francisco.

Once all immediate duties were done, and a stop at the hospital showed Joshua to be resting in the ward, Mary asked to be taken back to the ship.

"There is unfinished business there, and our belongings to be gathered."

"My boat is at your disposal," said Martino.

"Your kindness, sir, seems to have no bounds," Mary said, her emotions nearly overcoming her.

As they were leaving the hospital, they saw Dr. Harris, who had met them at the dock and had since attended Joshua. He, too, was on his way out. Seeing Mary, he removed the hat he had just placed upon his head.

Dr. Harris was a tall, angular man of about sixty. His hair and neatly trimmed beard were both gray, with his blue eyes providing a hint of younger days. When he spoke, they sparkled with benevolent friendliness.

"Good afternoon, Mrs. Patten. I was hoping to see you before I left."

Mary, with visible eagerness, said, "Have you news?"

"Oh, no," said the doctor. "No, I have nothing new to report. Your husband is very ill. But you already know that."

"Yes. That I know." When the doctor said nothing else, Mary said, "I suppose it will be some time before we know anything."

The doctor smiled benignly. "Yes, give us a day or so. Perhaps by then I will have formed an opinion." His voice was deep and gravelly, but with a soft touch from years of developing a bedside manner.

"I do have a few questions to ask," he said. "The answers may help make a diagnosis."

"Of course," said Mary. "Anything at all."

"You were on your way out, I see. Perhaps I could just walk along with you."

"Yes, please do. We were on our way back to the ship."

"Good," said the doctor. "My office is in that direction."

He walked with Mary and Martino all the way to the docks, listening to Mary's account of the voyage. Once at the dock, he followed them onto Martino's boat and rode along across the bay to *Neptune's Car*. He was especially interested in the physical con-

frontation with Keeler, and asked several questions to clarify its possible connection to Joshua's collapse.

On board, Mary showed him the cabin where Joshua had spent
so many weeks confined to bed. She showed him the medical book
that had provided such scant knowledge and the box of medical
supplies that had proved so useless.

He assured her she had done all she could, that her care was
blameless for the lingering of the illness.

"Your words are very kind," she said, "but cannot erase those
helpless weeks."

Dr. Harris looked sympathetic. "I can scarcely imagine the despair
you felt." He sat in the wing back, watching Mary as she checked that
the wardrobe and all drawers were empty of personal belongings. The
large trunk, occupying the center of the room, had been packed during the days becalmed of the headlands of the bay, and she now finished packing the remaining luggage. Into the two smaller valises she
put the last vestiges of her and Joshua's life aboard the ship. Sad to
be leaving, she was glad for the presence of the doctor.

"For almost two years," she said, "this has been our home.
Around the world and halfway again. It is difficult to imagine never
seeing it again."

From a drawer containing Joshua's things, she took a small fold
of white cloth. She looked at it with a little curiosity for a moment
before placing it in the bag. The doctor leaned forward in the chair.

"What was that?"

Mary picked the cloth back up. "This? It is Joshua's. Something
to do with being a member of the Masons."

"I thought so. May I see it?"

Dr. Harris took the cloth and unfolded it. Spread across his knees
it became a small apron, the lambskin used in formal Masonic ceremony. He looked at it thoughtfully.

"Captain Patten is a Mason?"

"Yes. In New York."

"If he is a Mason in New York, he is a Mason here."

She nodded, wondering what the doctor was leading up to.

"Mrs. Patten," he said. "Do you know anyone in San Francisco?
Anyone to comfort and assist you?"

"No," she answered.

"You have no acquaintance to rely upon? No friend of your husband?"

"No. No one at all."

"You may be mistaken about that." He smiled. "I, too, have such an apron."

"You are a Mason?"

"Yes. And I believe you will find the local lodge sympathetic to your needs."

The doctor, having watched her move about the cabin, said, "Is there anything else we need to discuss?"

"Such as?"

"Such as your own condition."

Mary stopped packing. "I suppose we could."

"I've been waiting for you to mention it. Is everything going normally?"

"I hardly know, Doctor, what normal is. And I have been around no one to ask."

"Well, there is probably nothing to be concerned about. I only asked because of the strain you have been under."

"I'm glad you did. I have been dying to tell someone."

"You have told no one?"

"No."

"Not even your husband?"

"Oh, yes. I have told him. But only a few days ago, during his brief recovery while we were becalmed."

Dr. Harris smiled. "Was he pleased?"

"Very much so. And to think I almost did not tell him. I was afraid to cause him worry."

Dr. Harris looked thoughtful. "I understand your concern. But I'm glad you did."

Mary considered the import of the doctor's words. If Joshua did not know by now, he seemed to be saying, he might never know. She finished packing in silence.

Over the ensuing days, Mary found that Dr. Harris was correct about the Masons. Members of the San Francisco lodge were ready at every turn to help her. They waited with her at the hospital, where she kept the same vigil as she had done on the ship. They helped her around the city, assisting in business of the ship. Wives accompanied her to the shops, helping buy new clothes to fit her growing form. Masons arranged runners for errands, provided escorts about the streets, and sent messages by steamship to Joshua's home lodge in New York.

They also fended off the reporters pressing Mary for a story, for she soon found that her story was considered newsworthy.

The first reporter appeared at the door of her hotel room on the morning after her arrival, and during that day and the next she was besieged by men with notebooks. No sooner had she given her story, in considerable detail, to the *Alta California*, the leading newspaper of the city, than a reporter from the *Daily Evening Bulletin* called, asking for the same.

Others followed. Even the faraway *New York Times Herald*, she learned, had a man in San Francisco to send dispatches back to his home newspaper.

They all wanted to hear her story. At first she did not mind, and was even pleased that there was an interest in letting the world know what tragedy had befallen her husband. Soon, though, she tired of the attention. Despite their arrival in San Francisco and its medical help, Joshua's condition was scarcely improving, and she found it difficult to put on a pleasant face for the interviews. The attention directed at herself, she also felt, was unwarranted.

"I performed," she said, "only the plain duty of a wife towards a good husband, stricken down by what we now fear to be a hopeless disease."

Others did not see it that way. As the days passed, the actions taken by the captain's brave wife became known in places far removed from the destination port. That the New York and Boston papers would carry the story was not unexpected, but Mary was surprised to learn that accounts of the voyage were printed in newspapers across the country. She was soon being called the "Florence Nightingale of the Seas," and received messages of comfort and commendation almost daily.

Though pleased by the support and secretly proud of the praise, Mary was decidedly uncomfortable with the attention. Again and again she insisted that what she had done was no more than any wife would do, but no amount of modesty diminished the celebrity. Seeking out her steadfast companion of the last two months, she lamented her plight to Timothy Hare. She found him on the ship, now tied to the wharf, where its cargo had been off-loaded to the rightful owners. Hare still tended to duties of command after nearly two weeks in port, although no one had ever officially given him any authority.

"The simple act of attending to an ill husband has been a cause of more fame than one would expect," she said. "And I cannot seem to put it to rest."

"Maybe they see you as deserving it," Hare said.

"I can hardly see that I deserve all this. Having the story in the papers was innocuous enough, but it does not stop there. Now I am hearing from those calling themselves women's reformers or feminists, promoting the notion of equal rights for women."

"Equal rights?"

"Yes. That women are equal to men, and they deserve the same rights. They want to hold me up as proof that a woman can do anything a man can do."

Hare looked incredulous. "But they can't. There's some things — sometimes, well, well, what do you think?"

Mary felt a certain joy in seeing him get flustered. Upon first hearing of the budding women's movement, she had thought back to Joshua's quote after lightning struck the ship by saying she "was uncommon handy aboard a ship, and would doubtless be of service, if a man." She remembered wondering what being a man had to do with anything, and understood the position of the new feminists, but could not agree with them.

"What do I think? No, Mr. Hare, we are not equal. In some ways, men are no doubt superior. In some ways, women are. We are simply different."

"Then what is your response to these — what did you call them?"

"Feminists. I don't know. I think they are wasting their time on an intangible ideal, but I suppose I cannot stop them from using me as some sort of example. But I am no better than any other woman."

"But you have had circumstances."

"And that is the only difference."

While talking, the two had migrated from the middle of the quarterdeck to the railing, and now stood side by side, both looking out over the bay and its clustered ships. Beyond the masts, the city of San Francisco rose from the edge of the water to sprawl over the sides of the close hills. Hare changed the subject.

"I have heard of your condition," he said.

"Oh?"

"You kept it a well-guarded secret."

Mary looked down at her stomach, now showing plainly to anyone who paid attention. "If the voyage had lasted another week it would not have been so secret."

"Why didn't you tell me? I could have done more."

"What more could you have done?"

Hare said nothing for a moment. Then, he said, "Something."

"We all had burdens enough, Mr. Hare."

"A shared burden is much easier to bear."

"Perhaps I should have told you. Toward the last, I was feeling overwhelmed. Very overwhelmed."

"I could have helped."

"I know."

Another silence fell between them.

"Have you heard from the company about a new captain?" she asked.

"Not yet."

"In the meanwhile, you are just waiting."

"Yes. No matter. There is plenty to keep me busy."

"You feel obliged to stay with the ship?"

Hare shrugged. "I've nothing better to do."

Mary felt a surge in her heart for the young mate. Half the ships in the harbor needed hands. Hare's reputation, enhanced by his service aboard *Neptune's Car*, would enable him to find a mate's position on almost any of them. His devotion to his ship kept him where he was.

"I am so happy to see you," she said. "I have missed your familiar face. These last days ashore have been, in some ways, as trying as those at sea."

Hare cast a wondering look at her. "Surely it is not as bad as all that," he said. "Are the memories of the trials we faced fading so soon?"

Mary smiled. "I suppose you are right. Still, being in San Francisco is not the panacea I had hoped it would be. Joshua is still not recovering, although I am grateful to have physicians attending to him. I was weary of the duty. I so fear, though, that I will never get him home to Boston."

"You mustn't despair, ma'am."

They stood together awhile longer. Mary felt a comfort from Timothy Hare's nearness. A half hour passed in small talk, neither wanting the responsibility of speaking of substance.

Finally, Mary said, "I should go."

Hare said, "I wish you could stay longer. The hours get long sitting out here."

"I will come again. Or you can visit us."

"I shall. Count upon it."

Mary smiled. "I have counted upon you for so much, Mr. Hare."

He returned the smile. "Just as you did only your duty as a good wife, I have only done the duty as a good mate."

Mary felt her eyes moisten. "Oh, you have been much more than a mate, Mr. Hare."

Without realizing she was moving, Mary found herself turned toward Timothy Hare and in a tearful embrace. He held her tight, and she him, and she could smell the wool of his coat. She felt his warmth and the strength in his chest, and she felt the tender and innocent emotions that had grown between them.

Over his shoulder she watched a ship gliding out of the harbor, and tears rolled down her cheeks at the thought of leaving Hare. Not of leaving him today, but leaving him for good, as she would soon be doing. Soon she would return to Boston with Joshua, whether he recovered or not, and Hare would sail away, either on this ship or another.

"It is entirely possible," she said, "that we will soon be separated by a world of ocean."

Hare took his arms from around her and held her shoulders with his hands. "That is true. Someday I will only be part of a very bad experience you once had."

"I don't think you will ever be only that."

Hare smiled. "I hope not."

Mary used a finger to wipe away her tears. "I should go."

"I know."

"Then you will visit the hospital?"

"Of course. I'll come tomorrow."

"I should go," Mary said again.

"Yes, you should. You probably have reporters waiting. Or more feminists."

Mary smiled, remembering what had brought her to the ship to begin with. Her public did not seem such a demand now.

"Thank you, Mr. Hare, for the shoulder to cry on."

She leaned forward to kiss his cheek, but instead kissed his lips, lightly, with restraint, but enough to taste them.

Then she turned and left the ship, walking alone down the docks to the street.

Epilogue

The stay in San Francisco lasted two months. Joshua spent the entire time in the Marine Hospital, regaining consciousness for only brief periods, and never with full lucidity. Timothy Hare came to visit, often at first and then less frequently. Dr. Harris came in nearly every day but offered little encouragement to go with his treatments. Another visitor was Captain Gardner of *Intrepid*, having arrived ten days after *Neptune's Car*. He, too, could offer only sympathy.

Most of the patients in the open ward were also men of the sea. They were thousands of miles from home and those who might love them, and so lay silent in their individual beds. Mary kept a chair by Joshua, but found that it did both her and the other patients good when she moved about, visiting each one.

As Christmas passed and the new year began, and Mary continued to grow in her pregnancy, she wondered how she would get Joshua and her coming child back to Boston. It was the dedication of the good Dr. Harris that eventually provided a way. He arranged passage by steamship to Panama, then overland by rail to another steamer bound for New York, and even accompanied the couple on the journey.

The March 18, 1857, edition of London's *Daily News* described the scene of Joshua and Mary Patten's arrival in New York:

One day last month the people in the streets of New York
observed a litter, evidently containing a sick person, carried
up from the shipping to the Battery Hotel. Beside the litter
walked a young creature who, but for her care-worn countenance and her being near her confinement, might have been
taken for a little school girl.

Joshua was carried ashore by fellow Masons, members of the
Polar Star Lodge alerted to the arrival of their fellow by Dr. Harris.
Mary did not want to put Joshua into a New York hospital, prefer-
ring to take him home to Boston. Knowing no place else to go, she
had his bearers deliver him to the same hotel where they had stayed
seven months before. The rooms may have been the same, but nothing else was. The nights and early mornings spent in tender love
were only memories, and the future was only something to fear.

As in San Francisco, the newspapers wanted to hear the story,
and the *New York Daily Tribune* obtained an interview with Mrs. Patten in their room at the hotel:

> She was assiduously attending her husband as heretofore;
> but the situation is such as to preclude all hope of
> recovery. . . . He now lies upon his couch insensible to every-
> thing but the kind offices of his beloved companion, and so
> weak that he may expire at any moment. . . .
> With that modesty which generally distinguishes true
> merit, Mrs. Patten begged to be excused from speaking
> about herself. She said that she had done no more than her
> duty, and as the recollection of her trials and sufferings evi-
> dently gave her pain, we could not do otherwise than respect
> her feelings. Her health is very much impaired from the
> hardships which she has undergone, and she is very near the
> period of maternity. Yet she does not spare herself in the
> least, but is most faithful and constant in her attentions to
> her husband.

While Mary was still in New York, a women's group in Boston
collected nearly $1,400 as a reward for her devotion to her duty.

When she protested, saying she did not deserve the money, the contributors insisted, saying that rather than a reward, it was intended to aid in paying Joshua's medical expenses.

Mary waited at the Battery Hotel until her brother arrived to assist her. They took Joshua home to Boston, arriving in late February. On March 10, 1857, she gave birth to a son, Joshua A. Patten, Jr.

The insurance underwriters who had a stake in the voyage also sent Mary a reward of one thousand dollars. By their own admission, it was a small sum for recognition of her efforts:

> In all the varied painful or beautiful positions in which any of your sex have been placed, we know of no instance where the love and devotion of a wife have been more impressively portrayed than in your watchfulness and care of your husband during his long and painful illness. Nor do we know of an instance on record where woman has, from force of circumstances, been called upon, or assumed, command of a large and valuable vessel, and exercise a proper control over a large number of seamen, and by her own skill and energy impress them with a confidence and reliance making all subordinate and obedient to that command.

Again Mary protested, downplaying her contribution. In a letter from Boston, dated February 25, 1857, she responded to the consortium of underwriters. With this letter, we are able to hear Mary's own modest words and feel her devotion to her husband.

> Gentlemen:
>
> I received yesterday your communication of the 18th inst., and it is with mingled sensations of gratitude and embarrassment that I leave my post, as watcher of my husband's sick bed to reply.
>
> I am sincerely grateful to you and to all those you represent for the very kind expression of sympathy, and for the liberal enclosure which you have transmitted to me in their behalf. I feel very sensibly, gentlemen, that kindness has prompted you to commend the manner in which I have en-

deavored to perform that which seemed to me, under the circumstances, only the plain duty of a wife towards a good husband, stricken down by (what we now fear to be) a hopeless disease, and to perform for him, as well as I could, those duties which he could not perform himself, especially when it was to carry out his own expressed wish. But I am, at the same time, seriously embarrassed by the fear that you may have overestimated the value of those services, because I feel that without the services of Mr. Hare, the second officer, a good seaman, and the hearty cooperation of the men to aid our endeavors, the ship would not have arrived safely at her destined port.

Be assured, gentlemen, that through all the trials which may be before me, and while I live, your considerate kindness will ever be held in thankful remembrance by yours, very respectfully,

Mary A. Patten

Her husband held to life for almost five more months. Nothing is known of his last days, the last recorded comments of his condition being the newspaper reports of the arrival in New York. The term *brain fever,* used to describe his illness in contemporary accounts, is unknown today. It may have been meningitis, encephalitis, or a symptom of tuberculosis, which has often been mentioned as the cause in various articles written over the years. The possibility of a head injury suffered during an altercation with Keeler is also a matter of conjecture. All that is known with certainty is that some pivotal act resulted in Keeler's arrest, and after several days of extra duty Captain Patten fell ill.

Joshua Patten died at the Somerville Lunatic Asylum outside Boston on July 25, 1857. His funeral was conducted by Rev. W. S. Smithett, the same minister who had baptized Mary and performed her marriage to Joshua. As described in the *Boston Daily Courier*, Reverend Smithett closed the sermon by paying

a high tribute to the deceased as a man beloved by all who knew him, a kind husband and a faithful friend to all those to whom he could render any service, either on sea or land.

The church services were solemn, and many of those present shed tears. Mrs. Patten was assisted into the church by two of her friends, and was so deeply affected that she could hardly walk after the services were over.

For all the attention she received at the time of the voyage, little is known about Mary afterwards. The only public mention to be found begins in 1858 in the Boston city directory, which lists: "Patten, Mary A., widow, boards at 7 Unity Court."

She is listed again in 1859, and then she disappears until the Boston death records for 1861. The cause of her death is listed as *phthisis*, an old term for a form of tuberculosis. Whether she contracted the disease while caring for Joshua is not known. Mary Ann Patten was not quite twenty-four.

As a footnote, it could be added that there is some controversy concerning the date of Mary's death. The above date, supported by death records in Boston, an obituary in the March 18, 1861, *Boston Daily Courier*, and cemetery records, is contradicted by another death notice published some sixteen years later. This, found in the *New York Herald* of March 5, 1877, reports the death of Mary Patton (note the different spelling) of Bridge Street, Brooklyn. The article goes on to detail the noteworthy voyage on *Neptune's Car*, and seems in every respect to be speaking of the heroine of this novel. Resolving this discrepancy involved much looking through old records, with only minimal satisfaction.

New York death records for the time are often in disarray and incomplete due, apparently, to movements throughout the boroughs and the occasional fire. A search of the archived death records in Manhattan's central depository produced no record for any Mary Patton, Patten, or other spelling variation. The only other clue comes from, again, the city directories. There, for the 1875–1876 issue, we do find a Mary Patton, widow of Patrick, living on Sullivan Street in Brooklyn. The name does not appear in the following year's edition, suggesting she may have died. Was this the Mary Patton of the 1877 obituary? And if so, had Mary Patten, widow of Joshua, later married Patrick, of the same last name with a different spelling? Hardly likely.

Without a definite resolution to the mystery, it may be supposed that an earnest reporter, seeing the name and remembering the voyage, confused two different people and wrote the story to fit. That seems the most likely reason, and allows us to believe the white stone marker that stands next to Joshua's in Woodlawn Cemetery in Everett, Massachusetts. There, chiseled in granite, is MARY ANN PATTEN, BORN APRIL 6, 1837, DIED MARCH 17, 1861.

The son born after the voyage and so soon left an orphan is likewise buried there, next to his mother and father. Nothing is known of his life, only that his death, at age forty-three, occurred in the harbor at Rockland, Maine, the family home, in September 1900. The Rockland vital records lists the cause of death as accidental drowning.

The ship in distress met by *Neptune's Car* on the way around Cape Horn was the *Rapid*, partially demasted and woefully shorthanded. Of the ship's twenty-four-man crew, only ten were available to work. The rest were either dead or too badly injured to assist in manning the ship. *Rapid* eventually made it back to Rio de Janeiro for repairs, but its captain made a notation in his log, angry at the lack of response to his plea for help. That the ship suffered such damage attests to the weather occurring around the cape in that fierce winter of 1856.

As further testament to the dangers of life at sea, the other ships of this narrative suffered as well. In 1860, after four years of service, the *Intrepid* ran aground in the straits of Sumatra, where it was raided by Malaysian pirates and burned, the crew narrowly escaping. A year later, *Romance of the Seas* left Hong Kong for San Francisco and was never heard from again, with the loss of thirty-five hands.

The fate of *Neptune's Car* is less certain. After Mary and Joshua left San Francisco, the ship continued across the Pacific to China under the command of a Captain Bearse. It made two more New York–to–San Francisco runs, including one in 1861, during which it put in to Rio de Janeiro for repairs to a sprung mast.

In late 1862, *Neptune's Car* was sold at auction in Liverpool and probably put into service in the Australian wool trade. As late as 1870 it was still listed in Lloyd's Register under that name, but after that mention it disappears from history.

The glory days of the clipper ships, which began in the late 1840s, lasted for only about a decade. Thousands of years of sailing knowledge culminated with the sleek and graceful vessels. For a shining moment, the clippers ruled the waves under wings of white. As quickly as they came into dominance, however, they fell out, replaced by the coming age of steam.

Any mention in the historical record of Keeler, whose real first name is not known, ends with his arrest in San Francisco. The only clue to his fate is hidden somewhere in the court records, probably buried in the vast files of the National Archives regional depository in San Bruno, California. Unless someone accidentally comes across this file, the punishment for his actions will remain unknown.

Whether Hare (whose true first name is likewise not known) stayed with *Neptune's Car* when it left San Francisco is unknown. Nor is it known if he was able to progress up the ranks of command. For the duration of this voyage, his actions were significant and his life important, but in the broad sweep of history, he fades into anonymity. His story, like that of Joshua and Mary Patten, is a short one, lasting 138 days. All else is as fleeting and transient as a wake upon the ocean.

AUTHOR'S NOTE
AND
ACKNOWLEDGMENTS

The story within these pages first presented itself to me in December 1995. A good friend and teacher lent me a book about the Atlantic Ocean written back in 1957 by Leonard Outhwaite. In this old book, in a chapter devoted to the era of clipper ships, was a one-paragraph mention of a young woman who assumed the duties of her captain husband after his incapacitation. Intrigued, I reread the passage and made note of the name of the ship, *Neptune's Car*.

This, I remembered thinking at the time, would make a good story.

Two months later, business took me to San Diego, where, as luck would have it, my third-floor window in the Holiday Inn looked out over the harbor. Across the street was the 216-foot-long bark-rigged *Star of India*, centerpiece of the San Diego Maritime Museum. Thinking of my story, I wandered over that evening and paid my money.

Yes, they had a research library, but it was closed for the day. Come back tomorrow. I thanked the girl and went aboard the *Star of India*. I walked the old wooden deck, below the enormous masts and yardarms with their bewildering array of shrouds and lines, and stood by the helm, imagining how it must have felt to sail the ships of old. I walked forward and stood above the forecastle, looking out over the bowsprit as the sun set over Point Loma.

Darkness cloaked itself around me as I sat on a wooden box and absorbed the feel of the ship. It was a quiet, still evening, and I had the deck to myself, except for a couple with two small children that made a cursory two-minute tour and departed back down to the street. They could now say they had seen the ship. But they had not. They could not have, not without slowing down for just minute. They did not feel it move, swaying ever so slightly at its moorings, and did not hear the soft breeze in the rigging.

I sat awhile longer, having nothing more important to do than pretend I was at sea.

The next day I took my first steps into the world of research libraries. Going back to the San Diego Maritime Museum, I was ushered down a hall and into small rooms crammed with books. With the aid of the librarian, a stout young man in wire-rimmed glasses, I sat down at a large table and went to work. Most references were brief—one line here, another there, but over the next few hours, the history of *Neptune's Car* began to emerge from the others, and one particular voyage began to emerge as more noteworthy than the rest.

Too soon, I had to leave the books and go to the airport, where a plane waited for me to go back to my landlocked home. By the time I left San Diego, though, I knew I had a story to tell. Over the next three or four years I visited many libraries and research institutions, and corresponded with many others, as well as many patient and generous individuals.

Time spent peering into microfilm readers and leafing through "many a quaint and curious volume of forgotten lore," led me to feel as if I had a personal acquaintance with the captain and his wife, although it was far from easy to attain. The passing of a century and a half left their actions obscure, with gaps in the record of what really happened on that 1856 voyage. Even names were difficult. Contemporary accounts referred to the wife only as "Mrs. Patten." I was several months into my research when I finally learned that her name was Mary.

I will long remember the exhilaration of discovery I felt that day.

Throughout the research and writing of this book, I had help and encouragement from many people. First, my wife and children were ever so understanding. Jan was my first critic, often seeing the chapters before anyone else, occasionally steering me back on course before I even knew I was off. Anna and Sam patiently let me have the computer, even though they would have liked to have it for themselves. They often got up in the mornings to find me typing away, and they watched over Dad's shoulder while he wrote the book that never seemed to get finished.

Anita Paddock, my first writing teacher, who has become my mentor and, hopefully, lifelong friend, deserves (and insists upon) special mention. Her support and encouragement have been endless. Clara Jane Rubarth, who lent me *The Atlantic* in the first place and started all this, also ranks high on my list of influential people.

I also need to thank Joan Druett, whom I have never met but with whom I have corresponded through e-mail on a number of occasions. Joan fixed me up with Jack Butler and other experts on the Internet MARHIST maritime forum moderated by Walter Lewis and Maurice Smith at the Marine Museum of the Great Lakes at Kingston, Ontario.

Many others also rendered aid, especially David Lambert of the New England Genealogical and Historical Society, Richard Pueser and Becky Livingston at the National Archives, and Ted Miles and Irene Stachura at the San Francisco Maritime Museum. Craig Arnold was the librarian at the San Diego Maritime Museum who helped me get started. Steve Wolfe and Dave Swanson of the *Star of India* crew answered questions for hours and allowed me to help take down the sails one November day. Norman Brouwer and Jack Putnam at the South Street Seaport in New York were both kind and helpful. Peter Brosnan of Los Angeles, who wrote a magazine article about Mary Patten several years ago, graciously shared his accumulated research. I promised to dance at the Mariner's Museum librarian Elaine Killam's wedding for her assistance, and Paula Johnson of the ship's plans division of the Smithsonian Institution was very helpful. There is, indeed, a lot more to the Smithsonian than meets the eye.

Once the research was finished (although it was never actually completed so much as it ran out of thread), the writing of the story was a sometimes easy, sometimes difficult task. Sometimes the words just flowed from my pen or fingertips, and they were good. Other times I sat as becalmed as a ship on a flat sea, spending from dawn until midmorning writing a paragraph or two that I later threw out with the trash.

Through it all I had a group of writer friends who, with the patience of Job, patiently worked me through the storms and calms of this voyage. At the very real risk of leaving someone out, I must thank the above mentioned Anita and Clara Jane, as well as Joyce Thomas, Glenn Wigington, Susan Davis, Dixie Kline, Ken Maursy, Jerry Hoffman, Aldonna Rohrbough, Carla Ramer, and Billy Spruell. I also thank Jo Diehl for her reading of the manuscript and Rita Diehl for also reading and for her thoughts on nautical matters.

I should also thank my coworkers at Arkansas Best Corporation, who had to hear about this work in progress ad nauseam, and my superiors, who have allowed me to have a job that left me with many hours sitting around airport lobbies and lounges with time to write.

Once written, the book was fortunate to find its way into the hands of agent Robert Tabian, who took the new guy on, and Brian Tart, my editor at Dutton, and his assistants, Kara Howland and Amy Hughes. Brian had me fix many things I didn't know were broken, and the book is much better because of him.

With all these people who assisted my research and my writing, I share the pleasure of seeing this completed book, printed and bound in a real cover, with real pages in between. Now it can be shared with readers, which is, of course, why I wrote it in the first place.

A native of Fort Smith, Arkansas, Douglas Kelley now makes his home with his wife and two children just across the Oklahoma state line. From this landlocked base, a profession as a corporate pilot facilitated his travels to research this book of the sea. *The Captain's Wife* is his first novel.